D0463421

# The Works of George W. Cable

## Arlin Turner

### EDITOR

Old Creole Days (New York, 1879)
The Grandissimes (New York, 1880)
Madame Delphine (New York, 1881)
The Creoles of Louisiana (New York, 1884)
Dr. Sevier (Boston, 1885)
The Silent South (New York, 1885)
Bonaventure (New York, 1888)
Strange True Stories of Louisiana (New York, 1889)
The Negro Question (New York, 1890)
John March, Southerner (New York, 1894)
Strong Hearts (New York, 1899)
The Cavalier (New York, 1901)
Bylow Hill (New York, 1902)
Kincaid's Battery (New York, 1908)
"Posson Jone" and Père Raphael (New York, 1909)
Gideon's Band, A Tale of the Mississippi (New York, 1914)
The Amateur Garden (New York, 1914)
The Flower of the Chapdelaines (New York, 1918)
Lovers of Louisiana (New York, 1918)

# JOHN MARCH

# SOUTHERNER

BY

George W. Cable

*With an Introduction and Notes by*

ARLIN TURNER

GARRETT PRESS, INC.
*New York,* 1970

SBN 512-00074-3
Library of Congress Catalog Card
Number 73-96494


The text of this book is a photographic reprint of the first edition,
published in New York by Charles Scribner's Sons in 1894.
Reproduced from a copy in the Garrett Press Collection.


*First Garrett Press Edition Published 1970*


Copyright © 1970 by Garrett Press, Inc.


Manufactured in the United States of America

GARRETT PRESS, INC.
*Publishers*
250 West 54th Street, New York, N.Y. 10019

# INTRODUCTION

George W. Cable discovered Creole New Orleans for literature. In works extending from his first story in 1873 to his last novel in 1918, he gave his native city a full and discriminating embodiment such as perhaps no other American city has received in the writings of a literary figure. Although some of his works are set outside the city, particularly in outlying regions of Louisiana and Mississippi, his best and most characteristic fiction portrays the French and the American civilizations in their struggle, from the Louisiana Purchase onward, for dominance in New Orleans. He lived the first forty years of his life in the city and knew it from both observation and study. He was old enough to register impressions ten years before the Civil War, and through lively traditions in the family his memory seemed to extend back farther. A questioning observer of events around him and an eager student of local history, he stored up the materials which later entered his stories and novels. To an extent that holds for only a few, if any, of our other novelists, Cable's major works deal with the issues confronting his region in his time and derive in important ways from his own experiences and observations.

Cable was born in New Orleans on October 12, 1844, to parents who had migrated from Indiana after the panic of 1837. His father, George Washington Cable, was a native of Virginia; his mother, Rebecca Boardman, was of New England descent. They owned slaves and seem to have adjusted comfortably to life about them, while remaining aware that theirs was the most European of all American cities. The father died in 1859, leaving his widow and four children all but penniless. The son George dropped out of school and began work without finishing high school.

After the fall of New Orleans to the Union forces, an event that Cable witnessed at the levee and in the streets and afterward recounted in both historical and fictional works, he joined the Confederate cavalry on October 9, 1863. Only five feet two inches in height and weighing no more than a hundred pounds, he was wounded twice but stood up to the demands of the desperate campaigns in Mississippi and Alabama until the surrender. He was mustered out in May, 1865.

As a clerk and bookkeeper, he continued the reading and study he had done even as a soldier. In December, 1869, he was married to Louise Stewart Bartlett. The next year he became a reporter for a New Orleans daily, the *Picayune,* and for a year and a half also provided a column of miscellaneous comment entitled "Drop Shot," first weekly and later daily. His writings were still sought for the *Picayune* after he had returned to work in business, and he furnished occasional feature articles and editorials. He welcomed especially an invitation to write editorials in a futile war the *Picayune* waged in 1872 against the Louisiana Lottery Company. His interest in local history sent him to archival records and early newspapers to gather information for a series of newspaper articles published under the title "The Churches and Charities of New Orleans."

These inclinations toward history and toward social criticism and reforms were reflected in the stories that Cable, in 1873, began publishing in *Scribner's Monthly Magazine.* Since he thought of the present as an extension of the past, stories of earlier time were to his mind suitable vehicles for comment on current affairs. After collecting seven magazine stories in the volume *Old Creole Days* (1879), he wrote his first novel, *The Grandissimes* (1880),

pleased to have the greater scope of the novel for the
portrait of the Creole civilization he had already begun
drawing and for the criticism he wanted to level at current
society. He was also hopeful that the novel would yield the
income he must have before he could cut his business ties
and give full time to writing. In 1881 appeared the
novelette *Madame Delphine,* and in 1884 the novel *Dr.
Sevier* and a historical work, *The Creoles of Louisiana.*

Readers of these five books, all published in a span of
five years, were introduced to the Vieux Carré, the ancient
square that had been laid out when Bienville founded New
Orleans in 1718. In Cable's time the old square was still
occupied mainly by Creoles, proud descendants of French
and Spanish colonials, and as much as possible remained
separate from the American city across Canal Street
upriver. With interests already pricked by Bret Harte and
others who had written about the people and manners and
terrain of distant regions, readers were fascinated by the
characters and the life they encountered on Cable's pages.
Reviewers found the word "charm" all but essential in
commenting on the stories. Nathaniel Hawthorne's sister
Elizabeth, in a fragment preserved at the Huntington
Library, mentioned "Jean-ah Poquelin" to her niece, the
novelist's daughter Una, presumably soon after the story
was printed in *Scribner's Monthly* in May, 1875. It is "a
tale that struck me," she wrote; "it is original and
impressive, and lingers in my mind. It is a story of the
early days of American rule in Louisiana. I forget the
author's name, but whoever he is, he has genius, and a field
for its exercise, among the mixed races and strange
manners of the South West."

Cable recognized the literary ore everywhere around
him, waiting to be mined. It was his habit to make notes
on the spot as he encountered likely materials—to record a
descriptive detail, a dialectal phrase, the words of a *patois*

song, or its tune. He had an acute ear for speech and could write down the musical scores of songs he heard on the street. He tended in his early fiction to introduce excessive detail from history and observation—such at least was the opinion of his editors, who were more concerned than he was with the conventional elements of plot. Similarly, his pursuit of accuracy caused him to burden his early stories with something close to literal transcription of dialect—chiefly the English of his French-speaking characters at various levels of education and acquaintance with the language, but including also the dialect speech of Spanish, Italian, German, and Irish characters. Satisfactory methods of representing dialect in fiction—indeed the legitimacy of dialect in literature at all—had not yet been determined. With experience, and prompted by protests against his dialect from readers and editors, Cable evolved a method which would drop any attempt at full delineation in favor of bare suggestion, mainly by occasional locutions, pronunciations, or simple foreign phrases. In applying the new method, he revised *The Grandissimes* for a new edition in 1883 by simplifying the Creole dialect. The charm of his stories continued nevertheless to owe much to the dialect speech of his characters. Howells and Twain and Cable's friends among his publishers liked to insert dialect expressions in their letters to him or to declare that they talked nothing but Creole.

The stories of *Old Creole Days* recognizably belong to the same unique locality; but for all they have in common in setting, theme, and technique, there are wide variations among them, suggesting an inclination in the author toward experiment with materials, effects, and means. At one extreme in tone and emotional response is "Madame Délicieuse," the story of a young woman who employs her beauty and her talents to conquer both a lover and his father, a stubborn Creole of an older, unbending generation. The laughter of Creole women on the balconies along Royal Street in the old city, the fragrance of orange blossoms which meets the wedding party emerging from the church—such are the ingredients which produce the charm of the story. At the other extreme is "Jean-ah Poquelin," set at a mysterious, ancient dwelling on the bank of an overgrown drainage canal at the edge of the swamp. Stubborn Creole independence, antagonism to all encroachments of government and society, whispered rumors of slave-smuggling, fratricide, and even greater transgressions give way finally to the actualities of leprosy, death, and unsuspected self-sacrifice.

" 'Tite Poulette" delineates in low key but with great force the quadroon women of New Orleans: quiet, resigned victims of a social system they have no hope of escaping. The escape of 'Tite Poulette, because it can be proved that she is white, the daughter of Spanish immigrants, makes the doom of the quadroons the more inexorable. Over against the delicacy, the hinting, and the indirection of this story may be set the broad comedy, the gargantuan feats of strength performed in "Posson Jone' " by the intoxicated parson from the remote parishes, and the equally extravagant contrasting portrait of Jules St. Ange, a young Creole who is adept in all the ways to get along in the city. A different contrast, no less pronounced, is furnished by "Café des Exilés," in which intrigue, stealth, betrayal, and death are enacted through the confused intermingling of refugees from the Caribbean Islands engaged in gun-smuggling.

The stories of *Old Creole Days* portray the strange and the picturesque; and these elements, stressed by the local colorists, have some prominence in most of Cable's other fiction. Even his earliest stories, however, defy classification simply as local color fiction. For one thing, Cable often added touches of stern realism, although his materials might seem to belong to romance, and although he might throw over them the haze of remote indefiniteness. His inclination, as a matter of fact, was to admit unpleasantness of concept and language and to present qualities of human character and action not as a rule present in the American fiction of his time. All his works before 1900 were published first in magazines, and the editors often urged revision to make them acceptable in "family" magazines. Even so, much of their distinctive flavor remained. For another thing, Cable drew characters of a greater variety, with subtler qualities of mind and spirit and greater psychological realism than was usual with the local colorists. The title character in his first published story, " 'Sieur George," and Injun Charlie in the second story, "Belles Demoiselles Plantation," might be cited, and also the title character in "Jean-ah Poquelin." Moreover, the voice of social criticism is clear in several of the stories. The result is that, even in this early work, Cable brings his special region into real existence, while drawing characters who suggest the vitality and depth to be achieved in longer works, and while adding threads of social comment which give his fiction a direct relationship to its time and place.

As Cable read Louisiana history, its chief fact after 1803 was the political, commercial, and cultural rivalry of the Creoles and the intruding *Américains.* This rivalry echoes in the stories "Jean-ah Poquelin" and "Madame Délicieuse"; and it provides the structure of *The Grandissimes,* which was planned as a dramatization of the clash between the two civilizations.

Cable undertook to display in *The Grandissimes* the full sweep of peoples and forces in New Orleans in the first years after the Louisiana Purchase, when the Creoles were by no means ready to transfer their allegiance from the French Emperor to the American President, or the President's representative, Governor Claibourne. The multitudinous Grandissime family and the others within their sphere include one who accepts the new political and social order, another who allows no quarter to the forces of change, a young Creole widow and her daughter (whom Howells placed among his favorite characters of fiction), and others who represent the compact, interwoven Creole society.

Some of the Creoles objected that Cable chose too large a proportion of his Creole characters from the lower classes, and that the dialect speech he gave them was not accurate. Other Creoles testified in the New Orleans newspapers that they found his characters and their speech true to life. Cable often declared that he was fond of the Creoles, and he obviously admired much in their character, but he also found faults to condemn. The displeasure of the Creoles was in part, perhaps, what might be expected of any distinctive people who found themselves introduced into fiction—even if the writer was one of their own number, and surely if he was an outsider. Still, Cable could not conceal—did not try to conceal—his impatience with the Creoles' clannishness, with their lack of concern for social betterment, and with what to his mind was their lax morality. As a consequence, a Creole already critical of American encroachment on his Gallic culture could not help resenting books in which he was portrayed—rather than simply praised—by an American for other Americans.

Whatever resentment the Creoles felt on this account was inflamed when they found in *The Grandissimes* views on the race question which were anathema to them. Soon after the Civil War, Cable saw that the former slaves were often denied basic citizen's rights. As a newspaper reporter he had seen the folly of segregated schools, and in 1875 he wrote a letter on the matter to a New Orleans newspaper. But a rejoinder by the editor printed along with his letter and his failure to get a second letter published in any newspaper reminded him that his views were at odds with those held by his friends and business associates. He avoided the topic for the next ten years, except for indirect statements in his fiction, as in "Belles Demoiselles Plantation" and " 'Tite Poulette." The first story he had submitted in 1872, "Bibi," was rejected by several editors, mainly because of what it implied in picturing the tragic fate of a proud African prince in slavery. The story remained unpublished until it was incorporated in *The Grandissimes* as the episode of Bras Coupé. This novel, with its tone set by the elemental story of Bras Coupé, presents several victims of racial oppression: Clemence, the ancient purveyor of voodoo charms, who is shot in the back, in a sort of lynch killing, after she has been told to run for her life; the beautiful quadroon Palmyre, who hopelessly loves the white Honoré and scorns the love of Honoré Grandissime, f.m.c. (free man of color), who drowns himself because of his disappointment in love as well as in other areas which are controlled by the fact that he is not white. The white Honoré defies the taboos of his clan—and of the South at large—by entering into business partnership with his f.m.c. half-brother and thus pointing toward a future, the author implies, when the errors and the injustices of race would be left behind. The author speaks at times as author, and the character Frowenfeld has something of an authorial role as intermediary among the characters and as judge of all that takes place; even so, the social comment comes across to the readers mainly through situation and action. The reader is drawn into the life being portrayed and feels the forces bearing on the characters.

*The Grandissimes* succeeds in its purpose of recreating an era in the history of New Orleans. It delineates the social strata from the apex of the dominant race to the slaves newly brought from Africa, and activities from a parade of government officials to the making of a voodoo charm. The complicated plot reflects the complex inter-relations among individuals, families, and classes in the confused era represented. Though the action is set in a distant historical past and clarity is handicapped at times by indirection and indefiniteness and the play of conceal-ment and revelation in the narration, there is a firm sense of actuality, created in part by the density of the life portrayed.

In 1881 Cable published the novelette *Madame Del-phine,* which he said in the preface to a new edition in 1896 was written because a quadroon had charged him with falsifying the story of 'Tite Poulette. In this story he would tell the truth: the beautiful daughter is indeed a quadroon, but her mother swears a lie so that she can marry the white man she loves. When the mother has confessed the lie and has died in the confessional, the priest mutters, "Lord, lay not this sin to her charge!" Perhaps in no other work did Cable achieve such balance and mutual reinforcement of character, scene, and event, supported by such a consistent tone as in *Madame Delphine.*

Cable was glad to write *The Creoles of Louisiana* (1884), he said, to show his affection for the Creoles and dispel any belief that he had treated them unkindly in his fiction. He had first written, in connection with the Tenth Census of the United States, a work entitled *History and Present Condition of New Orleans* (1881). Afterward he adapted it for serial publication in the *Century Magazine,* January-July, 1883, with illustrations by Joseph Pennell, which were reproduced in the book. The materials of this history are of a type to invite a historian, or a novelist; the romance of the exploration and early settlement, the ravages of the cholera, yellow fever, and flood from the river, the vicissitudes of political ties—to France, Spain,

France again, the United States, the Confederacy, and the Union afterward. Here Cable had occasion to move extensively in the area he had already explored in his fiction. A comparison of the three published versions shows him successively reducing the proportion of bald facts in his account and approaching the methods of fiction.

Cable's second novel, *Dr. Sevier,* is set in New Orleans but is not a Creole story. It has only one Creole character, Narcisse, an auxiliary character who serves also to provide comedy in a story that is otherwise dark. In contrast to *The Grandissimes,* this novel has only three characters of any prominence, Dr. Sevier and a young couple, the Richlings, and the plot is simple. As first planned, this was to be a story of prison reform. Cable was at the time immersed in a campaign to reform the New Orleans prisons and asylums, but as composition progressed, this thread was superseded by an exploration of the themes of poverty, charity, work, pride, and the human relations which revolve about them. The New Orleans setting is all but ignored. Inundation and yellow fever are introduced, to be sure, but only as normal elements in the scene. It is likely that Cable wanted to show that he could write fiction which was not dependent on the Creoles and the romance of early New Orleans. But it seems more likely that the plot he conceived required ordinary people, such as the Richlings, who would face ordinary events in commonplace situations, and yet would suffer pain, ignominy, and tragedy which are no less severe for the unexcited way in which they present themselves. Cable had read Howells' *A Modern Instance* early in the composition of *Dr. Sevier* and undertook to employ Howellsian realism in presenting through different characters differing views of subjects he wanted to explore.

With the publication of *Dr. Sevier* in 1884, Cable was

established, at home and abroad, on the level of William
Dean Howells, Henry James, and Mark Twain. Indeed, it
was not uncommon for him to be ranked above one or
more of them. He was often compared with Nathaniel
Hawthorne and with the major French novelists of the
nineteenth century—without suffering in the comparison.
He continued to publish for another thirty-four years, but
his literary output never afterward equaled the rate or,
with possibly one or two exceptions, the quality of his
early work. His literary production fell off after 1884
because his platform readings from his works and his
reform work absorbed so much of his time and energy.

Soon after leaving his accountant's desk late in 1881,
Cable knew that his literary work would not furnish the
income he needed. By the end of 1883 he was popular in
the North and East as a platform reader. During four
months of 1884-1885 he traveled with Mark Twain on a
joint tour, which set the high mark in an era when many
authors gave public readings. These readings provided a
major part of his income for another twenty years. He
shared the platform on occasion with James Whitcomb
Riley, Hamlin Garland, and Eugene Field. In 1898 and
again in 1905, he went to England for a reading tour.

In the summer of 1884 Cable moved his family to
Simsbury, Connecticut, to be near his publishers and the
main lecture circuit. A year later he settled permanently in
Northampton, Massachusetts, where Smith College, he
said, offered an attraction for a man with six daughters. A
son had died of yellow fever in 1878 in New Orleans;
another son died in 1908 at the age of twenty-three.
Besides his own family, Cable furnished varying degrees of
support for his mother, his unmarried sister Mary Louise,
his widowed sister Antoinette Cox, and her two children,
all of whom moved to Northampton.

Cable was never long without a part in some reform

effort. From work in his church in New Orleans for social betterment, he moved on to organize a widely acclaimed program for reform of the New Orleans prisons and asylums. Next he studied the penitentiary reports from the twelve Southern states which leased convicts to labor for private contractors, and wrote an attack on the system which he delivered before the National Conference of Charities and Correction and published afterward in the *Century Magazine,* February, 1884, with the title "The Convict Lease System in the Southern States." His study of prison records had convinced him that former slaves received a special kind of justice in the courts. Under the title "The Freedman's Case in Equity," he opened the subject, first in an address before the American Social Science Association and afterward in the *Century Magazine* for January, 1885. The essay provoked intense opposition throughout the South, with the most persistent and virulent attacks printed by the New Orleans newspaper the *Times-Democrat,* which earlier had sponsored Cable's campaign for prison reform. The Creoles too now raised shrill voices in the outcry.

Cable was confident that once the subject was discussed openly, reasonable solutions could be reached. He visited the South regularly, to freshen his memory for the benefit of his fiction, he said, and to keep aware of developments. By writing, speaking, organizing others to debate the issues, and distributing his own and other pertinent writings, he undertook to speak for what he called "The Silent South" in the title of one of his essays—meaning the majority of Southerners who he thought held his views but were voiceless while the politicians and the journalists spoke in tones of reaction. A volume of his essays, *The Silent South,* appeared late in 1885; a second edition, with supplements, in 1889; and another volume, *The Negro Question*, in 1890. The essays in these books present the most inclusive, the most carefully reasoned argument yet published for extending full civil rights to the Negroes. His appeal was to reason, fairness, morality, and justice. Reducing the entire problem to a question of right and wrong, and therefore a problem having but one answer, he could make no room for expediency or gradualism. Thus he championed public education, universal suffrage, an end to segregation, and every assistance to help the freedman rise above the handicaps of slavery and deprivation.

Reluctantly and sadly, Cable realized by 1890 that there were no avenues for him to continue his efforts. The Southern states, with general approval in the North, were establishing legal barriers intended to keep the Negroes in a segregated, nonvoting status. The public platform was effectually closed to discussion of the great sore question, as he called it, and even his editors at the *Century Magazine* now rejected his polemical essays. He still had no doubt as to the ultimate outcome, and he wrote a prediction in his notes that the rise of the Negro race after emancipation would be "the great romance of American history."

In 1894 Cable published *John March, Southerner,* a novel in which he traced out with great care the bewildering intricacy of the Southern problem, and indicated not an exact program, but the direction in which he believed steps must be taken. The writing of the novel had been slow and painful, partly because he was embodying opinions only then being sifted out in his mind, and partly because he struggled—without success—to make the novel acceptable to the editor of the *Century*, Richard Watson Gilder, who wanted no further treatment of the Southern question, in fiction or otherwise. (The novel was finally serialized not in the *Century,* but in *Scribner's Magazine* and was published as a book by Charles Scribner.) Simply by introducing into *John March* the complex Southern mind, the tensions between classes and castes and sections, the tradition of the frontier, with its components of danger, heroism, and violence, the cult of chivalry—by drawing into his plot the full scope of the Southern character and experience following the Civil War, Cable moved a long way toward the modern Southern novel. He portrayed in realistic detail the post-Reconstruction South: the growth of industry, outside capital and outside management, development—or exploitation—of natural resources, public works, new stresses on schools and churches, political corruption, betrayal by Southern leaders. As in *Dr. Sevier* ten years earlier, various characters express in action and speech varied opinions on the issues.

John March progresses through misconception, error, and wrongheadedness. He has more humanity—more failings and aberrations—than Frowenfeld in *The Grandissimes*, or Honoré Grandissime. Like Dr. Sevier, he has abundant human contradictions. He comes to understand himself and to understand his region in the same process, for as the title indicates, he and the South are identical. Many aspects of his career and his outlook parallel the author's. His decision, finally, to decline the inviting opportunities outside the region and to dedicate his energy and talents to the future of the South may be taken to mean that Cable in some degree regretted moving north; at least it shows that he believed his move had lessened the effectiveness of his work for reform in the South.

Even before Cable realized that campaigning for Southern reform was no longer feasible, he had begun a program for social betterment in Northampton. He had begun in 1887 the reading clubs which evolved into the Home Culture Clubs, later the People's Institute, which remains active today. Another endeavor of his was the Northampton Prize Flower Garden Competition, which prompted one who had observed the competition several years to publish an article with the title "How One Man Made His Town Bloom." Cable's study of theories of gardening and his experience in the Northampton program resulted in a series of magazine essays and a book, *The Amateur Garden* (1914). His church work reached an apex in the Bible class he taught in the City Hall, which particularly invited non-church-goers and reached an attendance of 700 men.

Early in his career as an author, Cable planned to write about the Cajuns, descendants of the Acadians expelled from Nova Scotia in 1755 who had settled on the prairies and along the bayous of Southwest Louisiana. He had traveled in the Cajun country and had made warm friends there. Three magazine stories about the Cajuns were combined into *Bonaventure* (1888), though there is little to unify them except a few characters continued from one story to another and the simple life of the isolated communities. The stories presented a region and a people all but unknown to literature, but the homely, even primitive, virtues and faults of the characters, and their resignation to deprivation contrast sharply with the qualities which had proved so attractive in his Creole characters.

Three other separate stories were joined to make a volume, *Strong Hearts* (1899). Although set in or near New Orleans, these stories make little attempt to exploit the region or any of its particular inhabitants. Instead, they stress character delineation. The best of the three, "Gregory's Island," is a convincingly realistic study of a man who isolates himself on a remote island, with no means of escape for a predetermined period of battling against his thirst for drink. The novelette *Bylow Hill* (1902) is unique among Cable's works. It is set not in the South but in New England, though it has characters from the South, and it owes nothing to characters or events of the author's own observation. It is a study of abnormal psychology, in which a gifted young minister is destroyed by an irrational, blind jealousy of his wife. Although there is little in this work to suggest Cable's other fiction, the narrative method is well adapted to the plot, and the minister comes across as a believable character.

Beginning with *The Cavalier* (1900), Cable settled into a pattern which continued the rest of his life: writing slowly, with frequent interruptions occasioned by other demands on his time, drawing advances from his publisher to meet his expenses, and beginning a new novel before its predecessor was off the press. Thus were produced *The Cavalier* and three more novels: *Kincaid's Battery* (1908); *Gideon's Band* (1914); and *Lovers of Louisiana* (1918). He began still another novel, to be set in New Orleans at the time of World War I, but did not finish it.

In his later years Cable wintered in the South as a rule, but otherwise continued his routine and his community activities at Northampton. His first wife died in 1904. He married Eva C. Stevenson in 1906; and after her death in 1923, he married Mrs. Hanna Cowing. He died at St. Petersburg, Florida, January 31, 1925, and was buried at Northampton.

Cable's late novels are well made. They show a masterful handling of dramatic scene, dialogue, climax, and suspense. They draw heavily on the author's knowledge of Louisiana and the river, and especially his experiences as a soldier. These novels are what the author intended: romances of love and war or some other source of excitement and suspense, and they are skillfully managed. But instead of the sense of actuality which prevails in *The Grandissimes*, *Dr. Sevier*, and *John March*, his characters are idealized and their problems are neither profound nor moving.

*The Cavalier* had a larger immediate sale than any other book Cable wrote; and a dramatized version was successful on the stage. "The author did not have to read up to write this story," reads an inscription Cable wrote in a copy of the book. The narrator within the plot, Richard Thorndyke Smith, who had appeared earlier in stories and essays as an authorial spokesman, has experiences closely following Cable's war experiences. But everything is recalled over the haze of years. Nothing is said of the issues behind the war, or of the soldier's day-to-day experience of boredom, fear, and suffering. Cable had returned from that war thirty-five years earlier; he had returned from his individual campaign for Southern reform more recently and had turned from that defeat to write idealized romances instead of realistic novels of social criticism. He had kept up the struggle for reform more than a dozen years; reformers do not often exceed that term.

*Kincaid's Battery* is another romance of the war, with the artillery replacing the cavalry of *The Cavalier* and with the action centered around New Orleans instead of Northern Mississippi. Again the military action, the confusion and excitement of battle, reflects the author's familiarity with his materials, though his recollection is blurred by time and a deliberate idealization.

Cable called *Gideon's Band* a romance—and rightly. His plan was to recreate the steamboat traffic his father had known on the Mississippi River in the 1840's and 1850's. But the book suggests that Cable could no longer ignore the problems he had debated in his early works. Perhaps he realized that his treatment of those problems had given his early stories and novels the immediacy, actuality, and moral ballast which provided their strength. In the character Phyllis, the lot of the quadroons is again dramatized, but with only negative answers offered: the solution for Phyllis is not in flight to the North or in marriage to a white man. In the main plot, Cable returned to a theme repeated in his early work, both fictional and historical: the erosion of character which often resulted from the social dominance enjoyed by the aristocratic whites of the South, their wealth and pride, and especially their station above both poor whites and blacks.

In *The Flower of the Chapdelaines,* formed from three earlier stories and published in March, 1918, Cable returned to Creole characters and Creole speech and still more pointedly to the Southern questions he had argued more than thirty years earlier. In all three stories, which belong to slave times, and in the enveloping framework, which has its own love plot, Cable's views on the race question are implied rather than asserted. His last novel, *Lovers of Louisiana,* published later in the same year, opens all the old questions again. One member of the Durel family, Zéphire, has Creole narrowness and family pride in extravagant measure, but is repudiated by his father and by his sister Rosalie, who possesses the beauty and charm of Cable's earlier Creole women and has also an understanding of public affairs that would have been inappropriate to the earlier women. Her marriage to Philip Castleton represents a joining of the best from the Creole and the American civilizations and prophesies a better future for the South. Philip Castleton has much in common with John March, and he is identical with the author in much of what he does and what he thinks. He decides to remain in the South, hoping to help usher in the peace and justice so long absent. The character Ovid Landry, a Negro engaged in business with the Durel family, to the profit of all concerned, was modeled on a bookseller Cable knew while visiting New Orleans to gather materials for the book. *Lovers of Louisiana* is a novel of social criticism, Cable's first since *John March, Southerner* twenty-four years earlier. The presence of social comment, reflecting both conviction and feeling in the author, gives the novel some of the strength and interest of the early fiction.

The two threads of Cable's career—as social critic and reformer and as fiction writer—were fused in his best works and otherwise remained close and parallel. His "Drop Shot" newspaper column ran heavily to social comment and led him to begin writing stories. By the time his first stories were published in 1873, he realized that the former slaves were being denied the rights of citizenship, and he was convinced that, as had been true under slavery, both races would suffer as a consequence. But for another dozen years he confined his direct efforts for reform to areas such as prisons and asylums where he would have wide public approval. He dared broach the matter of Negro rights only indirectly in his fiction, especially in *The Grandissimes, Madame Delphine,* and several stories. His case for social reform gained strength from the force of these works and in turn furnished them with weight and immediacy they otherwise would have lacked.

When Cable launched his open campaign for greater Negro rights in 1884, he pushed his literary work to the back of his desk and published no extended work until *John March, Southerner,* ten years later. Although this novel has no equal in its detailed presentation and analysis of the Southern scene in the decade after Reconstruction, it is a successful work of fiction. It displays convincing realism of scene and character and a perceptive delineation of the relations present in a community during a transition period which demands radical changes in institutions and attitudes. Here, as in the early works, the social reformer and the novelist became one, and the reformer's zeal was an asset to the novelist.

With the Southern debate closed soon after 1890, Cable's reforming zeal found an outlet in the reading clubs and the flower garden competition. With publishers unreceptive to novels with the unpleasantness and the controversial social comment of *The Grandissimes* or *John March*, Cable turned to the historical romance. In a series of essays, he justified the romance not as a work that would convey the experience of real characters in real situations, whether current or historical, facing important social and moral problems—as he would have characterized *The Grandissimes;* rather, he justified the romance as a form of fiction that would "make you feel to-day that you are entertained, and find to-morrow that you are profited." Cable's books after 1900 conform to this pattern (though the last, *Lovers of Louisiana*, shows him less satisfied with it).

In only five of the forty-five years in Cable's literary career he produced most of his best work. Of his later writings, some belong with his best; most of them show great care in planning and execution and all but flawless management of the narration; and some of them contain memorable scenes or characters. But in his first five books Cable staked off a literary claim, Creole New Orleans, which no one has seriously challenged. He delineated the Creole and the American civilizations, confronting each other for more than a century, in a composite portrait in which each accentuates the qualities of the other; he reproduced the speech and songs of the region with a skill that Mark Twain declared had no equal; he portrayed a gallery of characters remarkable for their variety and their vividness; and running through his works is a firm, perceptive social commentary which normally augments the literary effectiveness.

## The Plan of This Edition

The nineteen volumes in the Collected Edition of George W. Cable in the American Authors Series includes all his major writings. Only two of the works he published separately have been excluded: *The Busy Man's Bible* (Meadville, Pa., 1889), composed from periodical articles on the study and teaching of the Bible; and *A Memory of Roswell Smith* (privately printed, 1892), a tribute to his publisher friend. Cable brought most of his magazine writings together in volumes of stories and essays, all of which are printed in the Collected Edition. The writings from his pen which do not appear in this edition include the contents of his "Drop Shot" column in the New Orleans *Picayune*, 1870-1872; miscellaneous uncollected sketches and essays in periodicals; a completed short story, an unfinished novel, and other fragments he left in manuscript; notebooks he kept at intervals, particularly during his visits to England in 1898 and 1905; and letters.

All volumes in the Collected Edition of Cable are reproductions of the first editions. For *The Silent South,* the appendix which Cable added in the 1889 edition is reproduced here from that edition. The preface in the 1896 edition of *Madame Delphine* is printed as an appendix in this edition.

Arlin Turner
*Duke University*

## Selected Bibliography

### Books

Biklé, Lucy L. C., *George W. Cable: His Life and Letters* (New York: Charles Scribner's Sons, 1928).

Butcher, Philip, *George W. Cable: The Northampton Years* (New York: Columbia University Press, 1959).

_____, *George W. Cable* (New York: Twayne Publishers, 1962).

Cardwell, Guy A., *Twins of Genius* (East Lansing: Michigan State University Press, 1953).

Dennis, Mary Cable, *The Tail of the Comet* (New York: E. P. Dutton, 1937).

Ekström, Kjell, *George Washington Cable: A Study of His Early Life and Work* (Upsala: Lundequistska Bokhandeln; Cambridge, Mass.: Harvard University Press, 1950).

Rubin, Louis D., Jr., *George W. Cable: The Life and Times of a Southern Heretic* (New York: Pegasus, 1969).

Turner, Arlin, *George W. Cable: A Biography* (Durham, N.C.: Duke University Press, 1956).

_____, *Mark Twain and George W. Cable: The Record of a Literary Friendship* (East Lansing: Michigan State University Press, 1960).

_____, *George W. Cable* (Austin, Tex.: Steck-Vaughn Company, 1969; Southern Writers Series).

### Articles

Bartlett, Rose, "How One Man Made His Town Bloom," *Ladies' Home Journal*, XXVII (March, 1910), 36, 80, 82.

Baskervill, William M., *Southern Writers* (Nashville, Tenn., 1897-1903, 2 vols.), I, 299-356.

Bentzon, Th. [Marie Thérèse Blanc], *Les Nouveaux Romanciers Américains* (Paris, 1885), pp. 159-226.

Butcher, Philip, "George W. Cable and Booker T. Washington," *Journal of Negro Education*, XVII (Fall, 1948), 462-68.

_____, "George W. Cable and Negro Education," *Journal of Negro History*, XXXIV (April, 1949), 119-34.

Eidson, John Olin, "George W. Cable's Philosophy of Progress," *Southwest Review*, XXI (Jan., 1936), 211-16.

Ekström, Kjell, "The Cable-Howells Correspondence," *Studia Neo-philologica,* XXII (1950), 48-61.

Hearn, Lafcadio, "The Scenes of Cable's Romances," *Century Magazine,* XXVII (Nov., 1883), 40-47.

Howells, W. D., *Heroines of Fiction* (New York, 1901, 2 vols.), II, 234-44.

Hubbell, Jay B., *The South in American Literature* (Durham, N.C., 1954), pp. 804-22.

Lorch, Fred W., "Cable and His Reading Tour with Mark Twain in 1884-1885," *American Literature,* XXIII (Jan., 1952), 471-86.

Manes, Isabel Cable, "George W. Cable, Fighter for Progress in the South," in *A Southerner Looks at Negro Discrimination: Selected Writings of George W. Cable* (New York, 1946), pp. 11-18.

Pattee, F. L., *A History of American Literature Since 1870* (New York, 1915), pp. 246-53.

Toulmin, Harry Aubrey, *Social Historians* (Boston, 1911), pp. 35-56.

Turner, Arlin, "George W. Cable's Revolt Against Literary Sectionalism," *Tulane Studies in English,* V (1955), 5-27.

_____, "George W. Cable's Beginnings as a Reformer," *Journal of Southern History,* XVII (May, 1951), 135-61.

_____, "George Washington Cable's Literary Apprenticeship," *Louisiana Historical Quarterly,* XXIV (Jan., 1941), 168-86.

_____, "A Novelist Discovers a Novelist: The Correspondence of H. H. Boyesen and George W. Cable," *Western Humanities Review,* V (Autumn, 1951), 343-72.

Wilson, Edmund, *Patriotic Gore* (New York, 1962), pp. 548-87, 593-604.

## Textual Note

*John March, Southerner* was serialized in *Scribner's Magazine,* January-December, 1894 (XV, 53-68, 154-70, 380-93, 461-76, 554-64, 740-53, XVI, 49-62, 236-40, 371-88, 489-510, 634-56, 768-89). The first separate edition, which is reproduced here, was published by Charles Scribner's Sons on November 24, 1894. Two bindings have been noted: one in green cloth and one in dark blue cloth. The original trim size of the book was 7-3/16 inches by 5 inches. See Jacob Blanck, *A Bibliography of American Literature,* II (New Haven, 1957), 8.

## Bibliography

Rubin, Louis D., Jr. "The Road to Yoknapatapha: George W. Cable and *John March, Southerner,*" in *The Faraway Country: Writers of the Modern South* (Seattle, Wash., 1963), pp. 21-42.

# JOHN MARCH

SOUTHERNER

## George W. Cable's Writings.

BONAVENTURE. A Prose Pastoral of Arcadian Louisiana. 12mo, paper, 50 cts ; cloth, $1.25.

DR. SEVIER. 12mo, paper, 50 cts ; cloth, $1.25.

THE GRANDISSIMES. A Story of Creole Life. 12mo, $1.25.

OLD CREOLE DAYS. 12mo, $1.25.

STRANGE TRUE STORIES OF LOUISIANA. Illustrated, 12mo, $2.00.

> *⁎* *New Uniform Edition of the above five volumes, cloth, in a box, $6.00.*

OLD CREOLE DAYS. Cameo Edition with Etching, $1.25.

OLD CREOLE DAYS. 2 vols. 16mo, paper, each 30 cts.

MADAME DELPHINE. 75 cts.

THE CREOLES OF LOUISIANA. Illustrated from drawings by Pennell. Small quarto, $2.50.

THE SILENT SOUTH, Together with the Freedman's Case in Equity and the Convict Lease System. With Portrait. 12mo, $1.00.

# JOHN MARCH

## SOUTHERNER

BY

GEORGE W. CABLE

NEW YORK
CHARLES SCRIBNER'S SONS
1894

THE CAXTON PRESS
NEW YORK

# CONTENTS

# JOHN MARCH, SOUTHERNER

### SUEZ

In the State of Dixie, County of Clearwater, and therefore in the very heart of what was once the "Southern Confederacy," lies that noted seat of government of one county and shipping point for three, Suez. The pamphlet of a certain land company—a publication now out of print and rare, but a copy of which it has been my good fortune to secure—mentions the battle of Turkey Creek as having been fought only a mile or so north of the town in the spring of 1864. It also strongly recommends to the attention of both capitalist and tourist the beautiful mountain scenery of Sandstone County, which adjoins Clearwater a few miles from Suez on the north, and northeast, as Blackland does, much farther away, on the southwest.

In the last year of our Civil War Suez was a basking town of twenty-five hundred souls, with rocky streets and breakneck sidewalks, its dwellings dozing most months of the twelve among roses and honeysuckles behind anciently whitewashed, much-broken fences, and all the place wrapped in that wide sweetness of apple and acacia scents that comes from whole mobs of dog-fennel.

The Pulaski City turnpike entered at the northwest corner and passed through to the court-house green with its hollow square of stores and law-offices—two sides of it blackened ruins of fire and war. Under the town's southeasternmost angle, between yellow banks and overhanging sycamores, the bright green waters of Turkey Creek, rambling round from the north and east, skipped down a gradual stairway of limestone ledges, and glided, alive with sunlight, into that true Swanee River, not of the maps, but which flows forever, "far, far away," through the numbers of imperishable song. The river's head of navigation was, and still is, at Suez.

One of the most influential, and yet meekest among the " citizens "—men not in the army—whose habit it was to visit Suez by way of the Sandstone County road, was Judge Powhatan March, of Widewood. In years he was about fifty. He was under the medium stature, with a gentle and intellectual face whose antique dignity was only less attractive than his rich, quiet voice.

His son John—he had no other child—was a fat-cheeked boy in his eighth year, oftenest seen on horseback, sitting fast asleep with his hands clutched in the folds of the Judge's coat and his short legs and browned feet spread wide behind the saddle. It was hard straddling, but it was good company.

One bright noon about the close of May, when the cotton blooms were opening and the cornsilk was turning pink; when from one hot pool to another the kildee fluttered and ran, and around their edges arcs of white and yellow butterflies sat and sipped and fanned themselves, like human butterflies at a seaside, Judge March

—with John in his accustomed place, headquarters behind the saddle—turned into the sweltering shade of a tree in the edge of town to gossip with an acquaintance on the price of cotton, the health of Suez and the last news from Washington—no longer from Richmond, alas!

"Why, son!" he exclaimed, as by and by he lifted the child down before a hardware, dry-goods, drug and music store, "what's been a-troublin' you? You a-got tear marks on yo' face!" But he pressed the question in vain.

"Gimme yo' han'ke'cher, son, an' let me wipe 'em off."

But John's pockets were insolvent as to handkerchiefs, and the Judge found his own no better supplied. So they changed the subject and the son did not have to confess that those dusty rivulet beds, one on either cheek, were there from aching fatigue of a position he would rather have perished in than surrender.

This store was the only one in Suez that had been neither sacked nor burned. In its drug department there had always been kept on sale a single unreplenished, undiminished shelf of books. Most of them were standard English works that took no notice of such trifles as children. But one was an exception, and this world-renowned volume, though entirely unillustrated, had charmed the eyes of Judge March ever since he had been a father. Year after year had increased his patient impatience for the day when his son should be old enough to know that book's fame. Then what joy to see delight dance in his brave young eyes upon that

volume's emergence from some innocent concealment—
a gift from his father!

Thus far, John did not know his a-b-c's. But education is older than alphabets, and for three years now
he had been his father's constant, almost confidential
companion. Why might not such a book as this, even
now, be made a happy lure into the great realm of letters? Seeing the book again to-day, reflecting that the
price of cotton was likely to go yet higher, and
touched by the child's unexplained tears, Judge March
induced him to go from his side a moment with the
store's one clerk—into the lump-sugar section—and
bought the volume.

---

## II.

### TO A GOOD BOY

In due time the Judge and his son started home.

The sun's rays, though still hot, slanted much as the
two rose into oak woodlands to the right of the pike and
beyond it. Here the air was cool and light. As they
ascended higher, and oaks gave place to chestnut and
mountain-birch, wide views opened around and far beneath. In the south spread the green fields and red
fallows of Clearwater, bathed in the sheen of the lingering sun. Miles away two white points were the spires
of Suez.

The Judge drew rein and gazed on five battle-fields
at once. " Ah, son, the kingdom of romance is at hand.

It's always at hand when it's within us. I'll be glad
when you can understand that, son."

His eyes came round at last to the most western
quarter of the landscape and rested on one part where
only a spray had dashed when war's fiery deluge rolled
down this valley. "Son, if there wa'n't such a sort o'
mist o' sunshine between, I could show you Rosemont
College over yondeh. You'll be goin' there in a few
years now. That'll be fine, won't it, son?"

A small forehead smote his back vigorously, not for
yea, but for slumber.

"Drowsy, son?" asked the Judge, adding a backward caress as he moved on again. "I didn't talk to you
enough, did I? But I was thinkin' about you, right
along." After a silence he stopped again.

"Awake now, son?" He reached back and touched
the solid little head. "See this streak o' black land
where the rain's run down the road? Well, that means
silveh, an' it's ow lan'."

They started once more. "It may not mean much,
but we needn't care, when what doesn't mean silveh
means dead loads of other things. Make haste an'
grow, son; yo' peerless motheh and I are only wait'n'—"
He ceased. In the small of his back the growing pressure of a diminutive bad hat told the condition of his
hidden audience. It lifted again.

"'Evomind, son, I can talk to you just as well asleep.
But I can tell you somepm that'll keep you awake. I
was savin' it till we'd get home to yo' dear motheh, but
yo' ti-ud an' I don't think of anything else an'—the
fact is, I'm bringing home a present faw you." He

looked behind till his eyes met a brighter pair. " What you reckon you've been sitt'n' on in one of them saddle pockets all the way fum Suez ? "

John smiled, laid his cheek to his father's back and whispered, " A kitt'n."

" Why, no, son ; its somepm powerful nice, but— well, you might know it wa'n't a kitt'n by my lett'n' you sit on it so long. I'd be proud faw you to have a kitt'n, but, you know, cats don't suit yo' dear motheh's high strung natu'e. You couldn't be happy with any- thing that was a constant tawment to her, could you ? "

The head lying against the questioner's back nodded an eager yes !

" Oh, you think you might, son, but I jes' know you couldn't. Now, what I've got faw you is ever so much nicer'n a kitt'n. You see, you a-growin' so fast you'll soon not care faw kitt'ns ; you'll care for what I've got you. But don't ask what it is, faw I'd hate not to tell you, and I want yo' dear motheh to be with us when you find it out."

It was fairly twilight when their horse neighed his pleasure that his crib was near. Presently they dis- mounted in a place full of stumps and weeds, where a grove had been till Halliday's brigade had camped there. Beyond a paling fence and a sandy, careworn garden of altheas and dwarf-box stood broadside to them a very plain, two-story house of uncoursed gray rubble, whose open door sent forth no welcoming gleam. Its windows, too, save one softly reddened by a remote lamp, reflected only the darkling sky. This was their home, called by every mountaineer neighbor " a plumb palace."

As they passed in, the slim form of Mrs. March entered at the rear door of the short hall and came slowly through the gloom. John sprang, and despite her word and gesture of nervous disrelish, clutched, and smote his face into, her pliant crinoline. The husband kissed her forehead, and, as she staggered before the child's energy, said :

" Be gentle, son." He took a hand of each. " I hope you'll overlook a little wildness in us this evening, my dear." They turned into a front room. " I wonder he restrains himself so well, when he knows I've brought him a present—not expensive, my deah, I assho' you, nor anything you can possible disapprove; only a B-double-O-K, in fact. Still, son, you ought always to remember yo' dear mother's apt to be ti-ud."

Mrs. March sank into the best rocking-chair, and, while her son kissed her diligently, said to her husband, with a smile of sad reproach :

" John can never know a woman's fatigue."

" No, Daphne, deah, an' that's what I try to teach him."

" Yes, Powhatan, but there's a difference between teaching and terrifying."

" Oh ! Oh ! I was fah fum intend'n' to be harsh."

" Ah ! Judge March, you little realize how harsh your words sometimes are." She showed the back of her head, although John plucked her sleeves with vehement whispers. " What *is* it child ? "

Her irritation turned to mild remonstrance. "You shouldn't interrupt your father, no matter how long you have to wait."

"Oh, I'd finished, my deah," cried the Judge, beaming upon wife and son. "And now," he gathered up the saddle-bags, "now faw the present!"

John leaped—his mother cringed.

"Oh, Judge March—before supper?"

"Why, of co'se not, my love, if you——"

"Ah, Powhatan, please! Please don't say if I." The speaker smiled lovingly—"I don't deserve such a rebuke!" She rose.

"Why, my deah!"

"No, I was not thinking of I, but of others. There's the tea-bell. Servants have rights, Powhatan, and we shouldn't increase their burdens by heartless delays. That may not be the law, Judge March, but it's the gospel."

"Oh, I quite agree with you, Daphne, deah!" But the father could not help seeing the child's tearful eyes and quivering mouth. "I'll tell you mother, son— There's no need faw anybody to be kep' wait'n'. We'll go to suppeh, but the gift shall grace the feast!" He combed one soft hand through his long hair. John danced and gave a triple nod.

Mrs. March's fatigue increased. "Please yourself," she said. "John and I can always make your pleasure ours. Only, I hope he'll not inherit a frivolous impatience."

"Daphne, I——" The Judge made a gesture of sad capitulation.

"Oh, Judge March, it's too late to draw back now. That were cruel!"

John clambered into his high chair—said grace in a pretty rhyme of his mother's production—she was a poetess—and ended with:

"Amen, double-O-K. I wish double-O-K would mean firecrackers; firecrackers and cinnamon candy!" He patted his wrists together and glanced triumphantly upon the frowsy, barefooted waitress while Mrs. March poured the coffee.

The Judge's wife, at thirty-two, was still fair. Her face was thin, but her languorous eyes were expressive and her mouth delicate. A certain shadow about its corners may have meant rigidity of will or only a habit of introspection, but it was always there.

She passed her husband's coffee, and the hungry child, though still all eyes, was taking his first gulp of milk, when over the top of his mug he saw his father reach stealthily down to his saddle-bags and straighten again.

"Son."

"Suh!"

"Go on with yo' suppeh, son." Under the table the paper was coming off something. John filled both cheeks dutifully, but kept them so, unchanged, while the present came forth. Then he looked confused and turned to his mother. Her eyes were on her husband in deep dejection, as her hand rose to receive the book from the servant. She took it, read the title, and moaned:

"Oh! Judge March, what is your child to do with 'Lord Chesterfield's Letters to his Son?'"

John waited only for her pitying glance. Then the tears burst from his eyes and the bread and milk from his mouth, and he cried with a great and continuous voice, "I don't like presents! I want to go to bed!"

Even when the waitress got him there his mother could not quiet him. She demanded explanations and he could not explain, for by that time he had persuaded himself he was crying because his mother was not happy. But he hushed when the Judge, sinking down upon the bedside, said, as the despairing wife left the room,

"I'm sorry I've disappointed you so powerful, son. I know just how you feel. I made—" he glanced round to be sure she was gone—"just as bad a mistake one time, trying to make a present to myself."

The child lay quite still, vaguely considering whether that was any good reason why he should stop crying.

"But 'evomind, son, the ve'y next time we go to town we'll buy some cinnamon candy."

The son's eyes met the father's in a smile of love, the lids declined, the lashes folded, and his spirit circled softly down into the fathomless under-heaven of dreamless sleep.

## III.

### TWO FRIENDS

IT was nearly four o'clock of a day in early June. The sun shone exceptionally hot on the meagre waters of Turkey Creek, where it warmed its sinuous length through the middle of its wide battle-field. The turnpike, coming northward from Suez, emerged, white, dusty, and badly broken, on the southern border of this waste, and crossed the creek at right angles. Eastward, westward, the prospect widened away in soft heavings of fallow half ruined by rains. The whole landscape seemed bruised and torn, its beauty not gone, but ravished. A distant spot of yellow was wheat, a yet farther one may have been rye. Off on the right a thin green mantle that only half clothed the red shoulder of a rise along the eastern sky was cotton, the sometime royal claimant, unsceptred, but still potent and full of beauty. About the embers of a burned dwelling, elder, love-pop, and other wild things spread themselves in rank complacency, strange bed-fellows adversity had thrust in upon the frightened sweet-Betsy, phlox and jonquils of the ruined garden. Here the ground was gay with wild roses, and yonder blue, pink, white, and purple with expanses of larkspur.

A few steps to the left of the pike near the wood's strong shade, a beautiful brown horse in gray and yellow trappings suddenly lifted his head from the clover and gazed abroad.

"He knows there's been fighting here," said a sturdy voice from the thicket of ripe blackberries behind; "he sort o' smells it."

"Reckon he hears something," responded a younger voice farther from the road. "Maybe it's C'nelius's yodle; he's been listening for it for a solid week."

"He's got a good right to," came the first voice again; "worthless as that boy is, nobody ever took better care of a horse. I wish I had just about two dozen of his beat biscuit right now. He didn't have his equal in camp for beat biscuit."

"When sober," suggested the younger speaker, in that melodious Southern drawl so effective in dry satire; but the older voice did not laugh. One does not like to have another's satire pointed even at one's nigger.

The senior presently resumed a narrative made timely by the two having just come through the town. "You must remember I inherited no means and didn't get my education without a long, hard fight. A thorough clerical education's no mean thing to get."

"Couldn't the church help you?"

"Oh—yes—I, eh—I did have church aid, but—— Well, then I was three years a circuit rider and then I preached four years here in Suez. And then I married. Folks laugh about preachers always marrying fortunes—it was a mighty small fortune Rose Montgomery brought me! But she was Rose Montgomery, and I got her when no other man had the courage to ask for her. You know an ancestor of hers founded Suez. That's how it got its name. His name was Ezra and hers was Susan, don't you see?"

"I think I make it out," drawled the listener.

"But she didn't any more have a fortune than I did. She and her mother, who died about a year after, were living here in town just on the wages of three or four hired-out slaves, and——"

The younger voice interrupted with a question indolently drawn out: "Was she as beautiful in those days as they say?"

"Why, allowing for some natural exaggeration, yes."

"You built Rosemont about the time her mother died, didn't you?"

"Yes, about three years before the war broke out. It was the only piece of land she had left; too small for a plantation, but just the thing for a college."

"It is neatly named," pursued the questioner; "who did it?"

"I," half soliloquized the narrator, wrapped in the solitude of his own originality.

He moved into view, a large man of forty, unmilitary, despite his good gray broadcloth and wealth of gold braid, though of commanding and most comfortable mien. His upright coat-collar, too much agape, showed a clerical white cravat. His right arm was in a sling. He began to pick his way out of the brambles, dusting himself with a fine handkerchief. The horse came to meet him.

At the same time his young companion stepped upon a fallen tree, and stood to gaze, large-eyed, like the horse, across the sun-bathed scene. He seemed scant nineteen. His gray shirt was buttoned with locust thorns, his cotton-woolen jacket was caught under an old cartridge belt, his ragged trousers were thrust into bursted boots, and he was thickly powdered with white and yellow dust. His eyes swept slowly over the battle-ground to some low, wooded hills that rose beyond it against the pale northwestern sky.

"Major," said he.

The Major was busy lifting himself carefully into the saddle and checking his horse's eagerness to be off. But the youth still gazed, and said again, "Isn't that it?"

"What?"

"Rosemont."

"It is!" cried the officer, standing in his stirrups, and smiling fondly at a point where, some three miles away by the line of sight, a dark roof crowned by a white-railed lookout peeped over the tree-tops. "It's Rosemont—my own Rosemont! The view's been opened by cutting the woods off that hill this side of it. Come!"

Soon a wreath of turnpike dust near the broken culvert over Turkey Creek showed the good speed the travelers made. The ill-shod youth and delicately-shod horse trudged side by side through the furnace heat of sunshine. So intolerable were its rays that when an old reticule of fawn-skin with bright steel chains and mountings, well-known receptacle of the Major's private papers and stationery, dropped from its fastenings at the back of the saddle and the dismounted soldier stooped to pick it up, the horseman said: "Don't stop; let it go; it's empty. I burned everything in it the night of the surrender, even my wife's letters, don't you know?"

"Yes," said the youth, trying to open it, "I remember. Still, I'll take its parole before I turn it loose."

"That part doesn't open," said the rider, smiling, "it's only make-believe. Here, press in and draw down at the same time. There! nothing but my card that I pasted in the day I found the thing in some old papers I was looking over. I reckon it was my wife's grandmother's. Oh, yes, fasten it on again, though like as not I will give it away to Barb as soon as I get home. It's my way."

And the Reverend John Wesley Garnet, A.M., smiled at himself self-lovingly for being so unselfish about reticules.

"You need two thumbs to tie those leather strings, Jeff-Jack." Jeff-Jack had lost one, more than a year before, in a murderous onslaught where the Major and he had saved each other's lives, turn about, in almost the same moment. But the knot was tied, and they started on.

"Speakin' o' Barb, some of the darkies told her if she didn't stop chasing squir'ls up the campus trees and crying when they put shoes on her feet to take her to church, she'd be turned into a boy. What d' you reckon she said? She and Johanna—Johanna's her only playmate, you know—danced for joy; and Barb says, says she, 'An' den kin I doe in swimmin'?' Mind you, she's only five years old!" The Major's laugh came abundantly. "Mind you, she's only five!"

The plodding youth whiffed gayly at the heat,

switched off his bad cotton hat, and glanced around upon the scars of war. He was about to speak lightly; but as he looked upon the red washouts in the forsaken fields, and the dried sloughs in and beside the high-way, snaggy with broken fence-rails and their margins blackened by teamsters' night-fires, he fell to brooding on the impoverishment of eleven States, and on the hundreds of thousands of men and women sitting in the ashes of their desolated hopes and the lingering fear of unspeakable humiliations. Only that morning had these two comrades seen for the first time the procla-mation of amnesty and pardon with which the presi-dent of the triumphant republic ushered into a second birth the States of "the conquered banner."

"Major," said the young man, lifting his head, "you must open Rosemont again."

"Oh, I don't know, Jeff-Jack. It's mighty dark for us all ahead." The Major sighed with the air of being himself a large part of the fallen Confederacy.

"Law, Major, we've got stuff enough left to make a country of yet!"

"If they'll let us, Jeff-Jack. If they'll only let us; but will they?"

"Why, yes. They've shown their hand."

"You mean in this proclamation?"

"Yes, sir. Major, 'we-uns' can take that trick."

The two friends, so apart in years, exchanged a con-fidential smile. "Can we?" asked the senior.

"Can't we?" The young soldier walked on for several steps before he added, musingly, and with a cynical smile, "I've got neither land, money, nor education, but I'll help you put Rosemont on her feet again—just to sort o' open the game."

The Major gathered himself, exaltedly. "Jeff-Jack, if you will, I'll pledge you, here, that Rosemont shall make your interest her watchword so long as her interests are mine." The patriot turned his eyes to show Jeff-Jack their moisture.

The young man's smile went down at the corners, satirically, as he said, "That's all right," and they trudged on through the white dust and heat, looking at something in front of them.

---

## IV.

### THE JUDGE'S SON MAKES TWO LIFE-TIME ACQUAINT-ANCES, AND IS OFFERED A THIRD

THEY had been ascending a long slope and were just reaching its crest when the Major exclaimed, under his voice, "Well, I'll be hanged!"

Before them stood three rusty mules attached to a half load of corn in the shuck, surmounted by a coop of panting chickens. The wheels of the wagon were heavy with the dried mud of the Sandstone County road. The object of the Major's contempt was a smallish mulatto, who was mounting to the saddle of the off-wheel mule. He had been mending the rotten harness, and did not see the two soldiers until he lifted

again his long rein of cotton plough-line. The word to
go died on his lips.

"Why, Judge March!" Major Garnet pressed forward to where, at the team's left, the owner of these
chattels sat on his ill-conditioned horse.

"President Garnet! I hope yo' well, sir? Aw at
least," noticing the lame arm, "I hope yo' mendin'."

"Thank you, Brother March, I'm peart'nin', as they
say." The Major smiled broadly until his eye fell
again upon the mulatto. The Judge saw him stiffen.

"C'nelius only got back Sad'day," he said. The
mulatto crouched in his saddle and grinned down upon
his mule.

"He told me yo' wound compelled slow travel, sir;
yes, sir. Perhaps I ought to apologize faw hirin' him,
sir, but it was only pending yo' return, an' subjec' to
yo' approval, sir."

"You have it, Brother March," said Major Garnet
suavely, but he flashed a glance at the teamster that
stopped his grin, though he only said, "Howdy, Cornelius."

"Brother March, let me make you acquainted with
one of our boys. You remember Squire Ravenel, of
Flatrock? This is the only son the war's left him.
Adjutant, this is Judge March of Widewood, the
famous Widewood tract. Jeff-Jack was my adjutant,
Brother March, for a good while, though without the
commission."

The Judge extended a beautiful brown hand; the
ragged youth grasped it with courtly deference. The
two horses had been arrogantly nosing each other's

muzzles, and now the Judge's began to work his hinder end around as if for action. Whereupon :

"Why, look'e here, Brother March, what's this at the back of your saddle?"

The Judge smiled and laid one hand behind him. "That's my John—Asleep, son?—He generally is when he's back there, and he's seldom anywhere else. Drive on, C'nelius, I'll catch you."

As the wagon left them the child opened his wide eyes on Jeff-Jack, and Major Garnet said :

"He favors his mother, Brother March—though I haven't seen—I declare it's a shame the way we let our Southern baronial sort o' life make us such strangers— why, I haven't seen Sister March since our big union camp meeting at Chalybeate Springs in '58. Sonnie-boy, you ain't listening, are you?" The child still stared at Jeff-Jack. "Mighty handsome boy, Brother March—stuff for a good soldier—got a little sweet-heart at my house for you, sonnie-boy! Rosemont College and Widewood lands wouldn't go bad together, Brother March, ha, ha, ha! Your son has his mother's favor, but with something of yours, too, sir."

Judge March stroked the tiny, bare foot. "I'm proud to hope he'll favo' his mother, sir, in talents. You've seen her last poem : 'Slaves to ow own slaves —Neveh!' signed as usual, Daphne Dalrymple? Dalrymple's one of her family names. She uses it to avoid publicity. The Pulaski City *Clarion* reprints her poems and calls her 'sweetest of Southland song-sters.' Major Garnet, I wept when I read it! It's the finest thing she has ever written!"

"Ah! Brother March," the Major had seen the poem, but had not read it, "Sister March will never surpass those lines of her's on, let's see; they begin— Oh! dear me, I know them as well as I know my horse—How does that——"

"I know what you mean, seh. You mean the ballad of Jack Jones!

> "'Ho! Southrons, hark how one brave lad
> Three Yankee standards——'"

"Captured!" cried the Major. "That's it; why, my sakes! Hold on, Jeff-Jack, I'll be with you in just a minute. Why, I know it as—why, it rhymes with 'cohorts enraptured!'—I—why, of course!—Ah! Jeff-Jack it was hard on you that the despatches got your name so twisted. It's a plumb shame, as they say." The Major's laugh grew rustic as he glanced from Jeff-Jack, red with resentment, to Judge March, lifted half out of his seat with emotion, and thence to the child, still gazing on the young hero of many battles and one ballad.

"Well, that's all over; we can only hurry along home now, and——"

"Ah! President Garnet, *is* it all over, seh? *Is* it, Mr. Jones?"

"Can't say," replied Jeff-Jack, with his down-drawn smile, and the two pairs went their opposite ways.

As the Judge loped down the hot turnpike after his distant wagon, his son turned for one more gaze on the young hero, his hero henceforth, and felt the blood rush from every vein to his heart and back again as Mr.

Ravenel at the last moment looked round and waved
him farewell. Later he recalled Major Garnet's offer of
his daughter, but :

" I shall never marry," said John to himself.

------

## V.

### THE MASTER'S HOME-COMING

THE Garnet estate was far from baronial in its extent. Rosemont's whole area was scarcely sixty acres,
a third of which was wild grove close about three sides
of the dwelling. The house was of brick, large, with
many rooms in two tall stories above a basement. At
the middle of the north front was a square Greek porch
with wide steps spreading to the ground. A hall extended through and let out upon a rear veranda that
spanned the whole breadth of the house. Here two or
three wooden pegs jutted from the wall, on which to
hang a saddle, bridle, or gourd, and from one of which
always dangled a small cowhide whip. Barbara and
Johanna, hand in hand—Johanna was eleven and very
black—often looked on this object with whispering
awe, though neither had ever known it put to fiercer
use than to drive chickens out of the hall. Down in
the yard, across to the left, was the kitchen. And
lastly, there was that railed platform on the hip-roof,
whence one could see, in the northeast, over the tops of
the grove, the hills and then the mountains; in the

southeast the far edge of Turkey Creek battle-ground ;
and in the west, the great setting sun, often, from this
point, commended to Barbara as going to bed quietly
and before dark.

The child did not remember the father. Once or
twice during the war when otherwise he might have
come home on furlough, the enemy had intervened.
Yet she held no enthusiastic unbelief in his personal
reality, and prayed for him night and morning : that
God would bless him and keep him from being naughty
—" No, that ain't it—an' keep him f'om bein'—no, don't
tell me !—and ast him why he don't come see what a
sweet mom-a I'm dot ! "

People were never quite done marveling that even
Garnet should have won the mistress of this inheritance,
whom no one else had ever dared to woo. Her hair
was so dark you might have called it black—her eyes
were as blue as June, and all the elements of her outward beauty were but the various testimonies of a noble
mind. She had been very willing for Rosemont to be
founded here. There was a belief in her family that
the original patentee—he that had once owned the
whole site of Suez and more—had really from the first
intended this spot for a college site, and when Garnet
proposed that with his savings they build and open
upon it a male academy, of which he should be principal, she consented with an alacrity which his vanity
never ceased to resent, since it involved his leaving the
pulpit. For Principal Garnet was very proud of his
moral character.

On the same afternoon in which John March first

saw the Major and Jeff-Jack, Barbara and Johanna
were down by the spring-house at play. This structure
stood a good two hundred yards from the dwelling,
where a brook crossed the road. Three wooded slopes
ran down to it, and beneath the leafy arches of a
hundred green shadows that only at noon were
flecked with sunlight, the water glassed and crinkled
scarce ankle deep over an unbroken floor of naked
rock.

The pair were wading, Barbara in the road, Johanna
at its edge, when suddenly Barbara was aware of
strange voices, and looking up, was fastened to her footing by the sight of two travelers just at hand. One
was on horseback; the other, a youth, trod the step-
ping stones, ragged, dusty, but bewilderingly handsome.
Johanna, too, heard, came, and then stood like Barbara,
awe-stricken and rooted in the water. The next moment there was a whirl, a bound, a splash—and Barbara was alone. Johanna, with three leaping strides,
was out of the water, across the fence, and scampering
over ledges and loose stones toward the house, mad with
the joy of her news:

"Mahse John Wesley! Mahse John Wesley!"—
up the front steps, into the great porch and through the
hall—"Mahse John Wesley! Mahse John Wesley!
De waugh done done! De waugh ove' dis time fo' sho'!
Glory! Glory!"—down the back steps, into the
kitchen—"Mahse John Wesley!"—out again and off to
the stables—"Mahse John Wesley!" While old Virginia ran from the kitchen to her cabin rubbing the
flour from her arms and crying, "Tu'n out! tu'n out,

you laazy black niggers!    Mahse John Wesley Gyarnet a-comin' up de road!"

Barbara did not stir.    She felt the soldier's firm
hands under her arms, and her own form, straightened
and rigid, rising to the glad lips of the disabled
stranger who bent from the saddle; but she kept her
eyes on the earth.    With her dripping toes stiffened
downward and the youth clasping her tightly, they
moved toward the house.    In the grove gate the horseman galloped ahead; but Barbara did not once look
up until at the porch-steps she saw yellow Willis, the
lame ploughman, smiling and limping forward round
the corner of the house; Trudie, the house girl, trying
to pass him by; Johanna wildly dancing; Aunt Virginia, her hands up, calling to heaven from the red
cavern of her mouth; Uncle Leviticus, her husband,
Cornelius's step-father, holding the pawing steed; gladness on every face, and the mistress of Rosemont drawing
from the horseman's arm to welcome her ragged guest.

Barbara gazed on the bareheaded men and courtesy-
ing women grasping the hand of their stately master.

"Howdy, Mahse John Wesley.    Welcome home, sah.
Yass, sah!"

"Howdy, Mahse John Wesley.    Yass, sah; dass so,
sot free, but niggehs yit, te-he!—an' Rosemont niggehs
yit!"    Chorus, "Dass so!" and much laughter.

"Howdy, Mahse John Wesley.    Miss Rose happy
now, an' whensomever she happy, us happy.    Yass, sah.
De good Lawd be praise!    Now is de waugh over an'
finish' an' eended an' gone!"    Chorus, "Pra-aise
Gawd!"

The master replied. He was majestically kind. He commended their exceptional good sense and prophesied a reign of humble trust and magnanimous protection.— " But I see you're all—" he smiled a gracious irony— " anxious to get back to work."

They laughed, pushed and smote one another, and went, while he mounted the stairs; they, strangers to the sufferings of his mind, and he as ignorant as many a far vaster autocrat of the profound failure of his words to satisfy the applauding people he left below him.

In the hall Jeff-Jack let Barbara down. Thump-thump-thump—she ran to find Johanna. A fear and a hope quite filled her with their strife, the mortifying fear that at the brook Mr. Ravenel had observed—and the reinspiring hope that he had failed to observe—that she was without shoes! She remained away for some time, and came back shyly in softly squeaking leather. As he took her on his knee she asked, carelessly :

" Did you ever notice I'm dot socks on to-day ? " and when he cried " No ! " and stroked them, she silently applauded her own tact.

Virginia and her mistress decided that the supper would have to be totally reconsidered—reconstructed. Jeff-Jack and Barbara, the reticule on her arm, walked in the grove where the trees were few. The flat out-croppings of gray and yellow rocks made grotesque figures in the grass, and up from among the cedar sprouts turtle-doves sprang with that peculiar music of their wings, flew into distant coverts, and from one such to another tenderly complained of love's alarms and separations. When Barbara asked her escort where his home was, he said it was going to be in Suez, and on cross-examination explained that Flatrock was only a small plantation where his sister lived and took care of his father, who was old and sick.

He seemed to Barbara to be very easily amused, even laughing at some things she said which she did not intend for jokes at all. But since he laughed she laughed too, though with more reserve. They picked wild flowers. He gave her forget-me-nots.

They did not bring their raging hunger into the house again until the large tea-bell rang in the porch, and the air was rife with the fragrance of Aunt Virginia's bounty : fried ham, fried eggs, fried chicken, strong coffee, and hot biscuits—of fresh Yankee flour from Suez. No wine, and no tonic before sitting down. In the pulpit and out of it Garnet had ever been an ardent advocate of total abstinence. He never, even in his own case, set aside its rigors except when chilled or fatigued, and always then took ample care not to let his action, or any subsequent confession, be a temptation in the eyes of others who might be weaker than he.

Barbara sat opposite Jeff-Jack. What of that ? Johanna, standing behind mom-a's chair, should not have smiled and clapped her hands to her mouth. Barbara ignored her. As she did again, after supper, when, silent, on the young soldier's knee, amid an earnest talk upon interests too public to interest her, she could see her little nurse tiptoeing around the door out in the dim hall, grinning in white gleams of summer lightning, beckoning, and pointing upstairs. The best way to treat such things is to take no notice of them.

In the bright parlor the talk was still on public affairs. The war was over, but its issues were still largely in suspense and were not questions of boundaries or dynasties; they underlay every Southern hearthstone; the possibilities of each to-morrow were the personal concern and distress of every true Southern man, of every true Southern woman.

Thus spoke Garnet. His strong, emotional voice was the one most heard. Ravenel held Barbara, and responded scarcely so often as her mother, whose gentle self-command rested him. Not such was its effect upon the husband. His very flesh seemed to feel the smartings of trampled aspirations and insulted rights. More than once, under stress of his sincere though florid sentences, he rose proudly to his feet with a hand laid unconsciously on his freshly bandaged arm, as though all the pain and smart of the times were centring there, and tried good-naturedly to reflect the satirical composure of his late adjutant. But when he sought to make light of "the slings and arrows of outrageous fortune," he could not quite hide the exasperation of a spirit covered with their contusions; and when he spoke again, he frowned.

Mrs. Garnet observed Ravenel with secret concern. Men like Garnet, addicted to rhetoric, have a way of always just missing the vital truth of things, and this is what she believed this stripling had, in the intimacies of the headquarter's tent, discerned in him, and now so mildly, but so frequently, smiled at. "Major Garnet,"

she said, and silently indicated that some one was waiting in the doorway. The Major, standing, turned and
saw, faltering with conscious overboldness on the threshold, a tawny figure whose shoulders stared through
the rags of a coarse cotton shirt ; the man of all men to
whom he was just then the most unprepared to show
patience.

---

## VI.

### TROUBLE

OUTSIDE it was growing dark. The bright red dot
that, from the railed housetop, you might have seen on
the far edge of Turkey Creek battle-ground, was a
watch-fire beside the blackberry patch we know of.
Here sat Judge March guarding his wagon and mules.
One of them was sick. The wagon, under a load of
barreled pork and general supplies, had slumped into
a hole and suffered a "general giving-way." While in
Suez the Judge had paid Cornelius off, written a note to
be given by him to Major Garnet, and agreed, in recognition of his abundant worthlessness, to part with him
from date, finally.

Yet the magnanimous Cornelius, still with him when
the wagon broke, went back to Suez for help and horse
medicine, but trifled so sadly, or so gayly, that at sunset there was no choice but to wait till morning.

John, however, had to be sent home. But how? On

the Judge's horse, behind Cornelius? The father hesitated. But the mulatto showed such indignant grief
and offered such large promises, the child, of course, sid-
ing with the teamster, and after all, they could reach
Widewood so soon after nightfall, that the Judge sent
them. From Widewood, Cornelius, alone, was to turn
promptly back——

"Well, o' co'se, sah! Ain't I always promp'?"—

Promptly back by way of Rosemont, leave the note
there and then bring the Judge's horse to him at the
camp-fire. If lights were out at Rosemont he could
give the letter to some servant to be delivered next
morning.

"Good-bye, son. I can't hear yo' prayers to-night.
I'll miss it myself. But if yo' dear motheh ain't too
ti-ud maybe she'll hear 'em."

It suited Cornelius to turn aside first to Rosemont.

"You see, Johnnie, me an' Majo' Gyarnet is got some
ve'y urgen' business to transpiah. An' den likewise an'
mo'oveh, here's de triflin' matteh o' dis letteh. What
contents do hit contain? I's done yo' paw a powerful
favo', an' yit I has a sneakin' notion dat herein yo' paw
express hisseff wid great lassitude about me. An' thus,
o' co'se, I want to know it befo' han,' caze ef a man play
you a trick you don't want to pay him wid a favo'.
Trick fo' trick, favo' fo' favo', is de rule of Cawnelius
Leggett, Esquire, freedman, an' ef I fines, when Majo'
Gyarnet read dis-yeh letteh, dat yo' paw done inter-
callate me a trick, I jist predestinatured to git evm wid
bofe of 'm de prompes' way I kin. You neveh seed me
mad, did you? Well, when you see Cawnelius Leggett

mad you wants to run an' hide. He wou'n't hu't a chile no mo'n he'd hu't a chicken, but ef dere's a *man* in de way—jis' on'y in de *way*—an' specially a *white* man— Lawd! he betteh teck a tree!"

The windows of Rosemont had for some time been red with lamplight when they fastened their horse to a swinging limb near the springhouse and walked up through the darkening grove to the kitchen. Virginia received her son with querulous surprise. " Gawd's own fool," she called him, " fuh runnin' off, an' de same fool double' an' twisted fo' slinkin' back." But when he arrogantly showed the Judge's letter she lapsed into silent disdain while she gave him an abundant supper. After a time the child was left sitting beside the kitchen fire, holding an untasted biscuit. Throughout the yard and quarters there was a stillness that was not sleep, though Virginia alone was out-of-doors, standing on the moonlit veranda looking into the hall.

She heard Major Garnet ask, with majestic forbearance, " Well, Cornelius, what do you want? "

The teamster advanced with his ragged hat in one hand and the letter in the other. The Major, flushing red, lifted his sound arm, commandingly, and the mulatto stopped. " Boy, can it be that in my presence and in the presence of your mistress you dare attempt to change the manners you were raised to ? "

Cornelius opened his mouth with great pretense of ignorance, but——

" Go back and drop that hat outside the door, sir ! " The servant went.

" Now, bring me that letter ! " The bearer brought

it and stood waiting while the Major held it under his lame arm and tore it open.

Judge March wrote that he had found a way to dispense with Cornelius at once, but his main wish was to express the hope—having let a better opportunity slip— that President Garnet as the "person best fitted in all central Dixie to impart to Southern youth a purely Southern education," would reopen Rosemont at once, and to promise his son to the college as soon as he should be old enough.

But for two things the Major might have felt soothed. One was a feeling that Cornelius had in some way made himself unpleasant to the Judge, and this grew to conviction as his nostrils caught the odor of strong drink. He handed the note to his wife.

"Judge March is always complimentary. Read it to Jeff-Jack. Cornelius, I'll see you for a moment on the back gallery." His wife tried to catch his eye, but a voice within him commended him to his own self-command, and he passed down the hall, the mulatto following. Johanna, crouching and nodding against the wall, straightened up as he passed. His footfall sounded hope to the strained ear of the Judge's son in the kitchen. Virginia slipped away. In the veranda, under the moonlight, Garnet turned and said, in a voice almost friendly:

"Cornelius."

"Yass, sah."

"Cornelius, why did you go off and hire yourself out, sir?"

At the last word the small listener in the kitchen trembled.

"Dass jess what I 'llow to 'splain to you, sah."

"It isn't necessary. Cornelius, you know that if ever one class of human beings owed a lifelong gratitude to another, you negroes owe it to your old masters, don't you? Stop! don't you dare to say no? Here you all are; never has one of you felt a pang of helpless hunger or lain one day with a neglected fever. Food, clothing, shelter, you've never suffered a day's doubt about them! No other laboring class ever were so free from the cares of life. Your fellow-servants have shown some gratitude; they've stayed with their mistress till I got home to arrange with them under these new conditions. But you—you! when I let you push on ahead and leave me sick and wounded and only half way home—your home and mine, Cornelius—with your promise to wait here till I could come and retain you on wages—you, in pure wantonness, must lift up your heels and prance away into your so-called new liberty. You're a fair sample of what's to come, Cornelius. You've spent your first wages for whiskey. Silence, you perfidious reptile!

"Oh, Cornelius, you needn't dodge in that way, sir, I'm not going to take you to the stable; thank God I'm done whipping you and all your kind, for life! Cornelius, I've only one business with you and it's only one word! Go! at once! forever! You should go if it were only—— Cornelius, I've been taking care of my own horse! Don't you dare to sleep on these premises to-night. Wait! Tell me what you've done to offend Judge March?"

"Why, Mahse John Wesley, I ain't done nothin' to

Jedge Mahch ; no, sah, neither defensive nor yit offensive. An' yit mo', I ain't dream o' causin' you sich uprisin' he'plessness. Me and Jedge Mahch "—he began to swell—" has had a stric'ly private disparitude on the subjec' o' extry wages, account'n o' his disinterpretations o' my plans an' his ign'ance o' de law." He tilted his face and gave himself an argumentative frown of matchless insolence. " You see, my deah seh——"

Garnet was wearily turning his head from side to side as if in unspeakable pain ; a sudden movement of his free arm caused the mulatto to flinch, but the ex-master said, quietly :

" Go on, Cornelius."

" Yass. You see, Major, sence dis waugh done put us all on a sawt of equality——" The speaker flinched again.

" Great Heaven ! " groaned the Major. " Cornelius, why, Cor—*nelius* ! you *viper !* if it were not for dishonoring my own roof I'd thrash you right here. I've a good notion——"

" Ow ! leggo me ! I ain't gwine to 'low no daym rebel——"

Ravenel, stroking Barbara and talking to Mrs. Garnet, saw his hostess start and then try to attend to his words, while out on the veranda rang notes of fright and pain.

" Oh ! don't grabble my whole bres' up dat a-way, sah ! Please sah ! Oh ! don't ! You ain't got no mo' right ! Oh ! Lawd ! Mahse John Wesley ! Oh ! good Lawdy ! yo' han' bites like a *dawg !* "

Ravenel paused in his talk to ask Barbara about

the sandman, but the child stared wildly at her mother.
Johanna reappeared in the door with a scared face;
Barbara burst into loud weeping, and her nurse bore
her away crying and bending toward her mother, while
from the veranda the wail poured in.

"Oh! Oh! don't resh me back like that! Oh! Oh!
my Gawd! Oh! you'll bre'k de balusters! Oh! my
Gawd-A'mighty, my back; Mahse John Wesley, you
a-breakin' *my back!* Oh, good Lawd 'a' mussy! my
po' back! my po' back! Oh! don't dra—ag—you
ain't a-needin' to drag me. I'll walk, Mahse John
Wesley, I'll walk! Oh! you a-scrapin' my knees off!
Oh! dat whip ain't over dah! You can't re'ch it
down!—ef I bite——" There was a silent instant and
the mulatto screamed.

With sinking knees a small form slipped from the
kitchen and ran—fell—rose—and ran again across the
moonlight and into the grove toward the spring-house.

Barbara's crying increased. Ravenel said:

"Don't let me keep you from the baby"—while
outside:

"Oh! I didn't mean to bite you, sweet Mahse John
Wesley. 'Fo' Gawd I—oh!—o—oh—h—you broke
my knees!"

"If you'll excuse me," said the mother, and went
upstairs.

"Oh! mussy! mussy! yo' foot a-mashing my whole
breas' in'! Oh, my Gawd! De Yankees 'll git win' o'
dis an' you'll go to jail!"

The lash fell. "O—oh!—o—oh! Oh, Lawd!" Jeff-
Jack sat still and once or twice smiled. "Oh, Lawd 'a'

mussy! my back! Ow! It bu'ns like fiah!—o—oh!
—oh!—ow!"

"It doesn't hurt as bad as it ought to, Cornelius,"
and the blows came again.

"Ow! Dey won't git win' of it! 'Deed an 'deedy
dey won't, sweet Mahse John Wesley!—oh!—o—oh!
—Ow!—Oh, Lawd, come down! Dey des *shan't* git
win' of it! 'fo' Gawd dey shan't! Ow!—oh!—oh!—
oh!—a—ah—oo—oo!"

"Now, go!" said Garnet. Cornelius leaped up, ran
with his eyes turned back on the whip, and fell again,
wallowing like a scalded dog. "Oh, my po' back, my
po' back! M—oh! it's a-bu'nin' up—oh!"

The Major advanced with the broken whip uplifted.
Cornelius ran backward to the steps and rolled clear to
the ground. The whip was tossed after him. With a
gnashing curse he snatched it up and hurried off,
moaning and writhing, into the darkness, down by the
spring-house.

Garnet smiled in scorn, far from guessing that soon,
almost as soon as yonder receding clatter of hoofs
should pass into silence, the venomous thing from
which he had lifted his heel would coil and strike, and
that another back, a little one that had never felt the
burden of a sin or a task, or aught heavier than the
sun's kiss, was to take its turn at writhing and burning
like fire.

The memory of that hour, when it was over and
home was reached, was burnt into the child's mind forever. It was then late. Mrs. March, "never strong,"
and,—with a sigh,—"never anxious," had retired. Her

two handmaids, freedwomen, were new to the place, but already fond of her son. Cornelius found them waiting uneasily at the garden-fence. He had lingered and toiled with the Judge and his broken wagon, he said, "notwithstandin' we done dissolve," until he had got the worst "misery in his back" he had ever suffered. When they received John from him and felt the child's tremblings, he warned them kindly that the less asked about it the better for the reputations of both the boy and his father.

"You can't 'spute the right an' custody of a man to his own son's chastisement, naw yit to 'low to dat son dat ef ever he let his maw git win' of it, he give him double an' thribble."

When the women told him he lied he appealed to John, and the child nodded his head. About midnight Cornelius handed the horse over to Judge March, reassuring him of his son's safety and comfort, and hurried off, much pleased with the length of his own head in that he had not stolen the animal. John fell asleep almost as soon as he touched the pillow. Then the maid who had undressed him beckoned the other in. Candle in hand she led the way to the trundle-bed drawn out from under the Judge's empty four-poster, and sat upon its edge. The child lay chest downward. She lifted his gown, and exposed his back.

"Good Gawd!" whispered the other.

## VII.

### EXODUS

As Major Garnet's step sounded again in the hall, Barbara's crying came faintly down through the closed doors. He found Ravenel sitting by the lamp, turning the spotted leaves of Heber's poems.

"Mrs. Garnet putting Barb to bed?" he asked, and slowly took an easy chair. His arm was aching cruelly.

"Yes." The young guest stretched and smiled.

The host was silent. He was willing to stand by what he had done, but that this young friend with lower moral pretensions wholly approved it made his company an annoyance. What he craved was unjust censure. "I reckon you'd like to go up, too, wouldn't you? It's camp bedtime."

"Yes, got to come back to sleeping in-doors—might as well begin."

On the staircase they met Johanna, with a lighted candle. The Major said, as kindly as a father, "I'll take that."

As she gave it her eyes rolled whitely up to his, tears slipped down her black cheeks, he frowned, and she hurried away. At his guest's door he said a pleasant good-night, and then went to his wife's room.

Only moonlight was there. From a small, dim chamber next to it came Barbara's softened moan. The mother sang low a child hymn. The father sat down at a window, and strove to meditate. But his arm ached. The mother sang on, and presently he found himself waiting for the fourth stanza. It did not come; the child was still; but his memory supplied it:

> " And soon, too soon, the wintry hour
>     Of man's maturer age
>   May shake the soul with sorrow's power,
>     And stormy passion's rage."

He felt, but put aside, the implication of reproach to himself which lay in the words and his wife's avoidance of them. He still believed that, angry and unpremeditated as his act was, he could not have done otherwise in justice nor yet in mercy. And still, through this right doing, what bitterness had come! His wife's, child's, guest's—his own—sensibilities had been painfully shocked. In the depths of a soldier's sorrow for a cause loved and lost, there had been the one consolation that the unasked freedom so stupidly thrust upon these poor slaves was in certain aspects an emancipation to their masters. Yet here, before his child had learned to fondle his cheek, or his home-coming was six hours old, his first night of peace in beloved Rosemont had been blighted by this vile ingrate forcing upon him the exercise of the only discipline, he fully believed, for which such a race of natural slaves could have a wholesome regard. The mother sang again, murmurously. The soldier grasped his suffering arm, and returned to thought.

The war, his guest had said, had not taken the slaves away. It could only redistribute them, under a new bondage of wages instead of the old bondage of pure force. True. And the best and the wisest servants would now fall to the wisest and kindest masters. Oh, for power to hasten to-morrow's morning, that he might call to him again that menial band down in the yard, speak to them kindly, even of Cornelius's fault, bid them not blame the outcast resentfully, and assure them that never while love remained stronger in them than pride, need they shake the light dust of Rosemont from their poor shambling feet.

He rose, stole to the door of the inner room, pushed it noiselessly, and went in. Barbara, in her crib, was hidden by her mother standing at her side. The wife turned, glanced at her husband's wounded arm, and made a soft gesture for him to keep out of sight. The child was leaning against her mother, saying the last words of her own pr..yer.

"An' Dod bless ev'ybody, Uncle Leviticus, an' Aunt Jinny, an' Johanna, an' Willis, an' Trudie, an' C'nelius "—a sigh—" an mom-a, an'—that's all—an'——"

"And pop-a?"

No response. The mother prompted again. Still the child was silent. "And pop-a, you know—the best last."

"An' Dod bless the best last," said Barbara, sadly. A pause.

"Don't you know all good little girls ask God to bless their pop-a's?"

"Do they?"

"Yes."

"Dod bless pop-a," she sighed, dreamily; "an' Dod

bless me, too, an'—an' keep me f'om bein' a dood little dirl.—Ma'am?—Yes, ma'am.    Amen."

She laid her head down, and in a moment was asleep. Husband and wife passed out together.   The wounded arm, its pain unconfessed, was cared for, pious prayers were said, and the pair lay down to slumber.

Far in the night the husband awoke.   He could think better now, in the almost perfect stillness.   There were faint signs of one or two servants being astir, but in the old South that was always so.   He pondered again upon the present and the future of the unhappy race upon whom freedom had come as a wild freshet. Thousands must sink, thousands starve, for all were drunk with its cruel delusions.   Yea, on this deluge the whole Southern social world, with its two distinct divisions—the shining upper—the dark nether—was reeling and careening, threatening, each moment, to turn once and forever wrong side up, a hope-forsaken wreck.   To avert this, to hold society on its keel, must be the first and constant duty of whoever saw, as he did, the fearful peril.   So, then, this that he had done—and prayed that he might never have to do again—was, underneath all its outward hideousness, a more than right, a generous, deed.   For a man who, taking all the new risks, still taught these poor, base, dangerous creatures to keep the only place they could keep with safety to themselves or their superiors, was to them the only truly merciful man.

He drifted into revery.   Thoughts came so out of harmony with this line of reasoning that he could only dismiss them as vagaries.   Was sleep returning?   No, he laid wide awake, frowning with the pain of his wound. Yet he must have drowsed at last, for when suddenly he saw his wife standing, draped in some dark wrapping, hearkening at one of the open windows, the moon was sinking.

He sat up and heard faintly, far afield, the voices of Leviticus, Virginia, Willis, Trudie, and Johanna, singing one of the wild, absurd, and yet passionately significant hymns of the Negro Christian worship. Distance drowned the words, but an earlier familiarity supplied them to the grossly syncopated measures of the tune which, soft and clear, stole in at the open window:

> " Rise in dat mawnin', an' rise in dat mawnin',
>  Rise in dat mawnin', an' fall upon yo' knees.
> Bow low, an' a-bow low, an' a-bow low a little bit longah,
> Bow low, an' a-bow low; sich a conquerin' king!"

The eyes of wife and husband met in a long gaze.

"They're coming this way," he faltered.

She slowly shook her head.

"My love—" But she motioned for silence and said, solemnly:

" They're leaving us."

" They're wrong!" he murmured in grieved indignation.

"Oh, who is right?" she sadly asked.

" They shall not treat us so!" exclaimed he. He would have sprung to his feet, but she turned upon him suddenly, uplifting her hand, and with a ring in her voice that made the walls of the chamber ring back, cried,

" No, no ! Let them go ! They were mine when they were property, and they are mine now ! Let them go ! "

The singing ceased. The child in the next room had not stirred. The dumfounded husband sat motionless under pretence of listening. His wife made a despairing gesture. He motioned to hearken a moment more ; but no human sound sent a faintest ripple across the breathless air ; the earth was as silent as the stars. Still he waited—in vain—they were gone.

The soldier and his wife lay down once more without a word. There was no more need of argument than of accusation. For in those few moments the weight of his calamities had broken through into the under quicksands of his character and revealed them to himself.

---

## VIII.

### SEVEN YEARS OF SUNSHINE

POETS and painters make darkness stand for oblivion. But for evil things or sad there is no oblivion like sunshine.

The next day was hot, blue, and fragrant. John rose so late that he had to sit up in front of his breakfast alone. He asked the maid near by if she thought his father would be home soon. She " reckoned so."

" I wish he would be home in a hour," he mused,

aloud. " I wish he would be on the mountain road right now."

When he stepped down and started away she crouched before him.

" Whah you bound fuh, ole gen'leman, lookin' so sawt o' funny-sad ? "

" I dunno."

" W'at you gwine do, boss ? "

" I dunno."

" Well, cayn't you kiss me, Mist' I-dunno ? "

He paid the toll and passed out to his play. With an old bayonet fixed on a stick he fell to killing Yankees—colored troops. Pressing them into the woods he charged, yelling, and came out upon the mountain road that led far down to the pike. Here a new impulse took him and he moved down this road to form a junction with his father. For some time the way was comparatively level. By and by he came to heavier timber and deeper and steeper descents. He went ever more and more loiteringly, for his father did not appear. He thought of turning back, yet his longing carried him forward. He was tired, but his mother did not like him to walk long distances when he was tired, so it wouldn't be right to turn back. He decided to wait for his father and ride home.

Meantime he would go to the next turn in the road and look. He looked in vain. And so at the next—the next—the next. He went slowly, for his feet were growing tender. Sometimes he almost caught a butterfly. Sometimes he slew more Yankees. Always he talked to himself with a soft bumbling like a bee's.

But at last he ceased even this and sat down at the edge of the stony road ready to cry. His bosom had indeed begun to heave, when in an instant all was changed. Legs forgot their weariness, the heart its dismay, for just across the road, motionless beside a hollow log, what should he see but a cotton-tail rabbit. As he stealthily reached for his weapon the cotton-tail took two slow hops and went into the log. Charge bayonets!—pat-pat-pat—slam! and the stick rattled in the hole, the deadly iron at one end and the deadly boy at the other.

And yet nothing was impaled. Singular! He got his eyes to the hole and glared in, but although it was full of daylight from a larger hole at the other end, he could see no sign of life. It baffled comprehension. But so did it defy contradiction. There was but one resource: to play the rabbit was still there and only to be got out by rattling the bayonet every other moment and repeating, in a sepulchral voice, " I—I—I'm gwine to have yo' meat fo' dinneh!"

He had been doing this for some time when all at once his blood froze as another voice, fifteen times as big as his, said, in his very ear—

" I—I—I'm gwine to have yo' meat fo' dinneh."

He dropped half over, speechless, and beheld standing above him, nineteen feet high as well as he could estimate hastily, a Yankee captain mounted and in full uniform. John leaped up, and remembered he was in gray.

" What are you doing here all alone, Shorty?"

" I dunno."

" Who are you ?   What's your name ? "

" I dunno."

The Captain moved as if to draw his revolver, but brought forth instead a large yellow apple.   Then did John confess who he was and why there.   The Captain did as much on his part.

He had risen with the morning star to do an errand beyond Widewood, and was now getting back to Suez. This very dawn he had made Judge March's acquaintance beside his broken wagon, and had seen him ride toward Suez to begin again the repair of his disasters. Would the small Confederate like to ride behind him ?

Very quickly John gave an arm and was struggling up behind the saddle.   The Captain touched the child's back.

" Owch ! "

" Why, what's the matter ?   Did I hurt you ? "

" No, sir."

The horse took his new burden unkindly, plunged and danced.

" Afraid ? " asked the Captain.   John's eyes sparkled merrily and he shook his head.

" You're a pretty brave boy, aren't you ? " said the stranger.   But John shook his head again.

" I'll bet you are, and a tol'able good boy, too, aren't you ? "

" No, sir, I'm not a good boy, I'm bad.   I'm a very bad boy, indeed."

The horseman laughed.   " I don't mistrust but you're good enough."

" Oh, no.   I'm not good.   I'm wicked !   I'm noisy !

I make my ma's head ache every day! I usen't to be
so wicked when I was a little shaver. I used to be a
shaver, did you know that? But now I'm a boy.
That's because I'm eight. I'm a boy and I'm wicked.
I'm awful wicked, and I'm getting worse. I whistle.
Did you think I could whistle? Well, I can.   .   .   .
There! did you hear that? It's wicked to whistle in
the house—to whistle loud—in the house—it's sinful.
Sometimes I whistle in the house—sometimes." He
grew still and fell to thinking of his mother, and how
her cheek would redden with something she called sorrow at his shameless companioning with the wearer of
a blue uniform. But he continued to like his new
friend; he was so companionably " low flung."

"Do you know Jeff-Jack?" he asked. But the
Captain had not the honor.

"Well, he captures things. He's brave. He's
dreadful brave."

"No! Aw! you just want to scare me!"

"So is Major Garnet. Did you ever see Major
Garnet? Well, if you see him you mustn't make him
mad. I'd be afraid for you to make him mad."

"Why, how's that?"

"I dunno," said Johnnie, very abstractedly.

As they went various questions came up, and by and
by John discoursed on the natural badness of " black
folks "—especially the yellow variety—with imper-
fections of reasoning almost as droll as the soft dragging
of his vowels. Time passed so pleasantly that when
they came into the turnpike and saw his father coming
across the battle-field with two other horsemen, his good

spirits hardly had room to rise any higher. They rather fell. The Judge had again chanced upon the company of Major Garnet and Jeff-Jack Ravenel, and it disturbed John perceptibly for three such men to find him riding behind a Yankee.

It was a double surprise for him to see, first, with what courtesy they treated the blue-coat, and then how soon they bade him good-day. The Federal had smilingly shown a flask.

"You wouldn't fire on a flag of truce, would you?"

"I never drink," said Garnet.

"And I always take too much," responded Jeff-Jack.

I think we have spoken of John's slumbers being dreamless. A child can afford to sleep without dreaming, he has plenty of dreams without sleeping. No need to tell what days, weeks, months, of sunlit, forest-shaded, bird-serenaded, wide-awake dreaming passed over this one's wind-tossed locks between the ages of eight and fifteen.

Small wonder that he dreamed. Much of the stuff that fables and fairy tales are made of was the actual furnishment of his visible world—unbroken leagues of lofty timber that had never heard the ring of an axe; sylvan labyrinths where the buck and doe were only half afraid; copses alive with small game; rare openings where the squatter's wooden ploughshare lay forgotten; dark chasms scintillant with the treasures of the chemist, if not of the lapidary; outlooks that opened upon great seas of billowing forest, whence blue mountains peered up, sank and rose again like ocean monsters at play; glens where the she-bear suckled her drowsing cubs to the plash of yeasty waterfalls that leapt and whimpered to be in human service, but wherein the otter played all day unscared; crags where the eagle nested; defiles that echoed the howl of wolves unhunted, though the very stones cried out their open secret of immeasurable wealth; narrow vales where the mountain cabin sent up its blue thread of smoke, and in its lonely patch strong weeds and emaciated corn and cotton pushed one another down among the big clods; and vast cliffs from whose bushy brows the armed moonshiner watched the bridle-path below.

These dreams of other children's story-books were John's realities. And these were books to him, as well, while Chesterfield went unread, and other things and conditions, not of nature and her seclusions, but vibrant with human energies and strifes, were making, unheeded of him, his world and his fate. A little boy's life does right to loiter. But if we loiter with him here, we are likely to find our eyes held ever by the one picture: John's gifted mother, in family group, book in her lap—husband's hand on her right shoulder—John leaning against her left side. Let us try leaving him for a time. And, indeed, we may do the same as to Jeff-Jack Ravenel,

As he had told Barbara he would, he made his residence in Suez.

A mess-mate, a graceless, gallant fellow, who at the war's end had fallen, dying, into his arms, had sent by him a last word of penitent love to his mother, an aged widow. She lived in Suez, and when Ravenel brought this message to her—from whom marriage had torn all her daughters and death her only son—she accepted his offer, based on a generous price, to take her son's room as her sole boarder and lodger. Thus, without further effort, he became the stay of her home and the heir of her simple affections.

---

## IX.

### LAUNCELOT HALLIDAY

GENERAL HALLIDAY was a distant cousin of Mrs. Garnet. He had commanded the brigade which included Garnet's battalion, and had won fame. Garnet, who felt himself undervalued by Halliday, said this fame had been won by show rather than by merit. And in truth, Halliday was not so much a man of genuine successes as of an audacity that stopped just short of the fantastical, and kept him perpetually interesting.

"Launcelot's failures," said Garnet, "make a finer show than most men's successes. He'd rather shine without succeeding, than succeed without shining."

The moment the war ended, Halliday hurried back to his plantation, the largest in Blackland. This county's sole crop was cotton, and negroes two-thirds of its population. His large family—much looked up to—had called it home, though often away from it, seeking social stir at the State capital and elsewhere. On his return from the war, the General brought with him a Northerner, an officer in the very command to which he had surrendered. Just then, you may remember, when Southerners saw only ruin in their vast agricultural system, many Northerners thought they saw a new birth. They felt the poetry of Dixie's long summers, the plantation life—Uncle Tom's Cabin—and fancied that with Uncle Tom's good-will and Northern money and methods, there was quick fortune for them. Halliday echoed these bright predictions with brave buoyancy and perfect sincerity, and sold the conqueror his entire estate. Then he moved his family to New Orleans, and issued his card to his many friends, announcing himself prepared to receive and sell any shipments of cotton, and fill any orders for supplies, with which they might entrust him. The Government's pardon, on which this fine rapidity was hypothecated, came promptly—"through a pardon broker," said Garnet.

But the General's celerity was resented. He boarded at the St. Charles, and, famous, sociable, and fond of politics, came at once into personal contact with the highest Federal authorities in New Orleans. The happy dead earnest with which he "accepted the situation" and "harmonized" with these men sorely offended his old friends and drew the fire of the newspapers. Even Judge March demurred.

"President Garnet," John heard the beloved voice in front of him say, "gentlemen may cry Peace, Peace, but there can be too much peace, sir!"

The General came out in an open letter, probably not so sententiously as we condense it here, but in substance to this effect : " The king never dies ; citizenship never ceases ; a bereaved citizenship has no right to put on expensive mourning, and linger through a dressy widowhood before it marries again. . . . There are men who, when their tree has been cut down even with the ground, will try to sit in the shade of the stump. . . . Such men are those who, now that slavery is gone, still cling to a civil order based on the old plantation system. . . . They are like a wood-sawyer robbed of his saw-horse and trying to saw wood in his lap."

All these darts struck and stung, but a little soft mud, such as any editor could supply, would soon have drawn out the sting—but for an additional line or two, which gave poisonous and mortal offense. Blackland and Clearwater replied in a storm of indignation. The *Suez Courier* bade him keep out of Dixie on peril of his life. He came, nevertheless, canvassing for business, and was not molested, but got very few shipments. What he mainly secured were the flippant pledges of such as required the largest possible advances indefinitely ahead of the least possible cotton. Also a few Yankees shipped to him.

" Gen'l Halliday, howdy, sah ? " It was dusk of the last day of this tour. The voice came from a dark place on the sidewalk in Suez. " Don't you know me, Gen'l? You often used to see me an' Majo' Gyarnet togetheh ; yes, sah. My name's Cornelius Leggett, sah."

"Why, Cornelius, to be sure! I thought I smelt whiskey. What can I do for you?"

"Gen'l, I has the honor to espress to you, sah, my thanks faw the way you espress yo'self in yo' letteh on the concerns an' prospec's o' we' colo'ed people, sah. An likewise, they's thousands would like to espress the same espressions, sah."

"Oh, that's all right."

"Gen'l, I represents a quantity of ow people what's move' down into Blackland fum Rosemont and other hill places. They espress they'se'ves to me as they agent that they like to confawm some prearrangement with you, sah."

"Are you all on one plantation?"

"Oh, no, sah, they ain't ezac'ly on no plantation. Me? Oh, I been a-goin' to the Freedman' Bureau school in Pulaski City as they agent.

"Sah? Yass, sah, at they espenses—p-he!

"They? They mos'ly strowed round in the woods in pole cabins an' bresh arbors.—Sah?

"Yaas, sah, livin' on game an' fish.—Sah?

"Yaas, sah.

"But they espress they doubts that the Gove'ment ain't goin' to give 'em no fahms, an' they like to comprise with you, Gen'l, ef you please, sah, to git holt o' some fahms o' they own, you know; sawt o' payin' faw'm bes' way they kin; yass, sah. As you say in yo' letteh, betteh give 'm lan's than keep 'em vagabones; yass, sir. Betteh no terms than none at all; yass, sah." And so on.

From this colloquy resulted the Negro farm-village of

Leggettstown. In 1866–68 it grew up on the old Halliday place, which had reverted to the General by mortgage. Neatest among its whitewashed cabins, greenest with gourd-vines, and always the nearest paid for, was that of the Reverend Leviticus Wisdom, his wife, Virginia, and her step-daughter, Johanna.

In the fall of 1869 General Halliday came back to Suez to live. His wife, a son, and daughter had died, two daughters had married and gone to the Northwest, others were here and there. A daughter of sixteen was with him—they two alone. The ebb-tide of the war values had left him among the shoals; his black curls were full of frost, his bank box was stuffed with plantation mortgages, his notes were protested. He had come to operate, from Suez as a base, several estates surrendered to him by debtors and entrusted to his management by his creditors. This he wished to do on what seemed to him an original plan, of which Leggettstown was only a clumsy sketch, a plan based on his belief in the profound economic value of—" villages of small freeholding farmers, my dear sir !

" It's the natural crystal of free conditions ! " John heard him say in the post-office corner of Weed & Usher's drug-store.

Empty words to John. He noted only the noble air of the speaker and his hearers. Every man of the group had been a soldier. The General showed much more polish than the others, but they all had the strong graces of horsemen and masters, and many a subtle sign of civilization and cult heated and hammered through centuries of search for good

government and honorable fortune.  John stopped
and gazed.

"Come on, son," said Judge March almost sharply.
John began to back away.  "There!" exclaimed the
father as his son sat down suddenly in a box of sawdust
and cigar stumps.  He led him away to clean him off,
adding, "You hadn't ought to stare at people as you
walk away fum them, my son."

With rare exceptions, the General's daily hearers were
silent, but resolute.  They did not analyze.  Their
motives were their feelings; their feelings were their
traditions, and their traditions were back in the old en-
trenchments.  The time for large changes had slipped
by.  Haggard, of the *Courier*, thought it "Equally just
and damning" to reprint from the General's odiously
remembered letter of four years earlier, "If we can't
make our Negroes white, let us make them as white as
we can," and sign it "Social Equality Launcelot."  Parson Tombs, sweet, aged, and beloved, prayed from his
pulpit—with the preface, "Thou knowest thy servant
has never mixed up politics and religion"—that "the
machinations of them who seek to join together what
God hath put asunder may come to naught."

Halliday laughed.  "Why, I'm only a private citizen
trying to retrieve my private fortunes."  But—

"These are times when a man can't choose whether
he'll be public or private!" said Garnet, and the
*Courier* made the bankrupt cotton factor public every
day.  It quoted constantly from the unpardonable letter, and charged him with "inflaming the basest cupid-
ity of our Helots," and so on, and on.  But the General,

with his silver-shot curls dancing half-way down his shoulders, a six-shooter under each skirt of his black velvet coat, and a knife down the back of his neck, went on pushing his private enterprise.

"Private enterprise!" cried Garnet. "His jackals will run him for Congress." And they did—against Garnet.

The times were seething. Halliday, viewing matters impartially in the clear, calm light of petroleum torches, justified Congress in acts which Garnet termed "the spume of an insane revenge;" while Garnet, with equal calmness of judgment, under other petroleum torches, gloried in the "masterly inactivity" of Dixie's whitest and best—which Launcelot denounced as a foolish and wicked political strike. All the corruptions bred by both sides in a gigantic war—and before it in all the crudeness of the country's first century—were pouring down and spouting up upon Dixie their rain of pitch and ashes. Negroes swarmed about the polls, elbowed their masters, and challenged their votes. Ragged negresses talked loudly along the sidewalk of one another as "ladies," and of their mistresses as "women." White men of fortune and station were masking, night-riding, whipping and killing; and blue cavalry rattled again through the rocky streets of Suez.

Such was life when dashing Fannie Halliday joined the choir in Parson Tombs's church, becoming at once its leading spirit, and John March suddenly showed a deep interest in the Scriptures. He joined her Sunday-school class.

## X.

### FANNIE

Was sixteen—she said; had black eyes—the dilating kind—was pretty, and seductively subtle. Jeff-Jack liked her much. They met at Rosemont, where he found her spending two or three days, on perfect terms with Barbara, and treated with noticeable gravity, though with full kindness, by Mrs. Garnet, whom she called, warmly, "Cousin Rose."

Ravenel had pushed forward only two or three pawns of conversation when she moved at one step from news to politics. She played with the ugly subject girlishly, even frivolously, though not insipidly—at least to a young man's notion—riding its winds and waves like a sea-bird. Politics, she said, seemed to her a kind of human weather, no more her business and no less than any other kind. She never blamed the public, or any party for this or that; did he? And when he said he did not, her eyes danced and she declared she disliked him less.

"Why, we might as well scold the rain or the wind as the public," she insisted. "What publics do, or think, or say, or want—are merely—I don't know— sort o' chemical values. What makes you smile that way?"

"Did I smile? You're deep," he said.

"You're smiling again," she replied, and, turning, asked Garnet a guileless question on a certain fierce matter of the hour. He answered it with rash confidence, and her next question was a checkmate.

"Oh, understand," he cried, in reply; "we don't excuse these dreadful practices."

"Yes, you do. You-all don't do anything else—except Mr. Ravenel; he approves them barefaced."

Garnet tried to retort, but she laughed him down. When she was gone, "She's as rude as a roustabout," he said to his wife.

For all this she was presently the belle of Suez. She invaded its small and ill-assorted society and held it, a restless, but conquered province. John's father marked with joy his son's sudden regularity in Sunday-school. If his wife was less pleased it was because to her all punctuality was a personal affront; it was some time before she discovered the cause to be Miss Fannie Halliday. By that time half the young men in town were in love with Fannie, and three-fourths of them in abject fear of her wit; yet, in true Southern fashion, casting themselves in its way with Hindoo abandon.

Her father and she had apartments in Tom Hersey's Swanee Hotel. Mr. Ravenel called often. She entered Montrose Academy "in order to remain sixteen," she told him. This institution was but a year or two old. It had beeen founded, at Ravenel's suggestion, "as a sort o' little sister to Rosemont." Its principal, Miss Kinsington, with her sister, belonged to one of Dixie's best and most unfortunate families.

"You don't bow down to Mrs. Grundy," something prompted Ravenel to say, as he and Fannie came slowly back from a gallop in the hills.

"Yes, I do. I only love to tease her now and then. I go to the races, play cards, waltz, talk slang, and read novels. But when I do bow down to her I bow away down. Why, at Montrose, I actually talk on serious subjects!"

"Do you touch often on religion? You never do to the gentlemen I bring to see you."

"Why, Mr. Ravenel, I don't understand you. What should I know about religion? You seem to forget that I belong to the choir."

"Well, politics, then. Don't you ever try to make a convert even in that?"

"I talk politics for fun only." She toyed with her whip. "I'd tell you something if I thought you'd never tell. It's this: Women have no conscience in their intellects. No, and the young gentlemen you bring to see me take after their mothers."

"I'll try to bring some other kind."

"Oh, no! They suit me. They're so easily pleased. I tell them they have a great insight into female character. Don't you tell them I told you!"

"Do you remember having told me the same thing?"

She dropped two wicked eyes and said, with sweet gravity, "I wish it were not so true of you. How did you like the sermon last evening?"

"The cunning flirt!" thought he that night, as his kneeling black boy drew off his boots.

Not so thought John that same hour. Servants' delinquencies had kept him from Sunday-school that morning and made him late at church. His mother had stayed at home with her headache and her husband. Her son was hesitating at the churchyard gate, alone and heavy-hearted, when suddenly he saw a thing that brought his heart into his throat and made a certain old mortification start from its long sleep with a great inward cry. Two shabby black men passed by on plough-mules, and between them, on a poor, smart horse, all store clothes, watch-chain, and shoe-blacking, rode the president of the Zion Freedom Homestead League, Mr. Cornelius Leggett, of Leggettstown. John went in. Fannie, seemingly fresh from heaven, stood behind the melodeon and sang the repentant prodigal's resolve; and he, in raging shame for the stripes once dealt him, the lie they had scared from him at the time, and the many he had told since to cover that one, shed such tears that he had to steal out, and, behind a tree in the rear of the church, being again without a handkerchief, dry his cheeks on his sleeves.

And now, in his lowly bed, his eyes swam once more as the girl's voice returned to his remembrance: "Father, I have sinned against heaven and before thee, and am no more worthy to be called thy son."

He left his bed and stood beside the higher one. But the father slept. Even if he should waken him, he felt that he could only weep and tell nothing, and so he went back and lay down again. With the morning, confession was impossible. He thought rather of revenge, and was hot with the ferocious plans of a boy's helplessness.

## XI.

### A BLEEDING HEART

ONE night early in November, when nearly all Rosemont's lights were out and a wet brisk wind was flirting and tearing the yellowed leaves of the oaks, the windows of Mrs. Garnet's room were still bright. She sat by a small fire with Barbara at her knee. It had been election-day and the college was silent with chagrin.

"Is pop-a going to get elected, mom-a?"

"I don't think he is, my child."

"But you hope he is, don't you?"

"Listen," murmured the mother.

Barbara heard a horse's feet. Presently her father's step was in the hall and on the stairs. He entered, kissed wife and child, and sat down with a look first of care and fatigue, and then a proud smile.

"Well, Launcelot's elected."

A solemn defiance came about his mouth, but on his brow was dejection and distress.

"You know, Rose," he said, "that for myself, I don't care."

She made no reply.

He leaned on the mantlepiece. "My heart bleeds for our people! All they ask is the God-given right to a pure government. Their petition is spurned! Rose," —tears shone in his eyes—"I this day saw the sabres and bayonets of the government of which Washington

was once the head, shielding the scum of the earth
while it swarmed up and voted honor and virtue out of
office!" The handkerchief he snatched from his pocket
brought out three or four written papers. He cast
them upon the fire. One, under a chair, he overlooked.
Barbara got it later—just the thing to carry in her reticule when she went calling on herself. She could not
read its bad writing, but it served all the better for
that.

Next evening, at tea—back again from Suez—" Wife
did you see a letter in blue ink in your room this morning, with some pencil figures of my own across the face?
If it was with those papers I burned it's all right, but
I'd like to know." His unconcern was overdone.

Barbara was silent. She had battered the reticule's
inner latch with a stone. To get the paper out, the
latch would have to be broken. Silence saved it.

The election was over, but the turmoil only grew.
Mere chemicals, did Fannie call these incidents and
conditions? But they were corrosives and caustics
dropped blazing hot upon white men's bare hands and
black men's bare feet. The ex-master spurned political
fellowship with his slave at every cost; the ex-slave
laid taxes, stole them, and was murdered.

" Make way for robbery, he cries," drawled Ravenel;
"makes way for robbery and dies."

" Mr. Ravenel," said Judge March, " I find no place
for me, sir. I lament one policy and loathe the other.
I need not say what distress of mind I suffer. I doubt
not we are all doing that, sir."

" No," said Jeff-Jack, whittling a straw.

"I'll tell you what it is, Mr. Ravenel," said Fannie Halliday ; " it's a war between decency in the wrong, and vulgarity in the right."

"No," said Jeff-Jack again, and her liking for him grew.

Cornelius's explanation in the House was more elaborate.

"This, Mr. Speaker, are that great wahfare predicated in the New Testament, betwix the Republicans an' sinnehs on one side an' the Phair-i-sees on the other. The white-liners, they is the Phair-i-sees! They is the whited sculptors befo' which, notinstan'in' all they chiselin', the Republicans an' sinnehs enters fust into the kingdom ! "

So, for two more years, and John was fifteen.

Then the Judge decided to explain to him, confidentially, their long poverty.

" Daphne, dear "—he was going down into Blackland—" if you see no objection I'll take son with me.— Why, no, dear, not both on one hoss, you're quite right ; that wouldn't be kind to son."

" A merciful man, Powhatan, is merciful to——"

" Yes, deah ; Oh, I had the hoss in mind too ; indeed I had! Do you know, my deah, I can tend to business betteh when I have ow son along ? I'm gett'n' to feel like as if I'd left myself behind when he's not with me."

" You've always been so, Judge March." Her smile was sad. " Oh ! no, I mustn't advise. Take him along if you're determined to."

## XII.

### JOHN THINKS HE IS NOT AFRAID

"Son," said the father as they rode, "I reckon you've often wondered why, owning ow hund'ed thousand an' sixty acres, we should appeah so sawt o' reduced; haven't you?"

"Sir?"

The father repeated the question, and John said, dreamily:

"No, sir."

"Well, son, I'll tell you, though I'd rather you'd not mention it—in school, faw instance—if we can eveh raise money to send you to school.

"It's because, in a sense, we a-*got* so much lan'. Many's the time I could a-sole pahts of it, an' refused, only because that particulah sale wouldn't a-met the object fo' which the whole tract has always been held. It was yo' dear grandfather's ambition, an' his father's befo' him, to fill these lan's with a great population, p'osp'ous an' happy. We neveh sole an acre, but we neveh hel' one back in a spirit o' lan' speculation, you understan'?"

"Sir?—I—yes, sir."

"The plan wa'n't adapted to a slave State. I see that now. I don't say slavery was wrong, but slave an' free labor couldn't thrive side by side. But, now, son, you know, all labor's free an' the time's come faw a change.

" You see, son, that's where Gen'l Halliday's village projec' is bad. His villages are boun' han' an' foot to cotton fahmin' an' can't bring forth the higher industries ; but now, without concealin' anything fum him or anybody—of co'se we don't want to do that—if we can get enough of his best village residenters fum Leggettstown an' Libbetyville to come up an' take lan' in Widewood —faw we can give it to 'em an' gain by it, you know ; an' a site or two faw a church aw school—why, then, you know, when capitalists come up an' look at ow minin' lan's— why, first thing you know, we'll have mines an' mills an' sto'es ev'y *which* away !"

They met and passed three horsemen armed to the teeth and very tipsy.

" Why, if to-morrow ain't election-day ag'in ! Why, I quite fo'gotten that !"

At the edge of the town two more armed riders met them.

" Judge March, good mawnin', seh." All stopped. " Goin' to Suez ? "

" We goin' on through into Blackland."

" I don't think you can, seh. Our pickets hold Swanee River bridge. Yes, sah, ow pickets. Why *ow* pickets, they're there. 'Twould be strange if they wa'n't—three hund'ed Blackland county niggehs marchin' on the town to burn it."

" Is that really the news ? "

" That's the latest, seh. We after reinfo'cements." They moved on.

Judge March rode slowly toward Suez. John rode beside him. In a moment the Judge halted again, lifted his head, and listened. A long cheer floated to them, attenuated by the distance.

"I thought it was a charge, but I reckon it's on'y a meet'n of ow people in the square." He glanced at his son, who was listening, ashy pale.

"Son, we ain't goin' into town. I'm going, but you needn't. You can ride back a piece an' wait faw me; aw faw further news which'll show you what to do. On'y don't in any case come into town. This ain't yo' fight, son, an' you no need to get mixed in with it. You hear, son?"

"I"—the lad tried twice before he could speak—"I want to go with you."

"Why, no, son, you no need to go. You ain't fitt'n' to go. Yo' too young. You a-trembling now fum head to foot. Ain't you got a chill?"

"N-no, sir." The boy shivered visibly. "I've got a pain in my side, but it don't—don't hurt. I want to go with you."

"But, son, there's goin' to be fight'n'. I'm goin' to try to p'vent it, but I shan't be able to. Why, if you was to get hurt, who'd eveh tell yo' po' deah mother? I couldn't. I jest couldn't! You betteh go 'long home, son."

"I c-c-can't do it, father."

"Why, air you that sick, son?"

"No, sir, but I don't feel well enough to go home— Father—I—I—t-t-told—I told—an awful lie, one time, about you, and——"

"Why, son!"

"Yes, sir. I've been **tryin'** for **seven years** to— k—own up, and——"

"Sev—O Law, son, I don't believe you eveh done it at all. You neveh so much as told a fib in yo' life. You jest imagine you done it."

"Yes, I have father, often. I can't explain now, but please lemme go with you."

"Why, son, I jest can't. Lawd knows I would if I could."

"Yes, you can, father, I won't be in the way. And I won't be af-raid. You don't think I would eveh be a-scared of a nigger, do you? But if the niggers should kill you, and me not there, I wouldn't ever be any account no more! I haven't ever been any yet, but I will be, father, if you'll——"

Three pistol shots came from the town, and two townward-bound horsemen broke their trot and passed at a gallop. "Come on, Judge," laughed one.

"I declare, son, I don't know what *toe* do. You betteh go 'long back."

"Oh, father, don't send me back! Lemme go 'long with you. Please don't send me back! I couldn't go. I'd just haf to turn round again an' follow you. Lemme go with you, father. I want to go 'long with you. Oh—thank you, sir!" They trotted down into the town. "D' you reckon C'nelius 'll be there, father?— I—hope he will." The pallor was gone.

As the turnpike became a tree-shaded street, they passed briskly by its old-fashioned houses set deep in grove gardens. Two or three weedy lanes at right and left showed the poor cabins of the town's darker life shut and silent. But presently,

"Father, look there!"

The Judge and his son turned quickly to a turfy bank where a ragged negro lay at the base of a large tree. He was moaning, rocking his head, and holding a hand against his side. His rags were drenched with blood. The white eyes rolled up to the face of the Judge, as he tossed his bridle to his son.

" Watch," whispered the big lips, " watch."

John threw his father's bridle back, galloped through a gate, and came with a gourd full.

" Gimme quick, son, he's swoonin' away." The draught brought back some life.

"Shan't I get a doctor, father ? "

" Tain't a bit of use, son."

" No," moaned the negro. " I'm gwine fasteh dan docto's kin come. I'm in de deep watchs. Gwine to meet my Lawd Jesus. Good-by, wife ; good-by, chillun. Oh, Jedge March, dey shot me in pyo devilment. I was jist lookin' out fo' my boy. Dey was comin' in to town an dey sees me, an awdehs me to halt, an' 'stid o' dat I runs, thinkin' that'd suit 'em jist as well. Oh, Lawd !—Oh, Lawd ! Oh ! " He stared into the Judge's face, a great pain heaved him slowly, his eyes set, and all was over. A single sob burst from the boy as he gazed on the dark, dead features. The Judge hasted to mount.

" Now, son, I got to get right into town. But you see now, you betteh go along back to yo' motheh, don't you ? "

" I'm goin' with you."

## XIII.

### FOR FANNIE

THEY came where two men sat on horses in the way. "Sorry, Judge, but them's orders, seh; only enrolled men can pass."

But the speakers presently concluded that it could never have been intended to shut out such a personage as Judge March, and on pledge to report to Captain Shotwell, at the Swanee Hotel, or else to Captain Champion at the court-house, father and son proceeded. Montrose Academy showed no sign of life as they went by.

Yet John had never seen the town so populous. Saddled horses were tied everywhere. Men rode here or there in the yellow dust, idly or importantly, mounted, dismounted, or stood on the broken sidewalks in groups, some sober, some not, all armed and spurred, and more arriving from all directions. Handsome Captain Shotwell, sitting in civil dress, a sword belted on him and lying across his lap, explained to the Judge.

"Why, you know, Judge, how ow young men ah; always up to some ridiculous praank, jest in mere plaay, you know, seh. Yeste'd'y some of 'em taken a boyish notion to put some maasks on an' ride through Leggettstown in 'slo-ow p'ocession, with a sawt o' banneh marked, 'SEE YOU AGAIN TO-NIGHT.' They had guns—mo' f'om fo'ce o' habit, I reckon, than anything else—you know how ow young men ah, seh—one of 'em

carry a gun a yeah, an' nevah so much as hahm a
floweh, you know. Well, seh, unfawtunately, the
niggehs had no mo' sense than to take it all in dead
earnest. They put they women an' child'en into the
church an' ahmed theyse'ves, some thirty of 'em, with
shotguns an' old muskets—yondeh's some of 'em in the
cawneh. Then they taken up a position in the
road just this side the village, an' sent to Sherman an'
Libbetyville fo' reinfo'cements.

" Well, of co'se, you know, seh, what was jes' boun'
to happm. Some of ow ve'y best young men mounted
an' moved to dislodge an' scatteh them befo' they could
gatheh numbehs enough to take the offensive an' begin
they fiendish work. Well, seh, about daay-break,
while sawt o' reconnoiterin' in fo'ce, they come suddenly upon the niggehs' position, an' the niggehs,
without the slightes' p'ovocation, up an' fi-ud! P'ovi-
dentially, they shot too high, an' only one man was
inju'ed—by fallin' from his hawss. Well, seh, ow boys
fi-ud an' cha'ged, an' the niggehs, of co'se, run, leavin'
three dead an' fo' wounded; aw, accawdin' to latest
accounts, seven dead an' no wounded. The niggehs
taken sheltch in the church, ow boys fallen back fo'
reinfo'cements, an' about a' hour by sun comes word
that the niggehs, frenzied with raage an' liquo',
a-comin' this way to the numbeh o' three hund'ed, an'
increasin' as they come.—No, seh, I don't know that it
*is* unfawtunate. It's just as well faw this thing to
happm, an' to happm now. It'll teach both sides, as
Garnet said awhile ago addressin' the crowd, that the
gov'ment o' Dixie's simply got to paass, this time, away

f'om a raace that can't p'eserve awdeh, an' be undividedly transfehed oveh to the raace God-A'mighty appointed to gov'n!"

Judge March's voice was full of meek distress. "Captain Shotwell, where is Major Garnet, sir?"

"Garnet? Oh, he's over in the *Courier* office, consultin' with Haggard an' Jeff-Jack."

"Do you know whether Gen'l Halliday's in town, sir?"

The Captain smiled. "He's in the next room, seh. He's been undeh my—p'otection, as you might say, since daylight."

"Gen'l Halliday could stop all this, Captain."

"Stop it? He could stop it in two hours, seh! If he'd just consent to go under parole to Leggettstown an' tell them niggehs that if they'll simply lay down they ahms an' stay quietly at home—jest faw a day aw two—all 'll be freely fo'givm an' fo'gotten, seh! Instead o' that, he sits there, ca'mly smilin'—you know his way—an' threatenin' us with the ahm of the United States Gov'ment. He fo'gets that by a wise p'ovision o' that Gov'ment's foundehs it's got sev'l ahms, an' one holds down anotheh. The S'preme Cote—Judge March, you go in an' see him; you jest the man to do it, seh!"

John waited without. Presently father and son were seen to leave Captain Shotwell's headquarters and cross the square to the *Courier* office. There a crowd was reading a bulletin which stated that scouting parties reported no negro force massed anywhere. At the top of a narrow staircase the Judge and his son were let into the presence of Major Garnet and his advisers.

Here John had one more good gaze at Ravenel. He was in the physical perfection of twenty-six, his eyes less playful than once, but his smile less cynical. His dress was faultlessly neat. Haggard was almost as noticeable, though less interesting; a slender, high-strung man, with a pale face seamed by a long scar got in a duel. One could see that he had been trying to offset the fatigues of the night with a popular remedy. Garnet was dictating, Haggard writing.

"Captains Shotwell and Champion will move their forces at once in opposite circuits—through the disturbed villages—and assure all persons—of whatever race or party—that the right of the people peaceably to bear arms—is vindicated—and that order is restored—and will be maintained." A courier waited.

"At the same time," said Ravenel, indolently, "they can ask if the rumor is true that Mr. Leggett and about ten others are going to be absent from this part of the country until after the election, and say we hope it's so."

Haggard cast a glance at Garnet, Garnet looked away, the postscript was made, and the missive sent.

"Brother March, good-morning, sir." The Major kept the Judge's hand as they moved aside. But presently the whole room could hear—"Why, Brother March, the trouble's all over!—Oh, of course, if Halli-day feels any real *need* to confer with us he can do so; we'll be right here.—Oh—Haggard!"

The editor, in the doorway, said he would be back,

and went out. He was evidently avoiding Halliday. Judge March felt belittled and began to go.

"If you're bound for home, Brother March, I'll be riding that way myself, presently. You see, in a few minutes Suez'll be as quiet as it ever was, and I sent word to General Halliday just before you came in, that no one designs, or has designed, to abridge any personal liberty of his he may think safe to exercise." The speaker suddenly ceased.

Both men stood hearkening. Loud words came up the stairs.

"Your son stepped down into the street, Judge," said Ravenel. The next instant the three rushed out and down the stairway.

John had gone down to see the two armed bands move off. They had been gone but a few minutes when he noticed General Halliday, finely mounted, come from a stable behind the hotel and trot smartly toward him. The few store-keepers left in town stared in contemptuous expectation, but to John this was Fannie's father, and the boy longed for something to occur which might enable him to serve that father in a signal way and so make her forever tenderly grateful. The telegraph office was up these same stairs on the other side of the landing opposite the *Courier* office; most likely the General was going to send despatches. John's gaze followed the gallant figure till it disappeared in the doorway at the foot of the staircase.

Near the bottom the General and the editor met and passed. The editor stopped and cursed the General. "You jostled me purposely, sir!"

Halliday turned and smiled. " Jim Haggard, why should you shove me and then lie about it? can't you pick a fight for the truth?"

" Don't speak to me, you white nigger! Are you armed?"

" Yes!"

" Then, Launcelot Halliday," yelled the editor, backing out upon the sidewalk and drawing his re- peater, " I denounce you as a traitor, a poltroon, and a coward!" Men darted away, dodged, peeped, and cried—

" Look out! Don't shoot!" But John ran forward to the rescue.

" Put that thing up!" he called to the editor, in boy- ish treble. " Put it up!"

" Jim Haggard, hold on!" cried Halliday, following down and out with his weapon pointed earthward. " Let me speak, you drunken fool! Get that boy——"

" Bang!" went the editor's pistol before he had half lifted it.

" Bang!" replied Halliday's.

The editor's weapon dropped. He threw both hands against his breast, looked to heaven, wheeled half round, and fell upon his face as dead as a stone.

Halliday leaped into the saddle, answered one shot that came from the crowd, and clattered away on the turnpike.

" John was standing with arms held out. He turned blindly to find the doorway of the stairs and cried, " Father!" father!"

" Son!"

He started for the sound, groped against the wall, sank to his knees, and fell backward.

"Room, here, room!" "Give him air!" "By George, sir, he rushed right in bare-handed between 'em, orderin' Haggard"—"Stand back, you-all, and make way for Judge March!"

"Oh, son, son!" The father knelt, caught the limp hands and gazed with streaming eyes. "Oh, son, my son! air you gone fum me, son? Air you gone? Air you gone?"

A kind doctor took the passive wrist. "No, Judge, he's not gone yet."

Ravenel and the physician assumed control. "Just consider him in my care, doctor, will you? Shall we take him to the hotel?"

Garnet supported Judge March's steps. "Cast your burden on the Lord, Brother March. Bear up—for Sister March's sake, as she would for yours!"

Near the top stairs of the Ladies' Entrance Ravenel met Fannie.

"I saw it all, Mr. Ravenel; he saved my father's life. I must have the care of him. You can get it arranged so, Mr. Ravenel. You can even manage his mother."

"I will," he said, with a light smile.

Election-day passed like a Sabbath. General Halliday returned, voted, and stayed undisturbed. His opponent, not Garnet this time, was overwhelmingly elected. On the following day Haggard was buried "with great éclat," as his newspaper described it. Concerning John, the doctor said:

"Judge March, your wife should go back home. There's no danger, and a sick-room to a person of her——"

"Ecstastic spirit—" said the Judge.

"Exactly—would be only——"

"Yes," said the Judge, and Mrs. March went. To Fannie the doctor said,

"If he were a man I would have no hope, but a boy hangs to life like a cat, and I think he'll get well, entirely well. Move him home? Oh, not for a month!"

Notwithstanding many pains, it was a month of heaven to John, a heaven all to himself, with only one angel and no church. As long as there was danger she was merely cheerful—cheerful and beautiful. But when the danger passed she grew merry, the play of her mirth rising as he gained strength to bear it. He loved mirth, when others made it, and always would have laughed louder and longer than he did but for wondering how they made it. A great many things he said made others laugh, too, but he could never tell beforehand what would or wouldn't. He got so full of happiness at times that Fannie would go out for a few moments to let him come back to his ordinary self.

Two or three times, when she lingered long outside the door, she explained on her return that Mr. Ravenel had come to ask how he was.

Once Halliday met this visitor in the Ladies' Entrance, departing, and with a suppressed smile, asked, "Been to see how 'poor Johnnie' is?"

"Ostensibly," said the young man, and offered a cigar.

The General overtook Fannie in the hallway. He
shook his head roguishly. "Cruel sport, Fan. He'll
make the even dozen, won't he?"

"Oh, no, he'd like to make me his even two dozen,
that's all."

When the day came for the convalescent to go
home, he was not glad, although he had laughed much
that morning. As he lay on the bed dressed and waiting, he was unusually pale. Only Fannie stood by
him. Her hand was in both his. He shut his eyes,
and in a desperate, earnest voice said, under his breath,
"Good-by!" And again, lower still,—"Good-by!"

"Good-by, Johnnie."

He looked up into her laughing eyes. His color came
hot, his heart pounded, and he gasped, "S-say m-my
John! Won't you?"

"Why, certainly. Good-by, my Johnnie." She
smiled yet more.

"Will—will "—he choked—" will you b-be my—k—
Fannie—when I g-get old enough?"

"Yes," she said, with great show of gravity, "if
you'll not tell anybody." She held him down by
gently stroking his brow. "And you must promise to
grow up such a perfect gentleman that I'll be proud of
my Johnnie when "—She smiled broadly again.

—"Wh-when—k—the time comes?"

"I reckon so—yes."

He sprang to his knees and cast his arms about her
neck, but she was too quick, and his kiss was lost in
air. He flashed a resentful surprise, but she shook her
head, holding his wasted wrists, and said, "N-no, no, my

Johnnie, not even you; not Fannie Halliday, o-oh no!"
She laughed.

"Some one's coming!" she whispered. It was Judge
March. His adieus were very grateful. He called her
a blessing.

She waved a last good-by to John from the window.
Then she went to her own room, threw arms and face
into a cushioned seat and moaned, so softly her own ear
could not catch it—a name that was not John's.

## XIV.

### A MORTGAGE ON JOHN

As JOHN grew sound and strong he grew busy as
well. The frown of purpose creased at times his brow.
There was a "perfect gentleman" to make, and only a
few years left for his making if he was to be completed
in the stipulated time. Once in a while he contrived
an errand to Fannie, but it was always in broad day,
when the flower of love is never more than half open.
The perfect transport of its first blossoming could not
quite return ; the pronoun "my" was not again paraded.
Only at good-by, her eyes, dancing the while, would
say, "It's all right, my Johnnie."

On Sundays he had to share her with other boys
whom she asked promiscuously,

"What new commandment was laid on the disci-
ples?"—and——

"Ought not we also to keep this commandment?"

"Oh! yes, indeed!" said his heart, but his slow lips let some other voice answer for him.

When she asked from the catechism, "What is the misery of that estate whereinto man fell?" ah! how he longed to confess certain modifications in his own case. And yet Sunday was his "Day of all the week the best." Her voice in speech and song, the smell of her garments, the flowers in her hat, the gladness of her eyes, the wild blossoms at her belt, sometimes his own forest anemones dying of joy on her bosom—sense and soul feasted on these and took a new life, so that going from Sabbath to Sabbath he went from strength to strength, on each Lord's day appearing punctually in Zion.

One week-day when the mountain-air of Widewood was sweet with wild grapes, some six persons were scatteringly grouped in and about the narrow road near the March residence. One was Garnet, one was Ravenel, two others John and his father, and two were strangers in Dixie. One of these was a very refined-looking man, gray, slender, and with a reticent, purposeful mouth. His traveling suit was too warm for the latitude, and his silk hat slightly neglected. The other was fat and large, and stayed in the carryall in which Garnet had driven them up from Rosemont. He was of looser stuff than his senior. He called the West his home, but with a New England accent. He "didn't know's 'twas" and "presumed likely" so often that John eyed him with mild surprise. Ravenel sat and whittled. The day was hot, yet in his suit of gray summer stuffs he looked as fresh as sprinkled ferns. In a pause Major Garnet, with bright suddenness, asked:

"Brother March, where's John been going to school?"

The Judge glanced round upon the group as if they were firing upon him from ambush, hemmed, looked at John, and said:

"Why,—eh—who; son? —Why,—eh—to—to his mother, sir; yes, sir."

"Ah, Brother March, a mother's the best of teachers, and Sister March one of the most unselfish of mothers!" said Garnet, avoiding Ravenel's glance.

The Judge expanded. "Sir, she's too unselfish. I admit it, sir."

"And, yet, Brother March, I reckon John gets right smart schooling from you."

"Ah! no, sir. We're only schoolmates togetheh, sir—in the school of Nature, sir. You know, Mr. Ravenel, all these things about us here are a sort of books, sir."

Ravenel smiled and answered very slowly, "Ye-es, sir. Very good reading; worth thirty cents an acre simply as literature."

Thirty cents was really so high a price that the fat stranger gave a burst of laughter, but Garnet—"It'll soon be worth thirty dollars an acre, now we've got a good government. Brother March, we'd like to see that superb view of yours from the old field on to the ridge."

Ravenel stayed behind with the Judge. John went as guide.

"Judge," Ravenel said, as soon as they were alone, "how about John? I believe in your school of nature a little. Solitude for principles, society for character, somebody says. Now, my school was men, and hence the ruin you see——"

"Mr. Ravenel, sir! I see no ruin; I——"

"Don't you? Well, then, the ruin you don't see."

"Oh, sir, you speak in irony! I see a character——"

"Yes"—the speaker dug idly in the sand—"all character and no principles. But you don't want John to be all principles and no character? He ought to be going to school, Judge." The father dropped his eyes in pain, but the young man spoke on. "Going to school is a sort of first lesson in citizenship, isn't it? —'specially if it's a free school. Maybe I'm wrong, but I wish Dixie was full of good, strong free schools."

"You're not wrong, Mr. Ravenel! You're eminently right, sir."

Mr. Ravenel only smiled, was silent for a while, and then said, "But even if it were—I had an impression that you thought you'd sort o' promised John to Rosemont?"

The Judge straightened up, distressed. "Mr. Ravenel, I have! I have, sir! It's true; it's true!"

"I don't think you did, Judge, you only expressed an intention."

But the Judge waived away the distinction with a gesture.

"Judge," said the young man, slowly and gently,

"wouldn't you probably be sending John to Rosemont if Rosemont were free?"

The Judge did not speak or look up. He hunted on the ground for chips.

"Why don't you sell some land and send him?"

"Oh, Mr. Ravenel, we can't. We just can't! It's the strangest thing in the world, sir! Nobody wants it but lumbermen, and to let them, faw a few cents an acre, sweep ove' it like worms ove' a cotton field—we just can't do it! Mr. Ravenel, what *is* the reason such a land as this can't be settled up? We'll sell it to any real sett ehs! But, good Lawd! sir, where air they? Son an' me ain't got no money to impote 'em, sir. The darkies don't know anything but cotton fahmin'—they won't come. Let me tell you, sir, we've made the most flattering offers to capitalists to start this and that. But they all want to wait till we've got a good gov'- ment. An' now, here we've got it—in Clearwatch, at least—an' you can see that these two men ain't satis- fied!"

"What do you reckon's the reason?"

"Mr. Ravenel, my deah sir, they can't tell! The fat one can't and the lean one won't! But politics is at the bottom of it, sir! Politics keeps crowdin' in an' capital a-hangin' back, an'——"

"Johnnie doesn't get his schooling," said Ravenel.

The response was a silent gesture, downcast eyes, and the betrayal of an emotion, not of the moment, but of months and years of physical want and mental distress.

"We all get lots of politics," said Ravenel.

"Not son! not fum me, sir. Oh, my Lawd, sir,

that's one of the worst parts of it! I don't dare teach
him mine, much less unteach him his mother's. She's
as spirited as she's gentle, sir."

"Whatever was is wrong," drawled the young man.
"That's the new creed."

"Oh, sir, a new creed's too painful a thing fo' jest.
Ow South'n press, Mr. Ravenel, is gett'n' a sad facility fo'
recantin'. I don't say it's not sincere, sir—least of all
ow *Courier* since it's come into the hands of you an'
President Garnet!"

"Garnet! Oh, gracious!" laughed Jeff-Jack.
"Sincere—Judge, if you won't say anything about sincerity, I'll tell you what I'd like to do for John, sir.
I'll take your note, secured by land, for the money you
need to put John through Rosemont, and you needn't
pay it till you get ready. If you never get ready, I
reckon John'll pay it some day."

The moment the offer began to be intelligible, Judge
March tried to straighten up and look Jeff-Jack squarely
in the face, but when it was completed his elbows were
on his knees and his face in his slender brown hands.

Up in the old field Garnet had talked himself dizzy.
Northern travelers are by every impulse inquirers, and
Southern hosts expounders; they fit like tongue and
groove. On the ridge he had said:

"Now, Mr. Fair, here it is. I don't believe there's a
finer view in the world."

"Hm!" said the slender visitor.

The two guests had been shown the usual Sleeping
Giant, Saddle Mountain, Sugar Loaf, etc., that go with
such views. John had set Garnet right when he got

Lover's Leap and Bridal Veil tangled in the bristling pines of Table Rock and the Devil's Garden, and all were charmed with the majestic beauty of the scene.

On the way back, while Garnet explained to Mr. Gamble, the heavier guest, why negroes had to be treated not as individuals but as a class, John had been telling Mr. Fair why it was wise to treat chickens not as a class but as individuals, and had mentioned the names and personal idiosyncrasies of the favorites of his own flock; Mr. Fair, in turn, had confessed to having a son about John's age, and wished they knew each other. Before John could reply, the party gayly halted again beside his father and Mr. Ravenel. As they did so Mr. Fair saw Ravenel give a little nod to Garnet that said, "It's all arranged."

On another evening, shortly after this, father and son coming to supper belated, John brought his mother a bit of cross-road news. The "Rads" had given a barbecue down in Blackland, just two days before the visit of Jeff-Jack and those others to Widewood—and what did she reckon! Cornelius Leggett had there made a speech, declaring that he was at the bottom of a patriotic project to open a free white school in Suez, and "bu'st Rosemont wide open."

"Judge March," said the wife, affectionately, "I wonder why Mr. Ravenel avoided mentioning that to you. He needn't have feared your sense of humor. Ah! if you only had a woman's instincts!"

John said good-night and withdrew. He wished his mother loved his father a little less. They would all have a so much better time.

"No," Mrs. March was presently saying, "Mr. Ravenel's motives are not those that concern me most. Rosemont, to me, must always signify Rose Montgomery. It is to her presence—her spell—you would expose my child; she, who has hated me all her life. Ah! no, it's too late now to draw back, he shall go. Yes, without my consent! Oh! my consent! Judge March, you're jesting again!" She lifted upon him the smile of a heart really all but broken under its imaginary wrongs.

There was no drawing back. The mother suffered, but the wife sewed, and when Rosemont had got well into its season's work and November was nearly gone, John was ready for "college." One morning, when the wind was bitter and the ground frozen, father and son rode side by side down their mountain road. A thin mantle of snow made the woods gray, and mottled the shivering ranks of dry cornstalks. At each rider's saddle swung an old carpet-bag stuffed with John's clothes. His best were on him.

"Maybe they're not the latest cut, son, or the finest fit, but you won't mind; you're not a girl. A man's dress is on'y a sort o' skin, anyhow; a woman's is her plumage. And, anyhow, at Rosemont you'll wear soldier clothes. Look out son, I asked yo' dear motheh to mend——"

The warning came too late; a rope handle of one of the carpet-bags broke. The swollen budget struck the unyielding ground and burst like a squash. John sprang nimbly from the saddle, but the Judge caught his leg on the other carpet-bag and reached the ground in such a shape that his horse lost all confidence and began to back wildly, putting first one foot and then another into the scattered baggage.

One, or even two, can rarely get as much into a bursted carpet-bag, repacking it in a public road and perspiring with the fear that somebody is coming, as they can into a sound one at a time and place of their own choice. There's no place like home—for this sort of task; albeit the Judge's home may have been an exception. Time flew past while they contrived and labored, and even when they seemed to have solved their problem one pocket of John's trousers contained a shirt and the other was full of socks, and the Judge's heart still retained an anxiety which he dared neither wholly confess nor entirely conceal.

"Well, son, it's a comfort to think yo' precious motheh will never have the mawtification of knowin' anything about this."

"Yass, sir," drawled John, "that's the first thing I thought of."

---

## XV.

### ARRIVALS AT ROSEMONT

THE air was mild down on the main road which, because it led from Suez to Pulaski City, was known as the Susie and Pussie pike. The highway showed a mere dusting of snow, and out afield the sun had said

good-morning so cavalierly to some corn-shocks that the
powder was wholly kissed off one sallow cheek of each.
The riders kept the pike northwesterly a short way and
then took the left, saying less and less as they went on,
till the college came into view, their hearts sinking as it
rose.

The campus was destitute of human sounds; but birds
gossiped so openly on every hand concerning the tardy
intrusion that John was embarrassed, and hardly felt,
much less saw, what rich disorder the red and yellow
browns of clinging and falling leaves made among the
purple-gray trunks and olive-dappled boughs, and on
the fading green of the sod.

The jays were everywhere, foppish, flippant, the perfection of privileged rudeness.

It seemed a great way through the grove. At the
foot of the steps John would have liked to make the acquaintance of some fat hens that were picking around
in the weak sunshine and uttering now and then a
pious housewifely sigh.

There was an awful stillness as the two ascended the
steps, carrying the broken carpet-bag between them.
Glancing back down the campus avenue, John hoped
the unknown woman just entering its far gate was not
observing. So mild was the air here that the front door
stood open. In the hall a tall student, with a sergeant's
chevrons on his gray sleeve, came from a class-room
and led them into a small parlor. Major Garnet was
in Suez, but Mrs. Garnet would see them.

They waited. On the mantel an extremely Egyptian
clock—green and gilt—whispered at its task in servile

oblivion to visitors. John stared at a black-framed lithograph, and his father murmured,

"That's the poet Longfellow, son, who wrote that nice letteh to yo' dear motheh. This colo'ed picture's Napoleon crossing the Alps."

A footstep came down the hall, and John saw a pretty damsel of twelve or thirteen with much loose red-brown hair, stop near the door of the reception-room and gaze at someone else who must have been coming up the porch steps. He could not hear this person's slow advance, but presently a voice in the porch said, tenderly, "Miss Barb?" and gave a low nervous laugh.

Barbara shrank back a step. The soft footfall reached the threshold. The maiden retreated half a step more. Behind her sounded a faint patter of crinoline coming down the hall stairs. And then there came into view from the porch, bending forward with caressing arms, a slim, lithe negress of about nineteen years. Her flimsy dress was torn by thorns, and her hands were pitifully scratched. Her skirt was gone, the petticoat bemired, and her naked feet were bleeding.

"Miss Barb," said the tender voice again. From the inner stairs a lady appeared.

"What is it, son?" Judge March asked, and rising, saw the lady draw near the girl with a look of pitying uncertainty. The tattered form stood trembling, with tears starting down her cheeks.

"Miss Rose—Oh, Miss Rose, it's me!"

"Why, Johanna, my poor child!" Two kind arms opened and the mass of rags and mud dashed into

them.   The girl showered her kisses upon the pure garments, and the lady silently, tenderly, held her fast.
Then she took the black forehead between her hands.

" Child, what does this mean ? "

" Oh, it means nothin' but C'nelius, Miss Rose—same
old C'nelius !   I hadn't nowhere to run but to you, an'
no chance to come but night."

" Can you go upstairs and wait a moment for me in
my room?   No, poor child, I don't think you can !"
But Johanna went, half laughing, half crying, and
beckoning to Barbara in the old-time wheedling way.

" Go, Barbara."

The child followed, while John and his father stood
with captive hearts before her whom the youths of the
college loved to call in valedictory addresses the Rose
of Rosemont.   She spent a few moments with them,
holding John's more than willing hand, and then
called in the principal's first assistant, Mr. Dinwiddie
Pettigrew, a smallish man of forty, in piratical white
duck trousers, kid slippers, nankeen sack, and ruffled
shirt.   Irritability confessed itself in this gentleman's
face, which was of a clay color, with white spots.   Mr.
Pettigrew presently declared himself a Virginian, adding, with the dignity of a fallen king, that he—or his
father, at least—had lost over a hundred slaves by
the war.   It was their all.   But the boy could not
shut his ear to the sweet voice of Mrs. Garnet as, at one
side, she talked to his father.

"Sir ? " he responded to the first assistant, who was
telling him he ought to spell March with a final e, it
being always so spelled—in Virginia.   The   Judge

turned for a lengthy good-by, and at its close John went with his preceptor to the school-room, trying, quite in vain, to conceive how Mr. Pettigrew had looked when he was a boy.

---

## XVI.

### A GROUP OF NEW INFLUENCES

ALL Rosemonters were required to sit together at Sunday morning service, in a solid mass of cadet gray. After this there was ordinary freedom. Thus, when good weather and roads and Mrs. March's strength permitted, John had the joy of seeing his father and mother come into church; for Rosemont was always ahead of time, and the Marches behind. Then followed the delight of going home with them in their antique and precarious buggy, and of a day-break ride back to Rosemont with his father—sweetest of all accessible company. Accessible, for his mother had forbidden him to visit Fannie Halliday, her father being a traitor. He could only pass by her gate—she was keeping house now—and sometimes have the ecstasy of lingeringly greeting her there.

"Oh, my deah, she's his teacheh, you know. But now, suppose that next Sunday——"

"Please call it the sabbath, Powhatan."

"Yes, deah, the sabbath. If it should chance to rain——"

"Oh, Judge March, do you believe rain comes by chance?"

"Oh, no, Daphne, dear. But—if it should be raining hard——"

"It will still be the Lord's day. Your son can read and meditate."

"But if it should be fair, and something else should keep us fum church, and he couldn't come up here, and should feel his loneliness——"

"Can't he visit some of our Suez friends—Mary and Martha Salter, Doctor Coffin, or Parson Tombs, the Sextons, or Clay Mattox? I'm not puritanical, nor are they. He's sure of a welcome from either Cousin Hamlet Graves or his brother Lazarus. Heaven has spared us a few friends still."

"Oh, yes, indeed. Dead loads of them; if son would only take to them. And, Daphne, deah,"—the husband brightened—" I hope, yet, he will."

School terms came and went. Mrs. March attributed her son's failure to inherit literary talent to his too long association with his father. He stood neither first, second, nor last in anything. In spiritual conditions he was not always sure that he stood at all. At times he was shaken even in the belief that the love of fun is the root of all virtue, and although he called many a droll doing a prank which the law's dark lexicon terms a misdemeanor, for weeks afterward there would be a sound in his father's gentle speech as of that voice from which Adam once, in the cool of the day, hid himself. In church the sermons he sat under dwelt mainly on the technical difficulties involved in a sinner's salvation,

and neither helped nor harmed him ; he never heard
them.  One clear voice in the midst of the singing was
all that engaged his ear, and when it carolled, "He
shall come down like rain upon the mown grass," the
notes themselves were to him the cooling shower.

One Sabbath afternoon, after a specially indigestible
sermon which Sister Usher said enthusiastically to Major
Garnet ought to be followed by a great awakening—as,
in fact, it had been—Barbara, slim, straight, and fifteen,
softly asked her mother to linger behind the parting
congregation for Fannie.  As Miss Halliday joined
them John, from the other aisle, bowed so pathetically
to his Sunday-school teacher that when she turned
again to smile on Barbara and her mother she laughed,
quite against her will.  The mother and daughter
remained grave.

"Fannie," said Mrs. Garnet, her hand stealing into
the girl's, "I'm troubled about that boy."  Barbara
walked ahead pretending not to hear, but listening
hard.

"Law! Cousin Rose, so'm I!  I wish he'd get religion
or something.  Don't look so at me, Cousin Rose,
you *make* me smile.  I'm really trying to help him, but
the more I try the worse I fail.  If I should meet him
on the straight road to ruin I shouldn't know what to
say to him ; I'm a pagan myself."

## XVII.

### THE ROSEMONT ATMOSPHERE

ABOUT this time Barbara came into new surround-ings. She had been wondering for a month what mat-ter of disagreement her father and mother were trying to be very secret about, when one morning at breakfast her father said, while her mother looked out the window:

"Barb, we've decided to send you to Montrose to stay." And while she was still gazing at him speech-lessly, a gulping sob came from behind her mother's chair and Johanna ran from the room.

Barbara never forgot that day. Nor did her memory ever lose the picture of her father, as he came alone to see her the next day after her entrance into the academy, standing before the Misses Kin-sington—who were as good as they were thin, and as sweet as they were aristocratic—winning their im-petuous approval with the confession that the atmos-phere of a male college—even though it was Rose-mont—was not good for a young girl. While neither of the Misses Kinsington gave a hand to him either for welcome or farewell, when Mademoiselle Eglantine—who taught drawing, history, and French—happened in upon father and daughter a second time, after they had been left to say good-by alone, the hand of Mademoiselle lingered so long in his that Barbara concluded he had forgotten it was there.

"She's quite European in her way, isn't she, Barb?"

The daughter was mute, for she had from time to time noticed several women shake hands with her large-hearted father thus.

Twice a week Barbara spent an afternoon and night at Rosemont. Whether her father really thought its atmosphere desirable for her or not, she desired it, without ceasing and most hungrily. On Sunday nights, when the house had grown still, there would come upon her door the wariest of knocks, and Johanna would enter, choose a humble seat, and stay and stay, to tell every smallest happening of the week.

Not infrequently these recitals contained points in the history of John March.

Rosemont gave one of its unexpected holidays. John March and another senior got horses and galloped joyously away to Pulaski City, where John's companion lived. The seat of government was there. There, too, was the Honorable Mr. Leggett, his party being still uppermost in Blackland. He was still custodian, moreover, of the public school funds for the three counties.

Very late that night, as the two Rosemonters were about to walk past an open oyster saloon hard by the Capitol, John caught his fellow's arm. They stopped in a shadow. Two men coming from an opposite direction went into the place together.

"Who's that white man?" whispered John. The other named a noted lobbyist, and asked,

"Who's the nigger?"

"Cornelius Leggett." John's hand crept, trembling, to his hip pocket.

His companion grasped it. "Pshaw, March, are you crazy?"

"No, are you? I'm not going to shoot; I was only thinking how easy I could do it."

He stepped nearer the entrance. The lone keeper had followed the two men into a curtained stall. His back was just in sight.

"Let's slip in and hear what they say," murmured John, visibly disturbed. But when his companion assented he drew back. His fellow scanned him with a smile of light contempt. There were beads of moisture on his brow. Just then the keeper went briskly toward his kitchen, and the two youths glided into the stall next to the one occupied.

"Yass, seh," Cornelius was tipsily remarking, "the journals o' the day reputes me to have absawb some paucity o' the school funds. Well, supposen I has; I say, jess *supposen* it, you know. I antagonize you this question: did Napoleon Bonapawt never absawb any paucity o' otheh folks' things? An' yit he was the greates' o' the great. He's my patte'n, seh. He neveh stole jiss to be a-stealin'! An' yit wheneveh he found it assential of his *destiny* to steal anything, he stole it!

"O' co'se he incurred and contracted enemies; I has mine; it's useless to translate it. My own motheh's husban'—you riccolec' ole Unc' 'Viticus, don't you?— Rev'en' Leviticus Wisdom—on'y niggeh that eveh refused a office!"—he giggled—"Well, he ensued to tu'n

me out'n the church. Yass, seh, faw nothin' but fallin'
in love with his daughteh—my step-sisteh—sayin' I
run her out'n the county!

"But he couldn't p'ocure a sufficient concawdence o'
my fellow-citizens; much less o' they wives—naw evm
o' mine! No, seh! They brought in they verdic' that
jess at this junction it'd be cal'lated to ungendeh strife
an' could on'y do hahm." He giggled again.

"My politics save me, seh! They always will. An'
they ought to; faw they as pyo as the crystial fountain."

The keeper brought a stew of canned oysters. The
lobbyist served it, and Mr. Leggett talked on.

"Thass the diffunce 'twixt me and Gyarnit. That
man's afraid o' me—jess as 'fraid as a chicken-hawk is
of a gun, seh!—an' which nobody knows why essep'
him an' me. But thass jess the diff''ence. Nobody reputes him to steal, an' I don't say he do. I ain't ready
to say it yit, you un'stan'; but his politics—his politics,
seh; they does the stealin'! An' which it's the low-
downdest kind o' stealin', for it's stealin' fum niggers.
But thass the diff''ence; niggers steals with they claws,
white men with they laws. The claws steals by the
pound; the laws steals by the boatload!"

The lobbyist agreed.

"Jess so!" cried Mr. Leggett. "Ef Gyarnit'd vote
faw the things o' one common welfare an' gen'l progress
an' program, folks—an' niggers too—could affode faw
him to vote faw somepm fat oncet in a while an' to evm
take sugar on his vote—an' would sen' him to the ligis-
latur' stid o' me. Thass not sayin' I eveh did aw does

take sugar on my vote. Ef I wins a bet oncet in a while on whether a certain bill 'll pass, why, that, along o' my official emoluments an' p'crequisites evince me a sufficient plenty.

"Wife?—Estravagant?—No!—Oh! you thinkin' o' my secon' wife. Yes, seh, she was too all-fired estravagant! I don't disadmire estravagant people. I'm dreadful estravagant myseff. But Sophronia jess tuck the rag off'n the bush faw estravagance. Silk dresses, wine, jewelry—it's true she mos'ly spent her own green-backs, but thass jess it, you see; I jess had to paht with her, seh! You can asphyxiate that yo'seff, seh.

"Now this wife I got now—eh? No, I ain't never ezac'ly hear the news that the other one dead, but I suspicioned her, befo' she lef', o' bein' consumpted, an' —O anyhow she's dead to me, seh! Now, the nex' time I marries—eh?—O yes, but the present Mis' Leg-gett can't las' much longeh, seh. I mistakened myseff when I aspoused her. I'm a man o' rich an' abundant natu'e an' ought to a-got a spouse consistent with my joys an' destinies. I may have to make a sawt o' Emp'ess Josephine o' her—ef she lives.

"Y'ought to see the nex' one!—Seh?—Engaged?— No, not yit; she as shy as a crow an'—ezac'ly the same colo'!—I'm done with light-complected women, seh.—But y'ought to see this-yeh one!—Shy as a pa't'idge! But I'm hot on her trail. She put*tend* to be tarrible shocked—well, o' co'se thass right!—Hid away in the hills—at Rosemont. But I kin git her on a day's notice. All I got to espress myself is—Majo' Gyarnit, seh!—Ef you continues faw twenty-fo' hours mo' to harbor the girl Johanna, otherwise Miss Wisdom, the Black Diana an' sim'lar names, I shall imbibe it my jewty to the gen'l welfare an' public progress to reno- vate yo' rememb'ance of a vas'ly diff''ent an' mo' finan- cial matteh, as per my letteh to you of sich a date about seven year' ago an' not an's'd yit, *an' tell what I know about you.* Thass all I'll say. Thass all I haf to say! An' mebbe I won't haf to say that. Faw I'm tryin' love lettehs on her; wrote the fus' one this evenin'; on'y got two mo' to write. My third inevasively fetches 'em down the tree, seh! "

The lobbyist revived the subject of politics, the pub- lican went after hot water for a punch, and the eaves- droppers slipped away.

Early the following week Mr. Leggett reclined in his seat in the House of Representatives. His boots were on his desk, and he tapped them with his sword-cane while he waited to back up with his vote a certain bet of the Friday night before. A speaker of his own party was alluding to him as the father of free schools in Blackland and Clearwater; but he was used to this and only closed his eyes. A page brought his mail. It was small. One letter was perfumed. He opened it and sat transfixed with surprise, and a-tremble between vanity and doubt, desire and trepidation. He bent his beaded eyes close over the sweet thing and read its first page again and again. It might—it *might* be an im- posture; but it had come in a Rosemont envelope, and it was signed Johanna Wisdom.

The House began to vote. He answered to his name; the bill passed, his bet was won. Adjournment fol-

lowed.  He hurried out and away, and down in a suburban lane entered his snug, though humble, "bo'd'n'
house," locked his door, and read again.

Two or three well-known alumni of Rosemont and
two or three Northern capitalists—railroad prospectors
—were, on the following Friday, at the Swanee Hotel
to be the guests of the Duke of Suez, as Ravenel was
fondly called by the Rosemont boys.  To show Suez at
its best by night as well as by day, there was to be a
Rosemont-Montrose ball in the hotel dining-room.
Major Garnet opposed its being *called* a ball, and it was
announced as a musical reception and promenade.  Mr.
Leggett knew quite as well as Garnet and Ravenel that
the coming visitors were behind the bill he had just
voted for.

Johanna, the letter said, would be at the ball as an
attendant in the ladies' cloak-room.  It bade him meet
her that night at eleven on the old bridge that spanned
a ravine behind the hotel, where a back street ended at
the edge of a neglected grove.

"Lawd, Lawd! little letteh, little letteh! is you de
back windeh o' heavm, aw is you de front gate o' hell?
Th' ain't no way to tell but by tryin'!  Oh, how *kin* I
resk it?  An' yit, how kin I he'p but resk it?

"Sheh! ain't I resk my life time an' time ag'in jess
for my *abstrac' rights* to be a Republican niggeh?

"Ef they'd on'y shoot me!  But they won't.  They
won't evm hang me; they'll jess tie me to a tree and
bu'n me—wet me th'oo with coal-oil, tech a match—O
Lawd!"  He poured a tremendous dram, looked at it
long, then stepped to the window, and with a quaking

hand emptied both glass and bottle on the ground, as if he knew life depended on a silent tongue in a sober head.

And then he glanced once more at the letter, folded it, and let it slowly into his pocket.

"'Happy as a big sun-floweh,' is you? I ain't. I ain't no happier'n a pig on the ice. O it's mawnstus p'ecipitous! But it's gran'! It's mo'n gran'; it's muccurial! it's puffic'ly nocturnial!" With an exalted solemnity of face, half ardor, half anguish, he stiffened heroically and gulped out,

"I'll be thah!"

Friday came. John March and half-a-dozen other Rosemonters, a committee to furnish "greens" for garlanding the walls and doorways, hurried about in an expectancy and perturbation, now gay, now grave, that seemed quite excessive as the mere precursors of an evening dance. They gathered their greenery from the grove down beyond the old bridge and ravine, where the ground was an unbroken web of honeysuckle vines.

On this old bridge, at the late night hour fixed in the letter, Cornelius met a counterfeit, thickly-veiled Johanna, and swore to marry her.

"Black as you is? Yass! The blackeh the betteh! An' yit I'd marry you ef you wuz pyo white!—Colo' line!—I'll cross fifty colo' lines whenev' I feels like it!"

By midnight every Rosemonter at the ball had heard this speech repeated, and knew that it had hardly left the mulatto's throat before he had fled with shrieks of terror from the pretended ghosts of his earlier wives, and with the curses of a coward's rage from the vain clutches of his would-be captors.—But we go too fast.

## XVIII.

### THE PANGS OF COQUETRY

NIGHT fell. The hotel shone. The veranda was gay with Chinese lanterns. The muffled girls were arriving. The musicians tuned up. There were three little fiddles, one big one, a flageolet, and a bassoon.

> "Twinkling stars are laughing, love,
>   Laughing on you and me"

—sang the flageolet and little fiddles, while the double bass and the bassoon grunted out their corroborative testimony with melodious unction. Presently the instruments changed their mood, the flageolet pretended to be a mocking-bird, all trills, the fiddles passionately declared they were dreaming now-ow of Hallie—tr-r-r-ee! —dear Hallie—tr-r-r-ee!—sweet Hallie—tr-r-r-ee! and the bassoon and double bass responded from the depths of their emotions, "Hmmh! hmmh! hm-hm-hmmh!"

Ravenel and his guests appeared on the floor; Major Garnet, too. He had been with them, here, yonder, all day. Barbara remained at home, although her gowns were the full length now, and she coiled her hair. General Halliday and Fannie arrived. Her dress, they said, was the prettiest in the room. Jeff-Jack introduced everybody to the Northerners. The women all asked them if Suez wasn't a beautiful city, and the guests praised the town, its site, its gardens, "its possibilities," its ladies—!—and its classic river.

Try to look busy or dignified as he might, all these things only harried John March. He kept apart from Fannie. Indeed, what man of any self-regard—he asked his mangled spirit—could penetrate the crowd that hovered about her, ducking, fawning, giggling, attitudinizing—listening over one another's shoulders, guffawing down each other's throats? It hurt him to see her show such indiscriminating amiability; but he felt sure he knew her best, and hoped she was saying to herself, "Oh, that these sycophants were gone, and only John and I and the twinkling stars remained to laugh together! Why does he stay away?"

"O my darling Nellie Gray, they have taken you away," wept the fiddles, and "Who? who? who-who-who?" inquired the basses in deep solicitude.

Well, the first dance would soon come, now; the second would shortly follow, and then he and Fannie could go out on the veranda and settle all doubts. With certainty established in that quarter, whether it should bring rapture or despair, he hoped to command the magnanimity to hold over a terrified victim the lash of retribution, and then to pronounce upon him, untouched, at last, the sentence of exile. He spoke aloud, and looking up quickly to see if anyone had heard, beheld his image in a mirror. He knew it instantly, both by its frown and by the trick of clapping one hand on the front of the thigh with the arm twisted so as to show a large seal-ring bought by himself with money that should have purchased underclothes for his father. He jerked it away with a growl of self-scorn, and went to mingle with older men, to whom, he fancied, the world meant more than young women and old scores.

He stopped in a part of the room where two Northerners were laughing at a keen skirmish of words between Garnet and Halliday. These two had gotten upon politics, and others were drawing near, full of eager but unplayful smiles.

"Never mind," said Garnet, in retort, "we've restored public credit and cut the rottenness out of our government."

The Northerners nodded approvingly, and the crowd packed close.

"Garnet," replied the general, with that superior smile which Garnet so hated, "States, like apples—and like men—have two sorts of rottenness. One begins at the surface and shows from the start; the other starts from the core, and doesn't show till the whole thing is rotten."

For some secret reason, Garnet reddened fiercely for an instant, and then, with a forced laugh, addressed his words to one of the guests.

Another of the strangers was interested in the severe attention a strong-eyed Rosemont boy seemed to give to Halliday's speech. But it was only John March, who was saying, in his heart:

"She's got a perfect right to take me or throw me, but she's no right to do both!"

Only the Northerners enjoyed Halliday. The Suez men turned away in disdain.

The music struck a quadrille, sweetly whining and

hooting twice over before starting into doubtful history,

"In eighteen hundred and sixty-one—to the war! to the war!"

The dance springs out! Gray jackets and white trousers; tarlatan, flowers, and fans; here and there a touch of powder or rouge; some black broadcloth and much wrinkled doeskin. Jeff-Jack and Fannie move hand in hand, and despite the bassoon's contemptuous "pooh! pooh! poo-poo-pooh!" the fiddles declare, with petulant vehemence, that—

"In eighteen-hundred-and-sixty-one, the Yankees *they* the war *begun*, but we'll all! get! blind! drunk! when Johnnie comes marching home."

"You see we play the national—oh! no, I believe that's not one—but we do play them!" said a native.

John didn't march home, although when some one wanted a window open which had been decorated to stay shut, neither he nor his committee could be found. He came in, warm and anxious, just in time to claim Fannie for their schottische. At ten they walked out on the veranda and took seats at its dark end. She was radiant, and without a sign of the mild dismay that was in her bosom. When she said, "Now, tell me, John, why you're so sad," there was no way for him to see that she was secretly charging herself not to lie and not to cry.

"Miss Fannie," he replied, "you're breaking my heart."

"Aw, now, John, are you going to spoil our friendship this way?"

"Friendship!—Oh, Fannie!"

" Miss Fannie, if you please, Mister John."

" Ah! has it come to that? And do you hide that face?"—For Fannie had omitted to charge herself not to smile at the wrong time—"Have you forgotten the day we parted here five years ago?"

" Why, no. I don't remember what day of the week it was, but I—I remember it. Was it Friday? What day was it?"

" Fannie, you mock me! Ah! you thought me but a boy, then, but I loved you with a love beyond my years; and now as a man, I——"

"Oh! a man! Mr. March, there's an end to this bench. No! John, I don't mock you; I honor you; I've always been proud of you—Now—now, John, let go my hand! John, if you don't let go my hand I'll leave you; you naughty boy!—No, I won't answer a thing till you let me go! John March, let go my hand this instant! Now I shall sit here. You'll keep the bench, please. Yes, I do remember it all, and regret it!" She turned away in real dejection, saying, in her heart, "But I shall do no better till I die—or—or get married!"

She faced John again. "Oh, if I'd thought you'd remember it forty days it shouldn't have occurred! I saw in you just a brave, pure-hearted, sensible boy. I thought it would be pleasant, and even elevating—to you—while it lasted, and that you'd soon see how—how ineligible—indeed I did!" Both were silent.

" Fannie Halliday," said John at last, standing before her as slim and rank as a sapling, but in the dignity of injured trust, "when year after year you saw I loved you, why did you still play me false!"

"Now, Mr. March, you're cruel."

"Miss Fannie Halliday, have you been kind?"

"I meant to be! I never meant to cheat you! I kept hoping you'd understand! Sometimes I tried to make you understand, didn't I? I'm very sorry, John. I know I've done wrong. But I—I meant well. I really did!"

The youth waved an arm. "You've wrecked my life. Oh, Fannie, I'm no mere sentimentalist. I can say in perfect command of these wild emotions, 'Enchantress, fare thee well!'"

"Oh, fare thee fiddlesticks!" Fannie rose abruptly. "No, no, I didn't mean that, John, but—aw! now, I didn't *mean* to smile! Oh, let's forget the past—oh! now, yes, you can! Let's just be simple, true friends! And one of these days you'll love some sweet, true girl, and she'll love you and I'll love her, and—" she took his arm. He looked down on her.

"*I* love again!—*I*—? Ah! how little you women understand men! Oh, Fannie! to love twice is never to have loved. You are my first—my last!"

"Oh, no, I'm not," said Fannie, blithely and aloud, as they reëntered the room. Then softly, behind her fan, "I've a better one in store for you, now!"

"Two!" groaned the bass viol and bassoon. "Two! two! two-to-to-two!" and with a propitiative smile on John's open anguish, Fannie, gayer in speech and readier in laughter, but not lighter in heart, let a partner waltz her away. As John turned, one of his committee seized his arm and showed a watch.

## XIX.

### MR. RAVENEL SHOWS A "MORE EXCELLENT WAY"

URGED by all sorts and on all sides, the Northerners lingered a day or two more, visiting battle-fields and things. At Turkey Creek Halliday was talkative, Garnet overflowed with information, Captains Champion and Shotwell were boyish, and Colonel Proudfit got tight. They ate cold fried chicken and drank—

"Whew!—stop, stop!—I can't take—Why, half that would"—etc.

"Where's Mr. Ravenel?"

"Who, Jeff-Jack? Oh, he's over yonder pickin' blackberries—no, he seldom ever touches—he has to be careful how he—Yes, sometimes he disremembers."

In town again, Halliday led the way to the public grammar and high schools. Garnet mentioned Montrose boastfully more than once.

"Why don't we go there?" asked one of the projectors, innocently.

"Oh—ah—wha'd you say, Colonel Proudfit? Yess, that's so, we pass right by it on ow way to Rosemont"—and they did, to the sweet satisfaction of the Misses Kinsington, who were resolved no railroad should come to Suez if they could prevent it.

At Rosemont Mr. Dinwiddie Pettigrew told each Northerner, as soon as he could get him from Mrs. Garnet's presence, that Virginia was the Mother of

Presidents; that the first slaves ever brought to this country came in Yankee ships; that Northern envy of Southern opulence and refinement had been the mainspring of the abolition movement; and—with a smile of almost womanly heroism—that he—or his father at least—had lost all his slaves in the war.

At Widewood, whither Garnet and Ravenel led, the travelers saw only Judge March and the scenery. He brought them water to the fence in a piggin, and with a wavering hand served it out in a gourd.

"I could 'a' served it in a glass, gentlemen, but we Southe'ne's think it's sweeteh drank fum a gode."

"We met your son at the cotillion," said one, and the father lighted up with such confident expectation of a compliment that the stranger added, cordially, "He's quite noted," though he had not heard of the affair with Leggett.

On the way back Garnet praised everything and everybody. He wished they could have seen Daphne Dalrymple! If it were not for the Northern prejudice against Southern writers, her poems would—"See that fox—ah! he's hid, now."

But the wariest game was less coy than the poetess. She wrote, that day,

> "O! hide me from the Northron's eye!
> Let me not hear his fawning voice,
> I heard the Southland matron sigh
> And saw the piteous tear that " . . .

Thus it ended; "as if," said Garnet to John, who with restrained pride showed him the manuscript, " as if grief for the past choked utterance—for the present.

There's a wonderful eloquence in that silence, March, tell her to leave it as it is ; dry so."

John would have done this had he not become extremely preoccupied. The affair at the old bridge was everybody's burning secret till the prospectors were gone. But the day after they left it was everybody's blazing news. Oddly enough, not what anybody had done, but what Leggett had said—in contempt of the color line—was the microscopic germ of all the fever. From window to window, and from porch to porch, women fed alarm with rumor and rumor with alarm, while on every sidewalk men collaborated in the invention of plans for defensive vengeance.

" Well, they've caught him—pulled him out of a dry well in Libertyville."

" I beg your pardon, he crossed the Ohio this morning at daylight."

John March was light-headed with much drinking of praise for having made it practicable to "smash this unutterable horror in the egg ! "

Ravenel, near the *Courier* office, stopped at the beckon of Lazarus Graves and Charlie Champion. John was with them, laboring under the impression that they were with him. They wanted to consult Ravenel about the miscreant, and the "steps proper to be taken against him."

" When found," suggested Ravenel, and they pleasantly assented.

" Oh, yes," he said again, as the four presently moved out of the hot sun, " but if the color line hadn't been crossed already there wouldn't be any Leggett."

"But he threatens to cross it from the wrong side," replied John, posing sturdily.

Ravenel's smile broadened. "Most any man, Mr. March, could be enticed across."

The mouth of the enticer opened, but his tongue failed.

"A coat of tah and feathers will show him he mustn't even be enticed across," rejoined Lazarus.

Ravenel said something humorous about the new Dixie and a peace policy, and John's face began to show misgivings; but Captain Champion explained that the affair would be strictly select—best citizens—no liquor—no brawl—no life-taking, unless violent resistance compelled it; in fact, no individual act; but——

"Yes, I know," said Ravenel, "you mean one of those irresistable eruptions of a whole people's righteous indignation, that sweeps before it the whining hypercriticisms of effeminated civilizations," and the smile went round.

"Gentlemen, there's an easier way to get rid of Cornelius; one, Captain, that won't hurt more by the recoil than by the discharge."

They were all silent. John folded his arms. Presently Graves said, meditatively,

"We don't care to hang him, just at——"

"This juncture," said Ravenel; "no, better give him ten years in the penitentiary—for bigamy."

Sunshine broke on Mr. Graves's face, and he murmured, "Go 'way!"

"Champion, too, was radiant. "Hu-u-ush!" he said, "who'll get us the evidence?"

"Old Uncle Leviticus."

The more questions they asked the more pleased with the plan were John's two companions. "Why didn't you think of that?" asked each of the other in mock contempt. The youth felt his growing insignificance reach completeness as Ravenel said,

"In that case you'll not need Mr. March any longer."

"No, of course not," said John, quickly. "I was"— he forced a cough.

The other two waved good-by, and he turned to go with them, but was stopped.

"Don't you want to see me about something else, Mr. March?" said Ravenel, to detain him.

"No, sir," replied John, innocently. "Oh, no, I was——"

There came between them, homeward bound, an open parasol, a mist of muslin as sweet as a blossoming tree, a bow to Mr. Ravenel, and then a kinder one to John.

"Go," said Ravenel, softly. "Didn't you see? She wants you."

John overtook the dainty figure, lifted his military cap, and slackened his pace.

"Miss Fannie?" he caught step with her.

"Oh!—why good morning." She was delightfully cordial.

"Did you want to see me?" he asked. "Mr. Ravenel thought you did."

Fannie raised her brows and laughed.

"Why, really, Mr. Ravenel oughtn't to carry his thinking to such an excess. Still, I'm not sorry for the mistake—unless you are." She glanced at him archly. "Come on," she softly added, "I do want to see you."

---

## XX.

### FANNIE SUGGESTS

"Don't look so gruesome." She laughed.

John walked stiffly, frowned, and tried to twist the down on his upper lip. When only fenced and gardened dwellings were about them she spoke again.

"John, I'm unhappy."

"You, Miss Fannie?"

"Yes. As I passed you, you were standing right where you fell five years ago. For three days I've been thinking how deep in debt to you I've been ever since, and—how I've disappointed you."

The youth made no answer. He felt as if he would give ten years of his life to kneel at her feet with his face in her hands and whisper, "Pay me a little love." She laid her arm on her cottage gate, turned her face away, and added,

"And now you're disappointing me."

"I've got a right to know how, Miss Fannie, haven't I?"

Fannie's averted face sank lower. Suddenly she looked fondly up to him and nodded. "Come, sit on the steps a minute "—she smiled—" and I'll pick you a rose."

She skipped away. As she was returning her father came out.

"Why, howdy, Johnnie—Fan, I reckon I'll go to the office."

"You promised me you wouldn't!"

"Well, I'm better since I took some quinine. How's y' father, Johnnie?"

"Sir? Oh, she's not very well. She craves acids, and—Oh!—Father? he's very—I ain't seen him in a right smart while, sir. He's been sort o' puny for——"

"Sorry," said the General, and was gone.

Fannie held the rose.

"Thank you," said John, looking from it to the kindness in her eye. But she caressed the flower and shook her head.

"It's got thorns," she said, significantly, as she sat down on a step.

"Yes, I understand. I'll take it so."

"I don't know. I'm afraid you'll not want it when " —she laid it to her lips—" when I tell you how you've disappointed me."

"Yes, I will. For—oh! Miss Fannie——"

"What, John?"

"You needn't tell me at all. I know it already. And I'm going to change it. You shan't be disappointed. I've learned an awful lot in these last three days—and these last three hours. I've done my last sentimentalizing. I—I'm sure I have. I'll be too good for it, or else too bad for it! I'll always love you, Miss

Fannie, even when you're not—Miss Fannie any more; but I'll never come using round you and bothering you with my—feelings." He jerked out his handkerchief, but wiped only his cap—with slow care.

"As to that, John, I shouldn't blame you if you should hate me."

"I can't, Miss Fannie. I've not done hating, I'm afraid, but I couldn't hate you—ever. You can't conceive how sweet and good you seem to anyone as wicked as I've been—and still am."

"You don't know what I mean, John."

"Yes, I do. But you didn't know how bad you were f-fooling me. And even if you had of—it must be mighty hard for some young ladies not to—to——"

"Flirt," said Fannie, looking down on her rose. "I reckon those who do it find it the easiest and prettiest wickedness in the world, don't they?"

"Oh, I don't know! All my wickedness is ugly and hard. But I'm glad you expected enough of me to be disappointed."

"Yes, I did. Why, John, you never in your life offered me a sign of regard but I felt it an honor. You've often tripped and stumbled, but I—oh, I'm too bad myself to like a perfect boy. What I like is a boy with a conscience."

"My guiding star!" murmured John.

"Oh! ridiculous!—No, I take that back! But—but —why, that's what disappoints me! If you'd made me just your first mile-board. But it hurts me—oh, it hurts me! and—far worse—it's hurting Cousin Rose Garnet! to—now, don't flush up that way—to see

John March living by passion and not by principle!"

"H—oh! Miss Fannie!" He strained up a superior smile. "Is passion—are passions bound to be ignoble? But you're making the usual mistake——"

"How, John?" She put on a condescending patience.

"Why, in fancying you women can guide a man by——"

"Preaching?" the girl interrupted. Her face had changed. "I know we can't," she added, abstractedly. John was trying to push his advantage.

"Passion!" he exclaimed. "Passion? Miss Fannie, you look at life with a woman's view! We men—what are we without passion—all the passions? Furnaces without fire! Ships without sails!"

"True! John. And just as true for women. But without principles we're ships without rudders. Passion ought to fill our sails, yes; but if principles don't steer we're lost!"

"Now, are you not making yourself my guiding star?"

"No! I won't have the awful responsibility! I'm nothing but a misguided girl. Guiding star! Oh, fancy calling me that when your dear old——"

"Do—o—on't!"

"Then take it back and be a guiding star yourself! See here! D'you remember the day at the tournament when you were my knight? John March, can you believe it? I! me! this girl! Fannie Halliday! member of the choir! I prayed for you that day. I did, for a fact! I prayed you might come to be one of the few

who are the knights of all mankind; and here you—
John, if I had a thousand gold dollars I'd rather lose
them in the sea than have you do what you're this
day——"

"Miss Fannie, stop; I'm not doing it. It's not
going to be done. But oh! if you knew what spurred
me on—I can't expl——"

"You needn't. I've known all about it for years!
I got it from the girls who put you to bed that night.
But no one else knows it and they'll never tell. John,"
Fannie pushed her gaiter's tip with her parasol, "guess
who was here all last evening, smoking the pipe of
peace with pop."

"Jeff-Jack?"

"I mean besides · him. Brother Garnet! John,
what is that man mostly, fox or goose?"

"Oh, now, Miss Fannie, you're unjust! You're—
you're partisan!"

"Hmm! That's what pop called me. He says
Major Garnet means well, only he's a moss-back. Sakes
alive! That's worse than fox and goose in one!" Her
eyes danced merrily. "Why, that man's still in the
siege of Vicksburg, feeding Rosemont and Suez with its
mule meat, John."

"Miss Fannie, it's my benefactor you're speaking of."

"Aw! your grandmother! Look here. Why'd he
bring Mr. Ravenel here—for Mr. Ravenel didn't bring
him—to pow-wow with pop? Of course he had some
purpose—some plan. It's only you that's all sympa-
thies—no plans."

"Why, it's not an hour," cried John, rising, "since

Jeff-Jack told me he wasn't a man of plans, other men's plans were good enough for him!"

Fannie's mouth opened and her eyes widened with merriment. "Oh—oh—mm—mm—mm." She looked up at the sky and then sidewise at the youth. "Sit down, sit down; you need the rest! Oh!" She rounded her mouth and laughed.

"Now, see here, John March, you've no right to make me behave so. Listen! I have a sneaking notion that, with some reference to your mountain lands, Brother Garnet—whom, I declare, John, I wouldn't speak to if it wasn't for Cousin Rose—has for years built you into his plans, including those he brought here last night. In a few days you'll at last be through Rosemont; but I believe he'd be glad to see you live for years yet on loves, hates, and borrowed money. Oh! for your father's sake, don't please that man that way! Why can't you plan? Why don't you guide? You plan fast enough when passion controls you; plan with your passions under your control. Build men— *build him*—into your plans. Why, John, owning as much of God's earth as you do, you're honor bound to plan."

"I know it, Miss Fannie. I've been feeling it a long time; now I see it." He started to catch up the rose she had dropped, but the laugh was hers; her foot was on it.

"You—don't you dare, sir! John, there's my foot's sermon. D'you see? Everybody should put his own rose and thorn, both alike, under his own foot. Shod or unshod, sir, we all have to do it. Now, why can't

you bring Mr. Ravenel to see pop with a plan of your
own? I believe—of course I don't know, but I suspect
—Brother Garnet has left something out of his plan that
you can take into yours and make yours win. Would
you like to see it?" She patted her lips with her parasol handle and smiled bewitchingly.

"Would I—what do you mean, Miss Fannie?"

"Why, I've got it here in the house. It's a secret,
but "—lips and parasol again, eyes wickeder than ever—
"it's something that you can see and touch. Promise
you'll never tell, never-never-never?"

He promised.

"Wait here." She ran into the house, trolling a song.
As John sat listening for her return, the thought came
abruptly, "Hasn't Jeff-Jack got something to do with
this?" But there was scarcely time to resent it when
she reopened the door coyly, beckoned him in, passed
out, and closed it; and, watchworn, wasted, more dead
than alive, there stood before John the thing Garnet
was omitting—Cornelius Leggett.

When John passed out again Fannie saw purpose in
his face and smiled.

"Well?—Can you build him in?—into your
plans?"

The youth stared unintelligently. She laughed at
him.

"My stars! you forgot to try!"

It was late at night when Lazarus Graves and Captain Champion, returning from Pulaski City, where they
had been hurrying matters into shape for the prosecu-

tion of Leggett, rode down the Susie and Pussie Pike toward Suez. Where the Widewood road forked off into the forest on their left they stopped, having unexpectedly come upon a third rider bound the other way. He seemed quite alone and stood by his horse in deep shade, tightening the girth and readjusting blanket and saddle. Champion laughed and predicted his own fate after death.

"Turn that freckled face o' yo's around here, Johnnie March; we ain't Garnet and Pettigrew, an' th' ain't nothin' the matteh with that saddle."

"Howdy, Cap'm," said John, as if too busy to look up.

"Howdy yo'seff! What new devilment you up to now? None? Oh, then we didn't see nobody slide off fum behine that saddle an' slip into the bushes. Who was it, John? Was it Johanna, so-called?"

"No, it was Leggett," said John.

"Oh, I reckon!" laughed the Captain.

"Come on," grumbled Graves, and they left him.

--------

## XXI.

### MR. LEGGETT'S CHICKEN-PIE POLICY

THE youth whistled his charge out of the brush and moved on, sometimes in the saddle with the mulatto mounted behind, sometimes, where the way was steep, walking beside the tired horse. When both rode he had to bear a continual stream of tobacco-scented whisperings poured into his ear.

"Mr. March, that crowd wouldn't do me this a-way if they knowed the patri'tisms I feels to 'em. You see, it's they financialities incur the late rise in Clairwateh County scrip. Yass, seh; which I catch the fo'cas' o' they intentions in time to be infested in a good passle of it myseff."

"So that now your school funds are all straight again?"

"Ezac'ly! all straight an' comp'ehensive. An' what shell we say then? Shell we commit sin that grace may aboun'? Supposin' I has been too trancadillious; I say jis' *supposin'* I may have evince a rather too wifely pretendencies; what does they care fo' that? No, seh, all they wants is to git shet o' me."

"And do you think they're wrong?"

"Mr. March, I does! Thass right where they misses it. Why, they *needs* me, seh! I got a new policy, Mr. March. I 'llowed to espound it las' week on the flo' of the house, same day the guvneh veto that bill we pass; yass, seh. The guvneh's too much like Gyarnit; he's faw the whole hawg or none. Thass not my way; my visions is mo' perspectral an' mo' clairer. Seh? Wha'd you say?"

"Oh, nothing," laughed John. "Only a shudder of disgust."

"Yass, seh. Well, it is disgustin', ev'm to me. You see, I discerns all these here New Dixie projeckin'. I behole how they all a-makin' they sun'ry chicken-pies, which notinstanin' they all diff''ent, yit they all alike, faw they all tu'novers! Yass, seh, they all spreads hafe acrost the dish an' then tu'n back. I has been en-title Slick an' Slippery Leggett—an' yit what has I always espress myseff? Gen'le*men*, they must be suffi-ciend plenty o' chicken-pie to go round. An', Mr. March, if she don't *be* round, she won't *go* round. 'Tis true the scripter say, To them what hath shell be givened, an' to them what hath not shell be takened away that which seem like they hath; but the scripter's one thing an' chicken-pie's anotheh."

"Listen," whispered John, stopping the horse; and when Mr. Leggett would have begun again—"Oh, do shut your everlasting——"

"P-he-he-he-he!" tittered the mulatto under his breath. John started again and Leggett resumed.

"Whew! I'm that thusty! Ain't you got no sawt o' pain-killeh about yo' clo'es? Aw! Mr. March, mos' sholy you is got some. No gen'leman ain't goin' to be out this time o' night 'ithout some sawt o' corrective —Lawd! I wisht you had! Cayn't we stop som'er's an' git some? Lawd! I wisht we could! I'm jest a-honin' faw some sawt o' wetness.

"But exhumin' my subjec', Mr. March, thass anotheh thing the scripters evince—that ev'y man shall be jedge' by his axe. Yass, seh, faw of co'se ev'y man got his axe to grime. I got mine. You got yo's, ain't you? —Well, o' co'se. I respec' you faw it! Yass, seh; but right there the question arise, is it a public axe? An' if so, is it a good one? aw is it a private axe? aw is it both? Of co'se, ef a man got a good public axe to grime, he espec'—an' you espec' him—to bring his private axe along an' git hit grime at the same junction. Thass natchiul. Thass all right an' pufficly corrosive. On'y we must take tu'ns tunnin' the grime-stone. You grime my axe, I grime yo's. How does that strack you, Mr. March?"

John's reply was enthusiastic. "Why, it strikes me as positively mephitic."

"Mr. March, thass what it is! Thass the ve'y word! Now, shell me an' you fulfil the scripter—'The white man o' the mountains an' the Etheropium o' the valleys shell jine they han's an' the po' man's axe shell be grime'?' Ain't them words sweet? Ain't they jess pufficly syruptitious? My country, 'tis of thee! Oh, Mr. March, ef you knowed how much patri'tism I got!— You hear them Suez fellehs say this is a white man's country an' cayn't eveh be a rich man's country till it is a white man's——"

"See here, now; I tell you for the last time, if you value your life you'd better make less noise."

"Yass, seh. Lawd, I cayn't talk; I'm that thusty I'm a-spitt'n' cotton!—No, seh! White man ain't eveh goin' to lif hisseff up by holdin' niggeh down, an' that's the pyo chaotic truth; now, ain't it?"

"Best way is to hang the nigger up."

"Aw, Mr. March, you a-jokin'! You know I espress the truth. Ef you wants to make a rich country, you ain't got to make it a white man's country, naw a black man's country, naw yit mix the races an' make it a yaller man's country, much less a yaller woman's; no, seh! But the whole effulgence is jess this: you got to

make it a po' man's country!   Now, you accentuate yo'
reflections on that, seh!—Seh?"

"I say that's exactly what Widewood is."

"No, seh! no, seh!   I means a country what's good
faw a po' man, an' Widewood cayn't eveh be that
'ithout schoolhouses, seh!   But thass what me an' you
can make it, Mr. March.   Why, thass the hence an'
the whence that my constituents an' coefficients calls me
School-house Leggett.   Some men cusses me that I has
mix' the races in school.   Well, supposin' I has—a
little; I'se mix' myself.   You cayn't neveh mix 'em
hafe so fas' in school as they mixes 'em out o' school.
Yit thass not in the accawdeons o' my new policy.
Mr. March, I'm faw the specie o' schools we kin git an'
keep——"

John laughed again.   "Oh, yes, you're sure to keep
all the specie you get."

Mr. Leggett giggled.   "Aw! I means that *kine* o'
school.   An' jiss now that happ'm to be sep'ate schools.
I neveh was hawgish like my frien' Gyarnit.   Gyarnit's
faw Rosemont an' State aid *toe* Rosemont, an' faw nothin' else an' nobody else, fus', las', an' everlastin'.
Thass jess why his projeckin' don't neveh eventuate, an'
which it neveh will whilse I'm there to *pre*ventuate!
Whoever hear him say, 'Mr. School-house Leggett, aw
Mr. March, aw Mr. Anybody-in-God's-worl', pass yo'
plate faw a piece o' the chicken pie?'   What! you
heard it?   Oh, Mr. March, don't you be fool'!   An'
yit I favo's Rosemont——"

"Why, you've made it your standing threat to burst
Rosemont wide open!"

" Yass, te-he ! I has often prevaricate that intention. But Law' ! that was pyo gas, Mr. March. I favors Rosemont, an' State aid *toe* Rosemont—perwidin'— enough o' the said thereof to go round, an' the same size piece faw ev'y po' man's boy as faw ev'y rich man's boy. Of co's with gals it's diff''ent. Mr. March, you don't know what a frien' you been a-dislikin' ! "

" They say you're in favor of railroads."

" Why, o' co'se ! An' puttickly the Pussie an' Susie an' Great South Railroad an' State mawgage bawns in accawdeons—perwidin !—one school-house, som'er's in these-yeh th'ee counties, faw ev'y five mile' o' road they buil' ; an' a Leggettstown braynch road, yass, seh. An', Mr. March, yit, still, mo'over, perwiddin' the movin' the capital to Suez, away fum the corrup' influence of Pulaski City. Faw, Mr. March, the legislatu'e will neveh be pyo anywher's else esceptin' in Suez, an' not evm myseff ! Whew ! I'm that thusty——"

## XXII.

### CLIMBING LOVER'S LEAP

THE woods grew dense and pathless, and the whispering gave place to a busy fending off of the strong undergrowth. Presently John tied the horse, and the riders stepped into an open spot on a precipitous mountain side. At their left a deep gorge sank so abruptly that a small stone, casually displaced, went sliding and

rattling beyond earshot.  On their right a wasted moon
rose and stared at them over the mountain's shoulder;
while within hand's reach, a rocky cliff, bald on its
crown, stripped to the waist, and draped at its foot in
foliage, towered in the shadow of the vast hill.

"Why, good Lawd, Mr. March, this is Lover's Leap!
We cayn't neveh climb up here!"

"We've got to!  D' you reckon I brought you here
to look at it?  Come on.  We've only got to reach
that last cedar yonder by the dead pine."

The mulatto moaned, but they climbed.  As they
rose the black gorge seemed to crawl under them and
open its hungry jaws.

"Great Lawd!  Mr. March, this is sut'n death!
Leas'wise it is to me.  I cayn't go no fu'ther, Mr.
March; I inglected to tell you I'se got a pow'ful lame
foot."

"Keep quiet," murmured John, "and come on.
Only don't look down."

The reply was a gasp of horror.  "Oh! mussy me,
you spoke too late!  Wait jess a minute, Mr. March,
I'll stan' up ag'in in a minute.  I jess mus' set here a
minute an' enjoy the view; it's gr-gran'!

"Yass, seh.  I'se a-comin', seh.  I'll rise up in a few
minutes; I'm sick at my stomach, but it'll pass off if I
kin jiss set still a shawt while tell it passes off."

The speaker slowly rose, grabbling the face of the rock.

"Mr. March, wait a minute, I w-want to tell you.  Is-
is-is you w-waitin'?  Mr. March, this is pufficly safe and
haza'dous, seh, I feels that, seh, but I don't like this runnin' away an' hidin'!  It's cowardly; le's go down an'

face the thing like men! I'm goin' to crawl down back
'ards; thass the skilfullest way."

"Halt!" growled John, and something else added
"tick-tick."

"Oh! Mr. March, faw God's sake! Ef you mus'
shoot me, shoot me whah I won't fall so fuh! Why, I
was a-jokin'! I wa'n't a-dreamin' o' goin' back! Heah
I come, seh, look out! Oh, please put up that-ah
naysty-lookin' thing!—Thank you, seh!—Mr. March, escuse me jiss a minute whilse I epitomize my breath a
little, seh, I jess want to recover my dizziness—This is
fine, ain't it? Oh, Lawd! Mr. March, escuse my sink-
in' down this a-way! Oh, don't disfunnish yo'seff to
come back to me, seh; I's jiss faint and thusty. Mr.
March, I ain't a-scared; I'm jiss a-parishin' o' thust!
Lawd! I'm jiss that bole an' rackless I'd resk twenty
lives faw jiss one hafe a finger o' pyo whiskey. I dunno
what'll happm to me ef I don't git some quick. I ain't
had a drap sence the night o' the ball, an' thass what
make this-yeh flatulency o' the heart. Oh! please don't
tech me; ev'm ef you lif' me I cayn't stan'. Oh, Lawd!
the icy han' o' death is on me. I'll soon be in glory!"

"Glory!" answered an echo across the gorge.

John laughed. "We're nearly to the cave. If I
have to carry you it 'll double the danger."

"Oh, yass, seh! you go on, I'll jine you. I jis
wants a few minutes to myseff faw prayer."

"Cornelius," said the cautiously stooping youth, "I'm
going to take you where I said I would, if I have to
carry you there in three pieces. Here—wait—I'd better tote you on my back. Put your arms around my

neck.  Now give me your legs.  That's it.  Now, hold firm ; one false step and over we go."

He slowly picked his way.  Once he stopped, while a stone which had crumbled from under his tread went crashing through the bushes and into the yawning gulf. The footing was terribly narrow for several rods, but at length it widened.  He crouched again.  "Now, get off; the rest is only some steep climbing in the bushes."

"Mr. March, I ain't eveh goin' to git down to God's blessed level groun' ag'in ! "

"Think not ?   You'll be there in five seconds if you take hold of any dead wood.  Come on."

They climbed again, hugged the cliff while they took breath, climbed once more, forebore to look down, and soon, crowding into what had seemed but a shallow cleft, were stooping under the low roof of a small cavern.  Its close rocky bounds and tumbled floor sparkled here and there in the light of the matches John struck.  From their pockets the pair laid out a scant store of food.

"Now I must go," said John.  "I'll come again to-morrow night.  You're safe here.  You may find a snake or two, but you don't mind that, do you ? "

"Me?   Law, no! not real ones.  Di'mon'-back rattlesnake hisself cayn't no mo' scare me 'n if I was a hawg.  Good-by, seh."

How the heavy-eyed youth the next day finished his examinations he scarcely knew himself, but he hoped he had somehow passed.  He could not slip away from Rosemont until after bedtime, and the night was half gone when he reached the cliff under Lover's Leap.   A light rain increased the risk of the climb, but he reached the cave in safety only to find it deserted. On his way down he discovered ample signs that the promiscuous lover, an hour or two before, had slowly, safely, and in the "skilfullest way" reached the arms of his most dangerous but dearest love; "cooned it every step," John said, talking to his horse as they trudged back toward Rosemont. "What the rattlesnakes couldn't do," he added, "the bottle-snake has done."

Mr. Leggett's perils might not be over, but out of the youth's hands meant off his indulgent conscience, and John returned to his slighted books, quickened in all his wilful young blood by the knowledge that a single night of adventurous magnanimity had made him henceforth master of himself, his own purposes, and his own mistakes.

---

## XXIII.

### A SUMMONS FOR THE JUDGE

BACCALAUREATE SUNDAY. It was hot, even for Suez. The river seemed to shine with heat. Yet every convenient horse-rack was crowded with horses, more than half of them under side-saddles, and in the square neighing steeds, tied to swinging limbs because too emotionally noble to share their privileges with anything they could kick, pawed, wheeled, and gazed after their vanished riders as if to say, " 'Pon my word, if he hasn't gone to *church*."

The church, Parson Tombs's, was packed. Men were not few, yet the pews and the aisles, choked with chairs from end to end, were one yeast of muslins, lawns, and organdies, while everywhere the fans pulsed and danced a hundred measures at once in fascinating confusion.

In the amen pews on the right sat all Montrose; facing them, on the left, sat all Rosemont, except the principal; Garnet was with the pastor in the pulpit. The Governor of Dixie was present; the first one they of the old *régime* had actually gotten into the gubernatorial chair since the darkies had begun to vote. Two members of the Governor's staff sat in a front pew in uniform; blue!

"See that second man on the left?" whispered Captain Shotwell to an old army friend from Charleston; "that handsome felleh with the wavy auburn hair, soft mustache, and big, sawt o' pawnderin' eyes?"

"What! that the Governor? He can't be over thirty or thirty-one!"

"Governor, no! *he* wouldn't take the governorship; that's Jeff-Jack Ravenel, editor of the *Courier*, a-ablest man in Dixie. No, that's the Governor next to him."

"That old toad? Why, he's a moral hulk; look at his nose!"

"Yes, it's a pity, but we done the best we could—had to keep the alignment, you know. His brother leases and sublets convicts, five stockades of 'em, and ought to be one himself.

"These girls inside the altar-rail, they're the academy

chorus. That one? Oh, that's Halliday's daughter. Yass, beautiful, but you should 'a seen her three years ago. No use talkin', seh—I wouldn't say so to a Yankee, but—ow climate's hard on beauty. Teach in the acad'? Oh! no, seh, she jus' sings with 'em. Magnificent voice. Some Yankees here last week allowed they'd ruther hear her than Adelina Patti—in some sawngs.

"She's an awful man-killeh; repo'ted engaged to five fellehs at once, Jeff-Jack included. I don't know whether it's true or not, but you know how ow Dixie gyirls ah, seh. An' yet, seh, when they marry, as they all do, where'll you find mo' devoted wives? This ain't the lan' o' divo'ces, seh; this is the lan' o' loose engagements an' tight marriages.

" D' you see that gyirl in the second row of Montroses, soft eyes, sawt o' deep-down roguish, round, straight neck, head set so nice on it? That's Gyarnet's daughteh. That gyirl's not as old as she looks, by three years."

He ceased. The chorus under the high pulpit stood up, sang, and sat again. Parson Tombs, above them, rose with extended arms, and the services had begun. The chorus stood again, and the church choir faced them from the gallery and sang with them antiphonally, to the spiritual discomfort of many who counted it the latest agony of modernness. In the long prayer the diversity of sects and fashions showed forth; but a majority tried hard not to resent any posture different from their own, although Miss Martha Salter and many others who buried their faces in their own seats, knew that Mr. Ravenel's eyes were counting the cracks in the plastering.

Barbara knelt forward—the Montrose mode. She heard Parson Tombs confess the Job-like loathsomeness of everyone present; but his long-familiar, chanting monotones fainted and died in the portals of her ears like a nurse's song, while her sinking eyelids shut not out, but in, one tallish Rosemont senior who had risen in prayer visibly heavy with the sleep he had robbed from three successive nights. The chirp of a lone cricket somewhere under the floor led her forth in a half dream beyond the town and the gleaming turnpike, across wide fields whose multitudinous, tiny life rasped and buzzed under the vibrant heat; and so on to Rosemont, dear Rosemont, and the rose mother there.

Her fan stops. An unearthly sweetness, an unconditioned bliss, a heavenly disembodiment too perfect for ecstasy, an oblivion surcharged with light, a blessed rarefaction of self that fills the house, the air, the sky, and ascends full of sweet odors and soothing sounds, wafts her up on the cadenced lullaby of the long, long prayer. Is it finished? No.

"Oh, quicken our drowsy powers!" she hears the pastor cry on a rising wave of monotone, and starts the fan again. Is she in church or in Rosemont? She sees Johanna beckoning in her old, cajoling way, asking, as in fact, not fancy, she had done the evening before, for the latest news of Cornelius, and hearing with pious thankfulness that Leggett has reappeared in his official seat, made a speech that filled the house with laughter and applause, put parties into a better humor

with each other than they had been for years, and remains, and, for the present, will remain, unmolested.

Still Parson Tombs is praying. The fan waggles
briskly, then more slowly—slowly—slow-ly, and sinks
to rest on her white-robed bosom. The head, heavy
with luminous brown hair, careens gently upon one
cheek; that ineffably sweet dissolution into all nature
and space comes again, and far up among the dream-
clouds, just as she is about to recognize certain happy
faces, there is a rush of sound, a flood of consternation,
a start, a tumbling in of consciousness, the five senses
leap to their stations, and she sits upright fluttering her
fan and glancing round upon the seated congregation.
The pastor has said amen.

Garnet spoke extemporaneously. The majority, who
did not know every line of the sermon was written and
memorized, marvelled at its facility, and even some
who knew admitted it was wonderful for fervor, rhetor-
ical richness and the skill with which it "voiced the
times" without so much as touching those matters
which Dixie, Rosemont's Dixie, did not want touched.
Parson Tombs and others moaned "Amen," "Glory,"
"Thaynk Gawd," etc., after every great period. Only
General Halliday said to his daughter, "He's out of
focus again; claiming an exclusive freedom for his own
set."

The text was, "But I was born free."

Paul, the speaker said, was as profound a believer in
law as in faith. Jealous for every right of his citizenship, he might humble himself, but he never lightly
allowed himself to be humbled. Law is essential to

every civil order, but the very laying of it upon a man makes it his title-deed to a freedom without which obedience is not obedience, nor citizenship citizenship. No man is entirely free to fill out the full round of his whole manhood who is not in some genuine, generous way an author of the laws he obeys. "At this sacred desk and on this holy day I thank God that Dixie's noble sons and daughters are at last, after great tribulations, freer from laws and government not of their own choice than ever before since war furled its torn and blood-drenched banner! We have taught the world— and it's worth the tribulation to have taught the world —under God, that a people born with freedom in the blood cannot be forced even to do right! 'What you order me to do, alien lawmaker, may be right, but I was born free!' My first duty to God is to be free, and no freedom is freedom till it is purged of all indignity!

"But mark the limitation! Freemen are not made in a day! It was to a man who had bought his freedom that Paul boasted a sort that could not be bought! God's word for it, it takes at least two generations to make true freemen; fathers to buy the freedom and sons and daughters to be born into it! Wherefore let every one to whom race and inheritance have given beauty or talent, and to whom the divine ordering of fortune and social rank has added quality and scholarship, hold it the first of civic virtues to reply to every mandate of law or fate, Law is law, and right is right, but, first of all, I was born free, and, please God, I'll die so!

" Gentlemen of the graduating class : "

Nine trim, gray jackets rose, and John March was the tallest. The speaker proceeded, but he had not spoken many words before he saw the attention of his hearers was gone. A few smiled behind their hands or bit their lips; men kept a frowning show of listening to the address; women's faces exchanged looks of pity, and John turned red to his collar. For, just behind the Governor, the noble head and feeble frame of Judge March had risen unconsciously when his son rose, and now stood among the seated multitude, gazing on the speaker and drinking in his words with a sweet, glad face. The address went on, but no one heard it. Nor did any one move to disturb the standing figure; all Suez, nay, the very girls of Montrose knew that he who seemed to stand there with trembling knees and wabbling hands was in truth not there, but was swallowed up and lost in yonder boy.

Garnet was vexed. He shortened the address, and its last, eloquent sentence was already begun when Ravenel rose and through room swiftly made for him stepped back to Judge March. He was just in time to get an arm under his head and shoulders as he sank limply into the pew, looking up with a smile and trying to say nothing was wrong and to attend again to the speaker. Garnet's hearers were overcome, but the effect was not his. Their gaze was on the fallen man; and when General Halliday cleared his sight with an agitated handkerchief, and one by one from the son's wide open eyes, the hot, salt tears slipped down to the twitching corners of his mouth, and the aged pastor's voice trembled in a hurried benediction, women sobbed and few eyes were dry.

"Father," said John, "can you hear me? Do you know me?"

A glad light overspread the face for reply. But after it came a shadow, and Doctor Coffin said, softly,

"He's trying to ask something."

Fannie Halliday sat fanning the patient. She glanced up to Garnet just at John's back and murmured,

"He probably wants to know if——"

John turned an eager glance to his principal, and Garnet nodded "Yes."

"Father," cried John, "I've passed! I've passed, father; I've passed! Do you hear, dear father?"

The Major touched the bending youth and murmured something more. John turned back upon him a stare of incredulity, but Garnet smiled kindly and said aloud,

"I tell you yes; it will be announced to-morrow."

"Father," cried John, stooping close to the wandering eyes, "can you see me? I'm John! I'm son! Can you hear me, father? Father, I've got first honors—first honors, father! Oh, father, look into my eyes; it will be a sign that you hear me. Father, listen, look; I'm going to be a better son—to you and to mother—Oh, he hears me! He understands—" The physician drew him away.

They carried the sick man to the nearest house. Late in the afternoon Tom Hersey and two or three others were talking together near the post-office.

"Now, f'r instance, what right had he to give that boy first honors! As sho's you're a foot high, that's a piece o' pyo log-rollin'."—Doctor Coffin came by.— "Doctor, I understand Mrs. March has arrived. I hope the Jedge is betteh, seh.—What?—Why—why, you supprise—why, I'm mighty sorry to heah that, seh. —Gentle*men*, Jedge March is dead."

<hr>

## XXIV.

### THE GOLDEN SPIKE

ABOUT a week beyond the middle of June, 1878, when John March had been something like a year out of Rosemont and nine months a teacher of mountain lads and lasses at Widewood, Barbara finished at Montrose. She did not read her graduation essay. Its subject was Time. Its spelling was correct, and it was duly rosetted and streamered, but it was regretfully suppressed because its pages were mainly given to joyous emphasis of the advantages of wasting the hours. Miss Garnet had not been a breaker of rules; yet when she waved farewell and the younger Miss Kinsington turned back indoors saying,

"Dearest, best girl!" the sister added, affectionately— "That we ever got rid of."

On a day near the middle of the following month there began almost at dawn to be a great stir in and about Suez. The sun came up over Widewood with a shout, hallooing to Rosemont a promise for all Dixie of the most ripening hours, thus far, of the year, and woods, fields, orchards, streams, answered with a morning incense. Johanna stood whispering loudly at Barbara's bedside:

"Weck up, honey; sun high an' scoldin'! jess a-fussin' an' a-scoldin'!" One dark hand lifted back the white mosquito-net while the other tendered a cup of coffee.

Barbara winked, scowled, laid her wrists on the maid's shoulders and smiled into her black face. Johanna put away a brown wave of hair. "Come on, missie, dat-ah young Yankee gen'leman frien' up an' out."

Barbara bit her lip in mock dismay. "Has he depart-ed?" She had a droll liking for long words, and often deployed their syllables as skirmishers in the rear for her sentences.

Johanna tittered. "Humph! you know mawnstus well he ain't gone. Miss Barb, dass de onyess maan I eveh see wear a baang. Wha' fuh he do dat?"

"I must ask him," said Barbara, sipping her coffee. "It's probably in fulfillment of a vow."

The maid tittered again. "You cayn't ast as much as he kin. But dass my notice 'twix Yankees an' ow folks; Dixie man say, Fine daay, seh! Yankee say, You think it a-gwine fo' to raain? Dixie man—Oh, no, seh! hit jiss cayn't rain to-day, seh! Den if it jiss po' down Yankee say, Don't dis-yeh look somepm like raain? An' Dixie man—Yass, seh, hit do; hit look like raain, but Law'! hit ain't raain. You Yankees cayn't un'stan' ow Southe'n weatheh, seh!'"

Only Johanna laughed. Presently Barbara asked, "Have you seen pop-a?"

"Yo' paw? Oh, yass'm, he in de wes' grove, oveh whah we 'llowin' to buil' de new dawmontory. He jiss a-po'in' info'mations into de Yankee." Barbara laughed this time—at the Yankee—and Johanna mimicked: "Mr. Fair, yo' come to see a beautiful an' thrivin' town, seh. Suez is change' dat much yo' fatheh wouldn' know it ag'in!'"

"Pop-a's right about that, Johanna."

"Oh, yass'm." Johanna was rebuked; but Barbara smiled. By and by—"Miss Barb, kin I ax you a favo'?—Yass'm. Make yo' paw put me som'ers in de crowd to-day whah I ken see you when you draps de hammeh on de golden spike—Law'! dass de dress o' dresses! You looks highly fitt'n' to eat!'"

Young Fair had come to see the last spike driven in the Pulaski City, Suez and Great South Railroad.

At breakfast Mrs. Garnet poured the coffee. Garnet told the New Englander much about New England, touching extenuatingly on the blueness of its laws, the decay of its religion, and the inevitable decline of its industries. The visitor, with only an occasional "Don't you think, however"—seemed edified. It pleased Barbara to see how often, nevertheless, his eye wandered from the speaker to the head of the board to rest on one so lovely it scarce signified that she was pale and wasted; one whose genial dignity perfected the firmness with which she declined her daughter's offer to take her place and task, and smiled her down while Johanna smoothed away a grin.

The hour of nine struck. Fair looked startled. "Were we not to have joined Mr. Ravenel's party in Suez by this time?"

"Yes, but there's no hurry. Still, we'll start. Johanna, get your lunch-baskets. Sorry you don't meet Mr. March, sir; he's a trifle younger than you, but you'd like him. I asked him to go with us, but his mother—why, wa'n't that all right, Barb?"

"Oh, it wasn't wrong." Barbara smiled to her mother. "It was only useless; he always declines if I don't. We're very slightly acquainted. I hope that accounts for it." She arched her brows.

As she and the young visitor stood by the carriage while Johanna and the luncheon were being stowed he said something so graceful about Mrs. Garnet that Barbara looked into his face with delight and the Major had to speak his name twice befor he heard it.— "Ready? Yes, quite so. Shall I sit—oh! pardon; yes —in front, certainly."

The Major drove. The young guest would gladly have talked with Barbara as she sat back of him and behind her father; but Garnet held his attention. Crossing Turkey Creek battle-ground——

"Just look at those oats! See that wheat! Cotton, ah, but you ought to see the cotton down in Blackland!"

When the pike was dusty and the horses walked they were frequently overtaken and passed by cavalcades of lank, hard-faced men in dingy homespun, and cadaverous women with snuff-sticks and slouched sun-bonnets. Major Garnet bowed to them.

"Those are our Sandstone County mountaineers; our yeomanry, sir. Suez holds these three counties in a sort o' triple alliance. You make a great mistake, sir, to go off to-morrow without seeing the Widewood district. You've seen the Alps, and I'd just like to hear you say which of the two is the finer. There's enough mineral wealth in Widewood alone to make Suez a Pittsburg, and water-power enough to make her a Minneapolis, and we're going to make her both, sir!" The monologue became an avalanche of coal, red hematite, marble, mica, manganese, tar, timber, turpentine, lumber, lead, ochre, and barytes, with signs of silver, gold, and diamonds.

"Don't you think, however——"

"No, sir! no-o-o! far from it——"

A stifled laugh came from where Johanna's face darkened the corner it occupied. Barbara looked, but the maid seemed lost in sad reverie.

"Barb, yonder's where Jeff-Jack and I stopped to dine on blackberries the day we got home from the war. Now, there's the railroad cut on the far side of it. There, you see, Mr. Fair, the road skirts the creek westward and then northwestward again, leaving Rosemont a mile to the northeast. See that house, Barb, about half a mile beyond the railroad? There's where the man found his plumbago." The speaker laughed and told the story. The discoverer had stolen off by night, got an expert to come and examine it, and would tell the result only to one friend, and in a whisper. "'You haven't got much plumbago,' the expert had said, 'but you've got dead oodles of silica.' You know, Barb, silica's nothing but flint, ha-ha!'"

Fair smiled. In his fortnight's travel through the New Dixie plumbago was the only mineral on which he had not heard the story based.

A military horseman overtook the carriage and slackened to a fox-trot at Garnet's side. "Captain Champion, let me make you acquainted with Mr. Fair. Mr. Fair and his father have put money into our New Dixie, and he's just going around to see where he can put in more. I tell him he can't go amiss. All we want in Dixie is capital."

"Mr. Fair doesn't think so," said Barbara, with great sweetness.

"Ah! I merely asked whether capital doesn't seek its own level. Mustn't its absence be always because of some deeper necessity?"

Champion stood on his guard. "Why, I don't know why capital shouldn't be the fundamental need, seh, of a country that's been impoverished by a great waugh!"

Barbara exulted, but Garnet was for peace. "I suppose you'll find Suez swarming with men, women, and horses."

"Yes," said Champion—Fair was speaking to Barbara—"to say nothing of yahoos, centaurs, and niggehs." The Major's abundant laugh flattered him; he promised to join the party at luncheon, lifted his plumed shako, and galloped away. Garnet drove into the edge of the town at a trot.

"Here's where the reservoir's to be," he said, and

spun down the slope into the shaded avenue, and so to the town's centre.

"Laws-a-me! Miss Barb," whispered Johanna, "but dis-yeh town is change'! New hotel! brick! th'ee sto'ies high!" Barbara touched her for silence.

"But look at de new sto'es!" murmured the girl. Negroes—the men in dirty dusters, the women in smart calicoes, girls in dowdy muslins and boy's hats—and mountain whites, coatless men, shoeless women—hung about the counters dawdling away their small change

"Colored and white treated precisely alike, you notice," said Garnet, and Barbara suppressed a faint grunt from Johanna.

Trade had spread into side-streets. Drinking-houses were gayly bedight and busy.

"That's the new *Courier* building."

The main crowd had gone down to the railway tracks, and it was midsummer, yet you could see and feel the town's youth.

"Why, the nig—colored people have built themselves a six-hundred dollar church; we white folks helped them," said Garnet, who had given fifty cents. "See that new sidewalk? Our chain-gang did that, sir; made the bricks and laid the pavement."

The court-house was newly painted. Only Hotel Swanee and the two white churches remained untouched, sleeping on in green shade and sweet age.

The Garnet's wheels bickered down the town's southern edge and out upon a low slope of yellow, deep-gullied sand and clay that scarce kept on a few weeds to hide its nakedness while gathering old duds and tins,

"Yonder are the people, and here, sir," Garnet pointed to where the green Swanee lay sweltering like the Nile, "is the stream that makes the tears trickle in every true Southerner's heart when he hears its song."

"Still 'Always longing for the old plantation?'" asked the youth.

"Yes," said Barbara, defiantly.

The carriage stopped; half a dozen black ragamuffins rushed up offering to take it in charge, and its occupants presently stood among the people of three counties. For Blackland, Clearwater, and Sandstone had gathered here a hundred or two of their gentlest under two long sheds on either side of the track, and the sturdier multitude under green booths or out in the sunlight about yonder dazzling gun, to hail the screaming herald of a new destiny; a destiny that openly promised only wealth, yet freighted with profounder changes; changes which, ban or delay them as they might, would still be destiny at last.

Entering a shed Barbara laughed with delight. "Fannie!"

"Barb!" cried Fannie. A volley of salutations followed: "Good-morning, Major"—"Why, howdy, Doctor.—Howdy, Jeff-Jack.—Shotwell, how are you? Let me make you acquainted with Mr. Fair. Mr. Fair, Captain Shotwell. Mr. Fair and his father, Captain, have put some money into our "—A tall, sallow, youngish man touched the speaker's elbow—"Why, *hel*-lo, Proudfit! Colonel Proudfit, let me make you," etc.—"I hope you brought—why, Sister Proudfit, I decl'—aha, ha, ha!—You know Barb?"

General Halliday said, "John Wesley, how goes it?"

Garnet sobered. "Good-morning, Launcelot. **Mr.** Fair, let me make you acquainted with General Halliday. You mustn't believe all he says—ha, ha, ha! Still, when a radical does speak well of us you may know it's so! Launcelot, Mr. Fair and his father have put some money "—Half a dozen voices said "Sh-sh!"

"Ladies and gentle*men!*" cried Captain Shotwell. "The first haalf—the fro'—the front haalf of the traain—of the expected traain—is full of people from Pulaaski City! The ster'—the rear haalf is reserved faw the one hundred holdehs of these red tickets." (Applause.) "Ayfter the shor'—brief puffawn'—cerem'—exercises, the traain, bein' filled, will run up to Pulaaski City, leave that section of which, aw toe which, aw at least in which, that is, belonging toe—I mean the people containing the Pulaaski City section (laughter and applause)—or rather the section contained by the Pu—(deafening laughter)—I should saay the city containing the Pulaas'—(roars of laughter)—Well, gentlemen, if you know what I want to say betteh than I do, jest say it yo'se'ves an'——"

His face was red and he added something unintelligible about them all going to a terminus not on that road, while Captain Champion, coming to his rescue, proclaimed that the Suez section would be brought back, "expectin' to arrive hyeh an hou' by sun. An' now, ladies and gentle*men*, I propose three cheers faw that gallant an' accomplished gentleman, Cap'm Shotwell—hip-hip— ' " And the company gave them, with a tiger.

At that moment, faint and far, the whistle sounded. The great outer crowd ran together, all looking one way. Again it sounded, nearer; and then again, near and loud. The multitude huzzaed; the bell clanged; gay with flags the train came thundering in; out in the blazing sunlight Captain Champion, with sword unsheathed, cried "Fire!" The gun flashed and crashed, the earth shook, the people's long shout went up, the sax-horns sang "Way Down upon the Swanee River"—and the tears of a true Southerner leaped into Barbara's eyes. She turned and caught young Fair smiling at it all, and most of all at her, yet in a way that earned her own smile.

The speeches were short and stirring. When Ravenel began—"Friends and fellow-citizens, this is our Susie's wedding," the people could hardly be done cheering. Then Barbara, by him led forth and followed by Johanna's eager eyes, gave the spike its first wavering tap, the president of the road drove it home, and "Susie" was bound in wedlock to the Age. Married for money, some might say. Yet married, bound—despite all incompatibilities—to be shaped—if not at once by choice, then at last by merciless necessity—to all that Age's lines and standards, to walk wherever it should lead, partner in all its vicissitudes, pains and fates.

The train moved. Mr. Fair sat with Barbara. Major Grant secured a seat beside Sister Proudfit—"aha—ha-ha!"—"t-he-he-he-he!" Fannie gave Shotwell the place beside her, and so on. Even Johanna, by taking a child in her lap, got a seat. But Ravenel and Colonel Proudfit had to stand up beside Fannie and Barbara. Thus it fell out that when everyone laughed at a moonshiner's upsetting on a pile of loose telegraph poles, Ravenel, looking out from over the swarm of heads, saw something which moved him to pull the bell-cord.

"Two people wanting to get on," said Shotwell, as Ravenel went to the coach's rear platform. "They in a buggy. Now they out. Here they—Law', Miss Fannie, who you reckon it is? Guess! You *cayn't*, miss!"

Barbara, with studied indifference, asked Fair the time of day.

"There," said Shotwell, "they've gone into the cah behind us."

"Sister March and her son," observed Garnet to Mrs. Proudfit and the train moved on.

---

## XXV.

### BY RAIL

EVERYBODY felt playful and nearly everybody coquettish. When Sister Proudfit, in response to some sly gallantry of Garnet's used upon him a pair of black eyes, he gave her the whole wealth of his own. He must have overdone the matter, for the next moment he found Fannie's eyes levelled directly on him. She withdrew them with a casual remark to Barbara, yet not till they had said to him, in solemn silence:

"You villain, that time I saw you!"

Mrs. March had pushed cheerily into the rear Suez coach. Away from home and its satieties no one could be more easily or thoroughly pleased. Her son said the forward coach was better, but in there she had sighted Fannie and Barbara, and so——

"There's more room in here," she insisted with sweet buoyancy.

Hamlet Graves rose. "Here, Cousin Daphne!" His brother Lazarus stood up with him.

"Here, John, your maw'll feel better if you're a-sett'n' by her."

But she urged the seat, with coy temerity, upon Mr. Ravenel.

"How well she looks in mourning," remarked two Blackland County ladies. "Yes, she's pretty yet; what a lovely smile."

"Don't go 'way," she exclaimed, with hostile alarm, as John turned toward the coach's front. He said he would not, and chose a standing-place where he could watch a corner of Fannie's distant hat.

"You won't see many fellows of age staying with their mothers by choice instead o' running off after the girls," commented one of the Blackland matrons, and the other replied:

"They haven't all got such mothers!"

Mrs. March was enjoying herself. "But, Mr. Ravenel," she said, putting off part of her exhilaration,

" you've really no right to be a bachelor." She smiled aslant.

" My dear lady," he murmured, " people who live in gla——"

She started and tried to look sour, but grew sweeter. He became more grave. " You're still young," he said, paused, and then—" You're a true Daphne, but you haven't gone all to laurel yet. I wish—I wish I could feel half as young as you look; I might hope "—he hushed, sighed, and nerved himself.

" Why, Mr. Ravenel!" She glanced down with a winsome smile. " I'm at least old enough to—to stay as I am if I choose?"

" Possibly. But you needn't if you don't choose." He folded his arms as if to keep them from doing something rash.

Mrs. March bit her lip. " I can't imagine who would ever "—she bit it again. " Mr. Ravenel, do you remember those lines of mine—

" 'O we women are so blind'"?

" Yes. But don't call me Mr. Ravenel."

" Why, why not? "

" It sounds so cold." He shuddered.

" It isn't meant so. It's not in my nature to be cold. It's you who are cold." She hushed as abruptly as a locust. A large man, wet with the heat, stood saluting. Mr. Ravenel rose and introduced Mr. Gamble, president of the road, a palpable, rank Westerner; whereupon it was she who was cold. Mr. Gamble praised the " panorama gliding by."

" Yes." She glanced out over the wide, hot, veering landscape that rose and sank in green and yellow slopes of corn, cotton, and wheat. The president fanned his soaking shirt-collar and Mrs. March with a palm-leaf fan.

" Mercury ninety-nine in Pulaski City," he said to Ravenel, and showed a telegram. Mr. Ravenel began to ask if he might introduce——

" Mr. March! Well, you *have* changed since the day you took Major Garnet and Mr. Fair and *I* to see that view in the mounhns! If anybody'd a-told me that I'd ever be president of—Thanks, no sir." He wouldn't sit. He'd just been sitting and talking, he said, " with the two beauties, Miss Halliday and Miss Garnet." Didn't Mrs. March think them such?

She confessed they looked strong and well, and sighed an unresentful envy.

" Yes," said he, " they do, and I wouldn't give two cents on the dollar for such as don't."

Mrs. March smiled dyingly on John, and said she feared her son wouldn't either. John looked distressed and then laughed; but the president declared her the picture of robust health. This did not seem to please her entirely, and so he added,

" You've got to be, to write good poetry. It must be lots of fun, Mrs. March, to dash off a rhyme just to while away the time—ha, ha, ha! My wife often writes poetry when she feels tired and lazy. I know that whirling this way through this beautiful country is inspiring you right now to write half a dozen poems. I'd like to see you on one of those lovely hillsides in fine frenzy rolling "—He said he meant her eye.

The poetess blushed. A whimper of laughter came from somewhere, but one man put his head quickly out of a window, and another stooped for something very hard to pick up, while John explained that crowds and dust were no inspiration to his mother, who was here to-day purely for his sake. She sat in limp revery with that faint shade on her face which her son believed meant patience. He and the president moved a reverent step aside.

"I hear," said Gamble, in a business undertone, "that your school's a success."

"Not financially," replied John, gazing into the forward coach.

"Mr. March, why don't you colonize your lands? You can do it, now the railroad's here."

"I would, sir, if I had the capital."

"Form a company! They furnish the money, you furnish the land. How'd I build this road? I hadn't either money or lands. Why, if your lands were out West"——the speaker turned to an eavesdropper, saying sweetly, "This conversation is private, sir," but with a look as if he would swallow him without sauce or salt.

John mused. "My mother has such a dislike,"— he hesitated.

"I know," the president smiled, "the ladies are all that way. If a thing's theirs it just makes 'em sick to see anybody else make anything out of it. I speak from experience. They'll die poor, keeping property enough idle to make a dozen men rich. What's a man to do? Now, you "—a long pause, eye to eye—" your lands won't colonize themselves."

" Of course not," mused John.

The president showed two cigars. " Would you like to go to the smoking-car ? "

March glanced toward his mother. She was looking at her two kinsmen with such sweet sprightliness that he had trouble to make her see his uplifted cigar. She met his parting smile with a gleam of terror and distrust, but he shook his head and reddened as Hamlet winked at Lazarus.

" It means some girl," observed one of the Blackland matrons.

" Well, I hope it does," responded the other.

" Wait," said the giver of the cigar, " we're stopping for wood and water. It'll be safer to go round this front coach than through it." John thought it would not, but yielded.

" Now, Mr. March," they stood near the water-tank —" if you could persuade your mother to give you full control, and let you get a few strong men to go in with you—see? They could make you—well—secretary ! —with a salary ; for, of course, you'd have to go into the thing, hot, yourself. You'd have to push like smoke ! "

" Of course," said John, squaring his handsome figure; as if he always went in hot, and as if smoke was the very thing he had pushed like, for years.

" I shouldn't wonder if you and I "—Gamble began again, but the train started, they took the smoker and found themselves with Halliday, Shotwell, Proudfit, and a huge Englishman, round whom the other three were laughing.

## XXVI.

### JOHN INSULTS THE BRITISH FLAG

THE Briton had seen, on the far edge of Suez, as they were leaving the town, a large building.

"A nahsty brick thing on top a dirty yellow hill," he said; what was it?

"That?" said Shotwell, "that's faw ow colo'ed youth o' both sexes. That's Suez University."

"Univer—what bloody nonsense!"

All but March ha-haed. "We didn't name it!" laughed the Captain.

John became aware that some one in a remote seat had bowed to him. He looked, and the salute came again, unctuous and obsequious. He coldly responded and frowned, for the men he was with had seen it.

Proudfit touched the Briton. "In the last seat behind you you'll see the University's spawnsor; that's Leggett, the most dangerous demagogue in Dixie."

"Is that your worst?" said the Englishman; "ye should know some of ours!"

"O, yes, seh," exclaimed Shotwell, "of co'se ev'y country's got 'em bad enough. But here, seh, we've not `on'y the dahkey's natu'al-bawn rascality to deal with, but they natu'l-bawn stupidity to boot. Evm Gen'l Halliday'll tell you that, seh."

"Yes," said the General, with superior cheerfulness, "though sometimes the honors are easy."

"O, I allow we don't always outwit 'em "—everybody laughed—" but sometimes we just haf to."

"To save out-shooting them," suggested the General.

"O, I hope we about done with that."

"But you're not sure," came the quick retort.

"No, seh," replied the sturdy Captain, "we're not shore. It rests with them." He smoked.

"Go on, Shot," said the General, "you were going to give an instance."

"Yes, seh. Take Leggett, in the case o' this so-called University."

"That's hardly a good example," remarked Proudfit, who, for Dixie's and Susie's sake, regretted that Shot-well was talking so much and he so little.

"Let him alone," said Halliday, thoroughly pleased, and Shotwell went on stoutly.

"The concern was started by Leggett an' his gang— excuse my careless terms, Gen'l—as the public high-school. They made it ve'y odious to ow people by throwin' it wide open to both raaces instead o' havin' a' sep'ate one faw whites. So of co'se none but dahkeys went to it, an' they jest filled it jam up."

"What did the whites do?" asked the Briton.

"Why, what *could* they do, seh? You know how ow people ah. That's right where the infernal outrage come in. Such as couldn't affode to go to Rosemont aw Montrose jest had to stay at home!" The speaker looked at John, who colored and bit his cigar.

"So as soon as ow crowd got control of affairs we'd a shut the thing up, on'y faw Jeff-Jack. Some Yankee missiona'y teachers come to him an' offe'd to make it a college an' spend ten thousand dollahs on it if the State would on'y go on givin' it hafe o' the three counties' annual high-school funds."

The Englishman frowned perplexedly and Proudfit put in—

"That is, three thousand a year from our three counties' share of the scrip on public lands granted Dixie by the Federal Government."

"Expressly for the support of public schools," said General Halliday, and March listened closer than the foreigner, for these facts were newest to John.

"Still," said March, "the State furnishes the main support of public education."

"No," responded Shotwell, "you're wrong there, John; we changed that. The main suppote o' the schools is left to the counties an' townships."

"That's stupid, all round," promptly spoke the Briton.

"I thought," exclaimed John, resentfully, "we'd changed our State constitution so's to forbid the levy of any school tax by a county or township except on special permission of the legislature."

"So you have," laughed the General.

"The devil!" exclaimed the Englishman.

"O, we had to do that," interposed Proudfit again, and Gamble testified,

"You see, it's the property-holder's only protection."

"Then Heaven help his children's children," observed the traveler. John showed open disgust, but the General touched him and said, "Go on, Shotwell."

"Well, seh, we didn't like the missiona'y's proposition. We consid'ed it fah betteh to transfeh oveh that three thousan' a year to Rosemont, entire; which we did so. Pub—? No, seh, Rosemont's not public, but it really rep'esents ow people, which, o' co'se, the otheh don't."

"Public funds to a private concern," quietly commented the Englishman—"that's a steal." John March's blood began to boil.

"O," cried Shotwell—"ow people—who pay the taxes—infinitely rather Rosemont should have it."

"I see," responded the Briton, in such a tone that John itched to kick him.

"Well, seh," persisted the narrator, "you should 'a' heard Leggett howl faw a divvy!" All smiled. "Worst of it was—what? Wha'd you say, Gen'l?"

"He had the constitution of the State to back him."

"He hasn't now! Well, seh, the bill faw this ve'y raailroad was in the house. Leggett swo' it shouldn't even so much as go to the gove'neh to sign *aw* to veto till that fund—seh? annual, yes, seh—was divided at least evm, betwix Rosemont an' the Suez high school."

"Hear, hear!"

"Well, seh"—the Captain became blithe—"Jeff-Jack sent faw him—you remembeh that night, Presi-*dent* Gamble—this was the second bill—ayfteh the first hed been vetoed—an' said, s'e, 'Leggett, if I give you my own word that you'll get yo' fifteen hund'ed a year as soon as this new bill passes, will you vote faw it?'— 'Yass, seh,' says Leggett—an' he did!"

Proudfit laughed with manly glee, and offered no other interruption.

"Well, seh, then it come Jeff-Jack's turn to keep his word the best he could."

"Which he's done," said Gamble.

"Yes, Jeff-Jack got still anotheh bill brought in an' paassed. It give the three thousan' to Rosemont entieh, an' authorized the three counties to raise the fifteen hund'ed a year by county tax." The Captain laughed.

"Silly trick," said the Englishman, grimly.

"Why, the dahkeys got they fifteen hund'ed!"

"Don't they claim twenty-two fifty?"

"Well, they jess betteh not!"

"Rascally trick!"

"Sir," said John, "Mr. Ravenel is my personal friend. If you make another such comment on his actions I shall treat it as if made on mine."

"Come, Come!" exclaimed Gamble, commandingly; "we can't have——"

"You'll have whatever I give, sir!"

Three or four men half rose, smiling excitedly, but sank down again.

"You think, sir," insisted John, to the Englishman's calmly averted face, "that being in a free country—" he dashed off Shotwell's remonstrant hand.

"'Tain't a free country at all," said the Briton to the outer landscape. "There's hardly a corner in Europe but's freer."

"Ireland, for instance," sneered John.

"Ireland be damned," responded the foreigner, still still looking out the window. "Go tell your nurse to give you some bread and butter."

John leaped and swept the air with his open palm. Gamble's clutch half arrested it in front, Shotwell hindered it from behind, neither quite stopped it.

"Did he slap him?" eagerly asked a dozen men standing on the seats.

"He barely touched him," was the disappointed reply of one.

"Thank the Lawd faw evm that little!" responded another.

Shotwell pulled March away, Halliday following. Near the rear door——

"Johnnie," began the General, with an air of complete digression, but at the woebegone look that came into the young man's face, the old soldier burst into a laugh. John whisked around to the door and stood looking out, though seeing nothing, bitter in the thought that not for the Englishman's own sake, but for the sake of the British capital coveted by Suez, a gentleman and a Rosemonter was forbidden to pay him the price of his insolence.

"I'd like to pass," presently said someone behind him. He started, and Gamble went by.

"May I detain you a moment, sir?" said John.

The president frowned. "What is it?"

"In our passage of words just now—I was wrong."

"Yes, you were.    What of it?"

"I regret it."

"I can't use your regrets," said the railroad man. He moved to go. "If you want to see me about——"

John smiled. "No, sir, I'd rather never set eyes on you again."

As the Westerner's fat back passed into the farther coach his response came——

"What you want ain't manners, it's gumption." The door slammed for emphasis.

March presently followed, full of shame and indignation and those unutterable wailings with which youth, so often, has to be born again into manhood. Gamble had rejoined the Garnet group. John bowed affably to all, smiled to Fannie and passed. Garnet still sat with Mrs. Proudfit behind the others, and John, as he went by, was, for some cause supplied by this pair, startled, angered anew, and for the time being benumbed by conflicting emotions. He found his mother still talking joyously with the Graveses, who were unfamiliar with the graceful art of getting away. He found a seat in front of them, and sat stiff beside a man who drowsed.

"I'm a hopeless fool," he thought, "a fool in anger, a fool in love. A fool even in the eyes of that idiot of a railroad president in yonder smirking around Fannie.

"They'll laugh at me together, I suppose. O, Fannie, why can't I give you up? I know you're a flirt. Jeff-Jack knows it. I solemnly believe that's why he doesn't ask you to marry him!

"Yes, they're probably all laughing at me by now. O, was ever mortal man so uttterly alone! And these people think what makes me so is this silly temper. They say it! Mother assures me they say it! I believe I could colonize our lands if it wa'n't for that. O, I will colonize them! I'll do it all alone. If that jackanapes could open this road I can open our lands.

Whatever he used I can use; whatever he did I can do ! "

"Sir ? " said the neighbor at his elbow, " O excu—I thought you spoke."

" Hem ! No, I was merely clearing my throat.

" I can do it. I'll do it alone. She shall see me do it—they shall all see. I'll do it alone—all alone——"

He caught the steel-shod rhythm of the train and said over and over with ever bigger and more bitter resolution, " I'll do it alone—I'll do it alone ! "

Then he remembered Garnet.

----

## XXVII.

### TO SUSIE—FROM PUSSIE

On the return trip Garnet sat on the arm of almost every seat except Fannie's.

" No, sir; no, keep your seat ! " He wouldn't let anybody be " disfurnished " for him ! Proudfit had got the place next his wife and thought best to keep it.

" Mr. Fair," said Garnet, " I'd like you to notice how all this region was made in ages past. You see how the rocks have been broken and tossed,"—etc.

" Mr. Fair "—the same speaker—" I *wish* you'd change your mind and stay a week with us. Come, spend it at Rosemont. It's vacation, you know, and Barb and I shan't have a thing to do but give you a good time; shall we, Barb ? "

"It will give us a good time," said Barb.  Her slow, cadenced voice, steady eye, and unchallenging smile charmed the young Northerner.  He had talked about her to Fannie at luncheon and pronounced her "unusual."

"Why, really "—he began, looked up at Garnet and back again to Barbara.  Garnet bent over him confidentially.

"Just between us I'd like to advise with you about something I've never mentioned to a soul.  That is about sending Barb to some place North to sort o' round out her education and character in a way that—it's no use denying it, though it would never do for me to say so—a way that's just impossible in Dixie, sir."

The young man remembered Barbara's mother and was silent.

"Well, Barb, Mr. Fair will go home with us for a day or two, anyhow," Garnet was presently authorized to say.  "I must go into the next car a moment——"

John March, meditating on this very speaker with growing anger, saw him approach.  Garnet entered, beaming.

"Howdy, John, my son; I couldn't let you and Sister March——"

March had stepped before his mother:  He spoke in a deep murmur.

"I'm not your son, sir.  My mother's not your sister."

"Why, what in thun— why, John, I don't know whether to be angry or to laugh."

"Don't you dare to do either.  Go back to that other man's——"

"Speak more softly for heaven's sake, Mr. March, and don't look so, or you'll do me a wrong that may cost us both our lives!"

"Cheap enough," said the youth, with a smile.

"You've made a ridiculous mistake, John. Before God I'm as innocent of any——"

"Before God, Major Garnet, you lie. If you deny it again I'll accuse you publicly. Go back and fondle the hand of that other man's wife; but don't ever speak to my mother again. If you do, I—I'll shoot you on sight."

"I'll call you to account for this, sir," said Garnet, moving to go.

"You're lying again," was John's bland reply, and he turned to his seat.

"Why, John," came the mother's sweet complaint, "I wanted to see Brother Garnet."

"Oh, I'm sorry," said the complaisant son.

Garnet paused on the coach's platform to get rid of his tremors. "He'll not tell," he said aloud, the uproar of wheels drowning his voice. "He's too good a Rose-monter to tattle. At first I thought he'd got on the same scent as Cornelius.

"Thank God, that's one thing there's no woman in, anyhow. O me, O me! If that tipsy nigger would only fall off this train and break his neck!

"And now here's *this* calf to live in daily dread of. O dear, O *dear*, I ought to a-had more sense. It's all her fault; she's pure brass. They call youth the time of temptation—Good Lord! Why youth's armored from head to heel in its invincible ignorance. O me! Well —I'll pay him for it if it takes me ten years."

John's complacency had faded with the white heat of his anger, and he sat chafing in spirit while his elbow neighbor slept in the shape of an N. Across the car he heard Parson Tombs explaining to the Graves brethren and Sister March that Satan—though sometimes corporeal—and in that case he might be either unicorporeal or multicorporeal—and at other times incorporeal—as he might choose and providence permit—and, mark you, he might be both at once on occasion—was by no means omnipresent, but only ubiquitous.

Lazarus supposed a case: "He might be in both these cahs at once an' yet not on the platfawm between 'em."

"It's mo' than likely!" said the aged pastor, no one meaning anything sly. Yet to some people a parson's smiling mention of the devil is always a good joke, and the Graves laughed, as we may say. Not so, Sister March; she never laughed at the prince of darkness, nor took his name in vain. She spoke, now, of his "darts."

"No, Sister March, I reckon his darts, fifty times to one, ah turned aside fum us by the provi*dence* that's round us, not by the po' little patchin' o' grace that's in us."

John's heart jumped. Garnet looked in and beckoned him out. He went.

"John"—the voice was tearful—"I offer my hand in penitent gratitude." John took it. "Yes, my dear boy, my feet had well-nigh slipped."

"I oughtn't to have spoken as I did, Major Garnet."

"It was the word of the Lord, John. It saved me and my spotless name! The mistake had just begun, in mere play, but it might have grown into actual sin —of impulse, I mean, of course—not of action ; my life-long correctness of——"

"Oh, I'm sure of that sir ! I only wish *I*——"

"God bless you ! I've a good notion to tell your mother this whole thing, John, just to make her still prouder of you." He squeezed the young man's hand. "But I reckon for others' sakes we'd better not breathe it."

"O, I think so, sir ! I promise——"

"You needn't have promised, John. Your think-so was promise enough. And a mighty good thing for us all it's so. For, John March, you're the hope of Suez !

"You've got the key of all our fates in your pocket, John—you and your mother now, and you when you come into full charge of the estate next year. That's why Jeff-Jack's always been so willing to help me to help you on. But never mind that, only—beware of new friends. When they come fawning on you with offers to help you develop the resources of Widewood, you tell 'em——"

"That I'm going to develop them myself, alone."

"N-n-no—not quite that. O, you couldn't ! You've no idea what a—why, *I* couldn't do it *with* you, without Jeff-Jack's help, nor he without mine ! Why, just see what a failure the effort to build this road was, until " —the locomotive bellowed.

"Half-an-hour late, and slowing up again ! " exclaimed John. He knew the parson's wife was pressing his mother to spend the night with them, and he was afraid of having his soul asked after. "Why do we stop here, hardly a mile from town?"

"It's to let my folks off. They're going to walk over to the pike while I go on for the carriage and drive out; they and Jeff-Jack and the Hallidays."

The train stopped where a beautiful lane crossed the track between two fenced fields. Fair and Barbara alighted and stood on a flowery bank with the sun glowing in some distant tree-tops behind them. Fannie leaned from the train, took both Jeff-Jack's uplifted hands and fluttered down upon rebounding tiptoes; the bell sounded, the scene changed, and John murmured to himself in heavy agony,

"He's going to ask her! O, Fannie, Fannie, if you'd only refuse to say yes, and give me three years to show what I can do! But he's going to ask her before that sun goes down, and what's she going to say?"

## XXVIII.

### INFORMATION FOR SALE

"HOPE of Suez!" Garnet felt he had spoken just these three words too many. "Overtalked myself again," he said to himself while chatting with others; "a liar always does. But he shall pay for this. Ah me!"

He was right. The young man would have sucked down all his flattery but for those three words. Yet on one side they were true, and March guiltily felt them so as, looking at his mother, he thought again of that deep store of the earth's largess lying under their unfruitful custody. Suez and her three counties would have jeered the gaudy name from Lover's Leap to Liberty-ville though had they guessed better the meaning of the change into which a world's progress was irresistibly pushing them, whoever owned Widewood must have stood for some of their largest wishes and hopes, and they would have ceased to deride the blessed mutation and to hobble it with that root of so many world-wide evils—the calling still private what the common need has made public. The ghost of this thought flitted in John's mind, but would not be grasped or beckoned to the light.

"I wish I could think," he sighed, but he could only think of Fannie. The train stopped. The excursionists swarmed forth. The cannon belched out its thunderous good-byes, and John went for his horse and buggy, promising to give word for Garnet's equipage to be sent to him.

"I must mind Johanna and her plunder," said the Major; "but I'll look after your mother, too." And he did so, though he found time to part fondly with the Proudfits.

"He won't do," thought John, as he glanced back from a rise of ground. "Fannie's right. And she's right about me, too; the only way to get her is to keep away till I've shown myself fit for her; that's what she means; of course she can't say so; but I'm satisfied that's what she means!"

He passed two drunken men. Here in town at the

end of Suez's wedding so many had toasted it so often,
it was as if Susie's own eyes were blood-shot and her
steps uncertain. "It's my wedding, too," he soliloquized. "This Widewood business and I are married
this day; it alone, to me alone, till it's finished. Garnet shall see whether—humph!—Jake, my horse and
buggy!" And soon he was rattling back down the
stony slopes toward his mother.

"Hope of Suez!" he grimly laughed. "We'll be its
despair if we don't get something done. And I've got
to do it alone. Why shouldn't I? Yes, it's true,
times have changed; and yet if this was ever rightly a
private matter in my father's hands, I can't see why it
has or why it should become a public matter in
mine!"

He said this to himself the more emphatically because he felt, somehow, very uncertain about it. He
wished his problem was as simple as a railroad question.
A railroad can ask for public aid; but fancy him asking public aid to open and settle up his private lands!
He could almost hear Susie's horse-laugh in reply.
Why should she not laugh? He recalled with what
sweet unboastful tone his father had always condemned
every scheme and symptom of riding on public shoulders into private fortune. In the dear *old* Dixie there
had been virtually no public, and every gentleman was
by choice his own and only public aid, no matter what
—"Look out!"

He hauled up his horse. A man pressed close to the
side of the halted buggy, to avoid a huge telegraph
pole that came by quivering between two timber wheels.

He offered John a freckled, yellow hand, and a smile of maudlin fondness.

"Mr. Mahch, I admiah to salute you ag'in, seh. *Hasn't* we had a glo'ious day? It's the mos' obtainable day Susie eveh see, seh!"

"Well, 'pon my soul!" said John, ignoring the proffered hand. "If I'd seen who it was, I'd 'a' driven straight over you." Both laughed. "Cornelius, did you see my mother waiting for me down by the tracks?"

"I did, seh. Thah she a-set'n' on a pile o' ceda'-tree poles, lookin' like the las' o' pea-time—p-he-he-he!

"Majo' Gyarnit? O yass, seh, he thah, too. Thass how come I lingud thah, seh, yass, seh, in espiration o' Johanna. Mr. Mahch, I loves that creatu' yit, seh!— I means Johanna."

"Oh!—not Major Garnet," laughed John, gathering the reins.

Cornelius sputtered with delight, and kept between the wheels. "Mr. Mahch,"—he straightened, solemnly, and held himself sober—"I was jess about to tell you what I jess evise Majo' Gyarnit espressin' to yo' maw— jess accidental as I was earwhilin' aroun' Johanna, you know."

"What was it? What did he say?"

"O, it wan't much, what he say. He say, 'Sis' Mahch, you e'zac'ly right. Don't you on no accounts paht with so much's a' acre o' them lan's lessn——"

"Lord!—the lands—take care for the wheel."

But Mr. Leggett leaned heavily on the buggy.

" Mr. Mahch, I evince an' repose you in confidence to wit : that long as you do like Gyarnit say——"

John gave a stare of menace. " Major Garnet, if you please."

" Yass, seh, o' co'se ; Majo' Gyarnit. I say, long as you do like he say, Widewood stay jess like it is, an' which it suit him like grapes suit a coon ! " The informant's booziness had returned. One foot kept slipping from a spoke of the fore-wheel. With pretence of perplexity he examined the wheel. " Mr. Mahch, this wheel sick ; she mighty sick ; got to see blacksmiff befo' she can eveh see Widewood."

John looked. The word was true. He swore. The mulatto snickered, sagged against it and cocked his face importantly.

" Mr. Mahch, if you an' me was on'y in cahoots ! En we *kin* be, seh, we kin—why, hafe o' yo' lan's 'u'd be public lan's in no time, an' the res' 'u'd belong to a stawk comp'ny, an' me'n' you 'u'd be a-cuttin' off kewponds an' a-drivin' fas' hawses an' a-drinkin' champagne suppuz, an' champagne faw ow real frien's an' real pain faw ow sham frien's, an' plenty o' both kine—thah goes Majo' Gyarnit's kerrige to him." It passed.

" But, why, Cornelius, should it suit Major Garnet for my lands to lie idle ? "

" Mr. Mahch, has you neveh inspec' the absence o' green in my eye ? It suit him faw a reason known on'y to yo's truly, yit which the said yo's truly would accede to transfawm to you, seh ; yass, seh ; in considerations o' us goin' in cahoots, aw else a call loan, an' yit mo' stric'ly a call-ag'in loan, a sawt o' continial fee, yass, seh ; an' the on'y question, how much kin you make it ? "

John looked into the upturned face for some seconds before he said, slowly and pleasantly, "Why, you dirty dog !"  He gave the horse a cut of the whip.  Leggett smiling and staggering, called after him, to the delight of all the street,

"Mr.  Mahch, thass confidential, you know!  An' Mr.  Mahch !  Woe !  Mr.  Mahch."  John glanced fiercely back—"You betteh 'zamine that *hine* wheel ! caze it jess now pa-ass ovch my foot ! "

---

## XXIX.

### RAVENEL ASKS

THE Garnet carriage, Johanna on the back seat, came smartly up through the town, past Parson Tombs's, the Halliday cottage, and silent Montrose Academy, and was soon parted from the Marches' buggy, which followed with slower dignity and a growing limp.

" Well, Johanna," said Garnet, driving, " had a good time ? "

" Yass, seh."

" What's made Miss Barb so quiet all day ; doesn't she like our friend ? "

The answer was a bashful drawl—" I reckon she like him tol'able, seh."

"If you think Miss Barb would be pleased you can change to this seat beside me, Johanna." The master drew rein and she made the change. He spoke again. "You saw me, just now, talking with Cornelius, didn't you?"

"Yass, seh."

"His wife's dead, at last."

No answer.

"Johanna," he turned a playful eye, "what makes you so hard on Cornelius!"

She replied with a white glance of alarm and turned away. He would have pressed the subject but she murmured,

"Dah Miss Barb."

Barbara sat on a bare ledge of rock above the roadside, platting clovers. Fair stood close below, watching her fingers. She sprang to her feet.

"What did keep you so?" She moved to where Fair had stopped to hand her down, but laughed, turned away, waved good-by to Fannie and Ravenel out in a field full of flowers and western sunlight, and ran around by an easier descent to the carriage. Fair helped her in.

"Homeward bound," she said, and they spun away. As they turned a bend in the pike she glanced back with a carefully careless air, but saw only their own dust.

John, driving beside his mother, with eyes on the infirm wheel, was very silent, and she was very limp. The buggy top was up for privacy. By and by he

heard a half-spoken sound at his side, and turning saw
her eyes full of tears.

"O thunder!" he thought, but only said, "Why,
mother, what's the matter?"

"Ah! my son, that's what I wonder. Why have
you shunned me all day? Am I——"

"There are the Tombses waiting at their gate," interrupted the son. The aged pair had hurried away from
the train on foot to have their house open for Sister
March.

"Yes," said Daphne, sweetly yielding herself to their
charge, "John's fierce driving has damaged a wheel,
and we wont——"

"Go home till morning," said the delighted pastor
with a tickled laugh that drew from his wife a glance
of fond disapproval.

John drove alone to a blacksmith shop and left his
buggy there and his horse at a stable. For the blacksmith lay across his doorsill "sick." He had been
mending rigs and shoeing critters since dawn, and had
drunk from a jug something he had thought was water
and found—"it wusn't."

March sauntered off lazily to a corner where the lane
led westward like the pike, turned into it and ran at
full speed.

With a warm face he came again into the main
avenue at a point nearly opposite the Halliday's cottage
gate. General Halliday and the Englishman were just
going through it.

John turned toward the sun-setting at a dignified
walk. "I'm a fool to come out here," he thought.

"But I must see at once what Jeff-Jack thinks of my plan. Will he tell me the truth, or will he trick me as they say he did Cornelius? O I must ask him, too, if he did that! I can't help it if he is with her; I must see him. I don't want to see her; at least that's not what I'm out here for. I'm done with her—for a while; Heaven bless her!—but I must see him, so's to know what to propose to mother."

The day was dying in exquisite beauty. Long bands of pale green light widened up from the west. Along the hither slope of a ridge someone was burning off his sedge-grass. The slender red lines of fire, beautiful after passion's sort, but dimming the field's fine gold, were just reaching the crest to die by a roadside. The objects of his search were nowhere to be seen.

A short way off, on the left, lay a dense line of young cedars and pines, nearly parallel with the turnpike. A footpath, much haunted in term-time by Montrose girls, and leading ultimately to the rear of the Academy grounds, lay in the clover-field beyond this thicket. John mounted a fence and gazed far and near. Opposite him in the narrow belt of evergreens was a scarcely noticeable opening, so deeply curved that one would get almost through it before the view opened on the opposite side. He leaped into the field, ran to this gap, burst into the open beyond, and stopped, hat in hand—speechless. His quest was ended.

Not ten steps away stood two lovers who had just said that fearfully sweet "mine" and "thine" that keeps the world a-turning. Ravenel's right arm was curved over Fannie's shoulder and about her waist. His left hand smoothed the hair from her uplifted brow, and his kiss was just lighting upon it.

The blood leaped to his face, but the next instant he sunk his free hand into his pocket and smiled. John's face was half-anger, half-anguish.

"Pleasant evening," said Ravenel.

"For you, sir." John bowed austerely. "I will not mar it. My business can wait." He gave Fannie a grief-stricken look and was hurrying off.

"John March," cried Ravenel, in a voice breaking with laughter, "come right back here, sir." But the youth only threw up an arm in tragic disdain and kept on.

"John," called a gentler voice, and he turned. "Don't leave us so," said Fannie. "You'll make me unhappy if you do." She had drawn away from her lover's arm. She put out a hand.

"Come, tell me I haven't lost my best friend."

John ran to her, caught her hand in both his and covered it with kisses. Ravenel stood smiling and breaking a twig slowly into bits.

"There, there, that's extravagant," said Fannie; but she let the youth keep her hand while he looked into her eyes and smiled fondly through his distress. Then she withdrew it, saying:

"There's Mr. Ravenel's hand, hold it. If I didn't know how men hate to be put through forms, I'd insist on your taking it."

"I reckon John thinks we haven't been quite candid," said Ravenel.

"I'm not sure we have," responded Fannie. "And

yet I do think we've been real friends. You know John "—she smiled at her hardihood—" this is the only way it could ever be, don't you?" But John turned half away and shook his head bitterly. She spoke again. "Look at me, John." But plainly he could not.

"Are you going to throw us overboard?" she asked. There was a silence; and then—"You mustn't; not even if you feel like it. Don't you know we hadn't ever ought to consult our feelings till we've consulted everything else?"

John looked up with a start, and Fannie, by a grimace, bade him give his hand to his rival. He turned sharply and offered it. Ravenel took it with an air of drollery and John spoke low, Fannie loitering a step aside.

"I offer you my hand with this warning—I love her. I'm going on to love her after she's yours by law. I'll not make love to her; I may be a fool, but I'm not a hound; I love her too well to do that. But she's bound to know it right along. You'll see it. Everybody'll know it. That'll be all of it, I swear. But any man who wants to stop me from it will have to kill me. I believe I have the right, before God, to do it; but I'm going to do it anyhow. I prize your friendship. If I can keep it while you know, and while everybody else knows, that I'm simply hanging round waiting for you to die, I'll do it. If I can't—I can't." The hands parted.

"That's all right, John. That's what I'd do in your place."

March gazed a moment in astonishment. Then Fannie, still drifting away, felt Ravenel at her side and glanced up and around.

"O, you haven't let him go, have you? Why, I wanted to give him this four-leaf clover—as a sort o' pleasant hint. Don't you see?"

"I reckon he'll try what luck there is in odd numbers," said Ravenel, and they quickened their homeward step.

John went to tea at the Tombses in no mood to do himself credit as a guest. His mother was still reminding him of it next day when they alighted at home. "I little thought my son would give me so much trouble."

But his reply struck her dumb. "I've got lots left, mother, and will always have plenty. I make it myself."

--------

## XXX.

### ANOTHER ODD NUMBER

FANNIE expressed to Barbara one day her annoyance at that kind of men—without implying that she meant any certain one—who will never take no for an answer.

"A lover, Barb, if he's not of the humble sort, is the most self-conceited thing alive. He can no more take in the idea that your objection to him is *he* than a board can draw a nail into itself. You've got to hammer it in."

"With a brickbat," quoth Barbara, whose notions of carpentry were feminine, and who did not care to discuss the matter. But John March, it seemed, would not take no from fate itself.

"I don't believe yet," he mused, as he rode about his small farm, "that Jeff-Jack will get her. She's playing with him. Why not? She's played with a dozen. And yet, naturally, somebody'll get her, and he'll not be worthy of her. There's hope yet! She loves me far more than she realizes right now. That's a woman's way; they'll go along loving for years and find it out by accident—You, Hector! What the devil are you and Israel over in that melon-patch for instead of the corn-field?

"I've been too young for her. No, not too young for her, but too young to show what I can do and be. She waited to see, for years. The intention may not have been conscious, but I believe it was there! And then she got tired of waiting. Why, it began to look as though I would never do anything or be anybody! Great Cæsar! You can't expect a girl to marry an egg in hopes o' what it'll hatch. O let me make haste and show what I am! what I can—'Evermind, Israel, I see you. Just wait till we get this crop gathered; if I don't kick you two idle, blundering, wasting, pilfering black renters off this farm—as shore's a gun's iron!

"No, she and Jeff-Jack'll never marry. Even if they do he'll not live long. These political editors, if somebody doesn't kill 'em, they break down, all at once. Our difference in age will count for less and less every year. She's the kind that stays young; four years

from now I'll look the older of the two—I'll work myself old ! "

A vision came to the dreamer's fancy : Widewood's
forests filled with thrifty settlers, mines opened, factories
humming by the brooksides, the locomotive's whistle
piercing the stony ears of the Sleeping Giant ; Suez full
of iron-ore, coal, and quarried stone, and Fannie a
widow, or possibly still unwed, charmed by his successes,
touched by his constancy, and realizing at last the true
nature of what she had all along felt as only a friendship.

"That's it ! if I give men good reason to court me,
I'll get the woman I court !"—But he did not, for many
weeks, give men any irresistible good reason to court
him.

"Ah me ! here's November gone.  Talk of minutes
slipping through the fingers—the months are as bad as
the minutes !  Lord ! what a difference there is between
planning a thing and doing it—or even beginning to
do it ! "

Yet he did begin.  There is a season comes, sooner
or later, to all of us, when we must love and love must
nest.  It may fix its choice irrationally on some sweet
ineligible Fannie ; but having chosen, there it must
nest, spite of all.  Now, men may begin life not thus
moved ; but I never knew a man thus moved who still
did not begin life.  Love being kindled, purpose is
generated, and the wheels in us begin to go round.
They had gone round, even in John's father ; but not
only were time, place, and circumstance against the
older man, but his love had nested in so narrow a knot-

hole that the purposes and activities of his gentle soul died in their prison.

"Yes, that's one thing I've got to look out for," mused John one day, riding about the northwestern limits of his lands where a foaming brook kept saying, "Water-power!—good fishing!—good fishing!—water-power!" He dismounted and leaned against his horse by the brook's Widewood side, we may say, although just beyond here lay the odd sixty acres by which Widewood exceeded an even hundred thousand. The stream came down out of a steeply broken region of jagged rocks, where frequent evergreens and russet oaks studded the purple gray maze of trees that like to go naked in winter. But here it shallowed widely and slipped over a long surface of unbroken bed-rock. On its far side a spring gushed from a rocky cleft, leapt down some natural steps, ran a few yards, and slid into the brook. Behind it a red sun shone through the leafless tree-tops. The still air hinted of frost.

Suddenly his horse listened. In a moment he heard voices, and by an obscure road up and across the brook two riders came briskly to the water's edge, splashed into the smooth shallow and let their horses drink. They were a man and a maid, and the maid was Barbara Garnet. She was speaking.

"We can't get so far out of the way if we can keep this"—she saw John March rise into his saddle, caught a breath, and then cried:

"Why, it's Mr. March. Mr. March, we've missed our road!" Her laugh was anxious. "In fact, we're lost. Oh! Mr. March, Mr. Fair." The young men shook hands. Fair noted a light rifle and a bunch of squirrels at March's saddle-bow.

" You've been busier than we."

" Mighty poor sign of industry. I didn't come out for game, but a man's sure to be sorry if he goes into the woods without a gun. I mean, of course, Miss Garnet, if he's alone ! "

Barbara answered with a smile and a wicked drawl, " You've been enjoying both ad-van-tag-es. I used to wish I was a squirrel, they're so en-er-get-ic." She added that she would be satisfied now to remain as she was if she could only get home safe. She reckoned they could find the road if Mr. March would tell them how.

John smiled seriously. " Better let me show you." He moved down the middle of the stream. " This used to be the right road, long time ago. You know, Mr. Fair "—his voice rang in the trees, " our mountain roads just take the bed of the nearest creek whenever they can. Our people are not a very business people. But that's because they've got the rare virtue of contentment. Now ——"

" I don't think they're too contented, Mr. March," said Barbara, defensively. " Why, Mr. Fair, how much this creek and road are like ours at Rosemont ! "

" It's the same creek," called March.

By and by they left it and rode abreast through woods. There was much badinage, in which Barbara took the aggressive, with frequent hints at Fannie that gave John delicious pain and convinced him that Miss Garnet was, after all, a fine girl. Fair became so quiet that John asked him two or three questions.

"O no!" laughed Fair, he could stay but a day or two. He said he had come this time from "quite a good deal" of a stay in Texas and Mexico, and his father had written him that he was needed at home. "Which is absurd, you know," he added to Barbara.

"Per-fect-ly," she said. But he would not skirmish.

"Yes," he replied. "But all the same I have to go. I'm sorry."

"We're sorry at Rosemont."

"I shall be sorry at Widewood," echoed March.

"I regret it the more," responded Fair, "from having seen Widewood so much and yet so little. Miss Garnet believes in a great future for Widewood. It was in trying to see something of it that we lost——"

But Barbara protested. "Mr. Fair, we rode hap-hazard! We simply chanced that way! What should I know, or care, about lands? You're confusing me with pop-a! Which is doub-ly ab-surd!"

"Most assuredly!" laughed the young men.

"You know, Mr. March, pop-a's so proud of the Widewood tract that I believe, positively, he's jealous of anyone's seeing it without him for a guide. You'd think it held the key of all our fates."

"Which is triply absurd!"

"Superlatively!" drawled Barbara, and laughing was easy. They came out upon the pike as March was saying to Fair:

"I'd like to show you my lands; they're the key of my fate, anyhow."

"They're only the lock," said Barbara, musingly. "The key is—elsewhere."

John laughed. He thought her witty, and continued with her, though the rest of the way to Rosemont was short and plain. Presently she turned upon the two horsemen a pair of unaggressive but invincible eyes, saying, languorously,

"Mr. March, I want you to show Widewood to Mr. Fair—to-morrow. Pop-a's been talking about showing it to him, but I want him to see it with just you alone."

To Fair there always seemed a reserve of merriment behind Miss Garnet's gravity, and a reserve of gravity behind her brightest gayety. This was one thing that had drawn him back to Rosemont. Her ripples never hid her depths, yet she was never too deep to ripple. I give his impressions for what they may be worth. He did not formulate them; he merely consented to stay a day longer. A half-moon was growing silvery when John said good-by at the gate of the campus.

"Now, in the morning, Mr. Fair, I'll meet you somewhere between here and the pike. I wish I could say you'd meet my mother, but she's in poor health—been so ever since the war."

That night Garnet lingered in his wife's room to ask—
"Do you think Barb really missed the road, or was that——"

"Yes, they took the old creek road by mistake."

"Has Fair—said anything to her?"

"No; she didn't expect or wish it——"

"Well, I don't see why."

—"And he's hardly the sort to do unexpected things."

"They've agreed to ride right after breakfast.  What d'you reckon that's for?"

"Not what you wish.  But still, for some reason she wants you to leave him entirely to himself."

College being in session breakfast was early.

"Barb, you'll have to take care of Mr. Fair to-day, I reckon.  You might take my horse, sir.  I'll be too busy indoors to use him."

The girl and her cavalier took but a short gallop. They had nearly got back to the grove gate when he ventured upon a personal speech ; but it was only to charge her with the art of blundering cleverly.

She assured him that her blunders were all nature and her art accident.  "Whenever I want to be witty I get into a hurry, and haste is the an-ti-dote of wit."

"Miss Garnet," he thought, as her eyes rested calmly in his, "your gaze is too utterly truthful."

"Ah!" said Barbara, "here's Mr. March now."

Fair wished he might find out why Miss Garnet should be out-manœuvring her father.

---

## XXXI.

### MR. FAIR VENTURES SOME INTERROGATIONS

THE air was full of joy that morning, and John boyishly open and hearty.

"Fact is, Mr. Fair, I don't care for young ladies' company.  Half of them are frauds and the rest are a delusion and a snare —ha-ha-ha! Miss Garnet is new goods, as the boys say, and I'm not fashionable. Even our mothers ain't very well acquainted yet; though my mother's always regretted it; their tastes differ. My mother's literary, you know."

"They say Miss Garnet's a great romp—among other girls—and an unmerciful mimic."

"Don't you rather like that?"

"Who, me? Lord, yes! The finest girl I know is that way—dances Spanish dances—alone with other girls, of course. The church folks raised Cain about it once. O I—you think I mean Miss Halliday—well I do. Miss Garnet can tease me about her all she likes— ha, ha! it doesn't faze me! Miss .Fannie's nothing to me but a dear friend—never was! Why, she's older than I am—h-though h-you'd never suspect it."

"Well, yes, I think I should have known it."

"O go 'long! Somebody told you! But I swear, Mr. Fair, I wonder, sir, you're not more struck with Miss Halliday. Now, I go in for mind and heart. I don't give a continental for externals; and yet—did you ever see such glorious eyes as Fan—Miss Halliday's? Now, honest Ingin! *did* you, *ever?*"

Mr. Fair admitted that Miss Halliday's eyes danced.

"You say they do? You're right! Hah! *they* dance Spanish dances. I've seen black eyes that went through you like a sword; I've seen blue eyes that drilled through you like an auger; and I've seen gray ones that bit through you like a cold-chisel; and I've seen— now, there's Miss Garnet's, that just see through you without going through you at all—O I don't like any of 'em! but Fannie Halliday's eyes—Miss Fannie, I should say—they seem to say, 'Come out o' that. I'm not looking at all, but I know you're there!' O sir!— Mr. Fair, don't you hate, sir, to see such a creature as that get married to anybody? I say, to *anybody!* I tell you what it's like, Mr. Fair. It's like chloroform- ing a butterfly, sir! That's what it's like!"

He meditated and presently resumed—"But, Law' no! She's nothing to me. I've got too much to think of with these lands on my hands. D'you know, sir, I really speak more freely to you than if you belonged here and knew me better? And I confess to you that a girl like F—Miss Halliday—would be enough to keep me from ever marrying!"

"Why, how is that?"

"Why? O well, because!—knowing her, I couldn't ever be content with less, and, of course, I couldn't get her or make her happy if I got her. Torture for one's better than torture for two. Mind, that's a long ways from saying I ever did want her, or ever will. I'm happy as I am—confirmed bachelor—ha-ha-ha! What I do want, Mr. Fair, sir, is to colonize these lands, and to tell you the truth, sir—h—I don't know how to do it!"

"Are your titles good?"

"Perfect."

"Are the lands free from mortgage?"

"Free! ha-ha! they'd be free from mortgage, sir, but for one thing."

"What's that?"

"Why, they're mortgaged till you can't rest! The mortgages ain't so mortal much, but they've been on so long we'd almost be afraid to take them off. They're dried on sir!—grown in! Why, sir, we've paid more interest than the mortgages foot up, sir!"

"What were they made for? improvements?"

"Impr—O yes, sir; most of 'em were given to improve the interior of our smoke-house—sort o' decorate it with meat."

"Ah, you wasted your substance in riotous living!"

"No, sir, we were simply empty in the same old anatomical vicinity and had to fill it. The mortgages wa'n't all made for that; two or three were made to raise money to pay the interest on old ones—interest and taxes. Mr. Fair, if ever a saint on earth lived up to his belief 'my father did. He believed in citizenship confined to taxpayers, and he'd pay his taxes owing for the pegs in his shoes—he made his own shoes, sir."

"Who hold these mortgages?"

"On paper, Major Garnet, but really Jeff-Jack Ravenal. That's private, sir."

"Yes, very properly, I see."

"Do you? Wha' do you see? Wish I could see something. Seems like I can't."

"O, I only see as you do, no doubt, that any successful scheme to improve your lands will have to be in part a public scheme, and be backed by Mr. Ravenel's newspaper, and he can do that better if he's privately interested and supposed not to be so, can't he?"

March stared, and then mused. "Well, I'll be— doggoned!"

"Of course, Mr. March, that needn't be unfair to you.

Is it to accommodate you, or him, that Major Garnet lends his name?"

"O me!—At least—O! they're always accommodating each other."

"My father told me of these lands before I came here. He thinks that the fortunes of Suez, and consequently of Rosemont, in degree, not to speak "—the speaker smiled—" of individual fates, *is* locked up in them."

"I know! I know! The fact grows on me, sir, every day and hour! But, sir, the lands are my lawful inheritance, and although I admit that the public——"

"You quite misunderstand me! Miss Garnet said—in play, I know—that the key of this lock isn't far off, or words to that effect. Was she not right? And doesn't Mr. Ravenel hold it? In fact—pardon my freedom—is it not best that he should?"

"Good heavens, sir! why, Miss Garnet didn't mean—you say, does Jeff-Jack hold that key? He was holding it the last time I saw him! O yes. Even according to your meaning he thinks he holds it, and he thinks he ought to. I don't think he ought to, and incline to believe he won't! *Lift* your miserable head!" he cried to his horse, spurred fiercely, and jerked the curb till the animal reared and plunged. When he laughed again, in apology, Fair asked,

"Do you propose to organize a company yourself to —eh—boom your lands?"

"Well, I don't—Yes, I reckon I shall. I reckon I'll have to. Wha' do you think?"

"Might not Mr. Ravenel let you pay off your mortgages in stock?"

"I—he might.   But could I do that and still control
the thing ?   For, Mr. Fair, I've got to control !   There's
a private reason why I mustn't let Jeff-Jack manage
me.   I've got to show myself the better man.   He knows
why.   O !  we're good friends.   I can't explain it to you,
and you'd never guess it in the world !   But there's a
heavy prize up between us, and I believe that if I can
show myself more than a match for him in these lists—
this land business—I'll stand a chance for that prize.
There, sir, I tell you that much.   It's only proper that I
should.   I've got to be the master."

"Is your policy, then, to gain time—to put the thing
off while you——"

"Good Lord, no !  I haven't a day to spare !  I'll show
you these lands, Mr. Fair, and then if you'll accept the
transfer of these mortgages, I'll begin the work of opening these lands, somehow, before the sun goes down.   But
if I let Ravenel or Garnet in, I—" John pondered.

"Haven't you let them in already, Mr. March ?   I
don't see clearly why it isn't your best place for them."

March was silent.

## XXXII.

### JORDAN

BARBARA lay on a rug in her room, reading before the fragrant ashes of a perished fire. She heard her father's angry step, and his stern rap on her door. Before she could more than lift her brow he entered.

"Barb!—O what sort of posture—" She started, and sat coiled on the rug.

"Barb, how is it you're not with your mother?"

"Mom-a sent me out, pop-a. She thought if I'd leave her she might drop asleep."

He smiled contemptuously. "How long ago was that?"

"About fifteen minutes."

"It was an hour ago! Barb, you've got hold of another novel. Haven't you learned yet that you can't tell time by that sort of watch?"

"Is mom-a awake?" asked the girl, starting from the mantel-piece.

"Yes—stop!" He extended his large hand, and she knew, as she saw its tremor, that he was in the same kind of transport in which he had flogged Cornelius. In the same instant she was frightened and glad.

"I've headed him off," she thought.

"Barb, your mother's very ill—stop! Johanna's with her. Barb"—his tones sank and hardened—"why did that black hussy try to avoid telling me you were home and Fair had gone off with that whelp, John

March? What? Why don't you speak so I can hear? What are you afraid of ? "

" I'm afraid we'll disturb mom-a. Johanna should have told you plainly."

" Oh ! indeed ! I tell you, if it hadn't been for your mother's presence I'd have thrown her out of the window." An unintentional murmur from Barbara exasperated him to the point of ecstasy. He paled and smiled.

" Barb, did you want to keep me from knowing that Fair was going to Widewood ? " They looked steadily into each others' eyes. " Which of us is it you don't trust, that Yankee, or your own father ? Don't—" he lifted his palm, but let it sink again. " Don't move your lips that way again ; I won't endure it. Barbara Garnet, this is Fannie Halliday's work ! So help me, God, I'd rather I'd taken your little white coffin in my arms eighteen years ago and laid it in the ground than that you should have learned from that poisonous creature the effrontry to suspect me of dishonest—Silence ! You ungrateful brat, if you were a son, I'd shake the breath out of you. Have you *ever* trusted me ? Say ! " —he stepped close up— " Stop gazing at me like a fool and answer my question ! Have you ? "

" Don't speak so loud."

" Don't tell me that, you little minx ; you who have never half noticed how sick your mother is. Barb "— the speaker's words came through his closed teeth— " Mr. John March can distrust me and leave me out of his precious company as much as he damn pleases—if you like his favorite forms of speech—and so may your

tomtit Yankee. But you—sha'n't! You sha'n't repay
a father's careful plans with suspicions of underhanded
rascality, you unregenerate—see here! Do those two
pups know you didn't want me to go? Answer
me!"

She could not. Her lips moved as he had forbidden,
and she was still looking steadily into his blazing eyes,
when, as if lightning had struck, she flinched almost off
her feet, her brain rang and roared, her sight failed, and
she knew she had been slapped in the face.

He turned his back, but the next instant had wheeled
again, his face drawn with pain and alarm. "I didn't
mean to do that! Oh, good Lord! it wa'n't I! Forgive me, Barb. Oh, Barb, my child, as God's my wit-
ness, I didn't do it of my own free will. He let the
devil use me. All my troubles are coming together;
your suspicions maddened me."

Her eyes were again in his. She shook her head and
passed to her mirror, saying, slowly. "God shall smite
thee, thou whited wall." She glanced at the glass, but
the redness of its fellow matched the smitten cheek, and
she hurried to the door.

"Barb"—the tone was a deep whine—she stopped
without looking back. "Don't say anything to your
mother to startle her. The slightest shock may kill her."

Barbara entered the mother's chamber. Johanna
was standing by a window. The daughter beamed on
the maid, and turned to the bed; but consternation
quenched the smile when she beheld her mother's face.

"Why, mom-a, sweet."

A thin hand closed weakly on her own, and two

sunken blue eyes, bright with distress, looked into hers. " Where is he? " came a feeble whisper.

"Pop-a? Oh, he's coming. If he doesn't come in a moment, I'll bring him." The daughter's glance rested for refuge on the white forehead. " Shall I go call him?"

The pallid lips made no reply, the sunken eyes still lay in wait. Barbara racked her mind for disguise of words, but found none. There was no escape. Even to avoid any longer the waiting eyes would confess too much. She met them and they gazed up into hers in still anguish. Barbara's answered, with a sweet, full serenity. Then without a word or motion came the silent question,

" Did he strike you? "

And Barbara answered, audibly. " No."

She rose, adding, " Let me go and bring him." Conscience rose also and went with her. Just outside the closed door she covered her face in her hands and sank to the floor, moaning under her breath,

"What have I done? What shall I do? Oh God! why couldn't—why *didn't* I lie to *him?*" She ran down-stairs on tiptoe.

Her father, with Pettigrew at his side, was offering enthusiasm to a Geometry class. "Young gentlemen, a swift, perfect demonstration of a pure abstract truth is as beautiful and delightful to me—to any uncorrupted mind—as perfect music to a perfect ear."

But hearing that his daughter was seeking him, he withdrew.

The two had half mounted the stairs, when a hurried

step sounded in the upper hall, and Johanna leaned wildly over the rail, her eyes streaming.

"Miss Barb! Miss Barb! run here! run! come quick, fo' de love of God! Oh, de chariots of Israel! de chariots of Israel! De gates o' glory lif'n up dey head!"

Barbara flew up the stairs and into her mother's room. Mr. Pettigrew stood silent among the crystalline beauties of mathematical truth, and a dozen students leaped to their feet as the daughter's long wail came ringing through the house mingled with the cry of Johanna.

"Too late! Too late! De daughteh o' Zion done gone in unbeseen!"

Through two days more Fair lingered, quartered at the Swanee Hotel, and conferred twice more with John March. In the procession that moved up the cedar avenue of the old Suez burying-ground, he stepped beside General Halliday, near its end. Among the headstones of the Montgomeries the long line stopped and sang,

> "For oh! we stand on Jordan's strand,
>   Our friends are passing over."

In the midst of the refrain, each time, there trembled up in tearful ecstasy, above the common wave of song, the voices of Leviticus Wisdom and his wife. But only once, after the last stanza, Johanna's yet clearer tone answered them from close beside black-veiled Barbara, singing in vibrant triumph,

> "An' jess befo', de shiny sho'
>   We may almos' discoveh."

## XXXIII.

### THE OPPORTUNE MOMENT

Coming from the grave Fair walked with March.

"Yes, I go to-night; I shall see my father within three days. He may think better of your ideas than I do. Don't you suppose really—" etc. "You think you'll push it anyhow?"

"Yes, sir. In fact, I've got to."

After all others were gone one man still loitered furtively in the cemetery. He came, now, from an alley of arborvitæs with that fantastic elasticity of step which skilled drunkards learn. He had in hand a bunch of limp flowers of an unusual kind, which he had that day ridden all the way to Pulaski City to buy. He stood at the new grave's foot, sank to one knee, wiped true tears from his eyes, pressed apart the evergreens and chrysanthemums piled there, and laid in the midst his own bruised and wilted offering of lilies.

As he reached the graveyard gate in departing his mood lightened.

"An' now gen'le*men*," he said to himself, "is come to pa-ass the ve-y nick an' keno o' time faw a fresh staht. Frien' Gyarnit, we may be happy yit."

He came up behind Fair and March. Fair was speaking of Fannie.

"But where was she? I didn't see her."

"Oh, she stayed at Rosemont to look after the house."

"The General tells me his daughter is to be married to Mr. Ravenel in March."

John gave an inward start, but was silent for a moment. Then he said, absently,

"So that's out, is it?" But a few steps farther on he touched Fair's arm.

"Let's go—slower." His smile was ashen. "I—h-I don't know why in the devil I have these sickish feelings come on me at f-funerals." They stopped. "Humph! Wha'd' you reckon can be the cause of it—indigestion?"

Mr. Fair thought it very likely, and March said it was passing off already.

"Humph! it's ridiculous. Come on, I'm all right now."

The man behind them passed, looked back, stopped and returned. "Gen'le*men*, sirs, to you. Mr. Mahch, escuse me by pyo accident earwhilin' yo' colloquial terms. I know e'zacly what cause yo' sick transit. Yass, seh. Thass the imagination. I've had it, myseff."

March stopped haughtily, Fair moved out of hearing, and Cornelius spoke low, with a sweet smile. "Yass, seh. You see the imagination o' yo' head is evil. You imaginin' somepm what ain't happm yit an' jiss like as not won't happm at all. But thass not why I seeks to interrup' you at this junction.

"Mr. Mahch, I'm impudize to espress to you in behalfs o' a vas' colo'ed constituency—but speakin' th'oo a small ban' o' they magnates with me as they sawt o' janizary chairman—that Gen'l Halliday seem to be

ti-ud o' us an' done paass his bes' dotage, an' likewise
the groun's an' debasements on an' faw which we be
proud to help you depopulate yo' lan's, yass, seh, with
all conceivable ligislation thereunto."

"What business is it of yours or your Blackland
darkies what I do with my woods?"

"Why, thass jess it! Whass nobody's business is
ev'ybody's business, you know."

March smiled and moved toward Fair. "I've no
time to talk with you now, Leggett."

"Oh! no, seh, I knowed you wouldn't have. But
bein' the talk' o' the town that you an' this young
gen'leman"—dipping low to Fair—"is projeckin' said
depopulization I has cawdially engross ow meaju' in
writin' faw yo' conjint an' confidential consideration.
Yass, seh, aw in default whereof then to compote it in
like manneh to the nex' mos' interested."

"And, pray, who is the next most interested in my
private property?"

"Why, Majo' Gyarnit, I reck'n—an' Mr. Ravenel,
seein' he's the Djuke o' Suez—p-he!"

March let his hand accept a soiled document, saying,
"Well, he's not Duke of me. Just leave me this. I'll
either mail it to you or see you again. Good-by."

The title of the document as indorsed on it was:
"The Suez and Three Counties Transportation, Immigration, Education, Navigation, and Construction Co."

## XXXIV.

### DAPHNE AND DINWIDDIE: A PASTEL IN PROSE

"Professor" Pettigrew had always been coldly indifferent to many things commonly counted chief matters of life. One of these was religion; another was woman. His punctuality at church at the head of Rosemont's cadets was so obviously perfunctory as to be without a stain of hypocrisy. Yet he never vaunted his scepticism, but only let it exhale from him in interrogative insinuations that the premises and maxims of religion were refuted by the outcome of the war. To woman his heart was as hard, cold, and polished as celluloid. Only when pressed did he admit that he regarded her as an insipid necessity. One has to have a female parent in order to get into this world—no gentleman admitted without a lady; and when one goes out of it again, it is good to leave children so as to keep the great unwashed from getting one's property. Property!—humph! he or his father, at least—he became silent.

He often saw Mrs. March in church, yet kept his heart. But one night a stereoptican lecture was given in Suez. In Mrs. March's opinion such things, unlike the deadly theatre, were harmful only when carried to excess. To keep John from carrying this one to excess—that is, from going to it with anybody else—she went with him, and they "happened"—I suppose an agnostic would say—to sit next to Dinwiddie Pettigrew. John being in a silent mood Daphne and Dinwiddie found time for much conversation. The hour fixed for the lecture was half-past seven. Promptly about half-past eight the audience began to arrive. At a quarter of nine it was growing numerous.

"Oh! no," said General Halliday to the lecturer, "don't you fret about them going home; they'll stay like the yellow fever"—and punctually somewhere about nine "The Great Love Stories of History" began to be told, and luminously pictured on a white cotton full moon.

With lights turned low and everybody enjoined to converse only in softest whispers, the conditions for spontaneous combustion were complete in many bosoms, and at the close of the entertainment Daphne Dalrymple, her own asbestos affections warmed, but not ignited, walked away with the celluloid heart of Dinwiddie Pettigrew in a light blaze.

---

## XXXV.

### A WIDOW'S ULTIMATUM

AT the time of which we would here speak the lover had made one call at Widewood, but had not met sufficient encouragement to embolden him to ask that the lovee would give, oh, give him back a heart so damaged by fire, as to be worthless except to the thief;

though his manner was rank with hints that she might keep it now and take the rest.

Mrs. March was altogether too sacred in her own eyes to be in haste at such a juncture. Her truly shrinking spirit was a stranger to all manner of auctioning, but she believed in fair play, and could not in conscience quite forget her exhilarating skirmish with Mr. Ravenel on the day of Susie's wedding.

It had not brought on a war of roses. Something kept him away from Widewood. Was it, she wondered, the noble fear that he might subject her to those social rumors that are so often all the more annoying because only premature? Ah, if he could but know how lightly she regarded such prattle! But she would not tell him, even in impersonal verse. On the contrary, she contributed to the *Presbyterian Monthly*—a non-sectarian publication—those lines—which caught one glance of so many of her friends and escaped any subsequent notice—entitled,

" Love-Proof.

"She pities much, yet laughs at Love
For love of laughter! Fadeless youth "—

But the simple fact is that Mr. Ravenel's flatteries, when rare chance brought him and the poetess together, were without purpose, and justified in his liberal mind by the right of every Southern gentleman to treat as irresistible any and every woman in her turn.—"Got to do something pleasant, Miss Fannie; can't buy her poetry."

On the evening when March received from Leggett
the draft of An Act Entitled, etc., the mother and son
sat silent through their supper, though John was longing to speak.   At last, as they were going into the front
room he managed to say :

"Well, mother, Fair's gone—goes to-night."

He dropped an arm about her shoulders.

"Oh!—when I can scarcely bear my own weight!"
She sank into her favorite chair and turned away from
his regrets, sighing,

"Oh, no, youth and health never do think."

The son sat down and leaned thoughtfully on the
centre-table.

"That's so!  They don't think; they're too busy
feeling."

"Ah, John, you don't feel!   I wish you could."

"Humph!  I wish I couldn't."  He smoothed off a
frown and let his palm fall so flat upon the bare
mahogany that a woman of less fortitude than Mrs.
March would certainly have squeaked.   "Mother, dear,
I believe I'll try to see how little I can feel and how
much I can think."

"Providence permitting, my reckless boy."

"Oh, bless your dear soul, mother, Providence'll be
only too glad! yes, I've a notion to try thinking.
Fact is, I've begun already.   Now, you love solitude——"

"Ah, John!"

"Well, at any rate, you can think best when you're
alone."

"O John!"

"Well, father could. I can't. I need to rub against men. You don't."

"Oh!—h—h—John!" But when Mrs. March saw the intent was only figurative she drew her lips close and dropped her eyes.

Her son reflected a minute and spoke again. "Why, mother, just that Yankee's being here peeping around and asking his scared-to-death questions has pulled my wits together till I wonder where they've been. Oh, it's so! It's not because he's a Yankee. It's simply because he's in with the times. He knows what's got to come and what's got to go, and how to help them do it so's to make them count! He belongs—pshaw—he belongs to a live world. Now, here in this sleepy old Dixie——"

"Has it come to that, John?"

"Yes, it has, and it's cost a heap sight more than it's come to, because I didn't let it come long ago. I wouldn't look plain truth in the face for fear of going back on Rosemont and Suez, and all the time I've been going back on Widewood!" The speaker smote the family Bible with Leggett's document. His mother wept.

"Oh! golly," mumbled John.

"Oh! my son!"

"Why, what's the trouble, mother?"

Mrs. March could not tell him. It was not merely his blasphemies. There seemed to be more hope of sympathy from the damaged ceiling, and she moaned up to it,

"My son a Radical!"

He sprang to his feet. "Mother, take that insult back! For your own sake, take it back! I hadn't a thought of politics. If my words implied it they played me false!"

Mrs. March was anguished wonder. "Why, what else could they mean?"

"Anything! I don't know! I was only trying to blurt out what I've been thinking out, concerning our private interests. For I've thought out and found out —these last few days—more things that can be done, and must be done, and done right off with these lands of ours——"

"O John! Is that your swift revenge?"

"Why, mother, dear! Revenge for what? Who on?"

"For nothing, John; on widowed, helpless me!"

"Great Scott! mother, as I've begged you fifty times, I beg you now again, just tell me what to do or undo."

"Please don't mock me, John. You're the dictator now, by the terms of the will. They give you the legal rights, and the legal rights are all that count—with men. I'm in your power."

John laughed. "I wish you'd tell the dictator what to do."

"Too late, my son, you've taken the counsel of your country's enemies." She rose to leave the room. The son slapped his thigh.

"'Pon my soul, mother, you must excuse me. Here's a letter.

"Has Jeff-Jack accepted another poem?" he asked, as she read. "I wish he'd pay for it."

She did not say, though the missive must have ended very kindly, for in spite of herself she smiled.

"Ah, John! your vanity is so large it can include even your mother. I wish I had some of it; I might believe what my friends tell me. But maybe it's vanity in me not to think they know best." She let John press her hand upon his forehead.

"I wish I could know," she continued. "I yearn for wise counsel. O son! why do we, both of us, so distrust and shun our one only common friend? He could tell us what to do, son; and, oh, how we need some one to tell us!"

John dropped the hand. "I don't need Jeff-Jack. He's got to need me."

"Oh, presumptuous boy! John, you might say **Mr.** Ravenel. He's old enough to be your father."

"No, he's not! At any rate, that's one thing he'll never be!"

The widow flared up. "I can say that, sir, without your prompting."

"Why, mother! Why, I no more intended——"

"John, spare me! Oh, no, you were brutal merely by accident! I thank you! I *must* thank you for pointing your unfeeling hints at the most invincib—I mean inveterate—bachelor in the three counties."

"Inveterate lover, you'd better say. He marries Fannie Halliday next March. The General's telling every Tom, Dick and Harry to-day."

"John, I don't believe it! It can't be! I know better!"

"I wish you did, but they told me themselves, away

last July, standing hand in hand.  Mother, he's got no more right to marry her——"

"Than you have!  And he knows it!  For John, John!  There never was a more pitiful or needless mismatch!  Why, he could have—but it's none of my business, only—" she choked.

"No, of course not," said the son, emotionally, "and it's none of mine, either, only—humph!"  He rose and strode about.  "Why she could just as easily——Oh, me!"  He jostled a chair.  Mrs. March flinched and burst into tears.

"Oh, good heavens!  mother, what have I done now?  I know I'm coarse and irreverent and wilful and surly and healthy, and have got the big-head and the Lord knows what!  But I swear I'll stop everything bad and be everything good if you'll just quit off sniv—weeping!"

Strange to say, this reasonable and practicable proposition did not calm either of them.

"I'll even go with you to Jeff-Jack and ask his advice—oh!  Jane-Anne-Maria!  *now* what's broke?"

"Only a mother's heart!"  She looked up from her handkerchief.  "Go seek his advice if you still covet it;  I never trusted him;  I only feared I might doubt him unjustly.  But now I know his intelligence, no less than his integrity, is beneath the contempt of a Christian woman.  I leave you to your books.  My bed——"

"O mother, I wasn't reading!  Come, stay;  I'll be as entertaining as a circus."

"I can't;  I'm all unstrung.  Let me go while I can still drag——"

John rose. A horse's tread sounded. "Now, who can that be?"

He listened again, then rolled up his fists and growled between his teeth.

"Cawnsound that foo'—mother, go on up stairs, I'll tell him you've retired."

"I shall do nothing so dishonorable. Why should you bury me alive? Is it because one friend still comes with no scheme for the devastation of our sylvan home?"

Before John could reply sunshine lighted the inquirer's face and she stepped forward elastically to give her hand to Mr. Dinwiddie Pettigrew.

When he was gone, Daphne was still as bland as May, for a moment, and even John's gravity was of a pleasant sort. "Mother, you're just too sweet and modest to see what that man's up to. I'm not. I'd like to tell him to stay away from here. Why, mother, he's—he's courting!"

The mother smiled lovingly. "My son, I'll attend to that. Ah me! suitors! They come in vain—unless I should be goaded by the sight of these dear Widewood acres invaded by the alien." She sweetened like a bride.

The son stood aghast. She lifted a fond hand to his shoulder. "John, do you know what heart hunger is? You're too young. I am ready to sacrifice anything for you, as I always was for your father. Only, I must reign alone in at least one home, one heart! Fear not; there is but one thing that will certainly drive me again into marriage."

"What's that, mother?"

"A daughter-in-law. If my son marries, I have no choice—I must!" She floated up-stairs.

----

## XXXVI.

### A NEW SHINGLE IN SUEZ

NEXT day—"John, didn't you rise very early this morning?"

"No, ma'am."

He had not gone to bed. Yet there was a new repose in his face and energy in his voice. He ate breakfast enough for two.

"Millie, hasn't Israel brought my horse yet?"

He came to where his mother sat, kissed her forehead, and passed; but her languorous eyes read, written all over him, the fact that she had drawn her cords one degree too tight, and that in the night something had snapped; she had a new force to deal with.

"John"—there was alarm in her voice—he had the door half open—"are you so cruel and foolish as to take last evening's words literally?"

"That's all gay, mother; 'tain't the parson I'm going after, it's the surveyor."

He shut the door on the last word and went away whistling. Not that he was merry; as his horse started he set his teeth, smote in the spurs, and cleared the paling fence at a bound.

The surveyors were Champion and Shotwell. John worked with them. To his own surprise he was the life of the party. Some nights they camped. They sang jolly songs together; but often Shotwell would say:

"O Champion, I'll hush if you will; we're scaring the wolves. Now, if you had such a voice as John's— Go on, March, sing 'Queen o' my Soul.'"

John would sing; Shotwell would lie back on the pine-needles with his eyes shut, and each time the singer reached the refrain, "Mary, Mary, queen of my soul," the impassioned listener would fetch a whoop and cry, "That's her!" although everybody had known that for years the only "her" who had queened it over Shotwell's soul was John's own Fannie Halliday.

"Now, March, sing, 'Thou wert the first, thou aht the layst,' an' th'ow yo' whole soul into it like you did last night!"

"John," said Champion once, after March had sung this lament, "You're a plumb fraud. If you wa'n't you couldn't sing that thing an' then turn round and sing, 'They laughed, ha-ha! and they quaffed, ha-ha!'"

"Let's have it!" cried Shotwell. Paass tin cups once mo', gen'le*men!*"—tink—tink—

"March," said Champion, "if you'll excuse the personality, what's changed you so?"

John laughed and said he didn't think he was changed, but if he was he reckoned it was evolution. Which did not satisfy Shotwell, who had "quaffed, ha-ha!" till he was argumentative.

"Don't you 'scuse personal'ty 't all, March. I know wha's change' you. 'Tain't no 'sperience. You ain't been converted. You're gettin' *ripe!* 'S all is about it. Wha' changes green persimmons? 's nature; 'tain't 'sperience."

"Well, I'd like to know if sunshine an' frost ain't experiences," retorted Champion.

"Some experiences," laughed John, "are mighty hot sunshine, and some are mighty hard frosts." To which the two old soldiers assented with more than one sentimental sigh as the three rolled themselves in their blankets and closed their eyes.

When the survey was done they made a large colored map of everything, and John kept it in a long tin tube —what rare times he was not looking at it.

"How short-sighted most men are! They'll have lands to dispose of and yet not have maps made! How the devil do they expect ever"—etc. Sometimes he smiled to himself as he rolled the gorgeous thing up, but only as we smile at the oddities of one whom we admire.

He opened an office. It contained a mantel-piece, a desk, four chairs, a Winchester rifle, and a box of cigars. The hearth and mantel-piece were crowded with specimens of earths, ores, and building stones, and of woods precious to the dyer, the manufacturer, the joiner and the cabinet-maker. Inside the desk lay the map whenever he was, and a revolver whenever he was not—"Out. Will be back in a few minutes."

On the desk's top were more specimens, three or four fat old books from Widewood, and on one corner, by the hour, his own feet, in tight boots, when he read Washington's Letters, Story on the Constitution, or the

Geology of Dixie. What interested Suez most of all
was his sign. It professed no occupation. "John
March." That was all it proclaimed, for a time, in gilt,
on a field of blue smalts. But one afternoon when he
was—"Out of town. Will be back Friday"—some
Rosemont boys scratched in the smalts the tin word,
Gentleman.

"Let it alone, John," said the next day's *Courier.*
"It's a good ad., and you can live up to it." It stayed.

---

## XXXVII.

### WISDOM AND FAITH KISS EACH OTHER

IT came to pass in those days that an effort to start a
religious revival issued from Suez "University." It
seems the "Black-and-Tannery," as the Rosemont boys
called it, was having such increase in numbers that its
president had thought well to give the national thanks-
giving day special emphasis on the devotional side.
Prayer for gifts of grace to crown these temporal good
fortunes extended over into a second and third evening,
black young women and tan young men asked to be
prayed for, the president "wired" glad news to the
board in New York, the board "wired" back, "Speak
unto the children of Israel that they go forward!"—just
ten words, economy is the road to commendation—meetings were continued, and the gray-headed black janitor,

richest man in the institution, leading in prayer, promised that if the Lord would "come down" then and
there, "right thoo de roof," he himself would pay for
the shingles!

Since corner-stone day the shabby-coated president
had not known such joy. In the chapel, Sunday morning, he read the story of the two lepers who found the
Syrian camp deserted in the siege of Samaria; and
preached from the text, "We do not well: this day is a
day of good tidings, and we hold our peace; . . .
So they came and called unto the porter of the city."
That afternoon he went to Parson Tombs. The pastor
was cordial, brotherly; full of tender gladness to hear of
the " manifestations." They talked a great while, were
pleased-with each other, and came to several kind and
unexpected agreements. They even knelt and prayed
together. As to the president's specific errand—his
proposal for a week of union revival meetings in Parson
Tomb's church, with or without the town congregation,
the "university students" offering to occupy only the
gallery—the pastor said that as far as *he* was concerned,
he was much disposed to favor it.

"Why, befo' the wa' ow slaves used to worship with
us; I've seen ow gallery half full of 'm! And we'd be
only too glad to see it so again—for we love 'em yet,
seh—if they wouldn't insist so on mixin' religion an'
politics. I'll consult some o' my people an' let you
know."

When he consulted his church officers that evening
only two replied approvingly. One of them was the
oldest, whitest haired man in the church. "Faw my

part," he said, " I don't think the churches air a-behav-
in' theyse'ves like Christians to the niggehs anywheres.
I jest know ef my Lawd an' Master was here in Dixie
now he'd not bless a single one of all these separations
between churches, aw in churches, unless it's the separa-
tion o' the sexes, which I'm pow'ful sorry to see that
broke up. I'm faw invitin' them people, dry-so, an' I
don't give a cent whether they set up-stairs aw down"
—which was true.

The other approving voice was young Doctor Grace.

" Brethren, I believe in separating worshippers by
race. But when, as now, this is so fully and amicably
provided for, I would have all come together, joined, yet
separated, to cry with one shout, ' Lord, revive us ! '
And he'll do it, brethren ! I feel it right here ! " He
put his hand on the exact spot.

Garnet spoke. " Brother Grace, you say the separa-
tion is fully provided for—where'll the white teachers
of our colored brethren sit ? If they sit down-stairs we
run the risk of offending some of our own folks ; if they
sit in the gallery that's a direct insult to the whole community. It'll not be stood. When colored mourners
come up to the front—h-they'll come in troops—where'll
you put 'em ? "

" I'd put them wherever there's room for them," was
the heroic reply.

"Oh, there'd be room for them everywhere," laughed
Garnet, "for as far as *our* young folks are concerned,
the whole thing would be a complete frazzle. Why,
you take a graceless young fellow, say like John March.
How are you going to get him to come up here and

kneel down amongst a lot of black and saddle-colored bucks and wenches?—I word it his way, you understand. No, sir, as sure as we try this thing, we'll create dissension—in a church where everything now is as sweet and peaceful as the grave."

"Of course we mustn't have dissensions," said Parson Tombs.

Mr. Usher, who spoke last and very slowly, said but a word or two. He agreed with Brother Garnet. And yet he believed this was a message from on high to be up and a-doin'. "This church, brethren, has jest *got* to be replaastered, an' *I* don't see how we goin' to do it 'ithout we have a outpourin' o' the spirit that'll give us mo' church membehs."

So the good parson dropped the matter, and saw how rightly he had followed the divine guidance when only a day or two later the "university" insulted and exasperated all Suez by enrolling three young white women from Sandstone. The *Courier*, regretting to state that this infringed no statute, deprecated all violence, and while it extolled the forbearance of the people, yet declared that an education which educated backward, and an institution which sought to elevate an inferior race by degrading a superior, would compel the people to make laws they would rather not enact. The Black-and-Tannery's effort for a union revival meeting lay at the door of "our church," said Garnet smilingly to Sister Proudfit, "as dead as Ananias." The kind pastor was troubled.

Yet he was gladdened again when Barbara, on horseback, brought word from "pop-a" that he had found half a dozen of his students praying together for the conversion of their fellows, and that the merest hint of revival meetings in Suez had been met by them with such zeal that he saw they were divinely moved. " Get thee up, brother," the Major's note ended, " for there is a sound of abundance of rain."

" Is it good news? " asked Barbara. The white-haired man handed her the note, joyfully, and stood at her saddle-bow watching her face as she gravely read it.

" Bless the Lord," he said, " and bless you, too, my daughter, faw yo' glad tidin's. I'll see Mary and Martha Salter and Doctor Grace right off, and get ready to ketch the blessed shower. May the very first droppin's fall on you, my beautiful child. I've heard what a wise an' blessed help you've been to yo' father since yo'—here lately. Ain't you a-goin' to give yo' heart to Jesus, daughter ? "

She met his longing look with the same face as before; not blankly, yet denying, asking, confessing nothing. Truth there, but no fact.

" Well, good-by," said the old man, " I believe you're nearer the kingdom now than you know." His awkward kindness brought her nearer still.

Thus the revival began at Rosemont. The two congregations joined counsel, and decided to hold the meetings in Parson Tombs's church.

" I'm proud, Brother Tombs—or, rather, I'm grateful," said Garnet. " I look on this as a divine vindication against the missionary solicitude of an alien institution's ambitious zeal. My brethren, it's a heavenly proof of the superior vitality of Southern Christianity."

But they decided not to begin at once. Mary Salter thought they should, and so did the unmarried pastor of the other church, who, they said, was " sweet on her."

" All we need is faith ! " said Miss Mary.

" No, it's not," was Miss Martha's calm response, " we need a little common sense." She said the two pastors ought to preach at least two Sunday sermons, each " pointed toward the projected—that is to say expected—showers of blessing."

"Sort o' take the people's temperature," put in Doctor Grace, but she ignored him. By that time, she said, it would be too near Christmas to start anything of the kind before——

" Why, Christmas, Sister Martha, think what Christmas is ? It ought to be just the time ! "

" Yes, but it isn't."

" I think Miss Martha's right," said Parson Tombs, very sweetly to Mary ; " and I think," turning as affectionately to Martha, " that Miss Mary's right, too. We need faith *and* wisdom. The Lord promises both, and so we must use all we can *uv* both. Now, if we can begin a couple of days before New Year, so's to have things agoin' by New Year's eve, I *think* we'll find that wisdom and faith have kissed each other."

Miss Martha and Sister Tombs smiled softly at the startling figure. Miss Mary and the unmarried pastor dropped their eyes. But when Doctor Grace said, fervently, "That sounds good ! " all admitted the excellence of Parson Tombs's suggestion.

## XXXVIII.

### RUBBING AGAINST MEN

ABOUT three in the afternoon on the last day of the year John March was in the saddle loping down from Widewood.

He was thinking of one of the most serious obstacles to the furtherance of his enterprise: the stubborn hostility of the Sandstone County mountaineers. To the gentlest of them it meant changes that would make game scarcer and circumscribe and belittle their consciously small and circumscribed lives; to the wilder sort it meant an invasion of aliens who had never come before for other purpose than to break up their stills and drag them to jail. As he came out into the Susie and Pussie pike he met a frowsy pinewoodsman astride a mule, returning into the hills.

"Howdy, Enos." They halted.

"Howdy, Johnnie. Well, ef you ain't been a-swappin' critters ag'n, to be sho'! Looks mighty much like you a-chawed this time, less'n this critter an' the one you had both deceives they looks a pow'ful sight."

John expressed himself unalarmed and asked the news.

"I ain't pick up much news in the Susie," said Enos. "Jeff-Jack's house beginnin' to look mos' done. Scan'lous fine house! Mawnstus hayndy, havin' it jined'n' right on, sawt o', to old Halliday's that a way.

Johnnie, why don't *you* marry? You kin do it; the gal fools ain't all peg out yit."

" No," laughed John, " nor they ain't the worst kind, either."

" Thass so ; the wuss kine'is the fellers 'at don't marry 'em. Why, ef I was you, I'd have a wife as pooty as a speckle' hound pup, an' yit one 'at could build biscuits an' cook coffee, too! An' I'd jess quile down at home in my sock feet an' never git up, lessen it wus to eat aw go to bed. I wouldn't be a cavortin' an' projeckin' aroun' to settle up laynds which they got too many set- tlehs on 'em now, an' ef you bring niggehs we'll kill 'em, an' ef you bring white folks we'll make 'em wish they was dead."

The two men smiled good-naturedly. March knew every word bespoke the general spirit of Enos's neigh- bors and kin ; men who believed the world was flat and would trust no man who didn't ; who, in their own for- ests, would shoot on sight any stranger in store clothes ; who ate with their boots off and died with them on.

" Reckon I got to risk it," said John ; " can't always tell how things 'll go."

" Thass so," drawled Enos. " An' yit women folks seem like evm they think they kin. I hear Grannie Sugg, a-ridin' home fum church, 'llow ef Johnnie March bring air railroad 'ithin ten mile' o' her, he better leave his medjer 'ith the coffin man."

" Tell her howdy for me, will you, Enos ? " said John ; and Enos said he would.

Deeply absorbed, but clear in bloody resolve, March walked his horse down the turnpike in the cold sunshine and blustering air. He heard his name and looked back ; had he first recognized the kindly voice he would not have turned, but fled, like a partlet at sight of the hawk, from Parson Tombs.

"Howdy, John ! Ought to call you Mister March, I reckon, but you know I never baptized you Mister." They moved on together. " How's yo' maw ? "

John said she was about as usual and asked after the parson's folks.

" O they all up, thank the Lawd. Mr. March, this is the Lawd's doin' an' mahvellous in ow eyes, meetin' up with you this way. I was prayin' faw it as I turned the bend in the road ! He's sent me to you, Mr. March, I feel it ! "

March showed distress, but the parson continued bright.

" I jest been up to get Brother Garnet to come he'p us in ow protracted meet'n', an' to arrange to let the college boys come when they begin school ag'in, day after to-morrow. Mr. March, I wish you'd come, won't you ? to-night ! "

" I couldn't very well come to-night, Mr. Tombs. I —I approve of such meetings. I think it's a very pleasant way to pass—" he reddened. " But I'm too busy——"

" This is business, Mr. March ! The urgentest kind ! It's the spirit's call ! It may never call again, brotheh ! What if in some more convenient season Gawd should mawk when yo' fear cometh ? "

The young man drooped like a horse in the rain, and the pastor, mistaking endurance for contrition, pressed his plea. "You know, the holy book says, Come, faw *all* things ah *now* ready; it don't say *all* things will ever be ready again! The p'esumption is they won't! O my dear young brotheh, there's a wrath to come—real—awful—everlasting—O flee from it! Come to the flowing fountain! One plunge an' yo' saved! Johnnie—do I make too free? I've been prayin' faw you by name faw years!"

"O you hadn't ought to have done that, sir! I wa'n't worth it."

"Ah! yes you air! Johnnie, I've watched yo' ev'y step an' stumble all yo' days. I've had faith faw you when many a one was sayin' you was jess bound to go to the bad—which you know it did look that way, brotheh. But, s' I, Satan's a-siftin' of him! He's in the gall o' bitterness jess as I was at his age!"

"You! Ha-ha! Why, my dear Mr. Tombs, you don't know who you're talking about!"

"Yes, I do, brotheh. I was jess so! An' s' I, he'll pull through! His motheh's prayers 'll prevail, evm if mine don't! An' now, when ev'ybody sees you a-changin' faw the better——"

"Better! Great Sc——"

"Yes, an' yet 'ithout the least sign o' conversion—I say, s' I, it's restrainin' grace! Ah! don't I know? Next 'll come savin' grace, an' then repentance unto life. Straight is the way, an' I can see right up it!"

"Why, Mr. Tombs, you're utterly wrong! I've only learned a little manners and a little sense. All that's ever restrained me, sir, was lack of sand. The few bad things I've kept out of, I kept out of simply because I knew if I went into 'em I'd bog down. It's not a half hour since I'd have liked first-rate to be worse than I am, but I didn't have the sand for that, either. Why, sir, I'm worse to-day than I ever was, only it's deeper hid. If men went to convict camps for what they are, instead of what they do, I'd be in one now."

"Conviction of sin! Praise Gawd, brotheh, you've got it! O bring it to-night to the inquirer's seat!"

But the convicted sinner interrupted, with a superior smile : " I've no inquiries to offer, Mr. Tombs. I know the plan of salvation, sir, perfectly! We're all totally depraved, and would be damned on Adam's account if we wa'n't, for we've lost communion with God and are liable to all the miseries of this life, to death itself, and the pains of hell forever; but God out of his mere good pleasure having elected some to everlasting life, the rest of us—O I know it like a-b-c! Mother taught it to me before I could read. Yes, I must, with grief and hatred of my sin, turn from it unto God—certainly—because God, having first treated the innocent as if he were guilty, is willing now to treat the guilty as if he were innocent, which is all right because of God's sovereignty over us, his propriety in us, and the zeal he hath for his own worship—O——

" But, Mr. Tombs, what's the use, sir? Some things I can repent of, but some I can't. I'm expecting a letter to-day tha'll almost certainly be a favorable answer to an extensive proposition I've made for opening up my whole tract of land. Now, I've just been told by one of my squatters that if I bring settlers up there he'll kill 'em; and I know and you know he speaks for all of

them. Well, d' you s'pose I won't kill him the
minute he lifts a hand to try it?" The speaker's
eyes widened pleasantly. He resumed:

"There's another man down here. He's set his
worm-eaten heart on something—perfect right to do it.
I've no right to say he sha'n't. But I do. I'm just
*honing* to see him to tell him that if he values his health
he'll drop that scheme at the close of the year, which
closes to-day."

"O John, is that what yo' father—I don't evm say
yo' pious mother—taught you to be?"

"No, sir; my father begged me to be like my mother.
And I tried, sir, I tried hard! No use; I had to quit.
Strange part is I've got along better ever since. But
now, s'pose I should repent these things. 'Twouldn't
do any good, sir. For, let me tell you, Mr. Tombs,
underneath them all there's another matter—you can't
guess it—please don't try or ask anybody else—a matter
that I can't repent, and wouldn't if I could! Well,
good-day, sir, I'm sure I reciprocate your——"

"Come to the meeting, my brotheh. You love yo'
motheh. Do it to please her."

"I don't know; I'll see," replied John, with no intention of seeing, but reflecting with amused self-censure
that if anything he did should visibly please his mother,
such a result would be, at any rate, unique.

# XXXIX.

## SAME AFTERNOON

Suez had never seen so busy a winter. Never before in the same number of weeks had so much cotton been hauled into town or shipped from it. Goods had never been so cheap, gross sales so large, or Blackland darkeys and Sandstone crackers so flush.

And naturally the prosperity that worked downward had worked upward all the more. Rosemont had a few more students than in any earlier year; Montrose gave her young ladies better molasses; the white professors in the colored "university," and their wives, looked less starved; and General Halliday, in spite of the fact that he was part owner of a steamboat, had at last dropped the title of "Agent." Even John March had somehow made something.

Barbara, in black, was shopping for Fannie. Johanna was at her side. The day was brisk. Ox-wagons from Clearwater, mule-teams from Blackland, bull-carts from Sandstone, were everywhere. Cotton bales were being tumbled, torn, sampled, and weighed; products of the truck-patch and door-yard, and spoils of the forest, were changing hands. Flakes of cotton blew about under the wheels and among the reclining oxen. In the cold upper blue the buzzards circled, breasted the wind, or turned and scudded down it. From chimney tops the smoke darted hither and yon, and went to shreds in the cedars and evergreen oaks. On one small space of sidewalk which was quiet, Johanna found breath and utterance.

"Umph! dis-yeh town is busy. Look like jess ev'y-body a-makin' money." She got her mistress to read a certain sign for her. "Jawn Mawch, Gen'lemun! — k-he-he!—dass a new kine o' business. An' yit, Miss Barb, I heah Gen'l Halliday tell Miss Fannie 'istiddy dat Mr. Mawch done come out ahade on dem-ah tele-graph pole' what de contractors done git sicken' on an' th'ow up. He mus' be pow'ful smart, dat Mr. Mawch; ain't he, Miss Barb?"

"I don't know," murmured Barbara; "anybody can make money when everybody's making it." She bent her gaze into a milliner's window.

The maid eyed her anxiously. There were growing signs that Barbara's shopping was not for the bride-elect only, but for herself also, and for a long journey and a longer absence.

"Miss Barb, yondeh Mr. Mawch. Miss Barb, he de hayn'somess mayn in de three counties!"

"Ridiculous! Come, make haste." Haste was a thing they were beginning to make large quantities of in Suez. It has some resemblance to speed.

"Miss Garnet, pardon me." March gave the Rose-mont bow, she gave the Montrose. "Don't let me stop you, please." He caught step.

"Is General Halliday in town? I suppose, of course, you've seen Miss Fannie this morning?" His boyish eyes looked hungry for a little teasing. She stopped in a store doorway. Her black garb heightened the charm

of her red-brown hair, and of the countenance ready
enough for laughter, yet well content without it.

" Yes. I'm shopping for her now." Her smiling lip
implied the coming bridal, but her eyes told him teasing
was no longer in order. General Halliday was in
Blackland, she said, but would be back by noon.
March gave the Rosemont bow, she gave the Montrose,
Johanna unconsciously courtesied.

In the post-office John found two letters. One he
saw instantly was from Leggett. He started for his office, opening the other, which was post-marked Boston.
It ran:

" MY DEAR MR. MARCH.—My father has carefully
considered your very clear and elaborate plan, and,
while he freely admits his judgment may be wrong, he
deems it but just to be perfectly frank with you."

The reader's step ceased. A maker of haste jostled
him. He did not know it. His heart sank; he lost
the place on the page. He leaned against an awning-
post and read on:

" He feels bound to admire a certain masterly inven-
tiveness and courage in your plan, but is convinced it
will cost more than you estimate, and cannot be made
at the same time safe and commercially remunerative."

There was plenty more, but the wind so ruffled the
missive that, with unlifted eyes, he folded it. He looked
across the corner of the court-house square to his office,
whose second month's rent was due, and the first month's
not yet paid. He saw his bright blue sign with the
uncommercial title, which he had hoped to pay the

painter for to-day.   For, nad his proposition been accepted, the letter was to have contained a small remit-
tance.   A gust of wind came scurrying round the post-
office corner.   Dust, leaves, and flakes of cotton rose on
its wave, and—ah!—his hat went with them.

Johanna's teeth flashed in soft laughter as she waited
in a doorway.   " Run," she whispered, " run, Mr. Jawn
Mawch, Gen'lemun.   You so long gitt'n' to de awffice
hat cayn't wait.   Yass, betteh give it up.   Bresh de
ha'r out'n  yo' eyes an' let dat-ah niggeh-felleh ketch it.
K-he!   I 'clare, dat's de mos' migracious hat I eveh
see!   Niggeh got it!   Dass right, Mr. Mawch, give de
naysty niggeh a dime.   Po' niggeh!   now run tu'n yo'
dime into cawn-juice."

At his desk March read again:

" We appreciate  the  latent  value of  your  lands.
Time must bring changes which will liberate that value
and make it commercial; but it was more a desire to
promote these changes than any belief in their nearness
which prompted my father's gifts to Rosemont College
and Suez University.   Not that he shares the current
opinion that you are having too much politics.   Progress and thrift may go side by side with political storms,
and I know he thinks your State would be worse off to-
day if it could secure a mere political calm.

" In reply to your generous invitation to suggest
changes in your plan, I will myself venture one or two
questions.

" First—Is not the elaborateness of your plan an argument against it?   Dixie is not a new, wild country; and
therefore does not your scheme—to establish not only

mines, mills and roads, but stores, banks, schools and churches under the patronage and control of the company—imply that as a community and commonwealth you are, in Dixie, in a state of arrested development?

" Else why propose to do through a private commercial corporation what is everywhere else done through public government—by legislation, taxation, education, and courts? Cannot—or will not—your lawmakers and taxpayers give you their co-operation ?

"The spirit of your plan is certainly beyond criticism. It seeks a common welfare. It does not offer swift enrichment to the moneyed few through the use of ignorant labor unlifted from destitution and degradation, but rather the remuneration of capital through the social betterment of all the factors of a complete community. But will the plan itself pay? Have not the things around you which paid been those which cared little if savings-bank, church or school lived or died, or whether laws or customs favored them ?

" Suppose that on your own lands your colony should seem for a time to succeed, would you not be an island in an ocean of misunderstanding and indifference? If you should need an act of county or township legislation, could you get it? Is this not why capital seeks wilder and more distant regions when it would rather be in Dixie?

" I make these points not for their own sake, but to introduce a practical suggestion which my father is tempted to submit to you. And this, it may surprise you to find, is based upon the contents of the paper handed you as I was leaving Suez, by the colored man, Leggett, whose peculiar station doubtless makes it easy for him to see relations and necessities which better or wiser men, from other points of view, might easily overlook.

"This man would make your scheme as public as you would make it private, and my father is inclined to think that if public interest, action, and credit could be enlisted as suggested in Leggett's memorandum, your problem would have new attractions much beyond its present merely problematic interest, and might find financial backers. Alliance with Leggett is, of course, out of the question; but if you can consent and undertake to exploit your lands on the line of operation sketched by him we can guarantee the pecuniary support necessary to the effort, and you may at once draw on us at sight for the small sum mentioned in your letter, if your need is still urgent. With cordial regard,

"Yours faithfully,

"HENRY FAIR."

March started up, but sat again and gazed at the missive.

"Well, I will swear!" He smiled, held it at arm's length, and read again facetiously. "'Alliance with Leggett is, of course, out of the question; but if you can consent and undertake to exploit your lands on the line of operation sketched by him——'

"Now, where's that nigger's letter?—I wonder if I—" a knock at the door—" come in!—could have dropped it when my hat—O come in—ha! ha!—this isn't a private bedroom; I'm dressed."

## XL.

### ROUGH GOING

"Ah! Mr. Pettigrew, why'n't you walk right in, sir? I wasn't at prayer."

Mr. Pettigrew, his voice made more than usually ghostly by the wind and a cold, whispered that he thought he had heard conversation.

"O no, sir, I was only blowing up my assistant for losing a letter. Why, well, I'll be dog— You picked it up in the street, didn't you? Well, Mr. Pettigrew, I'm obliged to you, sir. Will you draw up a chair. Take the other one, sir; I threw that one at a friend the other day and broke it."

As the school-teacher sat down John dragged a chair close and threw himself into it loungingly but with tightly folded arms. Dinwiddie hitched back as if unpleasantly near big machinery. John smiled.

"I'm glad to see you, Mr. Pettigrew. I've been wanting a chance to say something to you for some time, sir."

Pettigrew whispered a similar desire.

"Yes, sir," said John, and was silent. Then: "It's about my mother, sir. Your last call was your fourth, I believe." He frowned and waited while the pipe-clay of Mr. Pettigrew's complexion slowly took the tint of old red sandstone. Then he resumed: "You used to tell us boys it was our part not so much to accept the protection of the laws as to protect them—from their own mistakes no less than from the mistakes of those who owe them reverence—much as it becomes the part of a man to protect his mother. Wasn't that it?"

The school-master gave a husky assent.

"Well, Mr. Pettigrew, I'm a man, now, at least bodily —I think. Now, I'm satisfied, sir, that you hold my mother in high esteem—yes, sir, I'm sure of that—don't try to talk, sir, you only irritate your throat. I know you think as I do, sir, that one finger of her little faded hand is worth more than the whole bad lot of you and me, head, heart, and heels."

The listener's sub-acid smile protested, but John—

"I believe she thinks fairly well of you, sir, but she doesn't really know you. With me it's just the reverse. Hm! Yes, sir. You know, Mr. Pettigrew, my dear mother is of a highly wrought imaginative temperament. Now, I'm not. She often complains that I've got no more romance in my nature than my dear father had. She idealizes people. I can't. But the result is I can protect her against the mistakes such a tendency might even at this stage of life lead her into, for they say the poet's heart never grows old. You understand."

The school-master bowed majestically.

"My mother, Mr. Pettigrew, can never love where she can't idealize, nor marry where she can't love; she's too true a woman for that. I expect you to consider this talk confidential, of course. Now, I don't know, sir, that she could ever idealize you, but against the bare possibility that she might, I must ask you not to call again. Hm! That's all, sir."

Mr. Pettigrew rose up ashen and as mad as an adder. His hair puffed out, his eyes glistened. John rose more leisurely, stepped to the hearth, picked up a piece of box stuff and knocked a nail out of one end.

"I'll only add this, sir: If you don't like the terms, you can have whatever satisfaction you want. But I remember "—he produced a large spring-back dirk-knife, sprung it open and began curling off long parings from the pine stick—"that in college, when any one of us vexed you, you took your spite out on us, and generally on me, in words. That's all right. We were boys and couldn't hold malice." A shaving fell upon Mr. Pettigrew's shoulder and stayed there. "But once or twice your venomous contempt came near including my father's name. Still that's past, let it go. But now, if you do take your spite out in words be careful to let them be entirely foreign to the real subject, and be dead sure not to involve any name but mine. Or else don't begin till you've packed your trunk and bought your railroad ticket; and you'd better have a transatlantic steamer ticket, too."

Mr. Pettigrew had drawn near the door. With his hand on it he hissed, "You'll find this is not the last of this, sir."

"I reckon it is," drawled John, with his eyes on his whittling. As the door opened and shut he put away his knife, and was taking his hat when his eye fell upon Cornelius's letter. He opened and read it.

The writing was Leggett's, but between the lines could be caught a whisper that was plainly not the mulatto's.

He was ready, he wrote, "to interjuce an' suppote that bill to create the Three Counties Colonization Company, Limited—which I has fo shawten its name an takened out the tucks.  The sed company will buy yo whole Immense Track, paying for the same one third $\frac{1}{3}$ its own stock—another one third $\frac{1}{3}$ to be subscribened by private parties—an the res to be takened by the three counties and paid for in Cash to the sed Company Limited—which the sed cash to be raised by a special tax to be voted by the People.  This money shell be used by the sed Company Limited to construc damns an sich eloquent an discomojus impertinences which then they kin sell the sed lans an impertinences to immigraters factorians an minors an in that means pay divies on the Stock an so evvybody get mo or less molasses on his finger an his vote Skewered.  Thattle fetch white immigration an thattle ketch the white-liner's vote.  But where some dever an as soon as any six miles square shell contain twenty white childen of school Age the sed Company Limited shell be boun to bill an equip for them a free school house.  An faw evvy school house so billden sed Company Limited shell be likewise boun to bill another sommers in the three Counties where a equal or greater number of collared children are without one.  Thattle skewer the white squatter and Nigger vote."

The next clause—there was only a line or two besides —brought an audible exclamation from the reader: "Lassly faw evvy sich school house so bilt the sed Co. Limited shell pay a sum not less than its cost to some white male college in the three counties older then the sed Company Limited."

John marvelled.  What was Garnet doing or promising, that Leggett should thus single out Rosemont for subsidies?  And who was this in the letter's closing line

—certainly not Garnet—who would " buy both fists full " of stock as soon as the bill should pass? He stepped out and walked along the windy street immersed in thought.

" John !"—General Halliday beckoned to him. The General and Proudfit were pushing into the lattice doors of a fragrant place whose bulletin announced " Mock Turtle Soup and Venison for Lunch To-day." March joined them. " Had your lunch, John? I heard you were looking for me."

" Well, yes, but there's no hurry." The three stood and ate, talking over incidents of war times, with John at a manifest disadvantage, and presently they passed from the luncheon trestles to the bar.

" No, Proudfit, if Garnet hadn't come in on our left just then and charged the moment he did we'd have lost the whole battery. Garnet was a poor soldier in camp, you're right ; but on the field you'd only to tease him and he'd fight like a wild bull."

They drank, lighted cigars, and sauntered out toward the General's office. " John, I've read what you wrote me. I can't see it. We'll never colonize any lands in Dixie, my boy, till we've changed the whole system of laws under which we rent land and raise crops. You might as well try to farm swamp lands without draining them."

" Why, General, my scheme doesn't include planta-tions at all."

" Yes, it does; Dixie's a plantation State, and you can't make your little patch of it prosper till our plant-ing prospers—can he, Proudfit ? "

The Colonel laughed. " No go, General ; I'm not

going to side with you. Our prosperity, all around,
hangs on the question whether you and the darkey may
tax us and spend the taxes as you please, or we shall
tax ourselves and spend the taxes as we please."

" Ah, Proudfit, you mean whether you may keep the
taxes low enough to hold the darky down or let them
be raised high enough to lift him up. Walk in, gentlemen. Proudfit, take the rocking-chair."

But the Colonel stood trying to return the General's
last thrust, and John was bored. "General, all I want
to see you about is to say that I'm going down into
Blackland in a day or two to get as many darkies as I
can to settle on my lands, and if you'll tell me the ones
that are in your debt, I'll have nothing to do with them
unless it is to tell them they've got to stay where they
are."

Proudfit whirled and stared. The General gave a
low laugh.

" Why, John, that sounds mighty funny to come from
you. Would you do such a thing as that?—run off
with another man's niggers?"

John bit his lip and looked at his cigar. "Are they
yours, General?"

" By Jove! my son, they're not yours! O! of course,
you've got the legal—pshaw! I'm not going to dispute
an abstraction with you. Go and amuse yourself; you
can't get 'em; the niggers that don't owe won't go;
that's the poetry of it. I'd rather you'd take the fellows that owe than the one's that don't; but you won't
get either kind."

" I can try, General."

"No, sir, you can't!" exclaimed Proudfit. His cigar went into the fireplace with a vicious spat, and his eyes snapped. "Ow niggehs ah res'less an' discontented enough now, and whether you'll succeed aw not you shan't come 'round amongst them tryin' to steal them away! Damned if we don't run you out of the three counties! So long, General!" He went by March to the door.

John stood straight, his jaws set, chin up, eyes down. Halliday, by grimaces, was adjuring him to forbear. "But, Colonel Proudfit," he said—Proudfit paused— "you'll not insist on the word 'steal?'"

"You can call it what you damn please, sir, but you mustn't do it." The speaker passed out, leaving the door invitingly ajar.

The General caught John's arm—"Wait, I want to see you."

"I'll be back in a minute, General."

"My boy, the grave's full of nice fellows going to be back in a minute. Son John, there's only one thing I'm thoroughly ashamed of you for——"

"I can see you half a dozen better, General; let me go."

"You've no need to go; Proudfit's coming right back; he's only gone for his horse. There's plenty of time to hear the little I've got to say. John March, I'm ashamed of this reputation you've got for being quick on the trigger. O, you're much admired for it— by both sexes! Ye gods! John, isn't it pitiful to see a fellow like you not able to keep a kindly contempt for the opinion of fools! My dear boy—my dear boy!

you'll never be worth powder enough to blow you to the devil till you've learned to let the sun go down on your wrath!"

John smiled and dropped his eyes, and the General, with an imperative gesture detaining some one at the young man's back, spoke on. "John, the old year's dying. For God's sake let it die in peace. Yes, and for your own sake, and for the sake of us old murderers of the years long dead, let as many old things as will die with it. I don't say bury anything alive—that's not my prescription; but ease their righteous death and give them a grave they'll stay in."

"General, all right! the Colonel may go for the present, but I'll tell you now, and I'll soon show him, that whatever the laws of my State give me leave to do I'll do if I choose, even if it's to help black men do what white men say shan't be done." John reached behind him for the latch.

His mentor smiled queerly. "Yes, even if it's to float a scheme drawing twice as much water as we've got on our political sandbar. Ah! John March, don't you know that the law's permission is never enough? Better get all the permissions you can, and turn your 'I' into the most multitudinous 'we' you can possibly make it. Seven legislatures can't dig you too much channel."

March's reply was cut short by a voice behind him, which said:

"You can have the *Courier's* permission."

As John wheeled about, Jeff-Jack came a step forward and Barbara Garnet shrank against a window.

" Well, Miss Garnet," laughed March, as Ravenel conversed with Halliday, " I *was* absorbed, wa'n't I? You and Miss Fannie going to watch the old year out and the new year in to-night?"

" No, sir, we're only going to the revival meeting," replied Barbara, with mellow gravity. " All bad people are cordially invited, you know. I reckon I've got to be there."

"Why, Miss Garnet, my name's Legion, too. I didn't know we were such close kin." He said good-day and departed, mildly wondering what the next incident would be. The retiring year seemed to be rushing him through a great deal of unfinished business.

---

## XLI.

### SQUATTER SOVEREIGNTY

It was really a daring stroke, so to time the revival that the first culmination of interest should be looked for on New Year's eve. On that day business, the dry sorts, would be apt to decline faster than the sun, and the nearness of New Year would make men—country buyers and horsemen in particular—social, thirsty, and adventurous.

In fact, by the middle of the afternoon the streets around the court-house square were wholly given up to the white male sex. One man had, by accident, shot his own horse. Another had smashed a window, also by accident, and clearly the fault of the bar-keeper, who shouldn't have dodged. Men, and youths of men's stature, were laying arms about each other's necks, advising one another, with profanely affectionate assumptions of superiority, to come along home, promising on triple oath to do so after one more drink, and breaking forth at unlooked-for moments in blood-curdling yells. Three or four would take a fifth or seventh stirrup cup, mount, start home, ride round the square and come tearing up to the spot they had started from, as if they knew and were showing how they brought the good news from Ghent to Aix, though beyond a prefatory catamount shriek, the only news any of them brought was that he could whip anything of his size, weight and age in the three counties. The Jews closed their stores.

Proudfit had gone home. Enos had met a brother and a cousin, and come back with them. John March, with his hat on, sat alone at his desk with Fair's and Leggett's letters pinned under one elbow, his map under the other, and the verbal counsels of Enos, General Halliday, and Proudfit droning in his ears. He sank back with a baffled laugh.

He couldn't change a whole people's habit of thought, he reflected. Even the *Courier* followed the popular whim by miles and led it only by inches. So it seemed, at least. And yet if one should try to make his scheme a public one and leave the *Courier* out—imagine it!

And must the *Courier*, then, be invited in? Must

everybody and his nigger "pass their plates?" Ah! how had a few years—a few months—twisted and tangled the path to mastership! Through what thickets of contradiction, what morasses of bafflement, what unimperial acceptance of help and counsel did that path now lead! And this was no merely personal fate of his. It was all Dixie's. He would never change his politics; O no! But how if men's politics, asking no leave of their owners, change themselves, and he who does not change ceases to be steadfast?

Behold! All the way down the Swanee River, spite of what big levees of prevention and draining wheels of antiquated cure, how invincibly were the waters of a new order sweeping in upon the "old plantation."

And still the old plantation slumbered on below the level of the world's great risen floods of emancipations and enfranchisements whereon party platforms, measures, triumphs, and defeats only floated and eddied, mere drift-logs of a current from which they might be cast up, but could not turn back.

He bent over the desk. "Jove!" was all he said; but it stood for the realization of the mighty difference between the map under his eyes and what he was under oath to himself to make it. What "lots" of men— not mountaineers only, but Blacklanders, too—had got to change their notions—notions stuck as fast in their belief as his mountains were stuck in the ground— before that map could suit him. To think harder, he covered his face with his hands. The gale rattled his window. He failed to hear Enos just outside his door, alone and very drunk, prying off the tin sign of John

March, Gentleman.  He did not hear even the soft click of the latch or the yet softer footsteps that brought the drunkard close before his desk ; but at the first word he glanced up and found himself covered with a revolver.

"Set still," drawled Enos.  In his left hand was the tin sign.  "This yeh trick looked ti-ud a-tellin' lies, so I fotch it in."

Without change of color—for despair stood too close for fear to come between—John fixed his eyes upon the drunken man's and began to rise.  The weapon followed his face up.

"Enos, point that thing another way or I'll kill you."  He took a slow step outward from the desk, the pistol following with a drunken waver more terrible than a steady aim.  Enos spoke along its barrel, still holding up the sign.

"Is this little trick gwine to stay fetch in?  Say 'yass, mawsteh,' aw I blow yo' head off.'"

But John still held the drunkard's eye.  As he took up from his desk a large piece of ore, he said, "Enos, when a man like you leaves a gentleman's door open, the gentleman goes and shuts it himself."

"Yass, you bet!  So do a niggah.  Shell I shoot, aw does you 'llow——"

"I'm going to shut the door, Enos.  If you shoot me in the back I swear I'll kill you so quick you'll never know what hurt you."  With the hand that held the stone, while word followed word, the speaker made a slow upward gesture.  But at the last word the stone dropped, the pistol was in March's hand, it flashed up and then down, and the drunkard, blinded and sinking from a frightful blow of the weapon's butt, was dragging his foe with him to the floor. Down they went, the pistol flying out of reach, March's knuckles at Enos's throat and a knee on his breast.

" 'Nough," gasped the mountaineer, " 'nough ! "

" Not yet ! I know you too well ! Not till one of us is dead ! " John pressed the throat tighter with one hand, plunged the other into his pocket, and drew and sprung his dirk. The choking man gurgled for mercy, but March pushed back his falling locks with his wrist and lifted the blade. There it hung while he cried,

" O if you'd only done this sober I'd end you ! I wish to God you wa'n't drunk ! "

" 'Nough, Johnnie, 'nough ! You air a gentleman, Johnnie, sir."

" Will you nail that sign up again ? "

" Yass."

The knife was shut and put away, and when Enos gained his feet March had him covered with his magazine rifle. " Pick that pistol up wrong end first and hand it to me ! Now my hat ! 'Ever mind yours ! Now that sign."

The corners of the tin still held two small nails.

" Now stand back again." March thrust a finger into his vest-pocket. " I had a thumb-tack." He found it. " Now, Enos, I'll tack this thing up myself. But you'll stand behind me, sir, so's if anyone shoots he'll hit you first, and if you try to get away or to uncover me in the least bit, or if anybody even cocks a gun, you die right there, sir. Now go on ! "

The sun was setting as they stepped out on the sidewalk. The mail hour had passed. The square and the streets around it were lonely. The saloons themselves were half deserted. In one near the *Courier* office there was some roystering, and before it three tipsy horsemen were just mounting and turning to leave town by the pike. They so nearly hid Major Garnet and Parson Tombs coming down the sidewalk on foot some distance beyond, that March did not recognize them. At Weed and Usher's Captain Champion joined the Major and the parson. But John's eye was on one lone man much nearer by, who came riding leisurely among the trees of the square, looking about as if in search of some one. He had a long, old-fashioned rifle.

"Wait, Enos, there's your brother. Stand still."

John levelled his rifle just in time. "Halt! Drop that gun! Drop it to the ground or I'll drop you!" The rifle fell to the earth. "Now get away! Move!" The horseman wheeled and hurried off under cover of the tree-trunks.

"Gentlemen!" cried Parson Tombs, "there'll be murder yonder!" He ran forward.

"Brother Tombs," cried Garnet, walking majestically after him, "for Heaven's sake, stop! you can't prevent anything that way." But the old man ran on.

Champion, with a curse at himself for having only a knife and a derringer, flew up a stair and into the *Courier* office.

"Lend me something to shoot with, Jeff-Jack, the Yahoos are after John March."

Ravenel handed from a desk-drawer, that stood open

close to his hand, a six-shooter. Champion ran down-stairs. Ravenel stepped, smiling, to a window.

March had turned his back and was putting up the sign, pressing the nails into their former places with his thumb. Men all about were peeping from windows and doors. Champion ran to the nearest tree in the square and from behind it peered here and there to catch sight of the dismounted horseman, who was stealing back to his gun.

"Keep me well covered, you lean devil," growled John to Enos, "or I'll shoot you without warning!" Working left-handed, he dropped the thumb-tack. With a curse between his teeth he stooped and picked it up, but could not press it firmly into place. He leaned his rifle against the door-post, drew the revolver and used its butt as a hammer. Champion saw an elbow bend back from behind a tree. The moun-taineer's brother had recovered his gun and was aiming it. The captain fired and hit the tree. March whirled upon Enos with the revolver in his face, the drunkard flinched violently when not to have flinched would have saved both lives, and from the tree-trunk that Champion had struck a rifle puffed and cracked. March heard the spat of a bullet, and with a sudden horrid widening of the eyes Enos fell into his bosom.

"Great God! Enos, your brother didn't mean to——"

The only reply was a fixing of the eyes, and Enos slid through his arms and sank to the pavement dead.

Champion had tripped on a root and got a cruel fall, losing his weapon in a drift of leaves; but as the brother of Enos was just capping his swiftly reloaded gun—

"Throw up your hands!" cried Parson Tombs, laying his aged eye along the sights of March's rifle; the hands went up and in a moment were in the clutch of the town marshal, while a growing crowd ran from the prisoner and from Champion to John March, who knelt with Parson Tombs beside the dead man, moaning,

"O good Lord! good Lord! this needn't 'a' been! O Enos, I'd better 'a' killed you myself! O great God, why didn't I keep this from happening, when I——"

Someone close to him, stooping over the dead under pretence of feeling for signs of life, murmured, "Stop talking." Then to the Parson, "Take him away with you," and then rising spoke across to Garnet, "Howdy, Major," with the old smile that could be no one's but Ravenel's. He and Garnet walked away together.

"Died of a gunshot wound received by accident," the coroner came and found. John March and the minister had gone into March's office, but Captain Champion's word was quite enough. It was nearly tea-time when John and the Parson came out again. The sidewalk was empty. As John locked the door he felt a nail under his boot, picked it up, and seeming not to realize his own action at all, stepped to the sidewalk's edge, found a loose stone and went back to the door, all the time saying,

"No, sir, I've made it perfectly terrible to think of God and a hereafter, but somehow I've never got so low down as to wish there wa'n't any. I—" his thumb pressed the nail into its hole in the corner of his sign—

"I do lots of things that are wrong, awfully wrong, though sometimes I feel—" he hammered it home with the stone—" as if I'd rather "—he did the same for the other two and the thumb-tack—" die trying to do right than live,—well,—this way. But—" tossing away the stone and wiping his hands—" that's only sometimes, and that's the very best I can say."

They walked slowly. The wind had ceased. By the *Courier* office John halted.

"Supper! O excuse me, Mr. Tombs! really I—I can't sir!—I—I'll eat at the hotel. I've got to see a gentleman on business. But I pledge you my word, sir, I'll come to the meeting." They shook hands. " You're mighty kind to me, sir."

The gentleman he saw on business was Ravenel. They supped together in a secluded corner of the Swanee Hotel dining-room, talking of Widewood and colonization, and by the time their cigars were brought—by an obsequious black waiter with soiled cuffs—March felt that he had never despatched so much business at one sitting in his life before.

" John," said Ravenel as they took the first puff, "there's one thing you can do for me if you will: I want you to stand up with me at my wedding."

March stiffened and clenched his chair. " Jeff-Jack, you oughtn't to 've asked me that, sir ! And least of all in connection with this Widewood business, in which I'm so indebted to you! It's not fair, sir ! "

Ravenel scarcely roused himself from reverie to reply, " You mustn't make any connection. I don't."

" Well, then, I'll not," said March. " I'll even

thank you for the honor.  But I don't deserve either the honor or the punishment, and I simply can't do it!"

" Can't you ' hide in your breast every selfish care and flush your pale cheek with wine ' ?  Every man has got to eat a good deal of crow.  It's not so bad, from the hand of a friend.  It shan't compromise you."

With head up and eyes widened John gazed at the friendly-cynical face before him.  " It would compromise me ; you know it would!  Yes, sir, you may laugh, but you knew it when you asked me.  You knew it would be unconditional surrender.  I don't say you hadn't a right to ask, but—I'm a last ditcher, you know."

" Well," drawled Ravenel, pleasantly, when they rose, " if that's what you prefer——"

" No, I don't prefer it, Jeff-Jack ; but if you were me could you help it ? "

" I shouldn't try," said Ravenel.

---

## XLII.

### JOHN HEADS A PROCESSION

By the afternoon train on this last day of the year there had come into Suez a missionary returning from China on leave of absence, ill from scant fare and overwork.

General Halliday, Fannie, and Barbara were at tea

when Parson Tombs brought in the returned wanderer. The General sprang to his feet with an energy that overturned his chair. "Why, Sammie Messenger, confound your young hide! Well, upon my soul! I'm outrageous proud to see you! Fan—Barb—come here! This is one of my old boys! Sam, this is the daughter of your old Major; Miss Garnet. Why, confound your young hide!"

Parson Tombs giggled with joy. "Brother Messenger is going to add a word of exhortation to Brother Garnet's discourse," he said with grave elation, and when the General execrated such cruelty to a weary traveler, he laughed again. But being called to the front door for a moment's consultation with the pastor of the other church, he presently returned, much embarrassed, with word that the missionary need not take part, a prior invitation having been accepted by Uncle Jimmie Rankin, of Wildcat Ridge. Fannie, in turn, cried out against this substitution, but the gentle shepherd explained that what mercy could not obtain official etiquette compelled.

"Tell us about John March," interposed the General. "They say you saved his life."

"I reckon I did, sir, humanly speakin'." The Parson told the lurid story, Fannie holding Barbara's hand as they listened. The church's first bell began to ring and the Parson started up.

"If only the right man could talk to John! He's very persuadable to-night and he'd take fum a stranger what he wouldn't take fum us." He looked fondly to the missionary, who had risen with him. "I wish you'd try him. You knew him when he was a toddler. He asks about you, freck-wently."

"You'd almost certainly see him down-town somewhere now," said Fannie.

Barbara gave the missionary her most daring smile of persuasion.

March was found only a step or two from Fannie's gate.

"Well, if this ain't a plumb Provi*dence!*" laughed the Parson. The three men stopped and talked, and then walked, chatted, and returned. The starlight was cool and still. At the Parson's gate, March, refusing to go in, said, yes, he would be glad of the missionary's company on a longer stroll. The two moved on and were quite out of sight when Fannie and Barbara, with Johanna close behind them, came out on their way to church.

"It would be funny," whispered Fannie, "if such a day as this should end in John March's getting religion, wouldn't it?"

But Barbara could come no nearer to the subject than to say, "I don't like revivals. I can't. I never could." She dropped her voice significantly—"Fannie."

"What, dear?"

"What were you going to say when Johanna rang the tea-bell and your father came in?"

"Was I going to say something? What'd you think it was?"

"I think it was something about Mr. Ravenel."

"O well, then, I reckon it wasn't anything much, was it?"

"I don't know, but—Johanna, you can go on into church." They loitered among the dim, lamp-lit shadows of the church-yard trees. "You said you were not like most engaged girls."

"Well, I'm not, am I?"

"No, but why did you say so?"

"Why, you know, Barb, most girls are distressed with doubts of their own love. I'm not. It's about his that I'm afraid. What do you reckon's the reason I've held him off for years?"

"Just because you could, Fannie."

"No, my dear little goosie, I did it because he never was so he couldn't be held off. I knew, and know yet, that after the wedding I've got to do all the courting. I don't doubt he loves me, but Barb, love isn't his master. That's what keeps me scared." They went in.

The service began. In this hour for the putting away of vanities the choir was dispensed with and the singing was led by a locally noted precentor, a large, pert, lazy Yankee, who had failed in the raising of small fruits. His zeal was beautiful.

"Trouble! 'Tain't never no trouble for me to do nawthin', an' even if 'twas I'd do it!" He sang each word in an argumentative staccato, and in high passages you could see his wisdom teeth. Between stanzas he spoke stimulating exhortations: "Louder, brethren and sisters, louder; the fate of immortal souls may be a-hangin' on the amount of noise you make."

As hymn followed hymn the church filled. All sorts
—black or yellow being no sort—all sorts came ; the
town's best and worst, the country's proudest and forlorn-
est; the sipper of wine, the dipper of snuff; acrid
pietist, flagrant reprobate, and many a true Christian
whose God-forgiven sins, if known to men, neither
church nor world could have pardoned ; many a soul
that under the disguise of flippant smiles or superior
frowns staggered in its darkness or shivered in its cold,
trembling under visions of death and judgment or
yearning for one right word of guidance or extrication ;
and many a heart that openly or secretly bled for some
other heart's reclaim. And so the numbers grew and
the waves of song swelled. The adagios and largos of
ancient psalmody were engulfed and the modern " hyme
toons," as the mountain people called them, were so
" peert an' devilish " that the most heedless grew attentive, and lovers of raw peanuts, and even devotees of
tobacco, emptied their mouths of these and filled them
with praise.

Garnet had never preached more effectively. For
the first time in Barbara's experience he seemed to her
to feel, himself, genuinely and deeply the things he said.
His text was, " Be sure your sin will find you out."
Men marvelled at the life-likeness with which he pictured the torments of a soul torn by hidden and
cherished sin. So wonderful, they murmured, are the
pure intuitions of oratorical genius! Yet Barbara was
longing for a widely different word.

Not for herself. It was not possible that she should
ever tremble at any pulpit reasoning of temperance and

judgment from the lips of her father. Three things in every soul, he cried, must either be subdued in this life or be forever ground to powder in a fiery hereafter; and these three, if she knew them at all, were the three most utterly unsubdued things that he embodied—will, pride, appetite. The word she vainly longed for was coveted for one whose tardy footfall her waiting ear caught the moment it sounded at the door, and before the turning of a hundred eyes told her John March had come and was sitting in the third seat behind her.

In the course of her father's sermon there was no lack of resonant Amens and soft groanings and moanings of ecstasy. But Suez was neither Wildcat Ridge nor Chalybeate Springs, and the tempering chill of plastered ceiling and social inequalities stayed the wild unrestraint of those who would have held free rule in the log church or under the camp-meeting bower. The academic elegance of the speaker's periods sobered the ardor which his warmth inspired, and as he closed there rested on the assemblage a silence and an awe as though Sinai smoked but could not thunder.

Barbara hoped against hope. At every enumeration of will, pride, and appetite she saw the Pastor's gaze rest pleadingly on her, and in the stillness of her inmost heart she confessed the evil presence of that unregenerate trinity. Yet when he rose to bid all mourners for sin come forward while the next hymn was being sung, she only mourned that she could not go, and tried in vain not to feel, as in every drop of her blood she still felt, there behind her, that human presence so different from all others on earth. "This call," she secretly cried, "this hour, are not for me.    Father in Heaven! if only they might be for him."

Before the rising precentor could give out his hymn Uncle Jimmie Rankin had sprung to his feet and started "Rock of Ages" in one of the wildest minors of the early pioneers.    At once the strain was taken up on every side, the notes swelled, Uncle Jimmie clapped hands in time, and at the third line a mountain woman in the gallery, sitting with her sun-bonnet pulled down over her sore eyes, changed a snuff-stick from her mouth to her pocket, burst into a heart-freezing scream, and began to thrash about in her seat.    The hymn rolled on in stronger volume.    The Yankee precentor caught the tune and tried to lead, but Uncle Jimmie's voice soared over him with the rapture of a lark and the shriek of an eagle, two or three more pair of hands clapped time, the other Suez pastor took a trochee, and the four preachers filed down from the high pulpit, singing as they came. Garnet began to pace to and fro in front of it and to exhort in the midst of the singing.

"Who is on the Lord's side?" he loudly demanded.

"Should my tears forever flow," sang the standing throng.

But no one advanced.

"Should my zeal no respite know," they sang on, and Garnet's "Whosoever will, let him come," and other calls swept across their chant like the crash of falling trees across the roar of a torrent.

"Oh, my brother, two men shall be in the field; the one shall be taken and the other left; which one will you be?    Come, my weary sister; come, my sin-laden brother. O, come unto the marriage! Now is the accepted time! The clock of God's patience has run down and is standing at Now! Sing the last verse again, Uncle Jimmie! This night thy soul may be required of thee! Two women shall be grinding together; the one shall be taken, the other left. O, my sweet sister, come! be the taken one!—flee as a bird! The angel is troubling the pool; who will first come to the waters? O, my unknown, yet beloved brother, whoever you are, don't you know that whosoever comes first to-night will lead a hundred others and will win a crown with that many stars? Come, brethren, sisters, we're losing priceless moments!"

Why does no one move? Because just in the middle of the house, three seats behind that fair girl whose face has sunk into her hands, sits, with every eye on them, the wan missionary from China, pleading with John March.

Parson Tombs saw the chance for a better turn of affairs. "Brethren," he cried, kneeling as he spoke, "let us pray! And as our prayers ascend if any sinner feels the dew o' grace fall into his soul, let him come forward and kneel with the Lord's ministers. Brother Samuel Messenger, lead us in prayer!"

The missionary prayed. But the footfall for which all waited did not sound; the young man who knelt beside the supplicant, with temples clutched in his hands, moved not. While the missionary's amen was yet unspoken, Parson Tombs, still kneeling, began to ask aloud,

"Will Brother Garnet——"

But Garnet was wiser. " Father Tombs," he cried " the Lord be with you, lead us in prayer yourself ! "

" Amen ! " cried the other pastor. He was echoed by a dozen of his flock, and the old man lifted his voice in tremulous invocation. The prayer was long. But before there were signs of it ending, the step for which so many an ear was strained had been heard. Men were groaning, " God be praised ! " and " Hallelujah ! " Fannie's eyes were wet, tears were welling through Barbara's fingers, mourners were coming up both aisles, and John March was kneeling in the anxious seat.

## XLIII.

### ST. VALENTINE'S DAY

ONE morning some six weeks after New Year's eve Garnet's carriage wheels dripped water and mud as his good horses dragged them slowly into the borders of Suez. The soft, moist winds of February were ruffling the turbid waters of Turkey Creek and the swollen flood of the Swanee. A hint of new green brightened every road-side, willows were full of yellow light, and a pink and purple flush answered from woods to fence-row, from fence-row to woods, across and across the three counties.

" This pike's hardly a pike at all since the railroad's started," said the Major, more to himself than to Barbara and Johanna ; for these were the two rear occupants of the carriage.

" Barb, I got a letter from Fair last night. You did too, didn't you ? "

" Yes, sir."

" He'll be here next week. He says he can't stop with us this time."

Barbara was silent, and felt the shy, care-taking glance of her maid. Garnet spoke again, in the guarded tone she knew so well.

" I reckon you understand he's only coming to see if he'll take stock in this land company we're getting up, don't you ? "

" Yes, sir."

" Doe she know you're going to spend these two weeks at Halliday's before you go North ? "

" I think he does."

The questioner turned enough to make a show of frowning solicitude. " What's the matter with you this morning ? sad at the thought of leaving home ? "

" No, sir "—the speaker smiled meditatively—" we only don't hit on a subject of interest to both."

The father faced to front again and urged the horses. He even raised the whip, but let it droop. Then he turned sharply and drew his daughter's glance. " Is Fair going to stay with John March ? "

They sat gaze to gaze while their common blood surged up to his brows and more gradually suffused her face. Without the stir of an eyelash she let her lips part enough to murmur, " Yes."

Before her word was finished Garnet's retort was bursting from him, " Thanks to you, you intermeddling —— " He was cut short by the lurch of the carriage into a hole. It flounced him into the seat from which he had half started and faced him to the horses. With a smothered imprecation he rose and laid on the whip. They plunged, the carriage sprang from the hole and ploughed the mire, and Garnet sat down and drove into the town's main avenue, bespattered with mud from head to waist.

Near the gate of the Academy grounds stood Parson Tombs talking to a youth in Rosemont uniform. The student passed on, and the pastor, with an elated face, waved a hand to Garnet. Garnet stopped and the Parson came close.

"Brother Tombs, howdy?"

"Why, howdy-do, Brother Garnet?—Miss Barb!—Johanna." He pointed covertly at the departing youth and murmured to Garnet, "He'll make ow fo'teenth convert since New Year's. And still there is room! —Well, brother, I've been a-hearin' about John March's an' yo'-all's lan' boom, but"—the good man giggled—"I never see a case o' measles break out finer than the lan' business is broke out on you!—And you don't seem to mind it no mo'n—Look here! air you a miracle o' grace, aw what air you?"

"Why, nothing, Brother Tombs, nothing! Nothing but an old soldier who's learned that serenity's always best."

The Parson turned to Barbara and cast a doting smile sidewise upon the old soldier. But Garnet set his face against flattery and changed the subject.

"Brother Tombs, speaking of John March, you know how risky it is for anybody—unless it's you—to say

anything to him. Oh, I dare say he's changed, but
when he hasn't been converted two months, nor a member of the church three weeks, we mustn't expect him to
have the virtues of an old Christian."

"He's changed mo'n I'm at libbety to tell you,
Brother Garnet. He's renounced dancing."

"Yes?—Indeed! He's quit dancing. But still he
carries two revolvers."

"Why, Brother John Wesley, I—that's so. I've
spoke to John about that, but—the fact is——"

Garnet smiled. "His life's in constant danger—
that's my very point. The bad weather's protected
him thus far, but if it should last five years without a
break, still you know that as soon as it fairs off——"

"*Uv* co'se! Enos's kinsfolks 'll be layin' faw him
behind some bush aw sett'n' fire to his house; an' so
what shall he do, brother, if we say he——"

"Oh, let him shoot a Yahoo or two if he must, but I
think you ought to tell him he's committing a criminal
folly in asking that young Yankee, Mr. Fair, to stop
with him at Widewood when he comes here next
week!"

"Why, Brother Garnet! Why, supposin' that
young stranger should get shot!"

"Yes, or if he should no more than see March shot
or shot at! What an impression he'd carry back
North with him! It's an outrage on our whole people,
sir, and God knows!—I speak reverently, my dear
brother—we've suffered enough of that sort of slander!
I'd tell him, myself, but—this must be between us, of
course——"

"Why, of co'se, Brother Garnet," murmured the Pastor and bent one ear.

"It's a pure piece of selfish business rivalry on John's part toward me. He's asked Fair to his house simply to keep him away from Rosemont."

"Why, Brother Garnet! Rosemont's right where he'd ought to go to!"

"In John's own interest!" said Garnet.

"In John's—you're right, my brother! I'm supprised he don't see it so!"

"O—I'm not! He's a terribly overrated chap, Brother Tombs. Fact is—I say it in the sincerest friendship for him—John's got no real talents and not much good sense—though one or two of his most meddlesome friends have still less." The Major began to gather up the reins.

"Well, I'll try to see him, Brother Garnet. I met him yeste'day—Look here! I reckon that young man's not goin' to stop with him after all. He told me yeste'day he was going to put a friend into Swanee Hotel because Sisteh March felt too feeble, aw fearful, aw somethin', an' he felt bound to stand his expenses."

"And so he "—the Major paused pleasantly. "How much did you lend him?"

"Aw! Brother Garnet, I didn't mean you to know that! He had to put shuttehs on his sitt'n'-room windows, too, you know, to quiet Sisteh March's ve'y natu'al fears. I only promised to lend him a small amount if he should need it."

"O, he'll need it," said the Major, and included Barbara in his broad smile. "Still, I hope you'll let

him have it. If he doesn't return it to you I will; I
loved his father. John should have come to me,
Brother Tombs, as he's always done. I say this to you
privately, you know. I'll consider the loan practically
made to me, for we simply can't let Fair go to Widewood, even if John puts shutters on all his windows."

Again the speaker lifted his reins and the Parson
drew back with a bow to Barbara, when Johanna spoke
and the whole group stared after two townward-bound
horsemen.

"Those are mountain people, right now," said the
Parson.

"Yes," replied Garnet, "but they're no kin to Enos."
He moved on to Halliday's gate.

It was the fourteenth of the month. The Major
stayed in town for the evening mail and drove home
after dark, alone, but complacent, almost jovial. He
had got three valentines.

---

## XLIV.

### ST. VALENTINE'S: EVENING

AT Widewood that same hour there was deep silence.
Since the first of the year the only hands left on the
place were a decrepit old negro and wife, whom even he
pronounced "wuthless," quartered beyond the stable-
yard's farther fence. For some days this "lady"
had been Widewood's only cook, owing to the fact that

Mrs. March's servant, having a few nights before seen a man prowling about the place, had left in such a panic as almost to forget her wages, and quite omitting to leave behind her several articles of the Widewood washing.

Within the house John March sat reading newspapers. His healthy legs were crossed toward the flickering hearth, and his strong shoulders touched the centretable lamp. The new batten shutters excluded the beautiful outer night. His mother, to whom the mail had brought nothing, was sitting in deep shadow, her limp form and her regular supply of disapproving questions alike exhausted. Her slender elbow slipped now and then from the arm of her rocking-chair, and unconscious gleams of incredulity and shades of grief still alternated across her face with every wrinkling effort of her brows to hold up her eyelids.

John was not so absorbed as he seemed. He felt both the silence and the closed shutters drearily, and was not especially cheered by the following irrelevant query in the paragraph before him:

"Who—having restored the sight of his jailer's blind daughter and converted her father from idolatry—was on this day beheaded?"

Yet here was a chance to be pleasant at the expense of a man quite too dead to mind.

"Mother," he began, so abruptly that Mrs. March started with a violent shudder, "this is February fourteenth. Did any ancient person of your acquaintance lose his head to-day?" He turned a facetious glance

that changed in an instant to surprise. His mother had
straightened up with bitter indignation, but she softened
to an agony of reproach as she cried:

"John!"

"Why, mother, what?"

"Ah! John! John!" She gazed at him tearfully.
"Is this what you've joined the church for?" To cloak
such——"

"My dear mother! I was simply trying to joke
away the dismals! Why,"—he smiled persuasively—
"if you only knew what a hard job it is." But the
ludicrousness of her misconstruction took him off his
guard, and in spite of the grimmest endeavor to prevent
it, his smile increased and he stopped to keep from
laughing.

Mrs. March rose, eloquent with unspoken resentment,
and started from the room. At the door she cast back
the blush of a martyr's forgiveness, and the next instant
was in her son's big right arm. His words were broken
with laughter.

"My dear, pretty little mother!" She struggled
alarmedly, but he held her fast. "Why, I know the
day is nothing to you, dear, less than nothing. I
know perfectly well that I am your own and only valentine. Ain't I? Because you're mine now, you
know, since I've turned over this new leaf."

The mother averted her face. "O my son, I'm so
unused to loving words, they only frighten me."

But John spoke on with deepening emotion. "Yes,
mother, I'm going to be your valentine, and yours only,
as I've never been or thought of being in all my life

before. I'm going to try my very best! You'll help me, won't you, little valentine mother?"

She lifted a glance of mournful derision. "Valentine me no valentines. You but increase my heart-loneliness. Ah! my self-deluded boy, your fickle pledges only mean, to my sad experience, that you have made your own will everything, and my wish nothing. Valentine me no valentines, let me go."

The young man turned abruptly and strode back to his newspapers. But he was too full of bitterness to read. He heard his mother's soft progress up-stairs, and her slow step in the unlighted room overhead. It ceased. She must have sat down in the dark. A few moments passed. Then it sounded again, but so strange and hurried that he started up, and as he did so the cry came, frantic with alarm, from the upper hall, and then from the head of the stairs:

"John! John!"

He was already bounding up them. Mrs. March stood at the top, pale and trembling. "A man!" she cried, "with a gun! I saw him down in the moon-light under my window! I saw him! he's got a gun!"

She was deaf and blind to her son's beseechings to be quiet. He caught her hands in his; they were icy. He led her by gentle force down-stairs and back to her sitting-room seat.

"Why, that's all right, mother; that's what you made me put the shutters on down here for. If you'd just come and told me quietly, why, I might a' got him from your window. Did you see him?"

"I don't know," she moaned. "He had a gun. I saw one end of it."

"Are you sure it was a gun? Which end did you see, the butt or the muzzle?"

Mrs. March only gasped. She was too refined a woman to mention either end of a gun by name. "I saw—the—front end."

"He didn't aim it at you, or at anything, did he?"

"No—yes—he aimed it—sidewise."

"Sideways! Now, mother, there I draw the line! No man shall come around here aiming his gun sideways; endangering the throngs of casual bystanders!"

"Ah! John, is this the time to make your captive and beleaguered mother the victim of ribald jests?"

"My dear mother, no! it's a time to go to bed. If that fellow's still nosing 'round here with his gun aimed sideways he's protection enough! But seriously, mother, whatever you mean by being embargoed and blockaded——"

"I did not say embargoed and blockaded!"

"Why, my dear mother, those were your very words!"

"They were not! They were not my words! And yet, alas! how truly——" She turned and wept.

"O Lord! mother——"

"My son, you've broken the second commandment!"

"It was already broke! O for heaven's sake, mother, don't cave in in this hysterical way!"

The weeper whisked round with a face of wild beseeching. "O, my son, call me anything but that! Call me weak and credulous, too easily led and misled!

Call me too poetical and confiding! I know I'm more lonely than I dare tell my own son! But I'm not— Oho! I'm not hysterical!" she sobbed.

So it continued for an hour. Then the lamp gave out and they went to bed.

The next morning John drove his mother to Suez for a visit of several days among her relatives, and rode on into Blackland to see if he could find "a girl" for Widewood. He spent three days and two nights at these tasks, stopping while in Blackland with—whom would you suppose? Proudfit, for all the world! He took an emphatic liking to the not too brainy colonel, and a new disrelish to his almost too sparkling wife.

As, at sunset of the third day, he again drew near Suez and checked his muddy horse's gallop at Swanee River Bridge, his heart leaped into his throat. He hurriedly raised his hat, but not to the transcendent beauties of the charming scene, unless these were Fannie Halliday and Barbara Garnet.

---

## XLV.

### A LITTLE VOYAGE OF DISCOVERIES

For two girls out on a quiet stroll, their arms about each other and their words murmurous, not any border of Suez was quite so alluring as the woods and waters seen from the parapet of this fine old stone bridge.

The main road from Blackland crossed here. As it reached the Suez side it made a strong angle under the town's leafy bluffs and their two or three clambering by-streets, and ran down the rocky margin of the stream to the new railway station and the old steamboat landing half a mile below. The bridge was entirely of rugged gray limestone, and spanned the river's channel and willow-covered sand-bars in seven high, rude arches. One Christmas dawn during the war a retreating enemy, making ready to blow up the structure, were a moment too slow, and except for the scars of a few timely shells dropped into their rear guard, it had come through those years unscathed. For, just below it, and preferable to it most of the year, was a broad gravelly ford. Beyond the bridge, on the Blackland side, the road curved out of view between woods on the right and meadows on the left. A short way up the river the waters came dimpling, green and blue in August, but yellow and swirling now, around the long, bare foot of a wooded island, that lay forever asleep in midstream, overrun and built upon by the winged Liliputians of the shores and fields.

The way down to this spot from the Halliday cottage was a grassy street overarched with low-branching evergreen oaks, and so terraced that the trees at times robbed the view of even a middle distance. It was by this way that Fannie and Barbara had come, with gathered skirts, picking dainty zigzags where, now and then, the way was wet. The spirit of spring was in the lightness of their draperies' texture and dyes—only a woman's eye would have noticed that Barbara was in mourning—and their broken talk was mainly on a plan for the celebration, on the twenty-second, not of any great and exceptionally truthful patriot's birthday— Captains Champion and Shotwell were seeing to that— but of Parson Tombs's and his wife's golden wedding.

When John March saw them, they had just been getting an astonishing amount of amusement out of the simple fact that Miss Mary Salter and the younger pastor were the committee on decorations. They were standing abreast the bridge's parapet, the evening air stirring their garments, watching the stern-wheeler, Launcelot Halliday, back out from the landing below into the fretting current for a trip down stream. John had always approved this companionship; it had tended to sustain his old illusion that Fannie's extra years need not count between her and him. But the pleasure of seeing them together now was but a flash and was gone, for something else than extra years was counting, which had never counted before. He had turned over a new leaf, as he said. On it he had subscribed with docile alacrity to every ancient grotesqueness in Parson Tombs's science of God, sin, and pardon; and then had stamped Fannie's picture there, fondly expecting to retain it by the very simple trick of garlanding it round with the irrefragable proposition that love is the fulfilling of the law! But not many days had the leaf been turned when a new and better conscience awoke to find shining there, still wet from God's own pen, the corollary that only a whole sphere of love can fulfil the law's broad circumference.

As Fannie and Barbara made their bow and moved

to pass on he hurriedly raised his hat and his good horse dropped into a swift, supple walk. The bridle hand started as if to draw in, but almost at the same instant the animal sprang again into a gait which showed the spur had touched her, and was quickly out of hearing.

"Barb," murmured Fannie, "you're thinking he's improved."

"Yes, only——"

"Only you think he'd have stopped if he'd seen us sooner. Why can't you think maybe he wouldn't? But you're not to blame; you simply have a girl's natural contempt for a boy's love. Well, a boy's love *is* silly; but when you see the constant kind, like John's, as sure as you live there are not many things entitled to higher respect. O Barb! I've never felt so honored by any other love that man ever offered me. He'll get over it, completely. I believe it's dying now, though it's dying hard. But the next time he loves, the girl who treats his love lightly—Let's go down in these woods and look for hepaticas. John can't bring them to me any more and Jeff-Jack never did. He sends candy. There's homage in a wild flower, Barb; but candy, oh—I don't know—it makes me ashamed."

"Why don't you tell him so?"

Fannie leaned close and whispered, "I'm afraid."

"Why, he gave me wild flowers, once."

"When? Who?" The black eyes flashed. "When did he ever give you flowers?"

"When I was five years old." They turned down a short descent into the woods.

Fannie smiled pensively. "Barb, did you notice that John——"

"Has been trading again! His love's not very constant as to horses."

"But what a pretty mare he's got! Barb, 'pon my word, when John March is well mounted, I do think, physically, he's——" The speaker hearkened. From the low place where they stood her eyes were on a level with the road. "It's him again; let's hide."

March came loping down from the bridge, slackened pace, and swept with his frowning glance the meadows on the left. Then he moved along the edge of the wood searching its sunset lights and glooms, and presently turned down into them, bending under the low boughs. And then he halted, burning with sudden resentment before the smiling, black-eyed girl who leaned against the tree, which had all at once refused to conceal her.

Neither spoke. Fannie's eyes were mocking and yet kind, and the resentment in John's turned to a purer mortification. A footstep rustled behind him and Barbara said:

"We're looking for wild flowers. Do you think we're too early?"

"No, I could have picked some this afternoon if I'd felt like it, but it's a sort o' belief with me that nobody ought to pick wild flowers for himself—ha-ha-ha!—Oh eh, Miss Garnet, I reckon I owe you an apology for charging down on you this way, but I just happened to think, after I passed you, that you could tell me where to find your father. He's president *pro tem.* of our land company, you know, and I want to consult him with

Mr. Gamble—you know Mr. Gamble, don't you?—president of the railroad? O! of course you do! Well, he's our vice-president."

"Why, no, Mr. March, I don't know where you'll find pop-a right now. I might possibly know when I get back to the house. If it's important I could send you word."

"O no! O no! Not at all! I'll find him easily enough. I hope you'll both pardon me, Miss Fannie, but it seems as if I learned some things pow'ful slow. I ought to know by this time when two's company and three's a crowd."

Before he had finished, the two listeners had seen the remoter significance of his words, and it was to mask this that Barbara drawled—

"Why, Mr. March, that's not nice of you!"

But the young man's confusion was sufficient apology, and both girls beamed kindly on him as he presently took his leave under the delusion that his face hid his inward mortification.

## XLVI.

### A PAIR OF SMUGGLERS

A SHORT way farther within the wood they began to find flowers.

"Well—yes," said Fannie, musingly. "And pop consented to be treasurer *pro tem.*, but that was purely to help John. You know he fairly loves John. They all think it'll be so much easier to get Northern capital if they can show they're fully organized and all interests interested, you know." She stooped to pick a blossom. Barbara was bending in another direction. Two doves alighted on the ground near by and began to feed, and, except for size, the four would have seemed to an onlooker to have been very much of a kind.

Presently Fannie spoke again. "But I think pop's more and more distrustful of the thing every day. Barb, I reckon I'll tell you something."

Barbara crouched motionless. "Tell on."

"O—well, I asked pop yesterday what he thought of this Widewood scheme anyhow, and he said, 'There's money in it for some men.' 'Well, then, why can't you be one of them,' I asked him, and said he, 'It's not the kind of money I want, Fan.'"

"O pshaw, Fannie, men are always saying that about one another."

"Yes," murmured Fannie.

"Fan," said Barbara, tenderly, "do stop talking

that way; you know I'm nearly as proud of your father as you are, don't you?"

"Yes, sweetheart."

"Well, then, go on, dear."

"I asked him if John was one," resumed Fannie, "and, said he, 'No, I shouldn't be a bit surprised to see John lose everything he and his mother have got.'"

Barbara flinched and was still again. "Has he told him that?"

"No, he says John's a very hard fellow to tell anything to. And, you know, Barb, that's so. I used to could tell him things, but I mustn't even try now."

"Why, Fan, you don't reckon Mr. Ravenel would care, do you?"

"Barb, I'll never know how much he cares about anything till it's too late. You can't try things on Jeff-Jack."

"I wish," softly said Barbara, "you wouldn't smile so much like him."

"Don't say anything against him, Barb, now or ever! I'm his and he's mine, and I wouldn't for both worlds have it any other way." But this time the speaker's smile was her own and very sweet. The two returned to the road.

"I asked pop," said Fannie, "where Jeff-Jack stands in this affair. He laughed and said, 'Jeff-Jack doesn't take stands, Fan, he lays low.'"

"Somebody ought to tell him."

"Tell who? Oh, John!—yes, I only wish to gracious some one would! But men don't do that sort of thing for one another. If a man takes such a risk as that for another you may know he loves him; and if a woman takes it you may know she doesn't."

"Fan," said Barbara, as they locked arms, "would it do for me to tell him?"

"No, my dear; in the first place you wouldn't get the chance. You can't begin to try to tell him till you've clean circumgyrated yourself away down into his confidence. It's a job, Barb, and a bigger one than you can possibly want. Now, if we only knew some girl of real sense who was foolish enough to be self-sacrificingly in love with him—but where are we going to find the combination?"

"And even if we could, you say no woman in love with a man would do it."

"There are exceptions, sweet Simplicity. What we want is an exception! Law, Barb, what a fine game a girl of the true stuff could play in such a case! Not having his love yet, but wanting it worse than life, and yet taking the biggest chance of losing it for the chance of saving him from the wreck of his career. O see!" They stopped on the bridge again to watch the sun's last beams gilding the waters, and Barbara asked,

"Do you believe the right kind of a girl would do that?"

"Why, if she could do it without getting found out, yes! Why, Law, I'd have done it for Jeff-Jack! You see, she might save him and win him, too; or she might win him even if she tried and failed to save him."

"But she might," said Barbara, gazing up the river, "she might even save him and still lose."

"Yes, for a man thinks he's doing well if he so much

as forgives a deliverer—in petticoats. Yet still, Barb, wouldn't a real woman sooner lose by saving him, than sit still and let him lose for fear she might lose by trying to save him?"

"I don't know; you can't imagine mom-a doing such a thing, can you?"

"What! Cousin Rose? Why, of all women she was just the sort to have done it. Barb, you'd do it!" Fannie expected her friend to look at her with an expression of complimented surprise. But the surprise was her own when Barbara gave a faint start and bent lower over the parapet. The difference was very slight, as slight as the smile of fond suspicion that came into Fannie's face.

"Fannie"—still looking down into the gliding water —"how does your father think Mr. March is going to lose so much; is he afraid he'll be swindled?"

"I believe he is, Barb."

"And do you think"—the words came very softly and significantly—"that that makes it any special matter of mine that he should be warned?"

"Yes, sweetheart, I do."

"Then"—the speaker looked up with distressed resolve—"I must do what I can. Will you help me, or let me help you, rather?"

"Yes, either way, as far as I can." They moved on for a moment. Then Barbara stopped abruptly, looking much amused. "There's one risk you didn't count!"

"What's that?"

"Why, if he should mistake my motive, and——"

"What? suspect you of being——"

" A girl of the true stuff! "

" O but, sweet, how could he? "

As they laughed Fannie generously prepared to keep her guess to herself, and to imply, still more broadly, that all she imputed to her friend was the determination secretly to circumvent a father's evil designs.

Barbara roused from a reverie. " I know who'll help us, Fan,—Mr. Fair." She withstood her companion's roguish look with one of caressing gravity until the companion spoke, when she broke into a smile as tranquil as a mother's.

" Barb, Barb, you deep-dyed villain ! "

The only reply of the defendant—they were once more in the shady lane—was to give her accuser a touch of challenge, and the two sprang up a short acclivity to where a longer vista opened narrowly before them. But here, as if rifles had been aimed at them, they shrank instantly downward. For in the dim sylvan light two others walked slowly before them, their heads hidden by the evergreen branches, but their feet perfectly authenticated and as instantly identified. One pair were twos, one were elevens, and both belonged to the Committee on Decorations. An arm that by nature pertained unto the elevens was about the waist that pertained unto the twos, and at the moment of discovery, as well as could be judged by certain sinuosities of lines below, there was a distance between the two pairs of lips less than any assignable quantity.

## XLVII.

### LEVITICUS

THE two maidens were still laughing as they re-entered their gate. Fannie threw an arm sturdily around her companion's waist and sought to repeat the pantomime, but checked herself at the sight of a buggy drawing near.

It was old, misshapen, and caked with wet and dry mud, as also was the mule which drew it. In the vehicle sat three persons. Two were negro women. One of them—of advanced years—was in a full bloom of crisp calico under a flaring bonnet which must have long passed its teens. The other was young and very black. She wore a tawdry hat that only helped to betray her general slovenliness. From between them a negro man was rising and dismounting. A wide-brimmed, crackled beaver rested on his fluffy gray locks, and there was the gentleness of old age in his face.

The spring sap seemed to have started anew in the elder woman's veins. She tittered as she scrambled to rise, and when the old man offered to help her, she eyed him with mock scorn and waved him off.

" G'way fum me, 'Viticus Wisdom — gallivantin' round here like we was young niggehs!—Lawd! my time is come I cayn't git up; my bones dun tuk dis-yeh shape to staay!"

"Come, come!" said the husband, in an undertone of

amiable chiding; and the buggy gave a jerk of thankful relief as its principal burden left it for the sidewalk, diffusing the sweet smell of the ironing-table.

While the younger woman was making her mincing descent, Fanny and Barbara came toward them in the walk.

" Miss Halliday," said Leviticus, lifting his beaver and bowing across the gate, " in response to yo' invite we—O bless the Lawd my soul! is that my little—Miss Barb, is that you ? "

Before he could say more Virginia threw both hands high. " Faw de Lawd's sake ! " She thrust her husband aside. " G'way, niggah ! lemme th'oo dis-yeh gate 'fo' I go ove' it ! " She snatched Barbara to her bosom. ' Lawd, honey ! Lawd, honey ! Ef anybody 'spec' you' ole Aunt Fudjinny to stan' off an' axe her baby howdy dey bettah go to de crazy house ! Lawd ! Lawd ! dis de fus' chance I had to hug my own baby since I been a po' ole free niggah ! " She held the laughing girl off by the shoulders.

" Honey, ef it's my las' ac', I "—she snatched her close again, kissed one cheek twice and the other thrice, and held her off once more to fix upon her a tearful, ravishing gaze. " Lawd, honey, Johanna done tole me how you growin' to favo' my sweet Miss Rose, an' I see it at de fun'l when I can't much mo'n speak to you, an' cry so I cayn't hardly see you ; but Lawd ! my sweet baby, dough you cayn't neveh supersede her in good looks, you jess as quiet an' beautiful as de sweet-potateh floweh !

" Howdy, Miss Fannie ? " She gave her hand and courtesied.

"Howdy, Uncle Leviticus?" said Barbara.

The old man lifted his hat again, bowed very low, and looked very happy. "I'm tol'able well, Miss Barb, thank the Lawd, an' hope an' trus' an' pray you're of the same complexion." Still including Barbara in his audience, he went on with an address to Fannie already begun.

"You know, Miss Fannie, yo' letteh say fo' Aunt Fudjinny an' me to come the twentieth—yass, ma'am, we understan'—but, you know, Mr. Mahch, he come down an' superscribe faw this young—ah———"

"Girl," suggested Barbara, with pretty condescension ; but Fannie covertly trod on her toe and said, "lady," with a twinkle at the dowdy maiden.

"P'ecisely ! " responded Leviticus to both speakers at once. "An' Mr. Mahch, he was bereft o' any way to fetch her to he's maw less'n he taken her up behime o' his saddle, an' so it seem' like the Lawd's call faw us to come right along an' bring her hencefah, an' then, if she an' his maw fin' theyse'ves agreeable, then Mr. Mahch—which his buggy happm to be here in Suez— 'llow to give her his transpotes the balance o' the way to-morrow in hit."

"And you and Aunt Virginia will stay through the golden wedding as our chief butler and chief baker, as I wrote you ; will you ? "

"Well, er, eh "—the old man scratched his head— " thass the question, Miss Fannie. Thass what I been a-revolvin', an' I sees two views faw revolution. On one side there is the fittenness o' we two faw this work."

"It's glaring," mused Fannie.

"Flagrant," as gravely suggested Barbara.

"P'ecisely! Faw, as you say in yo' letteh, we two was chief butler an' chief baker to they wedd'n' jess fifty year' ago, bein' at that time hi-ud out to 'Squi' Usher—the ole 'Squieh, you know—by Miss Rose' motheh, which, you know, Miss Tomb' she was a Usher, daughteh to the old 'Squi' Usher, same as she is still sisteh to the present 'Squieh, who was son to the ole 'Squieh, his father an' hern. The ole 'Squieh, he married a Jasper, an' thass how come the Tombses is remotely alloyed to the Mahches on the late Jedge's side, an' to you, Miss Barb, on Miss Rose's Montgomery side, an' in these times, when cooks is sca'ce an' butlehs is yit mo' so, it seem to me—it seem to me, Miss Fannie, like yo' letteh was a sawt o'—sawt o'——"

"Macedonian cry," said Fannie.

"Hark from the Tombses," murmured Barbara.

"And so you'll both come!" said Fannie.

"Why, as I say, Miss Fannie, thass the question, fo' there's the care o' my flock, you know."

"De laymbs," put in Virginia, "de laymbs is bleeds to be fed, you know, Miss Fannie, evm if dey is black."

"Yass, ma'am," resumed Leviticus; "an' if we speak o' mere yearthly toys, Fudjinia's pigs an' chickens has they claims."

"Well, whoever's taking care of them now can keep on till the twenty-second, Uncle Leviticus; and as for your church, you can run down there Sunday and come right back, can't you? Why can't you?"

"Uncle Leviticus," said Barbara, "we expect, of course, to pay you both, you know."

"Why, of course!" said Fannie, "you understood that, didn't you?"

"Yass'm, o' co'se," interposed Virginia, quickly, while Leviticus drawled,

"O the question o' pay is seconda'y!—But we'll have to accede, Fudjinia; they can't do without us."

"I think, Fannie," said Barbara, looking very business-like, "we'd better have them name their price and agree to it at once, and so be sure——"

"Lawd, honey!" cried Virginia, "we ain't goin' to ax no prices to you-all! sufficiend unto de price is de laboh theyof, an' we leaves dat to yo' generos'ty. Yass, dass right where we proud an' joyful to leave it —to yo' generos'ty."

"Well, now, remember, the Tombses mustn't know a breath about this. You'll find Johanna in the kitchen. She'll have to give you her room and sleep on the floor in Miss Barb's; she'll be glad of the excuse——"

"Thaank you, Miss Fannie," replied Virginia, with amiable complacency, "but we 'llowin' to soj'u'n with friends in town."

"O, indeed! Well"—Arrangements for a later conference were made. "Good-evening. I'm glad you're bringing such a nice-looking girl to Mrs. March. What is her—what is your name?"

"Daaphne."

"What!"

"Yass'm. Mr. Mahch say whiles I wuck faw he's

maw he like me to be naame Jaane, but my fo'-true name's Daaphne, yass'm."

"Barb," said Fannie, "I've just thought of something we must attend to in the house at once!"

---

## XLVIII.

### DELILAH

DAPHNE JANE was one of Leggettstown's few social successes. She was neither comely nor guileless, but she was tremendously smart. Her pious parents had sent her for two or three terms to the "Preparatory Department" of Suez University, where she had learned to read, write, and add—she had been born with a proficiency in subtraction. But she had proved flirtatious, and her father and mother had spent their later school outlays on her younger brothers and sisters. Daphne Jane had since then found sufficient and glad employ trying to pomatum the frizzles out of her hair, and lounging whole hours on her window-sill to show the result to her rivals and monopolize and cheer the passing toiler with the clatter of her perky wit and the perfumes of bergamot and cinnamon.

Cornelius Leggett had easily discovered this dark planet, but her parents were honestly, however crudely, trying to make their children better than their betters expected them to be, and they forbade him the house and her the lonely stroll.

The daughter, from the first moment, professed to look with loathing upon the much-married and probably equally widowed Cornelius, but her mother did not trust her chaste shudderings. When John March came looking for a domestic, she eagerly arranged to put her out to service in a house where, Leviticus assured her, Cornelius dared not bring his foot. John March, however, was not taken into this confidence. The maid's quick wit was her strong card, and even Leviticus did not think it just to her to inform a master or mistress that it was the only strong card she held.

So, thanks to Leviticus, the only man in Leggettstown who would stop at no pains to " suckumvent wickedness in high places," here she was, half-way to Widewood, and thus far safe against any unguessed machinations of the enemy or herself. In Suez, too, all went well. Before Mrs. March Jane seemed made of angelic " yass'ms," and agreed, with a strange, sweet readiness to go to Widewood and assume her duties in her mistress's absence, which would be for a few days only.

" And you'll go "—" yass'm "—" with my son "— " yass'm "—" in the buggy "—" yass'm "—" and begin work "—" yass'm " — " just as though "—" yass'm "— " I were there "—" yass'm." Mrs. March added, half to herself, half to her son, " I find Suez "—" yass'm "— " more lonely than "—" yass'm "—" our forest home." " Yass'm "—said the black damsel.

John was delighted with such undaunted and unselfish alacrity. He was only sorry not to take her home at once, but really this business with Garnet and Gam-

ble was paramount. It kept him late, and the next
morning was well grown when he sought his mother to
say that he could now take Jane to Widewood.

" My son, you cannot.   It's too late."

" Why, what's the matter? "

" Nothing, my dear John."

" Where's the girl ? "

" On the way to her field of labor."

" How is she getting there? "

" In our buggy."

" You haven't let her drive out alone? "

" My son, why should you charge me with both
cruelty and folly ? "

" Who took her out ? "

" One, my dear boy, who I little thought would ever
be more attentive to the widow's needs than her own son:
Cornelius Leggett."   Mrs. March never smiled her triumphs.   Her lips only writhed under a pleasant pain.

" Well, I'll be——"

" Oh ! "

" Why, what, mother?   I was only going to say I'll
be more than pleased if he doesn't steal the horse and
buggy.   I'll bet five dollars——"

"Oh ! "

" O, I only mean I don't doubt he's half ruined both
by now, and all to save a paltry hour."

"My son, it is not mine to squander.   Ah! John,
the hours are not ours ! "

" Why, what are they?   O! I see.   Well, I wish
whoever they belong to would come take 'em away ! "

Cornelius was at that moment rejoicing that this one

was peculiarly his. As he drove along the quiet Wide-wood road he was remarking to his charge :

"I arrove fum Pussy on the six o'clock train. One o' the fus news I get win' of is that you in town. Well! y'ought to see me!"

But his hearer refused to be flattered. "Wha'd you do—run jump in de riveh?"

"Jump in—I reckon not! I flew. Y'ought to see me fly to'a'ds you, sweet lady!"

The maiden laughed. "Law! Mr. Leggett, what a shoo-fly that mus' 'a' been! Was de conducto' ayfteh you?"

Mr. Leggett smiled undaunted. "My mos' num'ous thanks to yo' serenity, but I enjoys fum my frien' Presi-*dent* Gamble the propriety of a free paass ove' his road."

"Oh? does you indeed! *Is* dat so! Why you makes me proud o' myse'ff. You hole a free paass on de raailroad, an' yit you countercend to fly to me!" The manner changed to one of sweet curiosity. "Does you fly jess with yo' two feet, aw does you comp'ise de assistance o' yo' ears?"

"Why, eh—why, I declah 'pon my soul, you—you es peart es popcawn! You trebbles me to respond to you with sufficient talk-up-titude."

"Does I? Laws-a-me! I ax yo' pahdon, Mr. Leggett. But I uz bawn sassy. I ought to be jess ashame' o' myseff, talkin' dat familious to a gen'leman o' yo' powehs an' 'quaintances. Why you evm knows Mr. Mahch, don't you?"

"Who, me? Me know Johnnie Mahch? Why, my

dea'—escuse my smile o' disdaain—why Johnnie Mahch
—why—why, I ra-aise' Johnnie!"

"Why, dee Lawdy! Does you call him Johnnie to
his face?"

"Well, eh—not offm—ve'y seldom. 'Caze ef I do
that, you know, then, here, fus' thing, he be a-callin' me
C'nelius."

"I think C'nelius sounds sweet'n—" The speaker
clapped a hand to her mouth. "Escuse me! O, Mr.
Leggett, *kin* you escuse me?"

"Escuse you?"—his sidelong glance was ravishing—
"yo' beauty mo'n escuse you."

The maiden dropped her lashes and drew her feet out
of her protector's way. "An' you an' Mr. Mahch is
frien's! How nice dat is!"

"Yass, it nice faw him. An' it useful faw me. We
in cahoots in dis-yeh lan' boom. O, yass, me an' him an'
Gyarnit an' Gamble, all togetheh like fo' brethers. I
plays the fife, Johnnie beats the drum, Gyarnit wear the
big hat an' flerrish the stick, an' Gamble, he tote the ice-
wateh!" The two laughed so heartily as to swing
against each other.

"Escuse me!" said Mr. Leggett, with great fondness
of tone.

"You ve'y escusable," coyly replied the damsel. "Mr.
Leggett, in what similitude does you means you plays
de fife?"

"Why in the s'militude o' legislation, you know. But
Law'! Johnnie wouldn't neveh had the sense to 'range
it that-a way if it hadn't been faw my dea' ole-time
frien' an' felleh sodjer, Gyarnit."

"Is dat so? Well, well! Maajo' Gyarnit! You used to cook faw him in camp di'n' you? How much good sense he got, tubbe sho'!" A mixture of roguishness spoiled the pretence of wonder.

"Good sense? Law'! 'twant good sense in Gyarnit nuther. It was jess my pow' ove' him! my stra-ange, masmaric poweh! You know, the arrangements is jess this! Gyarnit got th'ee hund'ed sheers, I got fawty; yit I the poweh behime the th'one. Johnnie, he on'y sec'ta'y an' 'ithout a salary as yit, though him an' his maw got—oh! I dunno—but enough so he kin sell it faw all his daddy could 'a' sole the whole track faw—that is, perwidin' he kin fine a buyeh. Champion, Shotwell, the Graveses—all that crowd, they jess on'y the flies 'roun' the jug; bymeby they find theyse'ves onto the fly-papeh." The pair laughed again, and——

"Oh! escuse me!"

"My acci*dent*, seh. Mr. Leggett, hoccum you got all dat poweh?"

"Ah!" said the smiling gallant, "you wants to know the secret o' my poweh, do you? Well, that interjuce the ezacly question I'm jess a-honin' to ass you. You ass me the secret o' my poweh. Don't you know thass the ve'y thing what Delijah ass Saampson?"

"Yass, seh. I knows. Dass in de Bible, ain't it?"

"It is. It in the sacred scripters, which I hope that, like myseff, fum a chile thou hass known them, ain't you? Yass, well, thass right. I loves to see a young lady pious. I'm pious myseff. Ef I wan't a legislater *I'd* be a preacher. Now, you ass me the same riddle what Delijah ass Saampson. An' you know how he anseh her?

He assed a riddle to her.  An' likewise this my sweet
riddle to you : Is I the Saampson o' yo' hope an' dream
an' will you be my Deli—— Aw! now, don't whisk
away like that an' gag yo'seff with yo' handkercher! I's
a lawful widoweh, dearess."

The maiden quenched her mirth and put on great
dignity.  " Mr. Leggett, will you please to teck yo' ahm
fum roun' my wais'? "  She glanced back with much
whiteness of eyes.  " Teck it off, seh ; I ain't aansw'ed
you yit."

The arm fell away, but his whispering lips came close.
" Ain't I yo' Saampson, dearess o' the dear ?  Ain't
you the Delijah o' my haht ?  Answeh me, my julepina,
an' O, I'll reply you the secret o' my poweh aw any
otheh question in the wide, wide worl' ! "

" Mr. Leggett, ef you crowds me any wuss on dis-yeh
buggy seat I—I'll give you—I'll give you a unfavo'able
answeh !  Mr. Leggett "—she sniggered—" you don't
gimme no chaynce to think o' no objections even ef I
had any !  Will you please to keep yo' foot where yo'
foot belong, seh ?  Mr. Leggett—— "

" What is it, my sweet spirit o' nightshade ? "

" Mr. Leggett "—the eyes sparkled with banter—" I'll
tell you ef you'll fus' aansweh *me* a riddle ; will you ?
'Caze ef you don't I won't tell you.  Will you ? "

" Lawd !  I'll try !  On'y ass it quick befo' my haht
bus' wide opm.  Ass it quick ! "

" Well, you know, I cayn't ass it so scan'lous quick,
else I run de dangeh o' gettin' it wrong.  Now, dis is it :
When is—hol' on, lemme see—yass, dass it.  When is
two—aw! pshaw! you make me laaugh so I can't

ax it at all! When is two raace hawses less'n one?"

"Aw, sheh! I kin ans' that in five minutes! I kin ans' it in one minute! I kin ans' it now! Two hosses is—"

"Hol' on! I said raace hawses! Two raace hawses, I said, seh!"

"Well, dass all right, race hosses! Two race hosses less'n one when they reti-ud into the omlibus business."

"No, seh! no seh!" The maiden cackled till the forest answered back. "No, *seh!* two raace hawses less'n one when each one on'y jess abreas' o' the otheh!"

—"'Breas' o'—aw pshaw! you tuck the words right out'n my mouth! I seed the answeh to it fum the fus; I made a wrong espunction the fus time on'y jess faw a joke! Now, you ans' my question, dearess."

But the dearest had become grave and stately. "Mr. Leggett, befo' I comes to dat finality, I owes it to myseff an' likewise to my pa'ents to git yo' respondence to, anyhow, one question, an' ef you de man o' poweh you say you is, y' ought to be highly fitt'n' to give de correc' reply."

"Espoun' your question, miss! Espoun' yo' question!"

"Well, seh, de question is dis: Why is de—? No, dat ain't it. Lemme see. O yass, whass de diff'ence 'twix' de busy blacksmiff an' de loss calf? Ans' me dat, seh! Folks say C'nelius Leggett a pow'ful smaht maan! How I gwine to know he a smaht maan ef he cayn't evm ans' a riddle-diddle-dee?"

"I kin ans' it! I's ans'ed bushels an' ba'ls o' riddles! Now that riddle is estremely simple, an' dis is de inte'p'etation thereof! The diff''ence betwix' a busy blacksmiff' an' a loss ca-alf—thass what you said, ain't it?—Yass, well, it's because—O thass too easy! I dislikes to occupy my facilities with sich a trifle! It's jess simply because they both git so hawngry they crosseyed! Thass why they alike!"

"No, seh! no, seh! miss it ag'in! O fie, fo' shaame! a man o' sich mind-powehs like you! Didn't you neveh know de blacksmiff fill de air full o' bellows whilce de loss calf—aw shucks! you done made me fo'git it! Now, jess hesh up, you smaht yalleh niggeh! tryin' to meck out like you done guess it! Dis is it; de blacksmiff he fill de caalf full o' bellows, whilce——"

They both broke into happy laughter and he toyed innocently with one of her pinchbeck ear-rings.

"O! my sweet familiarity! you knows I knows it! But yo' sof' eyes is shot me th'oo to that estent that I don't know what I does know! I jess sets here in the emba'ssment o' my complacency a won'de'n' what you takes me faw!"

"How does you know I's tuck you at all yit; is I said so, Mr. Saampson?—Don't you tetch me, seh! right here in full sight o' de house! You's too late, seh! too late! Come roun' here, C'nelius Leggett, an' he'p me out'n dis-yeh buggy, else I dis'p'int you yit wid my aansweh.—No, seh! you please to take jess de tips o' my fingehs. Now, gimme my bundle o' duds!" the voice rose and fell in coquettish undulations—"now git back into de buggy—yass, seh; dass right. Thaank yo ve'y much, seh. Good-by. Come ag'in."

"Miss Daphne, y' ain't ans' my interrogutive yit."

"Yass, I is. Dass my answeh—come ag'in."

"Is dat all de respondence my Delijah got faw her Saampson?"

"Mr. Leggett, I ain't yo' Delijah! Thass fix! I ain't read the scripters in relations to dat young lady faw nuthin! Whetheh you my Saampson remain"— the smile and tone grew bewitching—"faw me to know an faw you to fine out."

"Shell I come soon?" murmured Mr. Leggett, for the old field hand and his wife were in sight; and the girl answered in full voice, but winsomely:

"As to dat, seh, I leaves you to de freedom o' yo' own compulsions."

He moved slowly away, half teased, half elated. At the last moment he cast a final look backward, and Daphne Jane, lagging behind the old couple, tossed him a kiss.

Quite satisfied to be idle, but not to be alone, the maiden so early contrived with her Leggettstown vivacity to offend the old field hands, that the night found her with only herself and her cogitations for company.

However, the house was still new to her, if not in its pantry, at least in its bureaus and wardrobes, and when she had spent the first evening hour counterfeiting the softly whimpered quavers of a little screech-owl that snivelled its woes from a tree in the back-yard, the happy thought came to her innocent young mind to try on the best she could find of her mistress's gowns and millinery. By hook and by crook, combined with a blithe assiduity, she managed to open doors and drawers, and if mimicry is the heaven of aspiring laziness, the maid presently stood unchallenged on the highest plateau of a sluggard's bliss. She minced before the mirror, she sank into chairs, she sighed and whined, took the attitudes given or implied by the other Daphne's portrait down-stairs, and said weary things in a faint, high key.

And then—whether the contagion was in the clothing she had put on, or whether her make-up and her acting were so good as to deceive Calliope herself—inspiration came ; the lonely reveler was moved to write. Poetry ? No! "Miss it ag'n!" She began a letter intended to inform "Mr. S. Cunnelius Leggett," that while alike by her parents and by Mrs. March she was forbidden to see "genlmun frens," an unannounced evening visitor's risks of being shot by Mr. March first, and the question of his kinship to the late Enos settled afterward, were probably—in the popular mind—exaggerated. The same pastime enlivened the next evening and the next. She even went farther and ventured into verse. Always as she wrote she endeavored to impersonate in numerous subtleties of carriage the sweet songstress whose gowns she had contrived—albeit whose shoes she still failed—to get into. And so, with a conscience void of offence, she was preparing herself to find out, what so many of us already know, that playing even with the muse's fire is playing with fire, all the same.

## XLIX.

### MEETING OF STOCKHOLDERS

AT sunrise of the twenty-second, Barbara started from her pillow, roused by the jarring thunder of a cannon. As it pealed a second time Fannie drew her down.

"It's only Charlie Champion in the square firing a salute. Go to sleep again."

As they stepped out after breakfast for a breath of garden air, they saw John March a short way off, trying to lift the latch of Parson Tombs's low front gate. He tried thrice and again, but each time he bent down the beautiful creature he rode would rear until it seemed as if she must certainly fall back upon her rider. The pastor had come out on his gallery, where he stood, all smiles, waiting for John to win in the pretty strife, which the rider presently did, and glanced over to the Halliday garden, more than ready to lift his hat. But Fannie and Barbara were busy tiptoeing for peach blossoms.

"Good-morning, Brother March; won't you 'light? I declare I don't know which you manage best, yo' horse aw yo' tempeh!" The parson laughed heartily to indicate that, however doubtful the compliment, his intentions were kind.

"Good-morning, sir," said John in the gateway as his pastor came bareheaded toward him; and after a word

or two more of greeting—" Mr. Tombs, there's to be
a meeting of stockholders in the parlor of the hotel
at ten o'clock.   My friend, Mr. Fair, got here yesterday
evening, and we want him to see that we mean business
and hope he does."

" I see," said Parson Tombs, with a momentous air.
" And I'll come.   I may be a little late in gett'n' there,
faw I've got to hitch up aft' a while and take Mother
Tombs to spend the day, both of us, with our daughters,
Mrs. Hamlet and Lazarus Graves.   I don't reckon anybody else has noticed it but them, but, John, my son,
Mother Tombs an' I will be married jess fifty years to-
night !   However that's neither here nor there ; I'll
come.   If I'm half aw three-quarters of an hour late,
why, I reckon that's no mo'n the rest of 'em will be,
is it ? "

John smiled and said he feared it wasn't.   As his
mare leaped from the sidewalk to the roadway he
noted the younger pastor going by on the other side,
evidently on a reconnoisance.   For the committee on
decorations was to come with evergreens to begin to deck
the Tombs parsonage the moment the aged pair should
get out of sight of it.

Three persons were prompt to the moment at the meeting of stockholders : Garnet, Gamble, and Jonas Crickwater, the new clerk of Swanee Hotel and a subscriber for
one share—face value one hundred dollars, cash payment
ten.   A moment later Cornelius entered, and with a
peering smile.

" Howdy, Leggett ? " said Garnet, affably ; but when

the tawny statesman moved as though he might offer to shake hands, the Major added with increased cordiality, "take a seat," and waved him to a chair against the wall; then, turning his back, he resumed conversation with the railroad president. Presently John March arrived, with a dignity in his gait and an energy in his eye that secretly amused the president of the road. John looked at his watch with an apologetic smile.

"I supposed you had gone some place to get Mr. Fair," said Garnet.

"He's in Jeff-Jack's office; they're coming over together." John busied himself with his papers to veil his immense satisfaction. Looking up from them he saw Leggett. "Oh!" he exclaimed, stepped forward, and, with a constrained bow, for the first time in his life gave him his hand. The mulatto bowed low and smiled eruptively, too tickled to speak.

At the end of half an hour the gathering numbered nine, and everybody was in conversation with somebody. Mr. Crickwater, after three gay but futile attempts to tell Gamble that they were from the same State in the North, leaned against a wall with anguish in his every furtive glance, hopelessly button-holed by Leggett.

"Ah!" cried Garnet, as Jeff-Jack and Fair entered together. The Major laughed out for joy. In a moment it was—"Mr. Fair, this man, and Mr. Fair, that one—you remember President Gamble, of course?— and Captain Champion? Mr. Fair, let me make you acquainted with Mr. Hersey. Mr. Weed I think you met the last time you were here. No! this is Mr. Weed, that's our colored representative, Mr. Leggett. He'd like to shake hands with you, too, sir."

"Mr. Fair," said Cornelius, "seh, to you; yass, I likes to get my sheer o' whateveh's a-goin'."

He was about to say much more, but Garnet purposely drowned his voice. "Gentlemen, we'll proceed to business. Mr. Crickwater, will you act as doorkeeper?" Mr. Crickwater assumed that office.

Secretary March having occasion to mention the number of subscribed shares represented by those present as six hundred and eleven, Garnet explained that besides his own subscription he represented one of fifteen shares and another of ten for two ladies, and Champion unintentionally uttered a lurid monosyllable as Shotwell stuck him under the leg with a pin. They were the shares, Garnet added, that General Halliday had failed to take.

Business went on. When, by and by, Mr. Crickwater admitted Parson Tombs, the pastor found the company listening to the Honorable Cornelius Leggett as he expounded the reasons for, and the purposes of, the various provisions of An Act to authorize the Counties of Blackland, Clearwater, and Sandstone to subscribe to the capital stock of the Three-Counties Land and Improvement Company, Limited, and to declare said counties to be bodies politic and corporate for the purposes therein mentioned.

"You see, gentlemen," interposed Garnet, "we make Mr. Leggett one of the principal advocates of this bill in order to secure the support of those, both in the Legislature and at the polls, who are likely to vote as he votes on the question of the three counties subscribing to this other thousand shares, the half of our capital stock reserved for the purpose."

Mr. Weed asked how many shares offered to voluntary subscribers on the ten-dollar instalment plan had been taken, and Garnet replied, "All. Those, together with the shares assigned me in exchange for the mortgages I hold on Widewood and propose to surrender, the forty for which Mr. Leggett pays five hundred dollars, and the two hundred retained by Mr. March and his mother, make six hundred and forty, leaving three hundred and sixty to be placed with capitalists willing to pay their face value. We have to-day an increased confidence that these reinforcements"—he smiled— "are not far off. When this is done we shall have raised the three-eighths of the face value of the one thousand private shares, as required, before the three counties' subscription to the other thousand shares can become effective. I have to state, gentlemen, that General Halliday has been compelled by the weight of other burdens to resign the treasurership; but on the other hand I have the pleasure to announce that Captain Charles Champion has consented to act as treasurer, and *also*, that Colonel Ravenel expresses his willingness to serve as one of the two trustees for the three counties on the— (applause)—on the very reasonable condition that he be allowed to name the other trustee. I believe there's no other formal business before the meeting, but before we adjourn I think a few brief remarks from one or two gentlemen who have not yet spoken will be worth far more than the time they occupy. I'll call on our vice-president, Mr. Gamble." (Applause.)

Gamble said his father used to tell him a man of words and not of deeds was like a garden full of weeds. Here he was silent so long that Champion whispered to Shotwell, " He's stuck ! "

But at length he resumed, that he attributed his own success in life to his always having believed in deeds !

"Indeed ! " echoed Shotwell in so audible a whisper that half the group smiled.

Gamble replied that his statement might surprise some that had been asleep for the last twenty years, but he guessed there wasn't any such person in this crowd. (Laughter.) However, he proposed to say in a few words, which should be as much like deeds as he could make 'em, what he was willing to do. He paused so long again that Champion winked at John and was afraid to look at Shotwell.

He remembered, the speaker finally began again, another good saying—couldn't seem to be sure whether it was from Shakespeare or the Bible—that " a fool and his money are soon parted." Now, he was far from intending that for anyone present——

" No-o," slowly interrupted Hersey, turning from a large spittoon, " we ain't any of us got any money to part with."

" Well, I haven't mistook any of you for fools, neither. But I think that proverb, or whatever you call it, is as much's to say just like this, that if a man ain't a fool, 'tain't easy to part him from his money ! " (Applause.)

" How about a fool and his land ? " asked John, with a genial countenance.

" O *you*'re all right," eagerly replied Gamble, and smiled inquiringly as the company roared with laughter. " Why, gentlemen, our able and efficient secretary *is* all right ! Land ain't always money, and the fool is the man who won't let his land go when he's got too much of it. (Applause.) But that's not what I was driving at. What I was driving at was this : that if we want to get any man or men to put big money into this thing out o' their own pockets, we've got to make 'em officers of the company an' give 'em control of it. Of course, our secretary is in to stay ; that's part of his pay for the land he gives ; but except as to him, gentlemen, there'll have to be a new slate. How's that, Mr. President ? "

" Certainly ; we're all pro tem. except Mr. March— and Colonel Ravenel."

" Yes, Colonel Ravenel, of course ; but the man he selects for the other trustee must be someone satisfactory to the men on the new slate, eh, Colonel ? "

Ravenel smiled, nodded, and as Gamble still looked at him, said, " All right."

" Now, gentlemen, if any of you don't agree to these things, now is the time to say it." A long pause. " If we are all agreed, then all I've got to add, Mr. President, is just this : you say there's three hundred and sixty shares for sale at their face value ; I'll take two hundred when anybody else will take the balance." (Applause.)

As Gamble sank down Garnet glanced over to Fair,

who was sitting next to Jeff-Jack; but Fair began to
read some of the company's printed matter and the
whole gathering saw Ravenel give Garnet a faint shake
of the head.

" Ravenel ! " suggested Champion, but Jeff-Jack
quietly replied, " Father Tombs," and five or six others
repeated the call. The pastor rose.

" I'm most afraid, my dea' friends an' brethren, I
oughtn't to try to speak to this crowd. I'm a man of
words and not of deeds, an' yet I'm 'fraid I shan't evm
say the right thing. I belong to the past. I've been
thinkin' of the past every minute I've been a-sitt'n' here.
Yo' faces ah all turned to the future an' ah lighted "—
he lifted his arm and waggled his hand—" by the
beams of a risin' sun reflected from the structu'es o' yo'
golden dreams. As I look back down the long an'
shining stair-steps o' the years I count seventy-two of
'em in the clear sight o' memory's eye besides fo' or five
that lie shrouded in the silve'y mist of earliest childhood." The pastor, ceased and his hearers were very
still.

"I don't tell my age to brag of it, but if I remind you-
all that I've baptized mo' Suez babies than there are
now Suez men an' women alive, an' have seen jest about
eve'y cawnehstone laid in this town that's ever been laid,
I needn't say my heart's in yo' fawtunes whether taw
this world aw the next.

" An' I don't doubt you goin' to be prospe'd. What
I'm bound to tell you I've my private fears of, an' yet
what I'm hopin' an' trustin' and prayin' the Lord will
delivch you fum— evm as a cawp'ate company— is

the debasin' sin o' money greed.  Gentle*men*, an' dea'
friends an' breth'en, may Gawd save you fum that as
he saved the two Ezra Jaspehs, the foundeh o' Suez an'
his cousin, the grantee of Widewood, fum the folly o'
lan' greed.  For I tell you they may not 'a' managed
either tract as well as some otheh men think they might
'a' done it, but they were saved the folly whereof I speak.
They's been some talk an' laugh here this mawnin' about
John March a-partin' with so much o' his lan'.   Well, if
that makes him a fool, he's a fool by my advice !  Faw
when he come to me with his plans all in the bud, so to
speak, I said to him there an' then, an' he'll remembeh :
Johnnie, s'I, I've set on the knees of both Ezra Jaspehs,
an' I'm tellin' you what I know of the one that was yo'
fatheh's grand-fatheh, as you say you know it of yo' own
sainted fatheh : that if the time had eveh come in his
life when paht'n' with Widewood tract would of seemed
any ways likely to turn it into sco'es an' hund'eds o'
p'osp'ous an' pious homes he would 'a' givm ninety-nine
hund'edths away faw nothin' rather than not see that
change ; yes, an' had mo' joy oveh the  one-hund'edth
left to him than oveh the ninety an' nine to 'a' kep' 'em
as the lan's of on'y one owneh an' one home.

   " Gentlemen, I'm free to allow, as I heah the explanations o' all the gue-ards an' counteh-gue-ards o' this
beautiful scheme—schools faw the well-to-do an' the
ill-to-do, imperatively provided as fast as toil is provided
faw the toiler and investments faw the investor—I have
cause to rejoice an' be glad.  An' yet !  It oughtn't to
seem strange to you-all if an' ole man, a man o' the quiet
ole ploughin' an' plantin', fodder-pullin', song-singin',

cotton-pickin', Christmas-keepin' days, the days o' wide
room an' easy goin', should feel right smaht o' solicitude
an' tripidation when he sees the red an' threatenin' dawn
of anotheh time, a time o' mines an' mills an' fact'ries
an' swarmin' artisans' an' operatives an' all the concom-
itants o' crowded an' complicated conditions, an' that
he should fall to prayin' aloud in the very highways
an' hotels, like some po' benighted believer in printed
prayehs an' litanies, the petition : Fum all Ole Worl'
sins an' New Worl' fanaticisms, fum all new-comers,
whetheh immigrants aw capitalists, with delete'ious
politics at va'iance fum ow own, which, heavm knows,
ah delete'ious enough, an' most of all fum the greed o'
money, good Lawd deliv' us!

" An' I have faith that he will.    Uphel' by that faith,
I've taken fifteen shares myself.    But O, if faith could
right here an' now be changed into sight, then would
this day be as golden in my hopes faw Suez an' her three
counties as it already is faw my private self in memory
o' past joys."

The speaker was sinking into his chair when Garnet
asked with a smile that everyone but the pastor understood, " Why, how's that Brother Tombs; is this day
something more than usual to you ? "

" Brother Garnet, if I've hinted that it is, it's mo'
than I started out to do, but I'm tempted, seein' so many
friends in one bunch so, to jest ask yo'-all's congratu-
lations on "—the eyes glistened with moisture—" the
golden anniversary o' my weddin' day."

The walls rang with applause, men crowded laughingly
around the Parson to shake his hand, and in ten minutes

the room was silent and the company gone, " every man to his tent," as the happy Parson said, each one as ready for his noontide meal as it was for him.

---

## L.

### THE JAMBOREE

THE social event of that midday was not the large family dinner where Mother Tombs sat between Hamlet and Lazarus, and Father Tombs between their wives; where Sister March was in the prettiest good humor conceivable and the puns were of the sort that need to be italicized, and the anecdotes were family heirlooms, and the mirth was as spontaneous as the wit was scarce, and not one bad conscience was hidden beneath it all. The true social event of that hour was the repast given by John March to Mr. Fair in Swanee Hotel, at which General Halliday, Captain Champion, and Dr. Coffin were on John's left, Ravenel sat at the foot of the board, and at John's right were Fair, in the place of honor, then Garnet, and then Shotwell in the seat appointed for Gamble, who had suddenly found he couldn't possibly stay.

Here were no mothers' quotations of their children's accidental wit, nor husbands' and wives' betrayals of silly sweetnesses of long-gone courtships and honeymoons. Passing from encomiums upon Parson Tombs's powers to the subject of eloquence in general, the allu-

sions were mainly to Edmund Burke, John C. Calhoun,
Sargent S. Prentiss, and Lorenzo Dow. The examples
of epigram were drawn from the times of Addison, those
of poetic wisdom from Pope, of witty jest from Douglas
Jerrold and Sidney Smith, of satire from Randolph of
Roanoke. John March told, very successfully, how a
certain great poet of the eighteenth century retorted
impromptu upon a certain great lord in a double-
rhymed and triple-punned repartee. Champion and
Shotwell, in happy alternation, recited two or three
incredible nonsense speeches attributed to early local
celebrities, and Garnet and Halliday gave the unpublished inside histories of three or four hitherto inexplicable facts, or seeming facts, in the personal or political
relations of Marshall, Jackson, Webster, and Clay.
Burns and Byron were there in spirit, and John could
have recited one of his mother's poems if anyone had
asked for it.

As for Ravenel and Fair, they had their parts and
performed them harmoniously with the rest, so that
John could see that he himself and everyone else were
genuinely interesting to those two and that they were
growingly interesting to each other. Both possessed
the art of provoking the others to talk ; they furnished
the seed of conversation and were its gardeners, while
the rest of the company bore its fruits and flowers.
Ravenel seemed always to keep others talking for his
diversion, Fair for his information.

John pointed this out to Miss Garnet that evening, at
the Parson's golden wedding, and noticed that she listened to him with a perfectly beautiful eagerness.

"It's because I talked about Fair," he said to himself as he left her—"Aha! there they go off together, now."

The scene of this movement was that large house and grounds, the "Usher home place," just beyond the ruined bridge where Cornelius had once seen ghosts. A pretty sight it was to come out on the veranda, as John did, and see the double line of parti-colored transparencies meandering through the dark grove to the gate and the lane beyond. Shotwell met him.

"Hello, March, looking for Fair? He's just passed through that inside door with Miss Garnet."

"I know it—I'm not looking for anyone—in particular."

Out here on the veranda it was too cool for ladies; John heard only male voices and saw only the red ends of cigars; so, although he was not—of course he wasn't! —looking for anyone—in particular—he went back into the crowded house and buzzing rooms.

"Hunt'n' faw yo' maw, John?" asked Deacon Sexton as he leaned on his old friend Mattox; "she's——"

"Why, I'm not hunting for anybody," laughed March; "do I look like I was?"

He turned away toward a group that stood and sat about Parson Tombs.

"I never suspicioned a thing," the elated pastor was saying for the third or fourth time. "I never suspicioned the first thing till Motheh Tombs and I got into ow gate comin' home fum the Graveses! All of a sudden there we *ware* under a perfec' demonstration o' pine an' ceda' boughs an' wreaths an' arborvitæ faschoons! Evm then I never suspicioned but what that was all until Miss Fannie an' Miss Barb come in an' begin banterin' not only Motheh Tombs but *me*, if you'll believe it, to lie down an' rest a while befo' we came roun' here to suppeh! Still I 'llowed to myself, s'I, it's jest a few old frien's they've gotten togetheh. But when I see the grove all lightened up with those Chinee lanterns, I laughed, an' s'I to motheh, s'I, ' I don't know what it is, but whatev' it is, it's the biggest thing of its kind we've eveh treed in the fifty years that's brought us to this golden hour ! ' An' with that po' motheh, she just had to let go all ho-holts; heh—heh cup run oveh.

" You wouldn't think so now, to see heh sett'n' oveh there smilin' like a basket o' chips, an' that little baag o gold dollahs asleep in heh lap, would you ? But that smile ain't change' the least iota these fifty years. What a sweet an' happy thought it was o' John March, tellin' the girls to put the amount in fifty pieces, one for each year. But he's always been that original. Worthy son of a worthy motheh ! Why, here he is ! Howdy, John ? I'm so proud to see Sisteh March here to-night ; she told me at dinneh that she 'llowed to go back to Widewood this evenin'."

" I see in the papeh she 'llowed to go this mawnin'," said Clay Mattox.

John showed apologetic amusement. " That's my fault, I reckon, I understood mother to say she couldn't stay this evening."

A finger was laid on his shoulder. It was Shotwell again. " John, Miss Fannie Halliday wants Jeff-Jack. Do you know where he is ? "

" No ! Where is Miss Fannie ? "

Shotwell lifted his hand again, with a soothing smile. "Don't remove yo' shirt; Ellen is saafe, fo' that thaynk Heavm, an' hopes ah faw the Douglas givm."

March flung himself away, but Shotwell turned him again by a supplicating call and manly, repentant air. "Law, John, don't mind my plaay, old man; I'm just about as sick as you ah. Here! I'll tell you where she is, an' then I'll tell you what let's do! You go hunt Jeff-Jack an' I'll staay with heh till you fetch him!"

"That would be nice," cheerfully laughed John.

In the next room he came upon Fannie standing in a group of Rosemont and Montrose youths and damsels. They promptly drew away.

"John," she said, "I want to ask a favor of you, may I?"

"You can ask any favor in the world of me, Miss Fannie, except one."

"Why, what's that?" risked Fannie.

"The one you've just sent Shotwell to do." He smiled with playful gallantry, yet felt at once that he had said too much.

Fannie put on a gayety intended for their furtive observers, as she murmured, "Don't look so! A dozen people are watching you with their ears in their eyes." Then, in a fuller voice—"I want you to get Parson Tombs away from that crowd in yonder. He's excited and overtaxing his strength."

"Then may I come back and spend a few minutes— no more—with you—alone? This is the last chance I'll ever have, Miss Fannie—I—I simply must!"

"John, if you simply must, why, then, you simply—

mustn t. You'll have the whole room trying to guess what you're saying."

"They've no right to guess!"

"We've no right to set them guessing, John." She saw the truth strike and felt that unlucky impulse of compassion which so often makes a woman's mercy so unmercifully ill-timed. "Oh!" she called as he was leaving.

He came back with a foolish hope in his face. She spoke softly.

"Everybody says there's a new John March. Tell me it's so; won't you?"

"I"—his countenance fell—"I thought there was, but—I—I don't know." He went on his errand. Champion met him and fixed him with a broad grin.

"I know what's the matter with you, March."

"O pooh! you think so, eh? Well, you never made a greater mistake! I'm simply tired. I'm fairly aching with fatigue, and I suppose my face shows it."

"Yes. Well, that's all I meant. Anybody can see by your face you're in a perfect agony of fatigue. You don't conceal it as well as Shotwell does."

"Shotwell!" laughed John. "He's got about as much agony to conceal as a wash-bench with a broken leg. O, I'll conceal mine if anybody'll tell me how."

Champion closed his lips but laughed audibly, in his stomach. "Well, then, get that face off of you. You look like a boy that'd lost all his money at a bogus snake-show."

When Fair came up to Barbara, she was almost as

'glad to see him as John supposed, and brought her every wit and grace to bear for his retention, with a promptness that satisfied even her father, viewing them from a distance.

"Miss Garnet, I heard a man, just now, call this very pleasant affair a jamboree. What constitutes a jamboree?"

"Why, Mr. Fair," said Barbara, in her most captivating drawl, "that's slang!"

"Yes, I didn't doubt. I hope you're not guilty of never using slang, are you?"

"O no, sir, but I never use it where I can't wear a shawl over my head. Still, I say a great many things that are much worse than slang."

"Miss Garnet, you say things that are as good as the best slang I ever heard."

"Ah!—that's encouraging. Did you ever hear the Misses Kinsington's rule· Never let your slang show a lack of wit or poverty of words! They say it's a sure cure for the slang habit. But if you really need to know, Mr. Fair, what constitutes a jamboree, I can go and ask Uncle Leviticus for you; that is, if you'll take me to him. He's our butler to-night, and he's one of the old slave house-servants that you said you'd like to talk with."

"But I want to talk with you, just now; definitions can wait."

"O you shall; there's every facility for talking there, and it's not so crowded."

The consumption of refreshments had been early and swift, and they found the room appropriated to it almost empty. Two or three snug nooks in it were occupied by one couple each. Leviticus was majestically superintending the coming and going of three or four maidservants. Just as he gathered himself up to define a jamboree, Virginia happened in and stood with a coffee-cup half wiped, eying him with quizzical approbation.

" A jamboree? You want to know what constitutes a jamboree? Well—What you want, Fudjinia? "

" Go on, seh, go on. Don't let me amba'as you. I wants jess on'y my civil rights. Go on, seh." She set her arms akimbo.

" A jamboree!" repeated Leviticus, giving himself a yet more benevolent dignity. " Well, you know, Miss Barb, to ev'ything they is a season, an' a time to ev'y puppose. A wedd'n' is a wedd'n', a infare is a infare, a Chris'mus dinneh is a Chris'mus dinneh! But now, when you come to a jamboree—a jam—Fudjinia "—he smiled an affectionate persuasion—" we ain't been appi'nted the chiefs o' this evenin's transactions to stan' idlin' round, is we? "

" Go on, seh, go on."

" Well, you know, Mr. Fair, when we South'enehs speak of a jamboree, a jamboree is any getherin' wherein the objec' o' the getherin' is the puppose fo' which they come togetheh, an' the joy and the jumble ah equal if not superiah to each otheh."

Virginia brought up a grunt from very far down, which might have been either admiration or amusement. " Umph! dat is a jamboree, faw a fac'! I wond' ef he git dat fum de books aw ef he pick it out'n his own lahnin'? "

"Miss Garnet," said Fair, "there are wheels within wheels. I am having a jamboree of my own."

---

## LI.

### BUSINESS

"This," replied Barbara, "has been a bright day for our whole town." And then, more pensively, "They say you could have made it brighter."

Whereat the young man lowered his voice. "Miss Garnet, I had hoped I could."

"And I had hoped you would."

"Miss Garnet, honestly, I'm glad I did not know it at the meeting. It was hard enough to disappoint Mr. March; but to know that I was failing to meet a hope of yours—"

Presently he added:

"Your hope implied a certain belief in me. Have I diminished that?"

"Why-y, no-o, Mr. Fair, you've rather aug-men-ted it."

He brightened almost playfully. "Miss Garnet, you give me more pleasure than I can quietly confess."

"Why, I didn't intend to do that."

"To be trusted by you is a glad honor."

"Well, I do trust you, Mr. Fair. I'm trusting you now—to trust me—that I really want to talk—man-talk. As a rule," continued Barbara, putting away her playfulness, "when a young lady wants to talk pure business, she'd better talk with her father, don't you think so?"

"As a rule, yes. And, as a rule, I make no doubt that's what you would do."

Barbara's reply was meditative. "One reason why I want to talk about this business at all this evening is also a strong reason why I don't talk about it to pop-a."

"I see; he's almost as fascinated with it as Mr. March is."

"It means so very much to the college, Mr. Fair, and you know he's always been over eyes and ears in love with it; it's his life." She paused and then serenely seized the strategic point at which she had hours before decided to begin this momentous invasion. "Mr. Fair, why, do you reckon, Mr. Ravenel has consented to act as commissioner?"

Fair laughed. "You mean is it trust or distrust?"

"Yes, sir; which do you reckon it is?"

He laughed again. "I'm not good at reckoning."

"You can guess," she said archly.

"Yes, we can both do that. Miss Garnet, I don't believe your *father* is actuated by distrust; he believes in the scheme. You, I take it, do not, and you are solicitous for him. Do I not guess rightly?"

"I don't think I'm more solicitous than a daughter should be. Pop-a has only me, you know. Didn't you believe in Mr. March's plan at one time, sir?"

"I believed thoroughly, as I do still, in Mr. March. I also had, and still have, some belief in his plan; but" —confidentially—" I have no belief in——"

"Certain persons," said Barbara so slowly and absently that Fair smiled again as he said yes. They sat in silence for some time. Then Barbara said, meditatively, "If even Mr. March could only be made to see that certain persons ought not to have part in his enterprise—but you can't tell him that. I didn't see it so until now. It would seem like pique."

"Or a counter scheme," said Fair. "Would you wish him told?"

"You admit I have a right to a daughter's solicitude?"

"Surely!" Fair pondered a moment. "Miss Garnet, if the opportunity offers, I am more than willing you should say to Mr. March——"

"I rarely meet him, but still——"

"That I expressed to you my conviction that unless he gets rid of——"

"Certain——" said Barbara.

"Persons," said Fair, "his scheme will end in loss to his friends and in ruin to him."

"And would that be"—Barbara rose dreamily—"a real service to pop-a?"

Fair gave his arm. "I think it the best you can render; only, your father——" He began to smile, but she lifted a glance as utterly without fear as without hardihood and said:

"I understand. He must never know it's been done."

"That's more than I meant," he replied, as Fannie Halliday came up. The two girls went for their wraps.

"March?" said Ravenel, as he and Fair waited to

escort them home.  "O, no, he left some time ago with his mother."

On the way to the Halliday cottage Fair said to Barbara:

"I'm glad of the talk we've had."

"You can afford to be so, Mr. Fair.  It showed your generosity against the background of my selfishness."

"Selfishness?  Surely it isn't selfish to show a daughter's care and affection for a father."

By her hand on his arm he felt her shrink at the last word.  "I love my father, yes.  But you're making mistakes about me.  Let's talk about Miss Fannie; she'll only be Miss Fannie about two weeks longer. You ought to stay to see her married, Mr. Fair."

"And you are to be bridesmaid!  But I *must* go to-morrow.  I wish my father and mother could reach here in time on their way home from New Orleans, but when they get this far your bridal party will have been two days married and gone."

Barbara mused a moment.  "You know, this plan for me to give a year to study in the North has been as much mine as pop-a's; but pop-a's entirely responsible for putting me into your father's and mother's care on the journey.  I've been in a state of alarm ever since."

"Really, that's wrong!  You're going to be a source of great pleasure to them.  And you'll like them, too, very much.  They are interesting in many ways and good in all, and as travelers they are perfect."

"You give me new courage, Mr. Fair.  But "—she spoke more playfully—"I'm afraid of New England, yet. There's a sort of motherly quality in our climate that I can't expect to find there. Won't the snow be still on the ground?"

"Very likely; the higher mountain tops, at least, will be quite covered."

"Well, I'm glad that doesn't mean what I once thought it did. I thought the snow in New England covered the mountain tops the same way the waters covered them in the Deluge."

Fair looked down into his companion's face under the leafy moonlight and halted in a quick glow of inspiration. "When first you see New England, Miss Garnet, nature will have been lying for four months in white, sacramental silence. But presently you will detect a growing change——"

"A stealing out of captivity?"

"Yes!—each step a little quicker than the one behind it——" So he went on for a full minute in praise of the New England spring.

Barbara listened with the delight all girls have for flowers of speech plucked for themselves.

"You know," she responded, as they moved on again, "it doesn't come easy for us Southerners to think of your country as being beautiful; but we notice that nearly all the landscapes in our books are made in 'barren New England,' and we have a pri-vate cu-ri-os-i-ty to know how you all in-vent them."

"If New England should not charm you, Miss Garnet," —Fair hurried his words as they drew near Ravenel and Fannie waiting at the cottage gate—"my disappointment would last me all my life."

"Why, so it would me," said Barbara, "but I do not expect it. Well, Fannie, Mr. Fair has at last been decoyed into praising his native land. Think of—— " She hushed.

A strong footstep approached, and John March came out of the gloom of the trees, saluting buoyantly. Ravenel reached sidewise for his hand and detained him.

"I took my mother away early," said March. "She can't bear a crowd long. I was feeling so fatigued, myself, I thought a brisk walk might help me. You still think you must go to-morrow, Mr. Fair? I go North, myself, in about a week."

The two girls expressed surprise.

"For the land company?" quickly prompted Fannie.

"Yes, principally. I'll take my mother's poems along and give them to some good publisher. O no-o, it's not exactly a sudden decision; its taken me all day to make it. My mother—O—no, she seems almost resigned to my going, but it's hard to tell about my mother, Miss Garnet; she has a wonderful control of her feelings."

---

## LII.

### DARKNESS AND DOUBT

THE paragraph in the *Courier* which purported to tell the movements of Mrs. March silently left its readers to guess those of her son. Two men whose abiding-places lay in different directions away from Suez had no sooner made their two guesses than they proceeded to act upon them without knowledge of, or reference to, the other.

About an hour after dark on the night of the golden wedding both these men were riding, one northward, the other southward, toward each other on the Widewood road. Widewood house was between them. Both moved with a wary slowness and looked and listened intently, constantly, and in every direction.

When one had ridden within a hundred yards or so of the Widewood house and the other was not much farther away, the rider coming up from the southward stopped, heard the tread of the horse approaching in front, and in hasty trepidation turned his own animal a few steps aside in the forest. He would have made them more but for the tell-tale crackle of dead branches strewed underfoot by the March winds. He sat for a long time very quiet, peering and hearkening. But the other had heard, or at least thought he had heard, the crackle of dead branches, and was taking the same precautions.

The advantage, however, was with the rider from the south, who knew, while the other only feared, there was something ahead it were better to see than be seen by. About the same time the one concluded his ears might have deceived him, the other had divined exactly what had happened. Thereupon the shrewder man tied his horse and stole noiselessly to a point from whose dense shade he could see a short piece of the road and the house standing out in the moonlight.

The only two front windows in it that had shades

were in Mrs. March's bed-chamber. The room was
brightly lighted and the shades drawn down. The rest
of the house was quite dark. The man hiding so near
these signs noted them, but drew no hasty conclusions.
He hoped to consider them later, but his first need was
to know who, or, at least where, the person was whom he
had heard upon the road.

Though already well hidden he crouched behind a
log, and upon the piece of road and every shadowy cover
of possible approach threw forward an alert scrutiny
supported by the whole force of his shrewdest conjec-
tures. The sounds and silences that belong to the night
in field and forest were far and near. Across the moon
a mottled cloud floated with the slowness of a sleeping
fish, a second, third, and fourth as slowly followed,
the shadow of a dead tree crawled over a white stone
and left it in the light ; but the enigma remained an
enigma still. It might be that the object of conjecture
had fled in the belief that the conjecturer was none
other than Widewood's master. But, in that same belief, who could say he might not be lying in ambush
within close gunshot of the horse to which the conjecturer dared not now return ? In those hills a man
would sometimes lie whole days in ambush for a neighbor, and one need not be a coward to shudder at the
chance of being assassinated by mistake. To wait on
was safest, but it was very tedious. Yet soon enough,
and near and sudden enough, seemed the appearance of
the man waited for, when at length, without a warning
sound, he issued from the bushy shadow of a fence into
the bright dooryard. In his person he was not formida-

ble. He was of less than medium stature, lightly built, and apparently neither sinewy nor agile. But in his grasp was something long and slender, much concealed by his own shadow, but showing now a glint of bright metal and now its dark cylindrical end; something that held the eye of the one who watched him from out the shadow. Neither the features nor yet the complexion of the one he watched were discernible, but the eyes were evidently on a third window of the lighted room not at its front, but on a side invisible to the watcher. This person rose from his log and moved as speedily as he could in silence and shadow until he came round in sight of this window and behind the other figure. Then he saw what had so tardily emboldened the figure to come forward out of hiding. This window also had a shade, the shade was lowered, and on it the unseen lamp perfectly outlined the form of a third person. Without a mutter or the slightest gesture of passion, the man under the window raised the thing in his grasp as high as his shoulder, lowered it again and glanced around. He seemed to tremble. The man at his back did not move; his gaze, too, was now fastened, with liveliest manifestations of interest, on the window-shade and the moving image that darkened it.

As the foremost of the two men began for the third time that mysterious movement which he had twice left unfinished, the one behind, now clearly discerning his intention, stole one step forward, and then a second, as if to spring upon him before he could complete the action. But he was not quick enough. The black and glistening thing rose once more to the level of its owner's shoulder, and the next instant on the still night air quivered the plaintive wail of—a flute.

At mortal risks both conjectured and unconjectured, it was an instrument of music, not of murder, which Mr. Dinwiddie Pettigrew was aiming sidewise.

## LIII.

### SWEETNESS AND LIGHT

YET the pulse of the man behind him, who did not recognize him, began to quicken with anger. Almost at the flute's first note the image on the window-shade started and hearkened. A moment later it expanded to grotesque proportions, the room swiftly grew dark, and in another minute the window of a smaller one behind it shone dimly as with the flame of a lamp turned low. The flutist fluted on. From the melody it appeared that the musician had at some date not indicated, and under some unaccountable influence, dreamt that he dwelt in marble halls with vassals and serfs at his side. The man at his back had come as near as the darkness would cover him, but there had stopped.

Presently the music ceased, but another sound, sweeter than all music, kissed, as it were, the serenader's ear. It was the wary lifting of a window-sash. He ran forward into the narrow shade of the house itself, and lost to the restraints of reason, carried away on transports of love, without hope of any reply, whispered,

" Daphne ! "

And a tender whisper came back—" Wait a minute."

" You'll come down ? " he whisperously asked ; but the window closed on his words, the dim light vanished, and all was still.

He was watching, on his left, the batten shutters of the sitting-room, when a small, unnoticed door near the dark, rear corner of the house clicked and then faintly creaked. Mr. Pettigrew became one tremolo of ecstasy. He glided to the spot, not imagining even then that he was to be granted more than a moment's interview through an inch or two of opening, when what was his joy to see the door swiftly spread wide inward by a dim figure that extended her arms in gracious invitation.

" O love ! " was all his passion could murmur as they clasped in the blessed dark, while she, not waiting to hear word or voice, rubbed half the rice powder and rouge from her lips and checks to his and cried,

" O you sweet, speckle', yalleh niggeh liah, you tol' me you on'y play de fife in de similitude o' ligislation ! "

As Dinwiddie silently but violently recoiled Daphne Jane half stifled a scream, sprang through a stair door, shot the bolt and rushed upstairs. At the same instant he heard behind him a key slipped from its lock. He glanced back in affright, and trembling on legs too limp to lift, dimly saw the outer door swing to. As the darkness changed to blackness he heard the key re-enter its lock and turn on the outside. The pirate was a prisoner.

Daphne Jane, locking everything as she fled, whirled into her mistress's room and out of her mistress's clothes.

Though quaking with apprehension so that she could scarcely button her own things on again, she was filled with the joy of adventure and a revel of vanity and mirth. The moment she could complete her change of dress and whisk her borrowed fineries back into their places she stole to a window over the door by which she had let the serenader in, softly opened it, and was alarmed afresh to hear two voices.

The words of the one in the room were quite indistinguishable, but those from the other on the outside, though uttered in a half whisper, were clear enough.

"No, seh, I ain't dead-sho' who you is, but I has examine yo' hoss, an' whilce I wouldn' swear you ah **Mr.** Pettigrew, thass the premonition I espec' to espress to my frien' Mr. March, lessn you tell me now, an' tell me true, who you ah.

"Yass, seh, I thought so. Yass, seh. No, seh, I know they ain't a minute to lose, but still I think the time ain't quite so pow'ful pressin' to me like what it is to you; I thought jess now I hyeard buggy-wheels, but mebbe I didn't.

"Yass, seh, I *does* think I has cause, if not to be mad, leas'wise to be ve'y much paained. You fus' kiss the young lady I destine faw my sultana, an' now you offeh me a briibe! Well, thass how I unde'stood it, seh.

"Seh? No, seh! that wouldn't be high tone'! But I tell you what I will do, seh. I'll let you out an' take yo' place an' make the young lady think her on'y mistake was a-thinkin' she was mistakened.

"Seh? Yass, I'm jess that se'f-sacrificin'. I'm

gen'ous as the whistlin' win'. An' I'll neveh whisp' a breath o' all this shaameful procedu'e evm to my dear frien' March, ef so be that—an' so long as—yo' gratichude—seh?

"O nothin'. I wus jess a-listenin' ef that soun' was buggy wheels, but I know that don't make no diff''ence to you, yo' courage is so vas'. I'm the bravess o' the brave, myseff, an' yit jess to think o' takin' yo' place fills me as full o' cole shivehs as a pup und' a pump.

"Seh? O I say I'll neveh whisp' it so long as yo' gratichude continue to evince itseff fresh an' lively at the rate of evm on'y a few dollahs per month as a sawt o' friendship's offerin'.

"Seh? I cayn't he'p it, seh; thass the ve'y bes' I can do; no otheh co'se would be hon'able."

The listening maid heard the door unlock and open and beheld liberty bartered for captivity with love for boot, and Mr. Pettigrew speed like a phantom across the moonlight and vanish in the woods. Before she could leave the window a sound of galloping hoofs told at last the coming of John March. Cornelius had barely time to scamper out into the night when the master of Widewood came trotting around the corner of the house and thence off to the stable, never to know of the farce which made Mr. Pettigrew thereafter the tool of Leggett, and which might even more easily have been a tragedy with the mountain people for actors and himself its victim.

## LIV.

### AN UNEXPECTED PLEASURE

RAVENEL and Fannie were married in church on an afternoon. The bridesmaids were Barbara and a very pretty cousin of Fannie's from Pulaski City, who would have been prettier yet had she not been revel-worn. The crowded company was dotted with notables; Garnet and Gamble took excellent care of the governor. But the bride's father was the finest figure of all.

"Old Halliday looks grand!" said Gamble.

"I'm glad he does," kindly responded Garnet; "it would be a pity for him to be disappointed in himself on such an occasion."

Parson Tombs kissed the bride, who, in a certain wildness of grateful surprise, gave him his kiss back again with a hug. When Ravenel's sister, from Flat-rock, said:

"Well, Colonel Ravenel, aren't you going to kiss me?" he gracefully did so, as if pleased to be reminded of something he might have forgotten. And then he kissed the aged widow with whom he had lived so long. Her cottage, said rumor, was not to be sold, after all, to make room for the new brick stores. No, the Salters' house had been bought for that purpose—it was ready to tumble down, anyhow—and on Miss Mary's marriage, soon to be, Miss Martha and her mother would take the Halliday cottage, the General keeping a room or two, but getting his meals at the hotel.

" It's a way of living I've always liked ! " he said, tossing his gray curls.

The bridal pair, everybody understood, were to leave
Suez on the Launcelot Halliday, and turn northward by
rail in the morning on an unfamilar route.

John March chose not to see the wedding. He remained in Pulaski City, where for three days he had
been very busy in the lobbies of the Capitol, and was
hoping to take the train for the north that evening.
Between the trifling of one and the dickering of another,
he was delayed to the last moment ; but then he flung
himself into a shabby hack, paid double fare for a pretence of double speed, and at the ticket window had to
be called back to get his pocket-book. The lighted train
was moving out into the night as a porter jerked him
and his valise on to the rear platform.

He stood there a moment alone silently watching the
lamps of the town sink away and vanish. His thought
was all of Fannie. She was Fannie Ravenel now. Fate
had laughed at him. He calculated that the pair
must about this time be rising from supper on the boat.

" Happy bridegroom !—and happy bride ! "

As the dark landscape perpetually spun away from
him he began with an inexperienced traveler's self-con-
sciousness to think of the strangeness of his own situation ;
but very soon Fannie's image came before him again in
a feverish mingling of gratitude and resentment. Had
she not made his life ? But for her he might yet be
teaching school in the hills of Sandstone. No doubt he
would have outgrown such work ; but when ? how soon ?
how tardily ? how fatally late ? She had lured and

fooled him; but she had lured and fooled him into a largeness of purpose, a breadth of being, which without her might never have come to him.

"I cannot be with her, I must not go near her; but I am here!" he exclaimed, catching a certain elation from his unaccustomed speed. "The prospect may be desert, but it's wide; it's wide!"

She had been good *for* him, he mused, not to him. She had been wiser than she meant; certainly she had not been kind. She was not cold-hearted. His welfare was dear to her. And yet she had cold-heartedly amused herself with him. She was light-minded. There! The truth was out! Just what he meant by it was not so clear; but there it was, half comforting him, half excusing her; she was light-minded! Well, she was Fannie Ravenel now. "Happy Fannie Ravenel!" He said it with a tempered bitterness and went in.

It was the sleeping-car he was on. Two steps brought him to the open entrance of its smoking-room—they were enough. With drooping eyelids its sole occupant was vacantly smiling at the failure of his little finger to push the ash from a cold cigar.

"Jeff-Ja'!" exclaimed March, "O my Lord!"

The bridegroom looked up with a smart exaggeration of his usual cynicism and said, "J—(h-h)—Johnnie, this 's 'n un'spec'—'spected pleasure!"

"I thought you were aboard the——" faltered John, and stood dumb, gnawing his lip and burning with emotions.

"John, o' frien', take a chair." The speaker waved a

hand in tipsy graciousness. " What made you think I was aboard—I look like one ? Wha'—(h-h)—kind o' board—sideboard ? S' down, John, make 'seff at home. Happm have cars all t' ourselves. Mr. March, this 's ufforshnate, ain't it ? Don't y' sink so ? One o' my p'culiar 'tacks. Come on 'tirely since leavin' Suez. Have—(h-h)—seat. My dear frien', I know what you're thinkin' 'bout. You're won'rin' where bride is an' feel del'cacy 'bout askin'. She's in state-room oth' end the car, locked in. She's not 'zactly locked in, but I'm locked out. Mrs. Ravenel is—(h-h)—annoyed at this, Mr. March ; ve'y mush annoyed."

He put on a frown. " John, 'll you do me a—(h-h)— favor ? "

" I'm afraid I can't, Ravenel. I've a good notion to get off at the next station."

" Tha's jus' what I's goin' t' ash you t' do. I'll stan' 'spence, John. You shan't lose anything."

" O no, if I get off I'll stand the expense myself. You've lost enough already, Jeff-Jack."

" No, sir ; *I'll* stan' 'spence. I can be gen'rous you are. Or 'f you'll stay 'n' take care Mrs. Ravenel I'll— (h-h)—get off m'seff! "

John shook his head, took up his bag and returned to the rear platform.

The train had stopped and was off again, when the porter came looking everywhere, the rear platform included.

" Whah dat gemman what get on at P'laski City ? "

Ravenel waved his cigar.

" He's out in back garden pickin' flowers ! Porter—

you—f—ond o' flowers? 'F you want to go an' pick some I'll—(h-h)—take care car for you. Porter!—here!—I—(h-h)—don't want to be misleading. Mr. March's simply stepped out s—see 'f he can find a f—four-leaf clover."

---

## LV.

### HOME-SICKNESS ALLEVIATED

On the second morning after the wedding and next trip of this train, the sleeping-car was nearly half filled with passengers by the time it was a night's run from Pulaski City. To let the porter put their two sections in order, a party of three, the last except one to come out of the berths, had to look around twice for a good place in which to sit together. They were regarded with interest.

"High-steppers," remarked a very large-eared commercial traveler to another.

"The girl's beautiful," replied the other, remembering that he was freshly shaved and was not bad-looking himself.

"Yes," said the first, "but the other two are better than that; they're comfortable. They're done raising children and ain't had any bad luck with 'em, and they've got lots of tin. If that ain't earthly bliss I'll bet you!"

"They're gett'n' lots of entertainment out of that daughter, seems like,"

" Reason why, she's not their daughter."

" How d'you know she's not ? "

" I mustn't tell—breach o' confidence. Guess."

" O I guess you're guessing. George! she's—what makes you think she's not their daughter ? "

" O nothin', only I'm a man of discernment, and besides I just now heard 'em call her Miss Garnet."

Their attention was diverted by the porter saying at the only section still curtained, " Breakfus' at next stop, seh. No, seh, it's yo' on'y chaynce till dinneh, seh. Seh? No, seh, not till one o'clock dis afternoon, seh."

" Is that gentleman sick ? " asked the younger commercial man, wishing Miss Garnet to know what a high-bred voice and tender heart he had.

" Who ? numb' elevm ? Humph ! he ain't too sick to be cross. Say he ain't sleep none fo' two nights. But he's gitt'n' up now."

The solicitous traveler secured a seat at table opposite Miss Garnet and put more majestic gentility into his breakfasting than he had ever done before. Once he pushed the sugar most courteously to the lady she was with, and once, with polished deference, he was asking the gentleman if he could reach the butter, when a tardy comer was shown in and given the chair next him. As this person, a young man as stalwart as he was handsome, was about to sit down, he started with surprise and exclaimed to Miss Garnet,

" Why ! You've begun—— Why, are we on the same train ? "

And she grew visibly prettier as she replied smilingly,

" You must be Number Eleven, are you not ? "

Coming out of the place the young lady's admirer heard her introduce Number Eleven to "Mr. and Mrs. Fair," and Mr. Fair, looking highly pleased, say,

"I don't think I ever should have recognized you!"

Something kept the train, and as he was joined by his large-eared friend—who had breakfasted at the sandwich counter—he said,

"See that young fellow talking to Mr. Fair? That's the famous John Marsh, owner of the Widewood lands. He's one of the richest young men in Dixie. Whenever he wants cash all he's got to do is to go out and cut a few more telegraph-poles—O laugh if you feel like it, but I heard Miss Garnet tell her friends so just now, and I'll bet my head on anything that girl says." The firm believer relighted his cigar, adding digressively, "I've just discovered she's a sister-in-law"—puff, puff— "of my old friend, General Halliday"—puff, puff— "president of Rosemont College. Well, away we go."

The train swept on, the smoking-room filled. The drummer with the large ears let his companion introduce "Mr. Marsh" to him, and was presently so pleased with the easy, open, and thoroughly informed way in which this wealthy young man discussed cigars and horses that he put aside his own reserve, told a risky story, and manfully complimented the cleanness of the one with which Mr. March followed suit.

A traveling man's life, he further said, was a rough one and got a fellow into bad ways. There wasn't a blank bit of real good excuse for it, but it was so.

No, there wasn't! responded his fellow-craftsman. For his part he liked to go to church once in a while

and wasn't ashamed to say so. His mother was a good
Baptist. Some men objected to the renting of pews,
but, in church or out of it, he didn't see why a rich
man shouldn't have what he was willing to pay for, as
well as a poor man. Whereupon a smoker, hitherto
silent, said, with an oratorical gesture,

"Lift up your heads, O ye gates, the rich and the poor
meet together, yet the Lord is the maker of them
all!"

March left them deep in theology. He found Mr.
and Mrs. Fair half hid in newspapers, and Miss Garnet
with a volume of poems.

"How beautiful the country is," she said as she made
room for him at her side. "I can neither write my
diary nor read my book."

"Do you notice," replied he, "that the spring here is
away behind ours?"

"Yes, sir. By night, I suppose, we'll be where it's
hardly spring at all yet."

"We'll be out of Dixie," said John, looking far
away.

"Now, Mr. March," responded Barbara, with a smile
of sweetest resentment, "you're ag-grav-a-ting my nos-
tal-gia!"

To the younger commercial traveler her accents
sounded like the wavelets on a beach!

"Why, I declare, Miss Garnet, I don't want to do
that. If you'll help me cure mine I'll do all you'll let
me do to cure yours."

Barbara was pensive. "I think mine must be worse
than yours; I don't want it cu-ured."

"Well, I didn't mean cured, either; I only meant solaced."

"But, Mr. March, I—why, my home-sickness is for all Dixie. I always knew I loved it, but I never knew how much till now."

"Miss Garnet!" softly exclaimed John with such a serious brightness of pure fellowship that Barbara dropped her gaze to her book.

"Isn't it right?" she asked, playfully.

"Right? If it isn't then I'm wrong from centre to circumference!"

"Why, I'm glad it's so com-pre-hen-sive-ly cor-rect."

The commercial traveler hid his smile.

"It's about all I learned at Montrose," she continued. "But, Mr. March, what is it in the South we Southerners love so? Mr. Fair asked me this morning and when I couldn't explain he laughed. Of course I didn't confess my hu-mil-i-a-tion; I intimated that it was simply something a North-ern-er can't un-der-stand. Wasn't that right?"

"Certainly! They *can't* understand it! They seem to think the South we love is a certain region and everything and everybody within its borders."

"I have a mighty dim idea where its Northern border is sit-u-a-ted."

"Why, so we all have! Our South isn't a matter of boundaries, or skies, or landscapes. Don't you and I find it all here now, simply because we've both got the true feeling—the one heart-beat for it?"

Barbara's only answer was a stronger heart-beat.

"It's not," resumed March, "a South of climate, like

a Yankee's Florida. It's a certain ungeographical South-within-the-South—as portable and intangible as —as——"

" As our souls in our bodies," interposed Barbara.

" You've said it exactly ! It's a sort o' something— social, civil, political, economic——"

" Romantic ? "

" Yes, romantic ! Something that makes——"

" ' No land like Dixie in all the wide world over ! ' "

" Good ! " cried John. " Good ! O, my mother's expressed that beautifully in a lyric of hers where she says though every endearing charm should fade away like a fairy gift our love would still entwine itself around the dear ruin—verdantly— I oughtn't to try to quote it. Doesn't her style remind you of some of the British poets? Aha ! I knew you'd say so ! Your father's noticed it. He says she ought to study Moore ! "

Barbara looked startled, colored, and then was impassive again, all in an instant and so prettily, that John gave her his heartiest admiration even while chafed with new doubts of Garnet's genuineness.

The commercial man went back to the smoking-room to mention casually that Mrs. March was a poetess.

" There's mighty little," John began, but the din of a passing freight train compelled him to repeat much louder—" There's mighty little poetry that can beat Tom Moore's ! "

Barbara showed herself so mystified and embarrassed that March was sure she had not heard him correctly. He reiterated his words, and she understood and smiled broadly, but merely explained, apologetically, that she had thought he had said there was mighty little pastry could beat his mother's.

John laughed so heartily that Mrs. Fair looked back at Barbara with gay approval, and life seemed to him for the moment to have less battle-smoke and more sunshine; but by and by when he thought Barbara's attention was entirely on the landscape, she saw him unconsciously shake his head and heave a sigh.

----

## LVI.

### CONCERNING SECOND LOVE

WHEN the train stopped at a station they talked of the book in her hand, and by the time it started on they were reading poems from the volume to each other. The roar of the wheels did not drown her low, searching tones; by bending close John could hear quite comfortably. Between readings they discussed those truths of the heart on which the poems touched. Later, though they still read aloud, they often looked on the page together.

In the middle of one poem they turned the book face downward to consider a question. Did Miss Garnet believe—Mr. March offered to admit that among the small elect who are really capable of a divine passion there may be some with whom a second love is a genuine and beautiful possibility—yet it passed his comprehension—he had never seen two dawns in one day—

but did Miss Garnet believe such a second love could ever have the depth and fervor of the first?

Yes, she replied with slow care, she did—in a man's case at least. To every deep soul she did believe it was appointed to love once—yes—with a greater joy and pain than ever before or after, but she hardly thought this was first love. It was almost sure to be first love in a woman, for a woman, she said, can't afford to let herself love until she knows she is loved, and so her first love—when it really is love, and not a mere consent to be loved——

"Which is frequently all it is," said John.

"Yes. But when it is a real love—it's fearfully sure and strong *because* it has to be slow. I believe when such a love as that leaves a woman's heart, it is likely to leave it hope-less-ly strand-ed."

"And you think it's different with a man?"

"Why, I hope it's sometimes different with a woman; but I believe, Mr. March, that with a man the chances are better. A man who simply must love, and love with his whole soul——"

"Then you believe there are such?"

"Yes, there must be, or God wouldn't create some of the women he makes."

"True!" said John, very gallantly.

"But don't you think, Mr. March, a man of that sort is apt to love prematurely and very faultily? His best fruit doesn't fall first. Haven't you observed that a man's first love is just what a woman finds it hardest to take in earnest?"

"Yes, I have observed that! And still—are you too

cynical to believe that there are men to whom first love
is everything and second love impossible?"

"No," said Barbara, with true resentment, "I'm not
too cynical. But—" she looked her prettiest—"still I
don't believe it."

John turned on her a hard glance which instantly
softened. It is a singular fact that the length and droop
of a girl's eyelashes have great weight in an argument.

"And yet," she resumed, but paused for John to
wave away the train-boy with his books.

"And yet what?" asked March, ever so kindly.

"And yet, that first love is everything, is what every
woman would like every man to believe, until he learns
better." Her steadfast gaze and slow smile made John
laugh. He was about to give a railing answer when the
brakeman announced twenty minutes for dinner.

"What! It can't——" he looked at his watch.
"Why, would you have imagined?"

O yes; her only surprise—a mild one—was that he
didn't know it.

At table she sat three seats away, with her Northern
friends between; and when they were again roaring
over streams, and through hills and valleys, and the
commercial travelers, whose number had increased to
four, were discussing aërial navigation, and March cut
short his after-dinner smoke and came back to resume
his conversation, he found Miss Garnet talking to the
Fairs, and not to be moved by the fact—which he felt
it the merest courtesy to state—that the best views were
on the other side of the car.

Thereupon he went to the car's far end and wrote a

short letter to his mother, who had exacted the pledge
of one a day, which she did not promise to answer.

In this he had some delay. A woman with a disabled mouth, cautiously wiping crumbs off it with a
paper napkin, asked him the time of day. She
explained that she had loaned her watch—gold—patent
lever—to her husband, who was a printer. She said
the chain of the watch was made of her mother's hair.
She also stated that her husband was an atheist, and had
a most singular mole on his back, and that she had
been called by telegraph to the care of an aunt taken
down with measles and whose husband was a steamboat pilot, and an excellent self-taught banjoist; that
she, herself, had in childhood been subject to mem-
branous croup, which had been cured with pulsatilla,
which the doctor had been told to prescribe, by his
grandmother, in a dream; also that her father, de-
ceased, was a man of the highest refinement, who
had invented a stump-extractor; that her sisters were
passionately fond of her; that she never spoke to
strangers when traveling, but, somehow, he, March, did
not seem like a stranger at all; and that she had
brought her dinner with her in a pasteboard shirt-box
rather than trust railroad cooking, being a dyspeptic.
She submitted the empty box in evidence, got him to
step to the platform and throw it away, and on his
return informed him that it was dyspepsia had disabled
her mouth, and not overwork, as she and her sisters had
once supposed.

Still March did finish his letter. Then he went and
smoked another cigar. And then he came again and

found the four traveling men playing whist, Mr. and Mrs. Fair dozing, and Miss Garnet looking out of a window on the other side in a section at the far end of the car, the only one not otherwise occupied.

" I'm in your seat," she said.

" O don't refuse to share it with me; you take away all its value."

She gradually remarked that she was not the sort of person wilfully to damage the value of a seat in a railroad car, and they shared it.

For a time they talked at random.    He got out a map and time-table and, while he held one side and she the other, showed where they had had to lie five hours at a junction the night before.    But when these were folded again there came a silent interval, and then John sank lower in his place, dropped his tone, and asked,

" Do you remember what we were speaking of before dinner ? "

Barbara dreamily said yes, and they began where they had left off.

Three hours later, on the contrary, they left off where they had begun.

## LVII.

### GO ON, SAYS BARBARA

MISS GARNET said she ought to rejoin her friends, and John started with her.

On their way the dyspeptic stopped them affectionately to offer Barbara a banana, and ask if she and the gentleman were not cousins. Miss Garnet said no, and John enjoyed that way she had of smiling sweetly with her eyes alone. But she smiled just as prettily with her lips also when the woman asked him if he was perfectly sure he hadn't relations in Arkansas named Pumpkinseed—he had such a strong Pumpkinseed look. The questioner tried to urge the banana upon him, assuring him that it was the last of three, which, she said, she wouldn't have bought if she hadn't been so lonesome.

Barbara sat down with her, to John's disgust, a feeling which was not diminished when he passed on to her Northern friends, and Mr. Fair tried very gently to draw him out on the Negro question! When he saw Mrs. Fair glancing about for the porter he sprang to find and send him, but lingered, himself, long among the mirrors to wash and brush up and adjust his necktie.

The cars stopping, he went to the front platform, where the dyspeptic, who was leaving the train, turned to thank him "for all his kindness" with such genuine gratitude that in the haste he quite lost his tongue, and for his only response pushed her anxiously off the steps. He still knew enough, however, to reflect that this probably left Miss Garnet alone, and promptly going in he found her—sitting with the Fairs.

Because she was perishing to have Mr. March again begin where he had left off, she conversed with the Fairs longer than ever and created half a dozen delays out of pure nothings. So that when she and John were once more alone together he talked hither and yon for a short while before he asked her where the poems were.

Nevertheless she was extremely pleasant. Their fellow-passenger just gone, she said, had praised him without stint, and had quoted him as having said to her, " It isn't always right to do what we have the right to do."

" O pshaw ! " warmly exclaimed John, started as if she had touched an inflamed nerve, and reddened, remembering how well Miss Garnet might know what that nerve was, and why it was so sore.

" I wish *I* knew how to be sen-ten-tious," said Barbara, obliviously.

" It was she led up to it." He laughed. " She said it better, herself, afterward ! "

" How did she say it ? "

" She ? O she said—she said her pastor said it— that nothing's quite right until it's noble."

" Well, don't you believe that principle ? "

" I don't know ! That's what I've asked myself twenty times to-day."

" Why to-day ? " asked Miss Garnet, with eyes down-cast, as though she could give the right answer herself.

" O "—he smiled—" something set me to thinking about it. But, now, Miss Garnet, is it true ? Isn't it sometimes allowable, and sometimes even necessary—absolutely, morally necessary—for a fellow to do what may look anything but noble?"

He got no reply.

"O of course I know it's the spirit of an act that counts, and not its look ; but—here now, for example,"—John dropped his voice confidentially—" is a fellow in love with a young lady, and—— Do I speak loud enough?"

"Yes, go on."

He did so for some time. By and by:

"Ah! yes, Mr. March, but remember you're only supposing a case."

"O, but I'm not only supposing it; it's actual fact. I knew it. And, as I say, whatever that feeling for her was, it became the ruling passion of his life. When circumstances—a change of conditions—of relations—made it simply wrong for him to cherish it any more it wasn't one-fourth or one-tenth so much the unrighteousness as the ignobility of the thing that tortured him and tortured him, until one day what does he up and do but turn over a new leaf. Do I speak too low?"

"No, go on, Mr. March."

Well, for about twenty-four hours he thought he had done something noble. Then he found that was just what it wasn't. It never is; else turning over new leaves would be easy! He didn't get his new leaf turned over. He tried; he tried his best."

"That's all God asks," murmured Barbara.

"What?"

"Nothing. Please don't stop. How'd it turn out?"

"O bad! He put himself out of sight and reach and went on trying, till one day—one night—without intention or expectation, he found her when, by the baseness —no, I won't say that, but—yes, I will!—by the baseness of another, she was all at once the fit object of all the pity and the sort of love that belongs with pity, which any heart can give."

"And he gave them!"

"Yes, he gave *them*. But the old feeling—whatever it was——" John hesitated.

"Go on. Please don't stop."

"The—the old feeling—went out—right there—like a candle in the wind. No, not that way, quite, but like a lamp drinking the last of its oil. Where he lodged that night——"

"Yes——"

"—He heard a clock strike every hour; and at the break of day that—feeling—whatever it was—with the only real good excuse to live it ever had—was dead."

"And that wasn't true love? Don't you believe it was?"

"Do you, Miss Barbara Garnet? Could true love lie down and give up the ghost at such a time and on such a pretext as that? Could it? Could it?"

"I think—O—I think it—you'll forgive me if——"

"Forgive! Why, how can you offend *me?* You don't imagine——"

"O no! I forgot. Well I think the love was true in degree; not the very truest. It was only *first* love; but it was the first love of a true heart."

"To be followed by a later and truer love, you think?"

"You shouldn't—O I don't know, **Mr. March.** What do you think?"

"Never! That's what I think. He may find refuge in friendship. I believe such a soul best fitted for that deep, pure friendship so much talked of and so rarely realized between man and woman. Such a heart naturally seeks it. Not with a mere hunger for comfort——"

"O no."

"——But because it has that to give which it cannot offer in love, yet which is good only when given; worthless to one, priceless to two. Sometimes I think it's finer than love, for it makes no demands, no promises, no compacts, no professions——"

"Did you ever have such a friendship?"

"No, indeed! If I had—oh pshaw! I never was or shall be fit for it. But I just tell you, Miss Garnet, that in such a case as we've spoken of, the need of such a heart for such a friendship can't be reckoned!"

He smiled sturdily, and she smiled also, but let compassion speak in her eyes before she reverently withdrew them. He, too, was still.

They were approaching a large river. The porter, growing fond of them, came, saying:

"Here where we crosses into Yankeedom. Fine view fum de rear platfawm—sun jes' a-sett'n'."

They went there—the Fairs preferred to sit still—and with the eddies of an almost wintry air ruffling them and John's arm lying along the rail under the window behind them, so as to clasp her instantly if she should lurch, they watched the slender bridge lengthen away

and the cold river widen under it between them and
Dixie.

Their silence confessed their common emotion.   John
felt a condescending expansion and did not withdraw
his arm even after the bridge was passed until he
thought Miss Garnet was about to glance around at it,
which she had no idea of doing.

"I declare, Miss Garnet, I—I wish——"

She turned her eyes to his handsome face lifted with
venturesome diffidence and frowning against the blustering wind.

"I'm afraid"—he gayly shook his head—"you won't
like what I say if you don't take it just as I mean it."
He put his hand over the iron-work again, but she was
still looking into his face, and he thought she didn't
know it.

"It wouldn't be fair to take it as you don't mean it,"
she said.   "What is it?"

"Why, ha-ha—I—I wish I were your brother!—ha-
ha!  Seriously, I don't believe you can imagine how
much a lone fellow—boy or man—can long and pine for
a sister.   If I'd had a sister, a younger sister—no boy
ever pined for an older sister—I believe I'd have
made a better man.   When I was a small boy——"

Barbara glanced at his breadth and stature with a
slow smile.

He laughed.   "O, that was away back yonder before you can remember."

"It certainly must have been," she replied, "and
yet——"

"And yet—" he echoed, enjoying his largeness.

" I thought all the pre-his-tor-ic things were big. But what was it you used to do? I know; you used to cry for a sister, didn't you?"

" Yes. Why, how'd you guess that?"

" I can't say, unless it was because I used to cry for a little brother."

" And why a little one?" he asked.

" I was young and didn't know any better."

" But later on, you——"

" I wanted the largest size."

" D'd you ever cry for a brother of the largest size?"

" Why, yes; I nearly cry for one yet, sometimes, when somebody makes me mad."

" Miss Garnet, I'm your candidate!"

" No, Mr. March. If you were elected you'd see your mistake and resign in a week, and I couldn't endure the mor-ti-fi-ca-tion."

John colored. He thought she was hinting at fickleness; but she gave him a smile which said so plainly, " The fault would be mine," that he was more than comfortable again—on the surface of his feelings, I mean.

And so with Barbara. The train had begun a downgrade and was going faster and faster. As she stood sweetly contemplating the sunset sky and sinking hills, fearing to move lest that arm behind her should be withdrawn and yet vigilant to give it no cause to come nearer, an unvoiced cry kept falling back into her heart—" Tell him!—For your misguided father's sake! Now!—Now!—Stop this prattle about friendship, love, and truth, and tell him his danger!"

But in reality she had not, and was not to have, the chance.

The young land-owner stood beside her staring at nothing and trying to bite his mustache.

He came to himself with a start. "Miss Garnet——"

As she turned the sky's blush lighted her face.

"That case we were speaking of inside, you know——"

"Yes, sir."

"Well, as I said, I knew that case myself. But, my goodness, Miss Garnet, you won't infer that I was alluding in any way to—to any experience of my own, will you?"

She made no reply.

"Law! Miss Garnet, you don't think I'd offer anybody a friendship pulled out of a slough of despond, do you?"

Barbara looked at him in trembling exaltation. "Mr. March, I know what has happened!"

He winced, but kept his guard. "Do you mean you know how it is I am on this train?"

"Yes, I know it all."

"O my soul! Have I betrayed it?"

"No, sir; the train conductor—I led him on—told us all about it before we were twenty miles from Suez."

"I ought to have guessed you'd find it out," said John, in a tone of self-rebuke.

"Yes," she replied, driving back her tears with a quiet smile, "I think you ought."

"Why—why, I—I—I'm overwhelmed. Gracious me! I owe you an humble apology, Miss Garnet. Yes, I do. I've thrust a confidence on you without your permission. I—I beg your pardon! I didn't mean to, I declare I didn't, Miss Garnet."

"It's safe."

"I know it. I'm surer of that than if you were any-one else I've ever known in my life, Miss Garnet."

"It shall be as if I had never heard it."

"O no! I don't see how it can. In fact—well—I don't see why it should—unless you wish it so. Of course, in that case——"

"That's not a con-tin-gen-cy," said Barbara, and for more than a minute they listened to the clangorous racket of the rails. Then John asked her if it did not have a quality in it almost like music and she bright-ened up at him as she nodded.

He made a gesture toward the receding land, bent to her in the uproar and cried, "It scarcely seems a moment since those hills were full of spring color, and now they're blue in the distance!"

She looked at them tenderly and nodded again.

"At any rate," he cried, holding his hat on and bending lower, "we have Dixie for our common mother." His manner was patriotic.

She glanced up to him—the distance was trivial— beaming with sisterly confidence, and just then the train lurched, and—he caught her.

"H-I conscience! wa'n't it lucky I happened to have my arm back there just at that moment?"

Barbara did not say. She stood with her back against the car, gazing at the track, her small feet braced forward with new caution, but she saw March lapse into reverie and heave another sigh.

However, she observed his mind return and rightly divined he was thinking her silence a trifle ungracious; so she lifted her hand toward a white cloud that rose above the vanished hills and river, saying:

"Our common mother waves us farewell."

"Yes," he cried with grateful pleasure. Seeing her draw her wrap closer he added, "You're cold?" And it was true, although she shook her head. He bent again to explain. "It'll be warmer when we leave this valley. You see, here——"

"Yes," she nodded so intelligently that he did not finish. Miss Garnet, however, was thinking of her chaperone and dubiously glanced back at the door. Then she braced her feet afresh. They were extremely pretty.

He smiled at them. "You needn't plant yourself so firmly," he said, "I'm not going to let you fall off."

O dear! That reversed everything. She had decided to stay; now she couldn't.

Once more the Northern pair received them with placid interest. Mr. Fair presently asked a question which John had waited for all day, and it was dark night without and lamp-light within, and they were drawing near a large city, before the young man, in reply, had more than half told the stout plans and hopes of this expedition of his after capital and colonists.

Mrs. Fair showed a most lively approval. "And must you leave us here?"

Barbara had not noticed till now how handsome she was. Neither had John.

"Yes, ma'am. But I shan't waste a day here if

things don't show up right. I shall push right on to New York."

Barbara hoped Mr. Fair's pleasantness of face meant an approbation as complete as his wife's, and, to hide her own, meditatively observed that this journey would be known in history as March's Raid.

John laughed and thanked her for not showing the fears of Captains Champion and Shotwell that he would " go in like a lion and come out like a lamb."

They hurried to the next section and peered out into the night with suppressed but eager exclamations. Long lines of suburban street-lamps were swinging by. Ranks of coke-furnaces were blazing like necklaces of fire. Foundries and machine-shops glowed and were gone; and, far away, close by, and far away again, beautifully colored flames waved from the unseen chimneys of chemical works.

"We've neither of us ever seen a great city," Miss Garnet explained when she rejoined her protectors. John had been intercepted by the porter with his brush, and Barbara, though still conversing, could hear what the negro was saying.

" I lef' you to de las', Cap. Seem like you 'ten'in' so close to business an' same time enjoyin' yo'seff so well, I hated to 'sturb—thank you, seh ! " The train came slowly to a stand. " O no, seh, dis ain't de depot. Depot three miles fu'theh yit, seh. We'll go on ag'in in a minute. Obacoat, seh? Dis yo' ambreel ? "

John bade his friends good-by. " And now, Miss Garnet "—he retained her hand a moment—" don't you go off and forget—Dixie."

She said no, and as he let go her hand she let him see deeper into her eyes than ever before.

A step or two away he looked back with a fraternal smile, but she was talking to Mrs. Fair as eagerly as if he had been gone three days. The train stood so long that he went forward to ask what the delay signified and saw the four commercial travelers walking away with their hand-bags. The porter was busy about the door.

" Big smash-up of freight-cyars in de yard ; yass, seh. No seh, cayn't 'zac'ly tell jis how long we be kep' here, but 'f you dislikes to wait, Cap, you needn'. You kin teck a street-cyar here what'll lan' you right down 'mongs' de hotels an' things ; yass, seh. See what ; de wreck ? No, seh, it's up in de yard whah dey don't 'llow you to pa-ass."

Out in the darkness beside the train March stood a moment. He could see Miss Garnet very plainly at her bright window and was wondering how she and her friends, but especially she, would take it if he should go back and help them while away this tiresome detention. If she had answered that last smile of his, or if she were showing, now, any tendency at all to look out the window, he might have returned ; but no, howdy after farewell lacked dignity. The street-car came along just then and Barbara saw him get into it.

## LVIII.

### TOGETHER AGAIN

MARCH did not put up at the most famous and pala-
tial hotel; it was full. He went to another much
smaller and quieter, and equally expensive. When he
had taken supper he walked the dazzling streets till
midnight, filled with the strangeness of the place and
the greater strangeness of his being there, and with
numberless fugitive reflections upon the day just gone,
the life behind it, and the life before, but totally without those shaped and ordered trains of thought which
no one has except in books.

Sometimes tenderly, sometimes bitterly, Fannie came
to mind, in emotions rather than memories, and as if
she were someone whom he should never see again.
Once it occurred to him that these ghost walkings of
thought and feelings about her must be very much like
one's thoughts of a limb shattered in some disaster and
lately cut off by a surgeon. The simile was not pleasant, but he did not see why he should want a pleasant
one. Only by an effort could he realize she was still of
this world, and that by and by they would be back
in Suez again, meeting casually, habitually, and in a
much more commonplace and uninteresting way than
ever they had done in the past. He shuddered, then he
sighed, and then he said ahem! and gave himself the
look of a man of affairs. On men who stared at him

he retorted with a frown of austere inquiry, not aware that they were merely noticing how handsome he was.

For a time he silently went through minute recapitulations of his recent colloquies with Miss Garnet, who seemed already surprisingly far away; much farther than any railroad speed could at all account for. He wished she were "further!"—for he could quote five different remarks of his own uttered to her that very day, which he saw plainly enough, *now,* nobody but a perfect fool could have made.

"Oh! Great Scott! What did possess me to drag her into my confidence?"

He "wondered if mesmerism had anything"—but rejected that explanation with disdain and dismissed the subject. And then this strange thing happened: He was standing looking into a show-window made gorgeous with hot-house flowers, when a very low voice close at hand moaned, "O Lord, no! I simply made an ass of myself," and when he turned sharply around no one was anywhere near.

He returned to his room and went to bed and to sleep wishing "to gracious" he might see her once more and once only, simply to show her that he had nothing more to confide—to her or any similar soft-smiling she!—The s's are his.

He did not rise early next morning. And in this he was wise. Rejoice, oh, young man, in your project, but know that old men, without projects, hearing will not hear—until they have seen their mail and their cashier; the early worm rarely catches the bird. John had just learned this in Pulaski City.

At breakfast he was again startled by a low voice very close to him. It was Mr. Fair.

" Mr. March, why not come over and sit with us? "

The ladies bowed from a table on the far side of the room. Mrs. Fair seemed as handsome as ever; while Miss Garnet!—well! If she was winsome and beautiful yesterday, with that silly, facing-both-ways traveling cap she had worn, what could a reverent young man do here and now but gasp his admiration under his breath as he followed his senior toward them?

Even in the lively conversation which followed he found time to think it strange that she had never seemed to him half so lovely in Suez; was it his oversight? Maybe not, for in Suez she had never in life been half so happy. Mrs. Fair could see this with her eyes shut, and poor Barbara could see that she saw it by the way she shut her eyes. But John, of course, was blind enough, and presently concluded that the wonder of this crescent loveliness was the old, old wonder of the opening rose. Meanwhile the talk flowed on.

" And by that time," said John, " you'd missed your connection. I might have guessed it. Now you'll take —but you've hardly got time——"

No, Mrs. Fair was feeling rather travel weary; this was Saturday; they would pass Sunday here and start refreshed on Monday.

In the crowded elevator, when March was gone, Barbara heard Mrs. Fair say to her husband,

" You must know men here whom it would be good for him to see; why don't you offer to——" Mrs.

Fair ceased and there was no response, except that
Barbara said, behind her smiling lips,

"It's because he's in bad hands, and still I have not
warned him!"

March did not see them again that day. In the
evening, two men, friends, sitting in the hotel's rotunda,
were conjecturing who yonder guest might be to whose
inquiries the clerk was so promptly attentive.

"He's a Southerner, that's plain; and a gentleman,
that's just as certain."

"Yes, if he were not both he would not be so perfectly at home in exactly the right clothes and yet look
as if he had spent most of his life in swimming."

"He hasn't got exactly the right overcoat; it's too
light and thin."

"No, but that's the crowning proof that he's a
Southerner." It was John.

They hearkened to the clerk. "He's just gone to
the theatre, Mr. March, he and both ladies. He was
asking for you. I think he wanted you to go."

"I reckon not," said John, abstractedly, and in his
fancy saw Miss Garnet explaining to her friends, with
a restrained smile, that in Suez to join the church was
to abjure the theatre. But another clerk spoke:

"Mr. March, did you—here's a note for you."

The clerk knew it was from Miss Garnet, and was
chagrined to see John, after once reading it, dreamily
tear it up and drop it to the floor. Still it increased
his respect for the young millionaire—Mr. March, that
is. It was as if he had lighted his cigar with a ten-
dollar bill.

John wrote his answer upstairs, taking a good deal of time and pains to give it an air of dash and haste, and accepting, with cordial thanks, Mr. and Mrs. Fair's cordial invitation to go with them (and Miss Garnet, writing at their request) next day to church. Which in its right time he did.

On his way back to the hotel with Miss Garnet after service, John was nothing less than pained—though he took care not to let her know it—to find how far astray she was as to some of the fundamental doctrines of Christianity. For fear she might find out his distress, he took his midday meal alone. And indeed, Miss Garnet may have had her suspicions, for over their ice-cream and coffee she said amusedly to Mrs. Fair, and evidently in reference to him,

"I am afraid it was only the slightness of our acquaintance that kept him from being pos-i-tive-ly pet-u-lent."

She seemed amused, I say, but an hour or so later, in her own room, she called herself a goose and somebody else another, and glancing at the mirror, caught two tears attempting to escape. She drove them back with a vigorous stamp of the foot and proceeded to dress for a cold afternoon walk among the quieted wonders of a resting city, without the Fairs, but not wholly alone.

## LIX.

### THIS TIME SHE WARNS HIM

As Miss Garnet and her escort started forth upon this walk, I think you would have been tempted to confirm the verdict of two men who, meeting and passing them, concluded that the escort was wasting valuable time when they heard him say,

"It did startle me to hear how lightly you regard what you call a memorized religion."

But this mood soon passed. A gentleman and lady, presently overtaking them, heard her confess, "I know I don't know as much as I think I do; I only wish I knew as much as I don't." Whereat her escort laughed admiringly, and during the whole subsequent two hours of their promenade scarcely any observer noticed the slightness of their acquaintance.

Across the fields around Suez their conversation would have been sprightly enough, I warrant. But as here they saw around them one and another amazing triumph of industry and art, they grew earnest, spoke exaltedly of this great age, and marvelled at the tangle of chances that had thrown them here together. John called it, pensively, a most happy fortune for himself, but Barbara in reply only invited his attention to the beauty of the street vista behind them.

Half a square farther on he came out of a brown study.

"Miss Barb"— It was the first time he had ever

said that, and though she lifted her glance in sober inquiry, the music of it ran through all her veins.

"—Miss Barb, isn't it astonishing, the speed with which acquaintance can grow, under favorable conditions?"

"Is it?"

"Oh, well, no, it isn't. Only that's not its usual way."

"Isn't the usual way the best?"

"Oh — usually — yes! But there's nothing usual about this meeting of ours. Miss Barb, my finding you and your friendship is as if I'd been lost at midnight in a trackless forest and had all at once found a road. I only wish"—he gnawed his lip—"I only wish these three last days had come to me years ago. You might have saved me some big mistakes."

"No," Barbara softly replied, "I'm afraid not."

"I only mean as a sister might influence an older brother; cheering—helping—warning."

"Warning!" murmured Barbara, with drooping head and slower step. "You don't know what an evil gift of untimely silence I've got. If I've failed all my life long as a daughter, in just what you're supposing of me——"

"O come, now, Miss——"

"Don't stop me! Why, Mr. March"—she looked up, and as she brushed back a hair from her ear John thought her hand shook; but when she smiled he concluded he had been mistaken—"I've been wanting these whole three days to warn you of something which, since it concerns your fortunes, concerns nearly everyone I know, and especially my father. Is it meddle-some for me to be solicitous about your ambitions and plans for Widewood, Mr. March?"

"Now, Miss Garnet! You know I'd consider it an honor and a delight—Miss Barb. What do you want to warn me against? Mind, I don't say I'll take your warning; but I'll prize the friendship that——"

"I owe it to my father."

"Oh, yes, yes! I don't mean to claim — aha! I thought that tolling was for fire! Here comes one of the engines!—Better take my arm a minute—I—I think you'd better—till the whirlwind passes."

She took it, and before they reached a crossing on whose far side she had promised herself to relinquish it, another engine rushed by. This time they stood aside under an arch with her hand resting comfortably in his elbow. It still rested there when they had resumed their walk, only stirring self-reproachfully when John incautiously remarked the street's restored quietness.

Barbara was silent. When they had gone some distance farther John asked,

"Have I forfeited your solicitude? Will you not warn me, after all?" He looked at her and she looked at him, twice, but speech would not come; her lips only parted, broke into a baffled smile, and were grave again.

"I suppose, of course, it's against measures, not men, as they say, isn't it?"

"It's against men," said Barbara.

"That surprises me," replied John, with a puzzled smile.

"Why, Mr. March, you can't suppose, do you, that your high ambitions and purposes——"

"Oh, they're not mine; they're my father's. The details and execution are mine——"

"But, anyhow, you share them; you've said so. You don't suppose your associates——"

"What; share them the same way I do? Why, no, Miss Barb; it wouldn't be fair to expect that, would it? And yet, in a certain way, on a lower plane—from a simply commercial standpoint—they do. I don't include your father with them! I only wish I could reflect the spirit of my father's wishes and hopes as perfectly as he does."

"Mr. March, don't men sometimes go into such enterprises as yours simply to plunder and ruin those that go in honestly with them?"

"Oh, undoubtedly. You see, in this case——"

"Mr. March——"

"Yes, Miss Barb——"

"I believe certain men are in your company with that intention."

"But you don't know it, do you? Else you would naturally tell your father instead of me. You only——" He hesitated.

"I only see it."

"Oh—oh! have you no other evidence—only an intuition?"

"Yes, I have other evidence."

"Ah!" laughed John. "You've got higher cards, have you?"

Her eyes softly brightened in response to his. The

next instant the hand in his arm awoke, but lay very still, as four men passed, solemnly raised their silk hats to March, and disappeared around a corner. They were the commercial travelers!

Her hand left his arm to brush something from her opposite shoulder, and did not return, but hid somewhere in her wrap, tingling with a little anguish all its own, in the realization that discovery is almost the only road to repentance. At the same time it could hear, so to speak, its owner telling, with something between a timorous courage and a calm diffidence, how, in Suez, she had drawn out a business man, unnamed, but well approved and quite disinterested, to say that she might tell Mr. March that, in his conviction, unless he got rid of certain persons—etc.

"I can tell you who it was, if you care to know. He said I might."

"No," said John, thoughtfully. "Never mind." And they heard their own footsteps for full two minutes. Then he said, "Miss Barb, suppose he is disinterested and sincere. Say he were my best friend. The thing's a simple matter of arithmetic. So long as your father and Jeff-Jack and I hang together there are not enough votes in the company to do anything we don't want done. I admit we've given some comparative strangers a strong foothold; but your father trusts them, and, if need be, can watch them. Does anybody know men better than Jeff-Jack does? But he knew just what we were doing when he consented to take charge of the three counties' interests; however, I admit that doesn't prove anything. Miss Barb, I know who said what you've told me, and I esteem and honor and love him as much as you do—wait, please. O smile ahead, if you like, only let me finish. You know we must take some risks, and while I thank him—and you, too, even if you do speak merely for your father's sake—I tell you the best moves a man ever makes are those he makes against the warnings of his friends! 'Try not the pass, the old man said,' don't you know?"

"This wasn't an old man."

"Wasn't it General Halliday?"

"No, sir, it was the younger Mr. Fair."

"Henry Fair," said John very quietly. He slackened his pace. He did not believe Fair cared that much for him; but it was easy to suppose he might seize so good a chance to say a word for Miss Garnet's own sake.

"Miss Barb, I don't doubt he thinks what he says. I see now why he failed to subscribe to our stock, after coming so far entirely, or almost entirely, to do it. He little knows how he disappointed me. I didn't want his capital, Miss Barb, half as much as his fellowship in a beautiful enterprise."

"He was as much disappointed as you, Mr. March; I happen to know it."

John looked at his informant; but her head was down once more.

"Well," he said, cheerily, "I'll just have to wait till —till I—till I've shown"—a beggar child was annoying him—"shown Fair and all of them that I'm not so green as I——" He felt for a coin, stood still, and turned red. "Miss—Miss Barb——" A smile widened over his face, and he burst into a laugh that grew till the tears came.

"What's the matter?" asked Barbara anxiously, yet laughing with him.

"Oh, I—I've let somebody pick my pockets. Yes, every cent's gone and my ticket to New York. I had no luck here yesterday, and I was going on to New York to-morrow." He laughed again, but ceased abruptly. "Good gracious, Miss Barb! my watch!—my father's watch!" The broad smile on his lips could not hide the grief in his eyes.

---

## LX.

### A PERFECT UNDERSTANDING

As they resumed their way Barbara did most of the talking. She tried so hard to make his loss appear wholly attributable to her, that only the sweetness of her throat and chin and the slow smoothness of her words saved her from seeming illogical. She readily got his admission that the theft might have been done in that archway as the engine rushed by. Very good! And without her, she reasoned, he would not have stopped. "Or, if you had stopped," she softly droned, with her eyes on her steps, "you would have had——"

"Oh, now, what would I have had?"

"Your hands in your pockets."

"That's not my habit."

"Oh, Mr. March!"

"My d-ear Miss Barb! I should think I ought to know!"

"Yes, sir; that's why I tell you." They laughed in partnership.

Mr. March was entirely right, Barbara resumed, not to tell his mishap to the Fairs, or to anyone, anywhere, then or thereafter. "But you're cruel to me not to let me lend you enough to avoid the rev-e-la-tion." That was the utmost she would say. If he couldn't see that she would rather *lose*—not to say lend—every dollar she had, than have anyone know where her hand was when his pocket was picked, he might stay just as stupid as he was. She remained silent so long that John looked at her, but did not perceive that she was ready to cry. She wore a glad smile as she said:

"I've got more money with me than I ought to be carrying, anyhow."

"Why, Miss Barb, you oughtn't to do that; how does that happen?" He spoke with the air of one who had never in his life lost a cent by carelessness.

"It's not so very much," was her reply. "It's for my share of Rosemont. I sold it to pop-a."

"What! just now when the outlook for Rosemont— why, Miss Barb, I do believe you did it to keep clear of our land company, didn't you?"

"Mr. March, I wish you would let me lend you some of it, won't you?"

"No, I'll be—surprised if I do. Oh, Miss Barb, I thank you just the same; but my father, Miss Barb, gave it to me, as a canon of chivalry, never to make a money bargain with a lady that you can't make with a bank. If I'm not man enough to get out of this pinch without—oh, pshaw!"

In the hotel, at the head of the ladies' staircase, they stood alone.

"Good-by," said John, unwillingly. "I'll see you this evening, shan't I, when I come up to say good-by to your friends?"

Barbara said he would. They shook hands, each pair of eyes confessing to the other the superfluity of the ceremony.

"Good-by," said John again, as if he had not said it twice already.

"Good-by. Mr. March, if you want to give securities—as you would to a bank—I—I shouldn't want anything better than your mother's poems."

He glowed with gratitude and filial vanity, his big hand tightening on hers. "Oh, Miss Barb! no, no! But God bless you! I wonder if anyone else was ever so much like sunshine in a prison window! Good-by!" She felt her hand lifted by his; but, when she increased its weight the merest bit, he let it sink again and slide from his fingers.

He was gone, and a moment later she was with the Fairs, talking slowly, with soft smiles; but her head swam, she heard their pleasant questions remotely as through a wall, and could feel her pulse to her fingers and feet. He had almost kissed her hand. "The next time—the next time—sweet heaven send this poor hand strength to resist just enough and—and not too much." So raved the prayer locked in her heart, or so it would have raved had she dared give it the liberty even of unspoken words.

Meanwhile, John March lay on his bed with the back of his head in his hands.

"I've offended her! There was no mistaking that last look. This wouldn't have happened if she hadn't let her hand linger in mine. Oh, I wish to heaven girls were not so senselessly innocent and sisterly! Great Cæsar! I'd give five hundred dollars not to have drooled that drivel about being her brother! George! She ought to know that only a fool or a scamp could make such an absurd proposal. I wonder if she still wants to lend me her money! I'd rather face a whole bank directorate with an overdrawn account than those Fairs this evening. I know exactly how they'll look. For it will be just like her to tell Mrs. Fair, who'll tell her husband, and they'll bury the thing right there with me under it, and 'Miss Garnet' will excuse herself on the plea of fatigue, and the conversation will drag, and I'll wish I had cut my throat in Pulaski City, and "—a steeple clock tolled the hour—— "Oh, can it be that that's only six!"

At tea he missed them. Returning to his room, he had hardly got his hands under his head again, trying not to think of his financial embarrassments because it was Sunday, when a new idea brought him to his feet. Church! Evening service! Would she go? He had not asked her when she had intimated that the Fairs would not. In his selfish enjoyment of her society he had quite forgotten to care for her soul! He ought to go himself. And all the more ought she, for he was numbered among the saved now, and she was not. She *must* go. But how could she unless he should take her? His Christian duty was clear. He would write an offer of his services, and by her answer he would know how he stood in her regard.

Her reply was prompt, affirmative, confined to the subject. And yet, in some inexplicable way it conveyed the impression that she had never suspected him of the faintest intention to carry her hand to his lips.

The sermon was only so-so, but they enjoyed the singing; particularly their own. Both sang from one book, with much reserve, yet with such sweetly persuasive voices that those about them first listened and then added their own very best. The second tune was "Geer," and, with John's tenor going up every time Barbara's soprano came down, and *vice versa*, it was as lovely see-sawing as ever thrilled the heart of youth with pure and undefiled religion. They sang the last hymn to "Dennis." It was,

> "Blest be the tie that binds
> Our hearts in Christian love!"

and they gratefully accepted the support of four good, sturdy, bass voices behind them. But it was the words themselves, of the fourth and fifth stanzas, that inspired their richest yet softest tones, while the four basses behind them rather grew louder:

> "When we asunder part
> It gives us inward pain,
> But we shall still be joined in heart
> And hope to meet again.

" This glorious hope revives
  Our courage by the way,
  While each in expectation lives
  And longs to see the day."

On the sidewalk the four basses again raised their four silk hats and vanished. They were the commercial travelers.

As the two worshippers returned toward their hotel, Barbara spoke glowingly of Mr. and Mrs. Fair; their perfect union; their beautiful companionship. John, in turn, ventured to tell of the unbounded esteem with which he had ever looked upon Barbara's mother. They dwelt, in tones of indulgent amusement, on the day, the hour, the scene, of John's first coming to the college, specially memorable to him as the occasion of his first real meeting of the Rose of Rosemont. Barbara said the day would always be bright to her as the one on which she first came into personal contact with Judge March. John spoke ardently of his father.

" And, by the bye, that day was the first on which I ever truly saw you."

" Or Johanna! " said Barbara. " Johanna's keeping Fannie Ravenel's new house. She's to stay with her till I get back." But John spoke again of Barbara's mother, asking permission to do so.

" Yes, certainly," murmured his companion. " In general I don't revere sacred things as I should," she continued, with her arm in her escort's, and " Blest be the tie "—still dragging in their adagio footsteps; " but my mother has all my life been so sacred to me—not that she was of the sort that they call otherworldly—I

don't care for otherworldliness nearly as much as I
should——"

"Don't you?" regretfully asked John; "that's one of
my faults too."

"No; but I've always revered mom-a so deeply that
except once or twice to Fannie, when Fannie spoke first,
I've never talked about her." Yet Barbara went on
telling of her mother from a full heart, her ears ravished
by the music of John's interjected approvals. They
talked again of his father also, and found sweet resem-
blances between the two dear ones. Only as they re-
entered the hotel were both at once for a moment silent.
Half way up the stairs, among the foliage plants of a
landing ablaze with gas, they halted, while John, beginning,

"Two hearts that love the same fair things"—

recited one of his mother's shorter poems.

"Why, Mr. March!" His hearer's whisper only
emphasized her sincere enthusiasm. "Did your mother
—why, that's per-fect-ly beau-ti-ful!"

They parted, but soon met again in one of the parlors.
Mrs. Fair came, too, but could not linger, having left
Mr. Fair upstairs asleep on a lounge. She bade Barbara
stay and hear all the manuscript poems Mr. March
could be persuaded to read, and only regretted that
her duty upstairs prevented her remaining herself.
"Good-by," she said to John. "Now, whenever you
come to Boston, remember, you're to come directly
to us."

John responded gratefully, and Barbara, as the two

sat down upon a very small divan with the batch of manuscript between them, told him, in a melodious undertone, that she feared she couldn't stay long.

"What's that?" she asked, as he took up the first leaf to put it by.

"This? Oh, this is the poem I tried to recite to you on the stairs."

"Read it again," she said, not in her usual monotone, but with a soft eagerness of voice and eye quite new to him, and extremely stimulating. He felt an added exaltation when, at the close of the middle stanza, he saw her hands knit into each other and a gentle rapture shining through her drooping lashes; and at the end, when she sighed her admiration in only one or two half-formed words, twinkled her feet and bit her lip, his exaltation rose almost to inebriety. He could have sat there and read to her all night.

Yet that was the only poem she heard. The title of the next one, John said as he lifted it, was, "If I should love again;" but Barbara asked a dreamy question of a very general character; he replied, then asked one in turn; they discussed—she introducing the topic—the religious duty and practicability of making all one's life and each and every part of it good poetry, and the inner and outer conditions essential thereunto; and when two strange ladies came in and promptly went out again John glanced at the mantel-clock, exclaimed his surprise at the hour, and gathering up the manuscript, rose to say his parting word.

"Good-by." His hand-grasp was fervent.

"Good-by," replied the maiden.

" Miss Barb "—he kept her hand—" I want a word, and, honestly—I—don't know what it is! Doesn't good-by seem to you mighty weak, by itself? "

" Why, that depends. It's got plenty of po-ten-ti-al-i-ty if you give it its old sig-nif-i-ca-tion."

" Well, I do—every bit of it! Do you, Miss Barb—to me? "

She gave such answer with her steady eyes that her questioner's mind would have lost its balance had she not smiled so lightly.

"Still," he responded, " good-by is such unclaimed property that I want another word to sort o' fence it in, you know."

The maiden only looked more amused than before.

" I don't want it to mean too much, you understand," explained he. The hand in his grew heavier, but his grasp tightened on it. " Yet don't you think these last three days' companionship deserves a word of its own? Miss Barb, you've been—and in my memory you will be henceforth—a crystalline delight! The word's not mine, it's from one of my mother's sweetest things. Can't I say good-by, thou ' crystalline delight ' ? "

" Why, Mr. March," said Barbara, softly pulling at her hand. " I don't particularly like the implication that I'm per-fect-ly trans-par-ent."

" Now, Miss Barb! as if I—oh pshaw! Good-by." He lifted her hand. She made it very light. He held it well up, looking down on it fondly. " This," he said, " is the little friend that wanted to help me out of trouble. Good-by, little friend; I "—his lips approached it—" I love you."

It flashed from his hand like a bird from the nest. " No-o ! " moaned its owner.

" Oh, Miss Gar—Miss Barb ! " groaned John, " you've utterly misunderstood."

" No "—Barbara had not yet blushed, but now she crimsoned—" I've not misunderstood you. I simply don't like that way of saying——"

" I didn't mean——"

" I know it, Mr. March. I know perfectly well you don't expect ever to mean anything to anybody any more ; you consider it a sheer im-pos-si-bil-i-ty. That's the keystone of our friendship."

John hemmed. " I wouldn't say impossibility ; I'd say impracticability. It's an impracticability, Miss Barb, that's all. Why, every time I think of my dear sweet little mother——"

" Oh, Mr March, that's right ! She *must* have your whole thought and care ! "

" She shall have it, Miss Barb, at every cost ! as completely as I know your father has and ought to have yours ! " He took her hand. " Good-by ! The understanding's perfect now, isn't it ? "

" I think so—I hope so—yes, sir."

" Say, ' Yes, John.' "

" Oh, Mr. March, I can't say that."

" Why, then, it isn't perfect."

" Yes, it is."

" Well, then, Miss Garnet, with the perfect understanding that the understanding is perfect, I propose to bid this hand good-by in a fitting and adequate manner, and trust I shall not be inter—!—rupted ! Good-by."

"Oh, Mr. March, I don't think that was either fair or right!" Her eyes glistened.

"Miss Barb, it wasn't! Oh, I see it now! It was a wretched mistake! Forgive me!"

Her eyes, staring up into his, filled to the brim. She waved him away and turned half aside. He backed to the door and paused.

"Miss Barb, one look! Oh, one look, just to show I'm not utterly unforgiven and cast out! I promise you it's all I'll ever ask—one look!"

"Good-by," she murmured, but could not trust herself to move.

He stifled a moan. She gave a start of pain. He thought it meant impatience. She took an instant more for self-command and then lifted a smile. Too late, he was gone!

---

## LXI.

### A SICK MAN AND A SICK HORSE

"THANK you, no," said Miss Garnet at the door of Mrs. Fair's room, refusing to enter. "I rapped only to say good-night."

To the question whether she had heard all the poems read she replied, "Not all," with so sweet an irony in her grave smile that Mrs. Fair wanted to tell her she looked like the starlight. But words are clumsy, and the admirer satisfied herself with a kiss on the girl's temple. "Good-night," she said; "dream of me."

Several times next day, as the three travelers wound their swift course through the mountains of Pennsylvania, Mrs. Fair observed Barbara sink her book to her lap and with an abstracted gaze on the landscape softly touch the back of her right hand with the fingers of her left. It puzzled her at first, but by and by—

"Poor boy!" she said to herself, in that inmost heart where no true woman ever takes anyone into council, "and both of you Southerners! If that's all you got, and you had to steal that, you're both of you better than I'd have been."

When about noon she saw her husband's eyes fixed on Barbara, sitting four seats away, she asked, with a sparkle: "Thinking of Mr. March?"

"Yes, I've guessed why he's stayed behind."

"Have you? That's quick work—for a man."

"It looks to-day as if he were out of the game, doesn't it?"

The lady mused. This time the husband twinkled:

"If he is, my dear, whom should we congratulate: all three or which two?"

"I don't know yet, my love. Wait. Wait till we've tried her in Boston."

At this hour John March was imperatively engrossed by an unforseen discovery. Tossing on his bed the night before, he had decided not to telegraph to Suez for money until he had searched all the hotels for some one from Dixie who would exclaim, "Why, with the greatest pleasure," or words to that effect. In the

morning he was up betimes and off on this errand, asking himself why he had not done it the evening before,
but concluding he must have foreborne out of respect
for the Sabbath.

At the first hotel his search had no reward. But in
the second he found a Pulaski City man, whose acquaintance he had never previously prized, yet from
whom he now hid four-fifths of his surprised delight
and still betrayed enough to flatter the fellow dizzy.
John took him back to his own hotel for breakfast,
made sure he had only to ask a loan to get it, and let
him go at last, unable to get the request through his
own teeth.

He went to a third hotel, but found only strangers.
Then he went to a fourth, explored its rotunda in vain,
turned three or four leaves of its register, and was giving a farewell glance to the back page, when he started
with surprise.

"I see," he said to the clerk, "I see you have—will
you kindly look this way a moment? Are these persons still with you?"

"They are, sir," said the clerk, gazing absently beyond him, and took March's card. "Front! I'll have
to send it to the lady, sir; Colonel Ravenel's sick. What?
Oh, well, sir, if *you* think pneumonia's slight— Yes,
sir, that's what he's got." He was turning away
contemptuously, but John said:

"Oh!—eh—one moment more, if you please."

"Well, sir, what is it?" The man gave his ear instead of his eye; but he gave both eyes, as John giving
both his, asked deferentially:

" Do you own all the hotels in this town, sir, or are you merely a clerk of this one ? "

The card went, and a bell-boy presently led the way to Fannie's door. It stood unlatched. The boy pushed it ajar, and John met only his frowning image reflected full length in the mirror-front of a folding-bed, until a door opened softly from the adjoining room and closed again, and Fannie, pale and vigil worn, but with ecstasy in her black eyes, murmured :

"Oh, John March, I never knew I could be quite so glad to see you ! "

She pressed his hand rapturously between her two, dropped it playfully, and saw that there had come between them a nearness and a farness different from any that had ever been. John felt the same thing, but did not guess that this was why her smile was grateful and yet had a pang in it. There was a self-oblivious kindness in his murmur as he refused a seat.

" No, I mustn't keep you a moment. Only tell me what I can do for you."

She explained that she would have to go back into the sick-room and return again, as the physician was in there, and Jeff-Jack was unaware, and ought probably to be kept unaware, of any other visitor's presence.

John said he would wait and hear the doctor's pronouncements and her commands. When she came the second time this person appeared with her. Beyond a soft introduction there were only a few words, and the two men went away together. As Fannie returned and bent cheerily over the bridegroom's bed, she was totally surprised by his feeble, bright-eyed request.

"When John March comes back with the medicine I want to see him."

The man to whom Fannie had introduced John was of a sort much newer to him than to travelers generally—a typical physician-in-ordinary to a hotel. He wore a dark-blue overcoat abundantly braided and frogged; his sheared mustaches were dyed black, and his diamond scarf-pin, a pendant, was chained to his shirt. As they drove to a favorite apothecary's some distance away, John told why he had come North, and the doctor said he had a cousin living at the hotel who had capital, and happened just then to be looking for investments. It would be no trouble at all to drive Mr. March back from the apothecary's and make him acquainted with Mr. Bulger. Was Mr. March fond of horses? Good! Bulger owned the fastest span in the city, and drove them every morning at ten.

In fact, before they quite reached the hotel again they came upon the capitalist, ribbons in hand, just leaving a public stable behind such a pair of trotters that John exclaimed at sight of them and accepted with alacrity a seat by his side. As for the medicine, the physician himself took it to Mrs. Ravenel, explained that John would be along in an hour or two, and said, "Yes, the patient could see Mr. March briefly, but must talk as little as possible."

Four or five times during the next seven or eight hours the sick man's eyes compelled Fannie to say: "I don't know why he doesn't come." And at evening with an open note in her hand, a smile on her lips, and a new loneliness in her heart, she announced: "He says he will be here early in the morning."

Mr. Bulger was large, heavy, and clean-shaven, as became a capitalist; but his overcoat was buff, with a wide trimming of fur, and his yellow hair was parted in the back and perfumed. March did not mind this, but he was truly sorry to notice, very quickly, that his companion's knowledge of horses was mostly a newspaper knowledge. While Mr. Bulger quoted turf records, John said to himself:

"Wonder how far he'll drive before he sees his nigh horse is sick."

But very soon the owner of the team remarked: "The mare seems droopy."

"Yes, Mr. Bulger," replied John, almost explosively, "she's going to be a very sick animal before you can get her back to the stable, if you ever get her back at all. If we don't do the right thing right off, you'll lose her. I wouldn't stop them, sir. My conscience! don't let her stand here, or she'll be so stiff, directly, you can't make her go!"

"Yes, I guess you're right," said Bulger, moving on. "If I can just get her home and out of harness and let her lie down——"

"If you do, sir, she'll never get up again."

"By Jo'!" exclaimed the owner of the horse. "I don't want that!" He looked grimly on the gentle sufferer. "See her," he presently said; "why, I never saw anything get sick so fast. Why, Mr. March, I'm afraid she's going to die right here! Half an hour ago I wouldn't 'a' sold that mare for two thousand dollars!

Mr. March, if you can save her you may have all the doctors you want, and I'll pay you a hundred dollars yourself as quick as I'd pay you one!"

"Give me the reins," was John's response. "Where's the very nearest good stable?"

There was one not far away. He turned and soon reached it. As they stopped in its door the beautiful creature in his care was trembling in all her flesh, and dripping sweat from every pore. The ready grooms helped him unharness.

"I'll send for a doctor, shan't I?" said Bulger, twice, before John heard him.

"Yes, if you know a real one; but I'll have everything done before he gets here. Here, you, fetch a blanket. Somebody bring me some fine salt—oh, a double handful—a tumblerful—to rub her back with— only be quick!"

In a moment the harness had given place to halter and blanket, and the weak invalid stiffly followed John's firm leading over the sawdust.

Three hours later Bulger said, "She's a good deal better, ain't she?" and when March smiled fondly on her and replied that he "should say so," her owner suggested luncheon.

"No," said John, "you go and eat; I shan't leave her till she's well. She mustn't lie down, and I can't trust anyone to keep her from doing it."

Two or three times more Bulger went and came again, and the lamps were being lighted in the streets when at last John remarked,

"Well, sir, you can harness her up now and drive

her home. Nice gyirl! Nice gyirl! Did you think us was gwine to let you curl up and die out yond' in the street? No, missie, no! you nice ole gyirl, doggone yo' sweet soul, no!"

"Mr. March," said Bulger, "I said I'd pay you a hundred dollars if you'd cure her, didn't I? Well, here's my check for half of it, and if you just say the word I'll make another for the other half."

John pushed away the proffering hand with a pleased laugh. "I can't take pay for doctoring a horse, sir, but I will ask a favor of you—in fact, I'll ask two; and the first is, Come and have dinner with me, will you?"

And when John called on Fannie the next morning, Mr. Bulger had taken a train for Suez, expecting to return in three days subscriber for all the land company's stock left untaken through the prudence of the younger Fair. John had treated himself to a handsome new pocketbook.

---

## LXII.

### RAVENEL THINKS HE MUST

"So you'll be leaving us at once!" said Fannie, as the two sat by Ravenel's bed.

"No, not till Mr. Bulger gets back. I can be up to my neck in work till then on the colonization side of the business." They bent to hear the bridegroom's words :

"Wish you wouldn't go East till Friday evening, and then go with us."

"Why Jeff-Jack Ravenel," exclaimed Fannie, with a careworn laugh, "what are you talking about?"

"Not much fun for John," was the languishing reply, "but big favor to us."

"But, my goodness!" said the bride, "the doctor won't even let you get up."

"Got to," responded the smiling invalid. "Got to be in Washington next Sunday."

"That's simply ridiculous," laughed Fannie, with a pretty toss, and sauntered into the next room, closing the door between. The sick man's smile increased:

"She's going in there to cry," he softly drawled.

"You can't go, Ravenel," said March. "Why, it'll kill you, like as not."

"Got to go, John. Politics."

"Oh, the other fellows can work it without you."

"Yes," replied the smiling lips, "that's why I've got to be there."

The subject was dropped. That was Tuesday morning. John called twice a day until Thursday evening. Each time he came Fannie seemed more and more wan and blighted, though never less courageous.

"She'll be sick herself if she doesn't hire a nurse and get some rest," said the doctor to John; but her idea of a hired nurse was Southern, and she would not hear of it. John was not feeling too honest these days. On the evening of Thursday he came nerved up to mention

Miss Garnet, whom, as a theme, he had wholly avoided whenever Fannie had spoken of her.   But the moment he met Fannie, in the outer room, he was so cut to the heart to see how her bridal beauty had wasted with her strength that he could only beg her to lie down an hour, two, three, half the night, the whole of it, while he would watch and tend in her place.   He would take it unkindly if she did not.

"Oh, John" she laughingly replied, "you forget!" He faintly frowned.

"Yes, Miss Fannie, I try to."   He did not add that he had procured assistance.

Her response was a gleam of loving approval.   John noticed seven or eight minute spots on her face and recognized for the first time in his life that they were freckles.

"John, did the doctor tell you it was my fault that Jeff-Jack got this sickness?"

"No, and I shouldn't have believed it if he had."

"Thank you, John"—her lifted eyes filled—"thank you; but it was; it was my fault, and nobody shall watch him in my place."   It would have made a difference to several besides herself, had she known that the doctor on both his last two visits had forgotten to say that no one need any longer sit up all night.

John called again Friday morning.   School himself as best he could, still an energy in his mien showed there was news from Suez.

"What is it, old man," asked the slow-voiced invalid, "have they made the new slate?"

"Yes, and the bill's passed empowering the three

counties to levy the tax and take the stock. Oh, Garnet's a wheel-horse, yes, sir-ee!—and Gamble and Bulger are a team! Bulger isn't coming back for a while
at all ; they've made him secretary."

A perceptible shade came over Ravenel's face, although he smiled as he said,

"Absence makes the heart grow fonder. Have they
made you vice-president ? "

" Yea, they have! I no more expected such a thing
—I knew Gamble, of course, would be president and
Champion treasurer ; but—Well, they say I can push
things better as vice-president, and I reckon that's so ; "
said John, and ceased without adding that his salary
was continued and that Bulger would draw none.

" Where does Major Garnet come in ? " asked Fannie.

" Oh, he still declines any appointment whatever, but
he's made up another company ; a construction company to take our contracts. Proudfit's president. It's
not strongly officered ; but, as Garnet says, better
have men we can dictate to than men who might try
to dictate to us. And besides, except Crickwater,
they're all Suez men. Mattox is treasurer ; Pettigrew's
secretary."

Fannie wanted to say that Proudfit had no means
except his wife's, but was still because a small rosy spot
on either cheek-bone of the invalid was beginning to
betray the intensity of his thought. She would have
motioned to John to tell no more, if she could have
done so unseen by Ravenel. However, the bridegroom
himself turned the theme.

" Are you going down there before you go East ? "

"No, Garnet and Bulger both urge me to go straight on. I'm mighty sorry I can't wait till you're well enough to go; but——"

On the pallid face in the pillow came the gentlest of smiles. Its fair, thin hand held toward Fannie a bunch of small keys, and their owner said,

"I wish, while you're getting your fare and berth tickets, you'd get two of each for us, John, will you?" He still smilingly held out the keys.

Fannie sat still. She tried to smile but turned very pale. "Jeff-Jack," she gasped, "you can't go. I beg you, don't try. I beg you, Jeff-Jack."

"Got to, Fannie." He sat up in the bed. John thrust a pillow behind him.

"Well, I——" her bloodless lips twitched painfully— "I can't let you go. The doctor says he mustn't, John."

Ravenel smiled on. "Got to, Fannie. Come, take these and get John my pocketbook."

Fannie rose. "No, I tell you the solemn truth, even if you could go, I can't. I shouldn't get there alive. You certainly wouldn't——" she tried to speak playfully —"leave me behind, would you?"

"Have to, Fannie. State interest—simply imperative. Leave you plenty money." He gave the keys a little shake. Her eyes burned through him, but he smiled on.

She took the keys. As she passed through the door between the two rooms she supported herself against the jamb. John rose hurriedly, but stood dumb. In a few seconds she returned. As she neared him she seemed to trip on the carpet, staggered, fell, and would have struck the floor at full length but for John's quick arms.  For an instant he held her whole slight weight.  Her brow had fallen upon his shoulder.  But quickly she lifted it and with one wild look into his face moaned, "No," and pushed herself from him into a rocking-chair.

The pocketbook lay on the floor.  He would have handed it to her, but she motioned for him to give it to her husband.  Ravenel drew from it three bank-notes, saying, as he passed them to John—"Better engage two berths, but buy only one ticket.  Then we can either——"

March, busy with his own pocketbook, made a sign that he understood.  His fingers trembled, but when he lifted his eyes from them there was a solemn calm in his face and his jaws were set like steel.  He handed back one of the notes, and with it something else which was neither coin nor currency.

"Does this mean——" quietly began Ravenel.

"Yes," said John, "I sell you my ticket.  I shan't leave town till Miss Fannie's fit to travel."

"Why, John!"  For a single instant the sick man reddened.  In the next he had recovered his old serenity.  "Why that's powerful kind of you."

"Oh, no," said March, with a boyish smile to Fannie, who was rising to move to a lounge, "it's a mighty old——"  He was going to say "debt," but before Ravenel could more than catch his breath or John start half a step forward she had struck the lounge like a flail.

March sprang to her, snatched up a glass of water, and seeing Ravenel's hand on the bell-pull at the bed's head cried, " Ring for the maid, why don't you ? She's fainted away."

" Keep cool, old man," said the bridegroom, with his quiet gaze on Fannie. Her eyes opened, and he withdrew his hand.

At seven that evening Ravenel, sitting in his sleeping-car seat, gave March his hand for good-by.

" Yes," said John, " and if the nurse I've got her isn't tip-top—George ! I'll find one that is ! "

" I'll trust you for that, John."

But John frowned. " What right have you got to trust me this way at all ? "

" Because, old man, this time you're in love with another girl."

" No, sir ! No, sir ! " said March, backing away as the train began to move. Don't you fool yourself with *that* notion."

" I shan't," drawled the departing traveler.

## LXIII.

### LETTERS AND TELEGRAMS

No one ever undertook to argue anything with Ravenel unless invited to do so, and very few ever got such an invitation. Fannie had not intended to be left behind. Out of her new care of him she had made her first and last effort to bend his will to hers, and even while she burned under the grief and shame of his treatment she would have gone with him at his beckon though death threatened her at every step.

At any rate so she felt as she came out of her faint and bravely resumed her care of him, retaining it even when the doctor declared she had a fever and ought to be in bed. But she felt also that Jeff-Jack knew he had only to beckon; and when he did not do so, either by hand or tone, she saved herself the idle torture of asking him to take a sick bride on a journey from which a sick bride could not deter him.

Yet she made one mistake, when she took at its face value the equal absence of fondness and resentment with which the bridegroom had behaved throughout. It was easy enough to read John March's deep indignation under the surface of his courteous silences; but neither she nor John guessed that the bridegroom's only reason for not being vexed with both of them was that he was not of the sort to let himself be vexed. Each had disappointed him seriously; Fannie by setting up domestic love and felicity as a purpose instead of an appliance, squandering her care and strength in a short-sighted devotion to his physical needs, and showing herself unfit to co-operate with him in the things for which he thought it no great matter to risk his life; and John by failing so utterly to discern the true situation in Suez that the only thing to do with him was to let him alone until time and hard luck might season him to better uses than anyone could make of him yet.

If Ravenel were going to allow himself the luxury of either vexation or chagrin, he had far more profound occasion in quite another person. Probably never before in their acquaintance had he been so displeased with Garnet. Some hours before he rose to dress for the train he had filled out two telegraph blanks. The contents of the first he read to Fannie and with her approval sent it to her father by wire. It read:

"Have been sick. Much better now. Fannie tired out, nursing. Wants Johanna. Send her in care Southern Express Company.                    R."

He did not read to her the second missive. But when he had made it ready—for the mail, not the telegraph,—getting her to address it in one of her envelopes and seal it with her own new seal, he said, with a pensive smile that made him very handsome, "Garnet will think it's from a woman—till he opens it."

It read as follows:

"Your Construction Company smells. *Courier* mum —but firm—money all got to stay in Three Counties, no matter who's on top. Last man one Yank too many. *Courier* may have to combine with Halliday.
                    "Yours to count on,        J. J."

John did not see Fannie that evening on his return from the station. He only received at second hand her request to call in the morning. She had gone to bed and taken her medicine, and was resting quietly, said the nurse. But when John asked if the patient was asleep, the nurse confessed she hardly thought so. She might have told how, listening kindly at the patient's door, she had heard her turn in bed and moan, " Oh, God! why can't I die?" But she had often heard such questions asked by persons with only a headache. And besides, there is always the question, To *whom* to to tell things. Where did this most winning young man stand? The only fact quite clear either to her, the clerks, bell-boys or chambermaids, was that when he stood in front of the bridegroom he completely hid him from view.

Though lost to sight, however, Fannie was still a tender care in the memory of John March—if we may adapt one of his mother's gracefulest verses. He went to his hotel fairly oppressed with the conviction that for Fannie's own sake it was his duty to drop a few brief lines to Barbara Garnet—ahem! Mr. March's throat was absolutely sound, but sometimes, when he wasn't watching, it would clear itself that way. To forestall any rumor that might reach Miss Garnet from Suez, it was but right to send her such a truthfully garbled account of the Ravenels and himself that she would see at a glance how perfectly natural, proper and insignificant it was for him to be lingering in a strange city with a sick bride whom he had once hoped to marry, the bridegroom being sick also and several hundred miles away. At the same time this would give him opportunity to explain away the still mortifying awkwardness of his last parting with Miss Garnet— without, however, really alluding to it. No use trying to explain a thing of that sort at all unless you can explain it without alluding to it.

He was ready, early in the evening, to begin; but lost some time trying to decide whether to open with Miss Garnet, or My Dear Miss Garnet, or Dear Miss Garnet, or My Dear Miss Barbara, or My Dear Miss Barb, or Dear Miss Barb, or just Dear Friend as you would to an ordinary acquaintance. He tried every form, but each in turn looked simply and dreadfully impossible, and at length he went on with the letter, leaving the terms of his salutation to the inspiration of the last moment. It was long after midnight when he finished. The night sky was inviting, and the post-office near by; he mailed the letter there instead of trusting the hotel. And then he stood by the mute slot that had swallowed it, and because he could not get it back for amendment called himself by as large a collection of flaming and freezing invectives as ever a Southern gentleman—"member in good standing of any Evangelical church"—poured upon himself in the privacy of his own counsels. He returned to his hotel, but was back again at sunrise smiling his best into a hand-hole, requesting so-and-so and so-and-so, while he pencilled and submitted examples of his hand-writing. To which a voice within replied,

"Oh, yes, the watchman; but the watchman told you wrong. I tell you again, that mail's gone."

"How long has—? However!—Oh, that's all right, sir; I only wanted—ahem!" The applicant moved away chewing his lip. What he had "only wanted" was to change the form of his letter's salutation. In the street it came to him that by telegraphing the post-master at the other end of the route he could —"Oh, thunder! Let it go!" He had begun it, "Dear Miss Barb."

And so it went its way, while he went his—on a business of whose pure unselfishness it is to be feared he was a trifle proud—I mean, to see how Mrs. Ravenel was and ask what more he could do for her. He was kindly received by a sweet little woman of thirty or so, who lived in a small high room of the hotel, taught vocal music in an academy, and had nothing to do on Saturdays and Sundays—this was Saturday. Through the doctor, who was her doctor, too, she had found access to Fannie's bedside and even into her grateful regard. Her soft, well-trained voice was of the kind that rests the sick and weary. The nurse, she said, was getting a little sleep on the lounge in Mrs. Ravenel's room. "Satisfactory?" Yes, admirable every way, and already as fond of Mrs. Ravenel as she herself.

"Isn't she lovely?" she exclaimed in melodious undertone, and hardly gave Mr. March time for a very dignified yes. "When she sat up in her pillows half an hour ago, with her breakfast, so delicate and tempting, lying before her forgotten, and she looking *so* frail and yet *so* pretty, with that look in her eyes as if she had been seeing ghosts all night, she seemed to me as though she'd just finished one life and begun another.

How long has she had that look, Mr. March? I noticed it the morning she arrived, though it wasn't anything like so plain as it is now. But it only makes her more interesting and poetical. If I were a man—hmph!—I'd wish I were Colonel Ravenel, that's all! No, I don't know that I should, either; but if I were not, I'm afraid I should give him trouble." John thought she watched him an instant there, but—

"Mr. March," she went on, "I wish you could hear the beautiful, tender, winning way in which she boasts of her husband. She's as proud of him for going and leaving her as she is of you for staying! Fact is, *I* can't tell which of you she's proudest of." She gave her listener a fascinated smile, with which he showed himself at such a loss to know what to do that she liked him still better than before.

"Mrs. Ravenel asked me to tell you how grateful she is. But she also——"

A bell-boy interrupted with two telegrams, both addressed to Fannie.

"She also what?" asked John, mantling.

"Mr. March, do you suppose either of these is bad news?"

"No, ma'am, one's probably from Suez to say the black girl's coming, and the other's from her husband; but if it were not good news, he was to send it to me."

She took the telegrams in and was soon with him again. "Oh, Mr. March, they're just as you said! Mrs. Ravenel says tell you she's better—which is true—and to thank you once more, but to say that she can't any longer—" the little musician poured upon him her most loving beams—"let you make the sacrifice you're——"

John solemnly smiled. "Why, she hasn't *been* letting me. She never asked me to stay and she needn't ask me to go. I gave my word to *him,* and I shall keep it—to myself." His manner grew more playful. "That's what you'd do, wouldn't you, if you were a man?"

But at that moment his hearer was not fancying herself a man; she was only wishing she were a younger woman. A gleam of the wish may have got into her look as she gave him her hand at parting, for somehow he began to have a sort of honey-sickness against feminine interests and plainly felt his land company's business crowding upon his conscience.

---

## LXIV.

### JUDICIOUS JOHANNA

ONE thing that gives play for sentiment concerning a three hours' belated railway train is the unapologetic majesty with which at last it rolls into a terminal station.

There had been rain-storms and freshets down in Dixie, and a subdued anxiety showed itself on Johanna's face as she stepped down from the crowded platform; but she shone with glad astonishment when she found John March taking her forgotten satchel from her hands and her checks from the express messenger.

A great many people looked at them, once for curiosity and again for pleasure; for she was almost as flattering a representative of her class as he of his, and in meeting each other they seemed happy enough to have been twins. The hotel's conveyance was an old-fashioned stage-coach, but very new and blue. It made her dumb with delight to see the owner-like serenity with which Mr. March passed her into it and by and by out of it into the gorgeous hotel. But to double the dose of some drugs reverses their effect, and her supper, served in the ladies' ordinary and by a white man-servant, actually brought her to herself. As she began to eat—blissfully, for only a yard or so away sat Mr. March smilingly holding back a hundred inquiries—she managed, herself, to ask a question or two. She grew pensive when told of Miss Fannie's sickness and of the bridegroom's being compelled to go to Washington, but revived in reporting favorably upon the health of Mrs. March, whom, she said, she had seen at a fair given by both the Suez churches to raise money to repair the graveyard fence—" on account o' de hawgs breakin' in so awfm."

" And you say everybody was there, eh ? " indolently responded John, as he resharpened his lead-pencil. " Even including Professor Pettigrew ? "

" No, seh, I observe he not 'mongs' de comp'ny, 'caze yo' maw's Jane, she call my notice to dat."

" I wonder how my mother likes Jane. Do you know ? "

Johanna showed a pretty embarrassment. " Jane say yo' maw like her. She say yo' maw like her 'caze she always done tole yo' maw ev'thing what happm when yo' maw not at home. Seh? Oh, no, seh," the speaker's bashfulness increased, "'tis on'y Jane say dat; same time she call my notice to de absence o' Pufesso' Pedigree—yass, seh."

John gave himself a heartier manner. " I reckon, Johanna, you'd be rather amazed to hear that I traveled nearly all the way from Pulaski City with yo' young missie and stayed at the same hotel here with her and her friends a whole Saturday and Sunday, wouldn't you ? "

Johanna's modest smile glittered across her face as she slowly replied, " No-o, seh, I cayn't 'zac'ly fine myseff ama-aze', 'caze Miss Barb done wrote about it in her letteh."

" Psheh ! " said John, playing incredulous, " you ain't got air letter from Miss Barb."

The girl was flattered to ecstasy. " Yass, seh, I is," she said ; but her soft laugh meant also that something in the way he faltered on the dear nickname made her heart leap.

" Now, Johanna," murmured John, looking more roguishly than he knew from under his long lashes, " you' a-foolin' me. If you had a letter you'd be monst'ous proud to show it. All you've got is a line or two saying, 'Send me my shawl,' or something o' that sort. "

Johanna glanced up with injured surprise and then tittered, " Miss Barb wear a shawl—fo' de Lawd's sa-ake ! Why, Mr. March, evm you knows betteh'n dat, seh." Her glow of happiness stayed while she drew forth a letter and laid it by her cup of coffee.

"Oh!"—the sceptic tossed his head—"seein's believin'; but I can't see so far off."

Johanna could hardly speak for grinning. "Dass heh letteh, seh, writ de ve'y same night what she tell you good-by."

"She wrote it"—John's heart came into his mouth—"that same night?"

"Dass what it saay, seh. D'ain't nothin' so ve'y private in it; ef yo' anteress encline you to read it, why——"

"Thank you," said the convert as his long arm took the prize.

There were three full sheets of it. He found himself mentioned again and again, but covertly drew his breath through his clenched teeth to see how necessary he had made himself to every page of her narrative and how utterly he was left out when not so needed. "She'll not get the same chance again," he thought as he finished.

"Johanna, have you—never mind, I was——" And he began to read it again.

Sitting thus absorbed, he was to the meek-minded girl before him as strong and fine a masculine nature as she had ever knowingly come near. But his intelligence was only masculine at last—a young man's intelligence. She kept her eyes in her plate; yet she had no trouble to see, perfectly, that her confidence was not ill-advised—a confidence that between the letter's lines he would totally fail to read what she had read.

One thing was disappointing. As often as read to her, the letter had seemed to sparkle and overflow with sweet humor and exquisite wit to that degree that she had to smother her laughter from beginning to end. Mr. March was finishing it a second time and had not smiled. Twice or thrice he had almost frowned. Yet as he pushed its open pages across the table he said ever so pleasantly,

"That's a mighty nice letter, Johanna; who's going to answer it for you?"

"Hit done answ'ed, seh. I ans' it same night it come. My fatheh writ de answeh; yass, seh, Unc' Leviticus."

"Oh, yes. Well, you couldn't 'a' chosen better— Oh! Miss Barb says here "—Mr. March gathered up the sheets again—'write me all you hear about the land company.' That's just so's to know how her father gets on, I reckon, ain't it?" He became so occupied with the letter that the girl did not have to reply. He was again reading it through. This time he repeatedly smiled, and as he folded it and gave it up he said once more,

"Yes, it's a nice letter. Does Miss Barb know where to mail the next one to you?"

"I ain't had no chaynce to sen' her word, seh."

"Why, that's a pity! You ought to do that at once, Johanna, and let her know you've got here safe and well—if only for her sake! I'll do it for you to-night, if you'd like me to."

Johanna thankfully assented.

Mr. March did not ponder, this time, as to what the

opening phrase of the letter should be ; and as he
sealed the " hurried note " he did so with the air of a
man who is confident he has made no mistake. It
began, " Dear Miss Barb."

## LXV.

### THE ENEMY IN THE REAR

A NEW week came in with animating spring weather.
On Monday Fannie sat up, and on Tuesday, when John
called, her own smile surprised him at the door, while
Johanna's reflected it in the background.

He felt himself taken at a disadvantage. His un-
ready replies to her lively promptings turned aimlessly
here and there; his thoughts could neither lead nor
follow them. The wine of her pretty dissembling went
to his head; while the signs of chastening in her fair
face joined strangely with her sprightliness in an
obscure pathetic harmony that moved his heartstrings
as he had felt youthfully sure they were never to
be moved again. His late anger against Ravenel
came back, and with it, to his surprise, the old tenderness for her, warmed by the anger and without
the bitterness of its old chagrin. He found himself
reminded of his letters to Johanna's distant mistress,
but instantly decided that the two matters had nothing
to do with each other, and gave himself rich comfort in
this visible and only half specious fulfilment of his

youth's long dream. The daily protection and care of this girl, her welcome, winsome gayeties and thanks, were his, his! with no one near to claim a division of shares and only honor to keep account with. His words were stumbling over these unconfessed distractions when she startled him by saying,

"I've telegraphed Jeff-Jack that I can travel."

His response was half-resentful. "Did the doctor say you might?"

She gave her tone a shade of mimicry. "Yes, sir, the doctor said I might." But she changed it to add, "You'll soon be free, John; it's a matter of only two or three hours." Her playfulness faded into a smile of gratefulest affection. Johanna, who was passing into the next room, could not see it, but she easily guessed it by the slight disconcertion which showed through the smile he gave back.

He dropped his eyes pensively. "To be free isn't everything."

"It is for you just now, John, mighty nearly. You've got a great work before you, and——"

"Oh, yes, so I've heard." He laughed apologetically and rose to go.

"You don't need to be reminded as badly as you used to," said Fannie, retaining his hand and looking into his face with open admiration. "You'll start East to-day, won't you?"

"That depends."

"Now, John, it doesn't do any such thing. It mustn't!"

"I'll let you know later," said John, freeing his

grasp. The pressure of her little hand had got into his pulse. He hurried away.

"She's right," he pondered, as he walked down the populous street, beset by a vague discomfort, "it mustn't depend. Besides, she's pretty sure not to stay here. It wouldn't be Jeff-Jack's way to come back; he'll wire to her to come to him at once. Reckon I'll decide now to go on that Washington express this evening. I can't afford to let my movements depend on F-Fannie's—hem! Heaven knows I've taxed the company's patience enough already."

He told the regretful clerks at his hotel that this was his farewell day with them, and tried to feel that he had thus burned the last bridge between himself and indiscretion. He only succeeded in feeling as you and I—and Garnet—used to feel when we had told our purpose to others and fibbed to ourselves about the motive. But Garnet had got far beyond that, understand.

So Vice-President March went to the day's activities paying parting calls from one private office to another in the interest of Widewood's industrial colonization. He bought his railroad ticket—returnable in case any unforeseen——

"Oh, that's all right, President March: yes, sir; good-day, sir."

At his hotel shortly after noon he found a note. He guessed at its contents. "She takes the same train I do." He forced himself to frown at the amusing yet agreeable accident. But his guess was faulty; the note read:

" I return immediately to Suez, where Jeff-Jack will arrive by the end of the week."

And thereupon John had another feeling known to us all—the dull shame with which we find that fate has defrauded us for our own good. However, he hurried to Fannie and put himself into her service with a gay imperiousness delightful to both and apparently amusing to the busy Johanna. By and by the music-teacher helped also, making Fannie keep her rocking-chair, and, as Mr. March came and went, dropped little melodious, regretful things to him privately about his own departure. Once she said that nothing gave her so much happiness as answering pleasant letters; but John only wondered why women so often talk obviously without any aim whatever!

" Well," at length he said to Fannie, " I'll go now and get myself off. Your train starts from the same station mine does; I'll say good-by there."

He packed his valise and hand-bag, and had given them to the porter, when he received a letter.

" My George ! " was his dismayed whisper to himself, " a duelist couldn't be prompter." He walked to the door, gazing at the superscription. " It feels like my letter sent back. Ah, well ! that's just what it ought to be. Confound the women, all ; I wonder how it feels for a man just to mind his own business and let them " —he rent the envelope—" mind—theirs ! "

He read the missive as he rode to the station. It wasn't very long, and it did seem to him a bit too formal ; and yet it was so gravely sweet that he had to smooth the happiness off his face repeatedly, and finally stole a private laugh behind the hand that twisted his small mustache, as he fondly sighed.

"Doggone your considerate little soul, you're just a hundred ton nicer and better than your father or anybody else is ever going to deserve!" But he read on:

"For you remember, do you not? that I was free to speak of yours and papa's ambitions and plans for Widewood? And so 1 enclose a page or two of a letter just received from our Johanna at home, because it states things about Colonel Proudfit's new construction company which Cornelius seems to have told your mother's black girl, Jane. They may be pure inventions; but if so, they must be his, not hers, although I should never have thought he would be so reckless as to tell such things to such a person——" Etc.

John unfolded the fragments of Johanna's letter with a condescending smile which began to fade before he had read five lines. A chill ran down his back, and then an angry flush mounted to his brow.

There is a kind of man—Mr. Leggett was such a one, Samson was another—who will tell his own most valuable or dangerous secrets to any woman on whose conquest he is bent, if she only knows how to bid for them. And there are "Delijahs" who will break any confidence and risk any fortune, nay, their own lives, to show a rival she has been eclipsed. There are also women, even girls, who are of such pure eyes they cannot discern obliquity anywhere. And there are others just as pure—the lily's own heart isn't purer—who, nevertheless—but why waste time or type. In short, Johanna first, and then Barbara, had seen how easily

Daphne Jane's tittle-tattle might be serious news to John March; which it certainly was if the dark cloud on his face was a true sign.

He found Fannie on her train and well cared for by Johanna and the music-teacher. In the silence which promptly followed his greeting, these two moved aside and Fannie murmured eagerly,

"What on earth's the matter?—Yes, there is, John; something's wrong; what is it? I saw you slip a letter into your pocket at the door. What does it mean?"

"Why, Fannie—it means I've got to go straight back to Suez."

She made a rapturous gesture. "And you're going on this train?" she whispered.

"No."

"Now, why not? John, you're foolish!—or else you think I am. You mustn't! You must go on this train. John, I—I want you to." She smiled up at his troubled gaze.

"Johanna," he said, and beckoned the maid a step aside. "Miss Barb has sent me that part of your letter to her that tells about the construction company."

"Yaas, seh," murmured Johanna. Her heart throbbed.

"You say, there, that Cornelius says its officers are mere tools in the power of men who have put them there; that Gamble's behind Crickwater, Bulger's behind Mattox, and he, Leggett, is behind Pettigrew—yes —don't interrupt, there isn't time—and that Colonel Proudfit got the money to buy stock enough to elect himself president, by persuading his wife to mortgage everything she has got. Yes; but you don't tell who Cornelius says is behind Colonel Proudfit. Didn't he say ? "

"Please, seh, Mr. March, ef Majo'——"

"That's all, Johanna, I'm much obliged to you. It may be, you know, that there isn't a word of truth in the whole thing; but in any case you'll never—No, that's right." He turned to Fannie. "I must change my ticket and check; I'm going with you."

---

## LXVI.

### WARM HEARTS, HOT WORDS, COOL FRIENDS

ABOUT that same hour the next day John stepped off the train at Suez and turned to let Fannie down; but a pair of uplifted arms came between the two, and Launcelot Halliday, with the back of his velvet coat close to the young man's face, said, "I'll take care of my daughter, John; you can look after any business of your own that may need you."

"Why, Pop!" exclaimed Fannie. The color flushed up to her brows. John gazed at him in haughty silence.

"Come on, Johanna," said the old General, heartily. "Good-by, John. When can I see you in your office?"

"Whenever I'm there, and not too busy!" replied March as he strode away.

"We'll go to the old house for to-night, Johanna,"

said Fannie, and did not speak again until she began to draw off her gloves in her father's parlor. Her face was white, her dark eyes wide; but her voice was slow and kind.

"Yes, Johanna, go along to my room. I'll be there directly." She shut the door and folded her gloves, smiling like a swordsman rolling up his sleeves.

"Pop, I've owed you a-many an explanation that I've never paid. You never owed me one in your life till now; but "—her eyes flashed—" you owe it this time to the roots of your hair."

"Fan, that's a mighty poor beginning for the explanation I expect from you."

His tone was one of forbearance, but before he could finish she was as red as a flower. "I belong to my husband! When I've anything to explain I'll explain to him."

"Fannie Halliday——"

"Ravenel, if you please, sir."

He smiled severely. "Have a chair, Mrs. Ravenel. Fan, you're married to a man who never asks an explanation."

The two gazed upon each other in silence. His accustomed belief in her and her ardent love for him were already stealing back into their hearts. Nevertheless——

"O, sir!" she exclaimed, "tell me something I don't know! Yes! But I'm married to a man who waits for things to explain themselves."

"Or till they're past all explanation, Fan."

"Yes, sir; yes! But more! I'm married to a man

who knows that nothing can explain conduct but conduct. That's the kind of explanation you still owe me, Pop, till you pay it to John March."

"Well, then," he replied with new warmth, "I'll owe it a long time. If he ever again shows his carelessness of conventional——"

Fannie laid a pale hand on her father's arm. "It wasn't his. He showed carefulness enough; I overruled it. It was his duty to come, Pop; and I had let him neglect duty for me long enough."

The General started. "Why, Fan." But when he looked into her sad eyes his soul melted. She smiled with her face close to his.

"Pop, you never meddled in my affairs before. Don't you reckon I'll manage this one all right."

"Why, yes, Fan. I was only anxious about you because——"

"Never mind your becauses, dear. Just say you'll make it all right with John."

"Go to bed, Fannie; go to bed; John and I will take care of ourselves."

When the General reached his office the next day the forenoon was well advanced. He was still there when at midday John March entered.

"John, howdy? Have a chair."

"Thank you, sir." But the young man continued to stand.

"Oh, take a seat, John; you can get up again if what I say doesn't suit you."

The speaker came from his desk, took a chair and pushed another to his visitor.

"John, I had a short talk with Fannie last night, and a long one again this morning. If my manner to you last evening impugned your motives, I owe you an apology."

"That's all I want to hear, General," said John, accepting the old soldier's hand.

"Yes, my boy; but it's not all I want to say. Fannie tells me you've been taking some business risks, so to speak, for her sake." John scowled. "Now, John, when she asked you to come home on her train she knew that was to her a social risk, and she took it for your sake in return. Not improper? I don't say it was. It was worse than improper, John; it was romantic! The gay half of Suez will never forget it, and the grim half will never forgive it! Oh, it was quite proper and praiseworthy if Pussie and Susie would just not misconstrue it, as they certainly will. Only a few months ago, you know, you were making it almost public that you would still maintain your highly poetical line of conduct and sentiment toward Fan after she should be married."

"General Halliday, I——"

"Let me finish, John. We didn't run you out of town, did we?"

March smiled a strong sarcasm and shook his head. The General went on.

"No, sir, we took you good-naturedly and trusted to your sober second thought. Well, Fan's scarcely ten days married, Jeff-Jack's a thousand miles away, and here you come full of good intentions, hell's pavement, you know——O John, the more I think of it the more amazed I am at all three of you. I don't blame Jeff-Jack for leaving Fan as he did—— "

" ' As he did ' ! By George! General Halliday, that's all I do blame him for ! "

" Why, do you mean—But never mind; that's probably none of my business; I don't see how you could ever think it was any of yours. Oh, now, please keep your seat ! No, at least, I don't blame him merely for leaving her; a politician's a soldier; he can't stop to comfort the sick. But he should have declined your offer to stay with her, in *italics*, John, and sent for me ! "

" Sent for—Oh, imagine him ! Besides, General Halliday, Jeff-Jack knew my offer was to myself; not to him at all, sir ! But he saw another thing—about me —as plainly as I did ; yes, plainer ! "

" I could do that myself, John. What was it—this time ? "

" He saw my sober second thought had come ! "

" H—, I wish I had his eyes ! Did he say so ? Wha'd he say ? "

" He said what wasn't true."

The old warrior smiled satirically. " What was it ? "

" 'Ever mind what it was ! I'm talked out.''

" My dear fellow, so am I ! John, honestly, I thank you for the—pardon me—the unusual patience with which you've taken my hard words." The speaker gripped his hearer's knee. " And you really think you've finished your first great campaign of mistakes— eh ? "

" Yes ! " They rose, laughing. " Yes, and I've every reason to hope it's my last." The General proposed drinks, but John hadn't time, and they only swapped cigars.

"I hear you leave us again this evening," said the General.

"No; they'd like me to go, but I'm—I'm very tired and anyhow——"

"You're wha-at? Tired! Why, John—O no, you don't mean tired, you mean insa-ane! Why, sir, that's going straight back on everything you've been saying! John, we're not going to stand this." The General grew red.

"Whom do you mean by 'we,' General?" Both men were forgetting to smoke.

"Everybody, sir! everybody in Suez with whom you have any relations? Why, look at it yourself! For a week running you neglect your own interests and your company's business to do—what? Just what you'd do if you were still under an infatuation which you've openly confessed for years!"

"But which, General Halliday, I tell you again——"

"Telling won't do, sir, when doing tells another story. Here are your directors astonished and vexed at you for coming back with not a word as to why you've come. O, how do I know it? It's the talk o' the town! They bid you go back to the field of work you chose yourself, and you tell *them*—business men—financiers—that you're 'tired and anyhow——' By Jupiter! John March——"

"General, stop! I'll manage my own business my own way, sir! It's no choice of mine to speak so to you, General Halliday, but I swear I'll not widen my confi-

dences—no, nor modify my comings and goings—to
provide against the looks of things. It's the culpable
who are careful, sir."

"Yes—yes—and 'the simple pass on and are pun-
ished.' I don't ask you to widen your confidences to
include me, John."

"Shan't widen them to include anyone, under pressure, General. But it's a pity when you know so much
about these things, you don't know more."

"I do, John. I know that when Jeff-Jack left here
he left his proxy—at your solicitation—with John Wesley Garnet!"

"Which, he gave me to understand, was just what he
intended to do, anyhow."

"O, gave you to understand, of course! But it
wasn't, John. Jeff-Jack's still got too many uses for
Garnet, to cross him without a good excuse. But he
knows what Gamble's influence is, and a different request
from you would have put his proxy in safer hands.
He would have saved you, John, if you hadn't yourself
rushed in and spoken for Garnet."

"And why should you assume that Garnet's holding
the proxy has made——"

"Oh, bah! Why, John, d'ye reckon I don't see that
he and Bulger have gone over to Gamble, and are out-
voting you—hauling you in hand over fist? It's written
in large letters and hung up where all Susie can read
it—except yourself!"

"Where?"

"In your face. And now you're staying here to stare
at a lost game. O, John, for your own sake, get away!

Clear out to-night! You can at least hide your helplessness. If you will, I'll call you back as soon as you can gain anything by coming. Yes, and I'll turn in and fight these fellows for you in the meantime!"

"Thank you, General, but you're mistaken; the game *isn't* lost. The moment Jeff-Jack and I——"

"Ah! John, the moment's gone! Ask yourself! Will Jeff-Jack ever join the forlorn hope of a man who won't dance to his fiddle? *His* self-sacrifices are not that sort."

"And yet that's the very sacrifice you think I ought to let you make for me!"

"By Joe! sir, it wouldn't be a sacrifice! If it will just get you out of town it will suit me perfectly!"

"Then, sir, you'll not be suited! I'm going to stay here and see what my enemies are up to; and if they're up to what I think they are, I'll break their backs if I have to do it single-handed and alone! Good-day, sir."

"Good-day, John; that's the way you'll have to do it, sir."

"Devil take him," added the General as he found himself alone, " *he's* crossed the bar. It's his heart that's safe. O, Fan, my poor child!"

## LXVII.

### PROBLEM: IS AN UNCONFIRMED DISTRUST NECESSARILY A DEAD ASSET?

JOHN went away heavy and bitter. Yet he remembered, this time, to take more care of his facial expression. He met Shotwell and Proudfit coming out of the best saloon. They stopped him, complimented his clothes and his legs, asked a question or two of genuine interest, poked him in the waistband, and regretted not meeting him sooner. Proudfit suggested, with the proper anathema, to go back and take a *re*-invigorator with Vice-President March. But the pleasant Shotwell said:

"You forget, Colonel, that ow a-able young friend belongs to Gideon's ba-and, now, seh."

Proudfit made a vague gesture of acknowledgment. "And anyhow"—his tongue thickened and his head waggled playfully—"anyhow, Shot, a ladies' man's just *got* to keep his breath sweet, ain't he?"

Shotwell looked as though the rolling earth had struck something. March paled, but he took the Captain's cigar to light his own as he remarked:

"I don't get the meaning of that expression as clear as I wish you'd make it, Colonel."

Shotwell pretended to burst with merriment. "Why, neither does the Colonel! That was only a sort o' glittering generality to hide his emba'assment—haw, haw, haw!"

Proudfit smiled modestly. "Shot, you're right again! He's right again, John. It was only one o' my grittlin' gen—my grilterin' geren—aw! Shot, hush yo' fuss! you confu-use me!"

John was laughing before he knew it. "Gentlemen, I've got to get along home. I slept at Tom Hersey's hotel last night, and haven't seen my mother yet. O— eh—Captain——"

Shotwell left Proudfit and walked away with March. Persons rarely asked advice of the ever-amiable Captain; they went by him to Charley Champion, whom he reverenced as well as loved. And so he was thoroughly pleased when John actually let Champion pass them and asked him, in confidence, what he thought of Proudfit's construction company.

"Well, of co'se, John, you know how fah Proudfit is fum being an a-able man; and so does he. He's evm fool enough to think he can sharpen his wits with whiskey, which *you* know, March, that if that was so I'd myself be as sharp as a ra-azor. But *I* don't suspicion but what everything's clean and square—Oh, I wouldn't swear nobody does; you know, yo'self, what double-ba'lled fools some men ah. I reckon just about everybody likes the arrangement, though; faw whetheh one company aw the otheh, aw both, make money, the money sta-ays. Yes, of co'se, we know he owes it to Garnet's influence, but I suspicion Garnet done as he did mo' to gratify Miz Proudfit's ambitions than fum any notion o' they being big money in it faw anybody; you know how fawnd Garnet's always been of both of 'em, you know. Oh, no, whateveh the thing is, it's square!

You might know that by Pettigrew bein' its seccata'y ; faw to *eh* is *human*—which Pettigrew *ain't*."

John mounted a horse and started for Widewood. He had to stop and shake hands with Parson Tombs over his front palings, and make an honest effort to feel annoyed by the old man's laughter-laden compliments on his energy, enterprise, and perspicacity. At the Halliday cottage he saw Fannie clipping roses from the porch trellis for Martha Salter, who stood by. She waved her hand.

"John March, I do believe you were going to gallop right a-past us without stopping!" said Fannie, as he tardily wheeled and rode slowly up to the low gate.

He answered awkwardly, and when she gave him a rose, looked across at Miss Salter, whose gravity increased his discomfort. A dash up the slope beyond the Academy was a partial relief only while it lasted, and at the top, where his horse dropped into a trot, he lifted the flower as if to toss it over the hedge, but faltered, bent forward, and stuck it into the animal's head-stall. As he straightened up he found himself in the company of a tall rider going his way, whom he had passed on the slope—the president of Suez University.

" I believe you're not often overtaken, once you're in the saddle, Mr. March."

John " reckoned that was so," and said that as he came up the hill he had been so busy thinking, that he had not recognized the quiet gray man in time to salute him. The poverty-chastened gentleman had " seen how it was," and began to speak of the great changes impending over Widewood and in Suez, principally due, he insisted with a very agreeable dignity, to Mr. March's courageous and untiring perseverance.

"It's true you couldn't have succeeded without some support from such resolute and catholic spirits as Major Garnet and President Gamble; but when I lately spoke to them they said emphatically that, in comparison with you, they had done nothing; and Mr. Leggett, who was present, confirmed them and included himself. He had brought them to me to urge me to take a few shares which were for the moment available. The holder, I believe, was the lady who teaches French here in the Academy, Mademoiselle Eglantine; yes. I have no money to invest, however, and Mr. Leggett tells me she has changed her mind again and will keep the stock, which I am sure is wise. The Construction Company?—I think it an excellent idea; admirable! I mustn't detain you, Mr. March, though I have a request to make. Possibly you know that our more advanced students gather for an hour or so once a week in what we've named our Social Hall, for various forms of profitable entertainment? Now and then we have the good fortune to have some man of mark address us informally, and if you, Mr. March, would do so, there's no one else in this region whom our young people would be so pleased to hear."

John thanked the president for the honor. If there was only something, anything, on which he was really qualified to speak—but——

"Mr. March, speak on the imperative need of organized effort harmoniously combined, for the accomplishment of almost all large undertakings! Or on the growing necessity men find to trust their interest in one another's hands! Oh! you can hardly be at a loss for a theme, I'm sure; but those are points which, it seems to me, our state of society here makes it especially needful to emphasize. Don't you think so, Mr. March?"

Mr. March thought so; ahem! There was a pause, and then they talked of the loveliness of the season. The temperature, they decided, must be about seventy-seven. And what a night the last one had been! Mr. March had attended a meeting of the land company's board, which did not adjourn until very late, but he simply had to take a long walk in the starlight afterward, and even when that was done he stayed up until an absurd hour writing a description of the glorious Southern night to a friend in New England who was still surrounded by frozen hills and streams.

"I hardly know an easier way to delight a New Englander's fancy at this time of year," said the gray president. "Or is your friend a Southern man?"

"Oh—eh—no, sir, she's a Southern girl. I—well, I had to write her on business, anyhow, and I just yielded to the impulse—wrote it, really, more to myself than——"

Mr. March dreamed a moment and presently spoke again.

"It's barely possible I shall have to leave town to-morrow or next day, sir; if I don't I'll try to meet your wish. Well, sir, good-day." He galloped on.

John had often before left Suez and crossed the old battle-field benumbed with consternation and galled with doubts of himself; but he had always breathed in new strength among the Widewood hills. Not so to-day. When once or twice he let his warm horse walk and his thought seek rest, the approbations of Proudfit and Shotwell, Parson Tombs, the president of Suez University, and such— Oh! they only filled him with gaspings. He tried to think what man of real weight there still was with whose efforts he might " harmoni-ously combine " his own; but he knew well enough there was not one who had not, seemingly through some error of his, drifted beyond his hail.

As the turnings of the mountain road led him from each familiar vista to the next, more and more griev-ously bore down upon his spirit the sacred charge which he had inherited along with this majestic forest. His father's presence and voice seemed with him again as at one point he halted a moment because it had been tne father's habit to do so, and gazed far down and away upon Suez and off in the west where Rosemont's roof and grove lay in a flood of sunlight.

" Oh, son," he could almost hear the dear voice say again, as just there it had once said, " I do believe it's fah betteh to get cheated once in a while than to be afraid to trust those who're not afraid to trust us. Why, son, we wouldn't ever a-been father and son at all, only for the sweet trustfulness of yo' dear motheh. Think o' that, son; you an' me neveh bein' any rela-tion to each otheh ! "

The rider's bosom heaved. But the next moment he was hearkening. A distant strain of human mirth came softly from farther up in the wooded hills; one and no more, as if those who made it had descended from some swell of the land into one of its tangled hollows. He listened in vain. All he heard was that beloved long-lost voice saying once more in his lonely heart, "Make haste and grow, son." He put in the spur.

Down a long slope, up a sudden rise, over a level curve where a fox-squirrel leaped into the road and scampered along it; up again, down into a hollow, across the ridge beyond—so he was going, when voices sounded again, then hoofs and wheels, and flashing and darkling in the woodland's afternoon shadows came a party of four, two under hats, two under bonnets, drawn by Bulger's handsome trotters in Garnet's carry-all. Garnet drove. Beside him sat Mrs. March luminous with satisfaction, and on the back seat with Bulger was a small thin woman whose flaxen hair was flattened in quince-seed waves on her pretty temples, and whom John knew slightly as Mrs. Gamble. Bulger and the ladies waved hands. Only Garnet's smile showed restraint.

In the board meeting of the night before, though surprise and annoyance at John's presence and attitude were obvious, only the Major and he had openly struck fire. When Gamble, Garnet, and Bulger were left alone, Bulger, who had all along been silent, remarked to Garnet:

"I never drive with a whip. There's lots of horse in a young fellow like March, and I never blame a horse for not liking what he don't understand. I give him lump-sugar. If he's vicious, that's another thing; but when he's only nervous—Got a match, Gamble?— Thanks. Now, I'll tell you what let's do first thing to-morrow morning." And this, with one or two happy modifications suggested by Garnet and Gamble, was now being done.

---

## LXVIII.

### FAREWELL, WIDEWOOD

JOHN was lost in a conflict of strong emotions. Sore beset, he forced them all aside for the moment and yielded only to a grateful wonder as he looked upon his pretty mother with her lap full of spring flowers. For the first time in their acquaintance her shapely ear was not waiting to receive, nor her refined lips to reject, his usual rough apologies. Her tone of resignation was almost playful as she said that the first news of his return had come to her through her present kind companions.

Mrs. Gamble put in that she had induced Mrs. March to join them, on their return from their mountain drive, by telling her that her son was so full of his work in his, her, and their common interest, that she could not expect him to come to her.

"And you all were bringing mother in to see me?" exclaimed John.

"Certing!" said blithe Mrs. Gamble, while Garnet faltered a smiling disclaimer, and the son wondered what hidden influence was making endurable to his mother the company of a woman who declared he would soon have this wilderness turned into a "frewtful garding." But as Mrs. Gamble turned from him and engaged Mrs. March's and Bulger's attention, Garnet gave him a beckoning nod, and as he came round, the Major leaned out and softly said, with a most amiable dignity:

"We were really looking for you, too. Don't you want, just for three or four hours, to forget last night's discord and come along with Sister March and us? We've got a pleasant surprise for her, and we'll enjoy it more, and so will she, if you take part in it."

"Why, Major Garnet—hm!—I can forget; I only can't recede, sir. But——"

"Better speak a little lower."

"Yes, sir. Where's mother going with you, sir? I suppose she knows that, of course?"

"O yes, she knows that. President Gamble and his wife have invited a few of us—the two Miss Kinsingtons, Mademoiselle, Brother and Sister Tombs, Proudfit, Sister Proudfit, Launcelot Halliday, and Fannie——"

"Professor Pettigrew?" asked John.

"No, just a few of us—to a sort of literary evening. But Sister March doesn't know that I've been asked to read a number of her poems; you'll be expected to recite others, and the evening will close with the announcement that we—that is, Mrs. Gamble, Bulger, and I—I'm afraid you'll think we've taken a great liberty in your absence, Brother March; I——"

"What have you been doing, Major Garnet?"

"Why, John, we've outrun your intended efforts and

—partly by mail, partly by telegraph—the news only came this morning—we've found Sister March a publisher."

"Why, Major Garnet!" whispered John, with girlish tenderness. Tears sprang to his eyes.

"They're a new house, just starting," continued Garnet, "but they'll print the poems at once."

"In Boston or New York?" interrupted John.

"Pittsburg."

"But how did they decide, Major, without seeing the poems?"

"They didn't; Sister March loaned me some of her duplicates."

"I hope you got good terms, did you?"

"Excellent. Thirty-three and a third per cent. royalty after the first five thousand. Why, John, Dixie alone will want that many."

John "reckoned so" and backed his horse. Mrs. Gamble ratified the Major's invitation, and the horseman replied to the smiling four that he must go home for one or two matters, but would make haste to join them in Suez. As Garnet lifted the reins Mrs. March settled herself anew at his side with a sweet glance into his face which disturbed her son, it seemed so fondly personal. But this disquietude quickly left him as he rode away, when he remembered the Major's daughter having lifted just such a look at himself, for whom, manifestly, she cared nothing, except in the most colorless way.

Daphne Jane, at Widewood, swinging on the garden-gate and cackling airily to a parting visitor, slipped to the ground as Widewood's master suddenly appeared, although just then the first light-hearted smile of that day broke upon his face. It was the parting visitor, also mounted, whose presence pleased him in a degree so unexpected even to himself that he promptly abated his first show of delight.

"Why, Johanna, you important adjunct! To what are we indebted for"—the tone grew vacant—"this —pleasure?" His gay look darkened to one of swift reflection and crushing inference. "Do—do you want to see me?" he blurted, and somewhere under her dark skin Johanna blushed. "No, of course you don't."

As he dismounted—"Jane," he said, "you no need to come in; finish your confab." Upstairs he tried to recall the errand that had brought him there, but Barbara's maid filled all his thought. He saw her from a window and silently addressed her.

"You're not yourself! You're your mistress and you know it! You're she, come all the way back from the land of snow to counsel me; and you're welcome. There's balm, at least, in a sweet woman's counsel, womanly given. Balm; ah, me! neither she nor I have any right—O! what am I looking for in this drawer?—No, I'll take just this word from her and then no more!" Down-stairs he paused an instant in passing his mother's portrait. "No, dear," he said, "we'll mix nothing else with our one good dream—Widewood filled with happy homes and this one, with just you and me in it, the happiest of them all!"

On the gate Daphne Jane still prattled, but after half

a dozen false starts Johanna, for gentle shame's sake, had felt obliged to go. Her horse paced off briskly, and a less alert nature than Daphne Jane's would have fancied her soon far on her way. As John came forth again he saw no sign that his mother's maid, slowly walking toward the house with her eyes down, was not engaged in some pious self-examination, instead of listening down the mountain road with both ears. But she easily guessed he was doing the same thing.

"Well, Jane," he said as he loosed his bridle from the fence, "been writing something for Johanna?" and when she said, "Yass, seh," he knew the bashful lie was part of her complicity in a matter she did not understand, but only hoped it was some rascality. A secret delight filled her bosom as he mounted and walked his horse out of sight. She stopped with lifted head and let her joy tell itself in a smiling whisper:

"Trott'n'!" She hearkened again; the smile widened; the voice rose: "Gallopin'!" Her eyes dilated merrily and she cried aloud:

"Ga-allopin', ga-allopin', lippetty-clip, down Zigzag Hill!" Her smile became a laugh, the laugh a song, the song a dance which joined the lightness of a butterfly with the grace of a girl whose mothers had never worn a staylace, and she ran with tossing arms and willowy undulations to kiss her image in Daphne's glass.

With a hundred or so of small stones rattling at his horse's heels John reached the foot of "Zigzag Hill," turned with the forest road once or twice more, noticed, by the tracks, that Johanna's horse was walking, and at another angle saw her just ahead timorously working her animal sidewise to the edge of the way.

" Johanna," he began as he dashed up—" O !—don't get scared—didn't you come out here in hopes to some-how let me know "—he took on a look of angry distress —" that the Suez folks are talking ? "

The girl started and stammered, but the young man knitted his brows worse. " Umhm. That's all right." His horse leaped so that he had to look back to see her, as he added more kindly :

" I'm much obliged to you, Johanna—Good-by."

The face he had thus taken by surprise tried, too late, to smile away the signs that its owner was grieved and hurt. A few rods farther on John wheeled around and trotted back. Her pulse bounded with gratitude.

" Johanna, of course, if I stay here I shall keep en-tirely out of Mrs. Ravenel's sight, or——"

The girl made a despairing gesture that brought John's frown again.

" Why, what ? " he asked with a perplexed smile.

" Law ! Mr. Mahch, you cayn't all of a sudden do dat ; dey'll on'y talk wuss."

" Well, Johanna—I'm not going to try it. I'm going to take the express train this evening." He started on, but checked up once more and faced around. " O—eh— Johanna, I'd rather you'd not speak of this, you under-stand. I natu'ly don't want Mrs. Ravenel to know why I go ; but I'm even more particular about General Halli-day. It's none o' his—hm ! I say I don't want him to know. Well, good-by. O—eh—Johanna, have you no word—of course, you know, the North's a mighty sizable place, and still it's just possible I might chance some day to meet up with—eh—eh—however, it's aft' all so utterly improbable, that, really—well, good-by ! "

A while later Johanna stopped at that familiar point which overlooked the valley of the Swanee and the slopes about Rosemont. The sun had nearly set, but she realized her hope. Far down on the gray turnpike she saw the diminished figure of John March speeding town-ward across the battle-field. At the culvert he drew rein, faced about, and stood gazing upon Widewood's hills. She could but just be sure it was he, yet her tender spirit felt the swelling of his heart, and the tears rose in her eyes, that were not in his only because a man —mustn't.

While she wondered wistfully if he could see her, his arm went slowly up and waved a wide farewell to the scene. She snatched out her handkerchief, flaunted it, and saw him start gratefully at sight of her and reply with his own. Then he wheeled and sped on.

"Go," she cried, "go ; and de Lawd be wid you, Mr. Jawn Mahch, Gen'lemun !—O Lawd, Lawd ! Mr. Jawn Mahch, I wisht I knowed a nigger like you ! "

## LXIX.

### IN YANKEE LAND

It was still early May when Barbara Garnet had been six weeks in college. The institution stood in one of New England's oldest towns, a place of unfenced greenswards, among which the streets wound and loitered, hunting for historic gambrel-roofed houses, many of which had given room to other sorts less picturesque and homelike. In the same search great elms followed them down into river meadows or up among flowery hills, casting off their dainty blossoms, putting on their leaves, and waving majestic greetings to the sower as he strode across his stony fields.

Yet for all the sudden beauty of the land and season Miss Garnet was able to retain enough of her "nostalgia" to comfort her Southern conscience. She had arrived in March and caught Dame Nature in the midst of her spring cleaning, scolding her patient children; and at any rate her loyalty to Dixie forbade her to be quite satisfied with these tardy blandishments. Let the cold Connecticut turn as blue as heaven, by so much the more was it not the green Swanee? She had made more than one warm friendship among her fellow-students, but the well-trimmed lamp of her home feeling waxed not dim. It only smoked a trifle even in Boston, that maze of allurements into which no Southerner of her father's generation ever sent his brother, no Southerness her sister, without some fear of apostasy.

Barbara had made three visits to that city, where Mrs. Fair, the ladies said, "did a great deal for her." Yet when Mrs. Fair said, with kind elation, "My dear, you have met Boston, and it is yours!" the smiling exile, as she put her hand into both hands of her hostess, remembered older friends and silently apologized to herself for having so lost her heart to this new one.

At that point came in one who was at least an older acquaintance—the son. Thoroughly as Barbara had always liked Henry Fair, he seemed to her to have saved his best attractiveness until now, and with a gentleness as masculine as it was refined, fitted into his beautiful home, his city, the whole environing country, indeed, and shone from them, in her enlivened fancy, like an ancestor's portrait from its frame. He came to take her to an exhibition of paintings, and thence to the railway station, where a fellow-student was to rejoin her for the trip back to college. Mrs. Fair had to attend a meeting of the society for something or other, of which she was president.

"These people make every minute count," wrote Barbara to Fannie; "and yet they're far from being always at work. I'm learning the art of recreation from them. Even the men have a knack for it that our Southern men know nothing about."

"You might endorse that 'Fair *versus* March,'" replied Ravenel to his wife, one evening, as he lingered a moment at tea. She had playfully shown him the passage as a timorous hint at better self-care; but he smilingly rose and went out. She kept a bright face, and as she sat alone re-reading the letter, said, laughingly,

"Poor John!" and a full minute afterward, without knowing it, sighed.

This may have been due, in part at least, to the fact that Barbara's long but tardy letter was the first one Fannie had received from her. It told how a full correspondence between the writer's father and his fellow college president had made it perfectly comfortable for her to appear at the institution for the first time quite unescorted, having within the hour parted from Mr. and Mrs. Fair, who, though less than three hours' run from their own home, would have gone with her if she could have consented. She had known that the dormitories were full and that like many other students she would have to make her home with a private family, and had found it with three very lovable sisters, two spinsters and a widow, who turned out to be old friends—former intimates—of the Fairs. And now this intimacy had been revived; Mrs. Fair had already been to see the monce, although to do so she had come up from Boston alone. How she had gone back the letter did not say. Fannie felt the omission.

"I didn't think Barb would do me that way," she mused; and was no better pleased when she recalled a recent word of Jeff-Jack's: that few small things so sting a woman as to disappoint her fondness and her curiosity at the same time. Now with men— However! All Barbara had omitted was that Mrs. Fair had gone back with her son, who on his way homeward from a trip to New York had been "only too glad" to join her here, and spend two or three hours under spring skies and shingle roof with the three pleasant sisters.

This was in the third of those six weeks during which Barbara had been at college. About half of the two or three hours was spent in a stroll along the windings of a small woodland river. The widow and Mrs. Fair led the van, the two spinsters were the main body, and Henry and Barbara straggled in the rear stooping side by side among white and blue violets, making perilous ventures for cowslips and maple blossoms, and commercing in sweet word-lore and dainty likes and dislikes.

When the procession turned, the two stragglers took seats on a great bowlder round which the stream broke in rapids, Barbara gravely confessing to the spinsters, as they lingeringly passed, that she had never done so much walking in her life before as now and here in a place where an unprotected girl could hire four hacks for a dollar.

The widow and Mrs. Fair left the others behind. They had once been room-mates at school, and this walk brought back something of that old relation. They talked about the young man at their back, and paused to smile across the stream at some children in daring colors on a green hillside getting sprouts of dandelion.

" Do you think," asked the widow, " it's really been this serious with him all along? "

" Yes, I do. Henry's always been such a pattern of prudence and moderation that no one ever suspects the whole depth of his feelings. He realizes she's very young, and he may have held back until her mind— her whole nature—should ripen ; although, like him, as you see, she's ripe beyond her years. But above all he's a dutiful son, and I believe he's simply been waiting till he could see her effect on us and ours on her. Tell me frankly, dear, how do you like her?"

The Yankee widow had bright black eyes and they twinkled with restrained enthusiasm as she murmured, "I hope she'll get him!"

"Ah!" Mrs. Fair smiled gratefully, made a pretty mouth and ended with a wise gesture and a dubious toss, as who should say, "I admit he's priceless, but I hope he may get her."

Whereupon the widow ventured one question more, and Mrs. Fair told her of John March. "Yes," she said at the end, "he happened to be in Boston for his company last Saturday when Miss Garnet was with us, and Henry brought him to the house. I wasn't half glad, though I like him, quite. He's a big, handsome, swinging fellow that everybody invites to everything. He makes good speeches before the clubs and flaunts his Southern politics just enough to please our Yankee fondness for being politely *sassed*."

"Why, dear, isn't that a rather good trait in us? It's zest for the overlooked fact, isn't it?"

"O!—it has its uses. It certainly furnishes a larger feeling of superiority to both sides at once than anything else I know of."

"You say Henry brought him to the house while Miss Garnet was with you——"

"Yes; and, my dear, I wish you might have seen those two Southerners meet! They didn't leave us any feeling of superiority then; at least *he* didn't. Except that they're both so Southern, they're not alike. She moved right in among us without the smallest misstep. He made a dozen delicious blunders. It was lovely to see how sweetly she and Henry helped him up and brushed him off, and the boyish manfulness with which he always took it. I couldn't tell, sometimes, which of the three to like best."

Those behind called them to hearken to the notes of a woodlark, and when Mrs. Fair asked her son the hour it was time to get to the station. Barbara would not say just when she could be in Boston again; but the classmate she liked best was a Boston girl, and by the time this college life had lasted six weeks her visits to the city had been three, as aforesaid. In every instance, with an unobtrusiveness all his own, Henry Fair had made her pleasure his business. On the second visit she had expected to meet Mr. March again—a matter wholly of his contriving—but had only got his telegram from New York at the last moment of her stay, stating that he was unavoidably detained by business, and leaving space for six words unused. The main purpose of her third visit had been to attend with Mrs. Fair a reception given by that lady's club. It had ended with dancing; but Mr. Fair had not danced to suit her and Mr. March had not danced at all, but had allowed himself to betray dejection, and had torn her dress. Back at college she had told the favorite classmate how she had chided Mr. March for certain trivial oversights and feared she had been severe; and when the classmate insisted she had not been nearly severe enough she said good-night and went to her room to mend the torn dress; and as she sewed she gnawed her lip, wished she had never left Suez, and salted her needle with slow tears.

Thus ended the sixth week—stop! I was about to forget the thing for which I began the chapter—and, anyhow, this was not Saturday, it was Friday! While Barbara was so employed, John March, writing to Henry Fair from somewhere among the Rhode Island cotton-spinners, said:

"To-night I go to New York, where I have an important appointment to-morrow noon, but I can leave there Monday morning at five and be in Springfield at ten-twenty-five. If you will get there half an hour later by the train that leaves Boston at seven, I will telegraph the Springfield men to meet us in the bank at eleven. They assure me that if you confirm my answers to their questions they will do all I've asked. Please telegraph your reply, if favorable, to my New York address."

About three o'clock of Saturday March was relieved of much anxiety by receipt of Fair's telegram. It was a long time before Monday morning, but in a sudden elation he strapped his valise and said to the porter— "Grand Central Depot."

"Back to Boston again?"

"Not much! But I'm not going to get up at four o'clock Monday morning either."

In Boston that evening a servant of the Fairs told one of their familiar friends who happened to drop in, that Mr. Fair, senior, was in, but that Mr. Henry had gone to spend Sunday at some Connecticut River town, he was not sure which, but—near Springfield.

## LXX.

### ACROSS THE MEADOWS

NEXT morning, John March, for the first time in his life, saw and heard the bobolink.

"Ah! you turncoat scoundrel!" he laughed in a sort of fond dejection, "you've come North to be a lover too, have you? You were songless enough down South!"

But the quivering gallant went singing across the fields, too drunk with the joy of loving to notice accusers.

On the previous evening March had come up by rail some fifteen miles beyond the brisk inland city just mentioned and stopped at a certain "Mount"—no matter what—known to him only through casual allusions in one or two letters of—a friend. Here he had crossed a hand-ferry, climbed a noted hill, put up at its solitary mountain house—being tired of walls and pavements, as he had more than once needlessly explained—and at his chamber window sat looking down, until most of them had vanished, upon a cluster of soft lights on the other side of the valley, shining among the trees of the embowered town where one who now was never absent from his thoughts was at school.

The knowledge that he loved her was not of yesterday only. He could count its age in weeks and a fraction, beginning with the evening when "those two Southerners" had met in Mrs. Fair's drawing-room. Since then the dear trouble of it had ever been with him, deep, silent, dark—like this night on the mountain—shot with meteors of brief exultation, and starlighted with recollections of her every motion, glance, and word.

At sunrise, looking again, he saw the town's five or six spires, and heard one tell the hour and the college bell confirm it. Care was on his brow, but you could see it was a care that came of new freedom. He was again a lover, still tremorous with the wonder of unsought deliverance from his dungeon of not-loving. And now the stern yet inspiring necessity was not to let his delivering angel find it out; to be a lover, but not a suitor. Hence his presence up here instead of down in the town beyond the meadows and across the river. He would make it very plain to her and her friends that he had not come, ahead of his business appointment, to thrust himself upon her, but to get a breath of heaven's own air—being very tired of walls and pavements—and to—to discover the bobolink!

Of course, being so near, he should call. He must anyhow go to church, and if only he could keep himself from starting too early, there was no reason why he should not combine the two duties and make them one pleasure. Should he ride or drive? He ordered the concern's best saddle-horse, walked mournfully half round him, and said, "I reckon—I reckon I'll drive. Sorry to trouble you, but——"

"Put him in the shafts, Dave," said the stable-keeper, and then to the guest, "No trouble, sir; if a man doesn't feel safe in a saddle he'd better not monkey with it."

"I dare say," sedately responded John. "I suppose a man oughtn't to try to learn to ride without somebody to go along with him."

The boy had just finished harnessing the animal, when March started with a new thought.  He steadied himself, turned away, drew something from his pocket, consulted and returned it—it was neither a watch nor a weapon—and rejoining the stable-keeper said, with a sweet smile and a red face:

"See here, it's only three miles over there.  If you'll let me change my mind——"

"You'll walk it—O all right!  If you change your mind again you can let us know on your return."

John took a way that went by a bridge.  It was longer than the other, by way of a ferry, but time, for the moment, was a burden and either way was beautiful.  The Sabbath was all smiles.  On the Hampshire hills and along the far meanderings of the Connecticut a hundred tints of perfect springtide beguiled the heart to forget that winter had ever been.  Above a balmy warmth of sunshine and breeze in which the mellowed call of church-bells floated through the wide valley from one to another of half a dozen towns and villages, silvery clouds rolled and unrolled as if in stately play, swung, careened, and fell melting through the marvellous blue, or soared and sunk and soared again.  Keeping his eyes much on such a heaven, our inexperienced walker thought little of close-fitting boots until he had to sit down, screened from the public road by a hillock, and, with a smile of amusement but hardly of complacency, smooth a cruel wrinkle from one of his very striped socks.  Just then a buckboard rumbled by, filled with pretty girls, from the college, he guessed, driving over to that other college town, seven miles across the valley, where a noted Boston clergyman was to preach to-day; but the foot-passenger only made himself a bit smaller and chuckled at the lucky privacy of his position. As they got by he stole a peep at their well-dressed young backs, and the best dressed and shapeliest was Barbara Garnet's. The driver was Henry Fair. It was then that the bobolink, for the first time in his life, saw and heard John March.

## LXXI.

### IN THE WOODS

THE sun mounted on to noon and nature fell into a reverent stillness; but in certain leafy aisles under the wooded bluffs and along that narrow stream where Mrs. Fair some three weeks earlier had walked with the widow, the Sabbath afternoon was scarcely half spent before the air began to be crossed and cleft with the vesper hymns and serenades of plumed worshippers and lovers.

It was a place to quicken the heart and tongue of any wooer. The breezes moved pensively and without a sound. On the middle surface of the water the sunshine lay in wide bands, liquid-bordered under overhanging boughs by glimmering shadows that wove lace in their sleep. Between the stream and the steep ground ran an abandoned road fringed with ferns, its

brown pine-fallings flecked with a sunlight that fell
through the twined arms and myriad green fingers of
all-namable sorts of great and lesser trees.  You would
have said the forest's every knight and lady, dwarf,
page, and elf—for in this magical seclusion all the
world's times were tangled into one—had come to the
noiseless dance of some fairy's bridal; chestnut and
hemlock, hazel and witch-hazel, walnut and willow,
birches white and yellow, poplar and ash in feathery
bloom, the lusty oaks in the scarred harness of their
winter wars under new tabards of pink and silver-
green, and the slim service-bush, white with blooms and
writhing in maiden shame of her too transparent gown.
In each tangled ravine Flora's little pious mortals of
the May—anemone, yellow violet, blood-root, mustard,
liverwort, and their yet humbler neighbors and kin—
heard mass, or held meeting—whichever it was—and
slept for blissful lack of brain while Jack-in-the-pulpit
preached to them, under Solomon's seal, and oriole,
tanager, warbler, thrush, up in the choir-loft, made love
between the hymns, ate tidbits, and dropped crumbs
upon wake-robin, baby-toes, and the nodding columbine.

Was it so?  Or was it but fantasy in the mind of
Henry Fair alone, reflected from the mood of the girl
at whose side he walked here, and whose "Herrick" he
vainly tried to beguile from her in hope that so she might
better heed his words?  It may be.  The joy of spring
was in her feet, the colors of the trees were answered
in her robes.  Moreover, the flush of the orchards and
breath of the meadows through which they had gone
and come again were on her cheek and in her parted

lips, the red-brown depths of the stream were in her hair and lashes, and above them a cunningly disordered thing of fine straw and loose ribbons matched the head and face it shaded, as though all were parts together of some flower unspoiled by the garden's captivity and escaped again into the woods.

To Barbara's ear Fair's speech had always been melodious and low. Its well-tempered pitch had her approval especially here, where not only was there the wild life of grove and thicket to look and listen for, but a subdued ripple of other girls' voices and the stir of other draperies came more than once along the path and through the bushes. But there are degrees and degrees, and in this walk his tones had gradually sunk to such pure wooing that "Herrick" was no protection and she could reply only with irrelevant pleasantries.

At length he halted, and with a lover's distress showing beneath his smile, asked :

"Why cannot you be serious with me—Barbara ? "

In make-believe aimlessness she swept the wood with a reconnoitring glance, and then with eyes of maidenly desperation fixed on him, said, tremblingly :

"Because, Mr. Fair, I know what you want to say, and I don't want you to say it."

He turned their slow step toward a low rock in an open space near the water's edge, where no one could come near them unseen. "Would you let me say it if we were down in Dixie? " he asked. "Is it because you are so far from home ? "

"No, Mr. Fair, I told you I really have no home. I'm sorry I did; I'm afraid it's led you to this, when everything I said—about taking myself into my own care and all—was said to keep you from it."

The lover shook his head. " You cannot. You must not. To be that kind is to be unkind. Sit here. You do not know exactly what I have to say; sit here, will you not? and while I stand beside you let me do both of us the simple honor to seal with right words what I have so long said in behavior."

Barbara hesitated. " O Mr. Fair, what need is there? Your behavior's always borne the seal of its own perfection. How could I answer you? If you only wanted any other answer but just the one you want, I could give it—the kindest answer in the world, the most unbounded praise—O I could give it with my whole heart and soul! Why, Mr. Fair "—as she sadly smiled she let him gaze into the furthest depth of her eyes—"as far as I can see, you seem to me to be ab-so-lute-ly fault-less."

The young man caught his breath as if for some word of fond passion, but the unfaltering eyes prevented him. As she began again to speak, however, they fell.

" And that's not because I can't see men's faults. I see them so plainly, and show so plainly I see them, that sometimes I wonder—" She left the wonder implied while she pinched lichens from the stone. He began in a tender monotone to say :

"All the more let me speak. I cannot see you put away unconsidered——"

She lifted her eyes again. " O ! I know what I'm putting away from me; a life! a life wider, richer than I ever hoped to live. Mr. Fair, it's as if a beautiful, great, strong ship were waiting to carry me across a summer sea, and I couldn't go, just for want of the right passport—the right heart! If I had that it might be ever so different. I have no other ship ever to come in. I say all this only to save you from speaking. The only thing lacking is lacking in me." She smiled a compassionate despair. "It's not you nor your conditions—you know it's none of those dear ones who love you so at home—it's only I that can't qualify."

They looked at each other in reverent silence. Fair turned, plucked a flower, and as if to it, said, "I know the passion of love is a true and sacred thing. But love should never be all, or chiefly, a passion. The love of a mother for her child, of brother and sister for each other, however passionate, springs first from relationship and rises into passion as a plant springs from its root into bloom. Why should not all love do so? Why should only this, the most perilous kind, be made an exception?"

"Because," softly interrupted Barbara, glad of a moment's refuge in abstractions, "it belongs to the only relationship that comes by choice!"

"Are passions ever the best choosers?" asked the gentle suitor. "Has history told us so, or science, or scripture, or anybody but lovers and romancers—and—Americans? Life—living and loving—is the greatest of the arts, and the passions should be our tools, not our guides."

"I believe life *is* an art to you, Mr. Fair; but to me it's a dreadful battle." The speaker sank upon the stone, half rose again, and then sat still.

"It hasn't scarred you badly," responded the lover. Then gravely: "Do you not think we may find it worth the fight if we make passions our chariot horses and never our charioteers?"

No answer came, though he waited. He picked another flower and asked : "If you had a brother, have you the faintest doubt that you would love him?"

"No," said Barbara, "I couldn't help but love him." She thrust away the recollection of a certain railway journey talk, and then thought of her father.

Fair dropped his voice. "If I did not know that I should not be here to-day. Barbara, kinship is the only true root of all abiding love. We cannot feel sure even of God's love until we call ourselves his children. Neither church, state, nor society requires lovers to swear that they love passionately, but that they will love persistently by virtue of a kinship made permanent in law."

Law! At that word Barbara inwardly winced, but Fair pressed on.

"These marriages on the American plan, of which we are so vain, are they the only happy ones, and are they all happy? When they are, is it because love began as a passion, or has it not been because the choice was fortunate, and love, whether from a large or small beginning, has grown, like that of Isaac and Rebecca, out of a union made stronger than the ties of blood, by troth and oath? Barbara, do you not know in your heart of hearts that if you were the wife of a husband, wisely but dispassionately chosen, you would love him with a wife's full love as long as he loved you? You do. You would."

Barbara was slow to reply, but presently she began,
"Unless I could commit my fate to one who already
loved me consumingly——" She gave a start of pro-
testation as he exclaimed:

"I love you consumingly! O Barbara, Barbara
Garnet, let that serve for us both! Words could not
tell my joy, if I could find in you this day a like passion for me. But the seed and soil of it are here to my
sight in what I find you to be, and all I ask is that you
will let reason fix the only relationship that can truly feed
the flame which I know—I *know*—my love will kindle."

"O Mr. Fair, I begged you not to ask!"

"Do not answer! Not now; to-morrow morning.
If you can't answer then——"

"I can answer now, Mr. Fair. Why should I keep
you in suspense?"

Such agitation came into the young man's face as
Barbara had never thought to see. His low voice
quivered. "No! No! I beseech you not to answer yet!
Wait! Wait and weigh! O Barbara! weigh well and
I will wait well! Wait! O wait until you have weighed
all things well—my fortune, love, life, and the love of
all who love me—O weigh them all well, beloved!
beloved one!"

Without warning, a grosbeak—the one whose breast
is stained with the blood of the rose—began his soft,
sweet song so close overhead that Barbara started up,
and he flew. She waited to catch the strain again, and
as it drifted back her glance met her lover's. She
smiled tenderly, but was grave the next moment and
said, "Let us go back."

Nevertheless they went very slowly, culling and exchanging wild flowers as they went. On her doorstep she said, "Now, in the morning——"

"How soon may I come?" he asked.

"Immediately after chapel."

---

## LXXII.

### MY GOOD GRACIOUS, MISS BARB

"Good-by," said Fair, with an ardent last look.

"Good-by," softly echoed Barbara, with eyelids down, and passed in.

According to a habit contracted since coming to college she took a brief glimpse of the hat-rack to see if it held any other than girls' hats. Not that she expected any visitor of the sort that can't wear that kind, but—you know how it is—the unexpected does sometimes call. Besides, Mr. Fair had told her whom he was to meet in Springfield next day. But the hat-rack said no. Nevertheless she glanced also into the tiny parlor. The widow sat there alone, reading the *Congregationalist*. She looked up with sweet surprise, and Barbara, not giving her time to speak, said:

"The woods are so per-fect-ly fas-ci-nat-ing I'm neg-lect-ing my cor-re-spond-ence."

She dangled her hat at her knee and slowly mounted to her room, humming a dance, but longing, as some sick wild thing, for a seclusion she had no hope to find.

The two college mates who had driven with her in the morning were lolling on her bed. They recognized the earliness of her return by a mischievous sparkle of eyes which only gathered emphasis from the absence of any open comment.

"Barbara," said one, as she doubled a pillow under her neck and took on the Southern drawl, " par-don my in-quis-i-tive-ness, but if it isn't an im-per-ti-nent ques-tion—or even if it is—how man-y but-ter-cups did you pro-cure, and alas! where are they now?"

"Heaow?" softly asked Barbara. But the other school-fellow cried :

"Barbara, dear, don't you notice that girl, she's bad. I'll give you a nice, easy question. I ask merely for information. Of course you're not bound to answer unless you choose——"

"I wan't to know!" murmured Miss Garnet.

"Of course you do; you don't want to criminate yourself when you haven't got to.

"And now, Miss Garnet—if that is still your name——"

"Don't call me Miss Garnet," said Barbara, with her chin in her hands, " call me honey."

"Honey," came the response, "where's our 'Herrick'?"

Barbara sprang to her feet with a gasp and vacancy of eye that filled the room with the laughter of her companions, and the next moment was speeding down the stairs and across the doorstep, crowding her hat on with one hand and stabbing it with the other as she went. Down from the streets into the wood she has-tened, gained the path, ran up it, walked by three or four pretty loiterers, ran again, and on the stone by the water-side found the volume as she had left it.

Then she lingered. As she leaned against the rock and gazed into the shaded depths of the mill-stream her problem came again, and the beautiful solitude whispered a welcome to her to revolve and weigh and solve it here. But when she essayed to do so it would no more be revolved or weighed by her alone than this huge bowlder at her side. Her baffled mind drifted into fantasy, and the hoary question, Whether it is wiser for a maiden to love first, hoping to be chosen accordingly, or to be chosen first and hope to love accordingly, became itself an age-worn relic from woman's earlier and harder lot, left by its glaciers as they had melted in the warmth of more modern suns.

She murmured a word of impatience at such dreaming and looked around to see if she was overheard; but the only near presence was two girls sitting behind and high above her, one writing, the other reading, under the pines. They seemed not to have heard, but she sauntered beyond their sight up the path, wondering if they were the kind in whom to love was the necessity it was in her, and, if so, what they would do in her case. What they would advise *her* to do depended mainly, she fancied, on whether they were in their teens or their twenties. As for married women, she shrank from the very thought of their counsel, whichever way it might tend, and mused on Fannie Ravenel, who, with eyes wide open, had chosen rather to be made unhappy by the one her love had lighted on than to take any other chance for happiness. She stopped her listless walk and found her wrists crossed and her hands knit, remembering one whom Fannie could have chosen and would not.

Burning with resentment against herself for the thought, she turned aside and sat down on the river's brink in a shade of hemlocks. "Come," her actions seemed to say, "I will think of Henry Fair; gentle, noble Henry Fair, and what he is and will and might be; of how I love his mother and all his kindred; of how tenderly I admire him; and of his trembling words, 'I love you consumingly!'"

Her heart quickened gratefully, as though he spoke again; but as she gazed down at the bubbles that floated by from a dipping bough she presently fell to musing anew on Fannie, without that inward shudder which the recollection of Fannie's course and fate commonly brought. "At least," she thought to herself, "it's heroic!" Yet before she could find a moment's comfort in the reflection it was gone, and she started up and moved on again, knowing that, whatever it may be for man, for true womanhood the better heroism is not to give a passionate love its unwise way at heroic cost, but dispassionately to master love in all its greatness and help it grow to passion in wise ways.

"If I take this step," she began to say to herself audibly as she followed the old road out into a neglected meadow, "I satisfy my father; I delight my friends; I rid myself at once and forever of this dreadful dependence on him." She bit her lip and shut her eyes against these politic considerations. "He tells me to weigh the matter well. How shall I, when there's nothing to weigh against it? Fannie could choose between the one who loved her and the one she loved. I have no choice; this is the most—most likely it is all—that will ever be offered me. There's just the one simple sane question before me—Shill I or shall I?" She smiled. "We make too much of it all!" she thought on. "A man's life depends upon the man he is, not on the girl he gets; why shouldn't it be so with us?" She smiled still more, and, glancing round the open view, murmured, "Silly little country girls! We begin life as a poem, we can't find our rhyme, we tell our mothers—if we have any—they say yes, it was the same with our aunts; so we decide with them that good prose will do very well; they kiss us—that means they won't tell—and—O Heaven! is that our best?" She dropped upon a bank and wept till she shook.

But that would never do! She dried her tears and lay toying with her book and sadly putting into thought a thing she had never more than felt before: that whatever she might wisely or unwisely do with it, she held in her nature a sacred gift of passion; that life, her life, could never bloom in full joy and glory shut out from wifehood and motherhood, and that the idlest self-deceit she could attempt would be to say she need-not marry. Suddenly she started and then lay stiller than before. She had found the long-sought explanation of her mother's tardy marriage—neither a controlling nor a controlled passion, but the reasoning despair of famishing affections. Barbara let her face sink into the grass

and wept again for the dear lost one with a new reverence and compassion. She was pressing her brow hard
against the earth when there came from the far end of
the meadow two clear, glad notes of nature's voice, that
entered her soul like a call from the pastures of Rosemont, a missing rhyme sent to make good the failing
poetry of love's declining day. She sprang to the top
of the rise with her open hand to her hat-brim, the dew
still in her lashes, her lips parted fondly, and her ear
waiting to hear again—the whistle of the quail. Many
a day in those sunny springtimes when she still ran wild
with Johanna had she held taunting parley with those
two crystal love-notes, and now she straightened to her
best height, pursed her lips, whistled back the brave
octave, and listened again. A distant cowbell tinkled
from some willows in another meadow across the river,
a breeze moved audibly by, and then the answer came.
"Bob—Bob White?" it inquired from the top of a
pine-covered bluff, round which the stream swept down
in bowlder-strewn rapids to its smoother course between
the two meadows. It may be the name was not just
that, but it was certainly two monosyllables! The
listener stepped quickly to the nearest bush, answered
again, and began to move warily from cover to cover in
the direction of the call. Once she delayed her response.
A man and wife with three or four children, loitering
down the river bank, passed so close to her as to be
startled when at last they saw her, although she was
merely sitting at the roots of a great tree deeply absorbed in a book. A few steps farther put a slight ridge
and a clump of bushes between the couple and the stu-

dent; and the man, glancing back, had just noticed it, when—

"Hear that quail!" he exclaimed, and stopped his wife with a touch.

"What of it?" asked the helpmate, who was stoop-shouldered.

"Why, we must have passed in a few feet of it! It's right there where we saw that girl!"

The woman's voice took on an added dreariness as she replied: "We might 'a' seen it if you hadn't been so taken up with the girl. James, come back! you know 'tain't that bird you're peekin' after. O land o' love! men *air* sich fools!"

The man found neither girl nor quail; the grassy seat beneath the tree was empty. But just as he was rejoining his partner—"Hark!" he said; "there he is again, farther up the river. Now if we listen like's not we'll hear another fellow answer him. Many's the time I've lain in the grass and called one of them right up. There! that was the answering challenge, away off yonder between here and that hill with the pines on it. There's going to be a beautiful little fight when those two birds meet, and that college girl's going to see it. I wish I— There's the other one again; they get closer each time! Didn't you hear it?"

The wife replied, mainly to herself, that she did not; that if he had her backache he wouldn't hear a brass band, and that her next walk would be by herself.

The partner did not venture to look back after that, but as they sauntered on, rarely speaking except when the mother rebuked the children, he listened eagerly, and after a silence of unaccountable length, finally heard the two calls once more, up near the rapids and very close to each other. He dared not prick his ears, but while he agreed with his wife that if they were ever going home at all it was time they were about it, he could not but think the outcome of a man's life depends largely on the sort of girl he gets.

At the upper end of the meadow, meantime, Barbara Garnet, with "Herrick" in one hand and her hat pressed against the back of her skirts in the other, was bending and peering round the trunk of an elm draped to the ground in flounces of its own green. The last response to her whistle had seemed to come from a spot so close in front of her that she feared to risk another step, and yet, peep and pry as she might, she could neither spy out nor nearer decoy the cunning challenger. In a sense of delinquency she noted the sky showing yellow and red through the hill-top pines, and seeing she must make short end of her play, prepared to rush out upon the rogue and have an old-time laugh at his pretty panic. So!—one for the money, two for the show, three to make ready, and four for to—"Ha, ha, ha!"—

"Good gracious alive!" exclaimed the quail, leaping from his back to his feet, and standing a fathom tall before the gasping, half-sinking girl. "Good gra'— why—why, my good gracious, Miss Barb! why—why, my good gracious!" insisted John March.

## LXXIII.

### IMMEDIATELY AFTER CHAPEL

THERE was a great deal of pleasure in the house of the three sisters that evening. The widow asked March to stay to tea, and when he opened his mouth to decline, the wrong word fell out and he accepted. He confided to Barbara his fear that in so doing he had blundered, but she softly scouted the idea, and with a delicious reproachfulness in her murmur, " wondered if he supposed they "—etc.

At table he sat next to her, in the seat the sisters had intended for Henry Fair. Neither Miss Garnet nor Mr. March gave the other's proximity more than its due recognition; they talked with almost everyone about almost everything, and as far as they knew said and did nothing to betray the fact that they were as happy as Psyche in a swing with Cupid to push and run under.

Nobody went to evening service. They sang hymns at the piano, selecting oftenest those which made best display of Miss Garnet's and Mr. March's voices. Hers was only mezzo-soprano and not brilliant, but Mr. March and a very short college girl, conversing for a moment aside, agreed that it was " singularly winsome." Another college girl, very tall, whispered Barbara that his was a " superb barrytone! " The young man entered deeper and deeper every moment into the esteem of the househould, and they into his. The very best of

the evening came last, when, at the widow's request, the
two Southerners sang, without the instrument, a hymn
or two of the Dixie mountaineers : " To play on the
golden harp " and " Where there's no more stormy
clouds arising."    Being further urged for a negro hymn,
John began " Bow low a little bit longer," which Barbara,
with a thrill of recollection and an involuntary gesture
of pain, said she couldn't sing, and they gave another
instead, one of the best, and presently had the whole
company joining in the clarion refrain of " O Canaan !
bright Canaan ! "    Barbara heard her college mates
still singing it in their rooms on either side of her after
she had said her prayers with her cheek on John
March's photograph.

To her painful surprise when she awoke next day she
found herself in a downcast mood.    She could not even
account for the blissful frame in which she had gone to
bed.    She had not forgotten one word or tone of all
John March had said to her while carried away from
his fine resolution by the wave of ecstasy which followed
their unexpected meeting, but the sunset light, their
thrilling significances, were totally gone from them.
Across each utterance some qualifying word or clause,
quite overlooked till now, cast its morning shadow.
Not so much as one fond ejaculation of his impulsive
lips last evening but she could explain away this
morning, and she felt a dull, half-guilty distress in the
fear that her blissful silences had embarrassed him into
letting several things imply more than he intended.
Before she was quite dressed one of her fellow-students
came in with an anguished face to show what a

fatal error she had made in the purchase of some ribbons.

Barbara held them first in one light and then in another, and at length shook her head over them in piteous despair and asked:

"How *could* you so utterly mistake both color and quality?"

"Why, my dear, I bought them by lamplight! and, besides, it wås an auction and I was excited."

"Yes," said Barbara, and took a long breath. "I know how that is."

Down in town two commercial travelers, one of whom we have met before, took an after-breakfast saunter.

"She was coming," said the one we remember, "to New England. I didn't know where or for what, and I don't know yet; but when my house said, 'Old boy, we'd like to promote you, just say what you want!' says I, 'Let the salary stand as it is, only change my district; gimme New England!'"

"That's the college," he continued, as they came up into Elm Street. "Those are the students, just coming out of the chapel: 'sweet girl graduates,' as Shakespeare calls them."

He clutched his companion's arm. Their eyes rested on one of the dispersing throng, who came last and alone, with a slow step and manifestly under some burdensome preoccupation, through the high iron gateway of the campus. She passed them with drooping eyelashes and walked in the same tardy pace before them.

Presently she turned from the sidewalk, crossed a small grassplot, and stood on the doorstep with her hand on the latch while they went by.

"Her?" said the one who thought he had quoted Shakespeare, "of course it's her; who else could it be? Ah, hmm! 'so near and yet so far!' Tom, I believe in heaven when I look at that girl—heaven and holiness! I read Taylor's 'Holy Living' when a boy!"

Presently they returned and passed again. She was still standing at the door. A few steps away the speaker looked over his shoulder and moaned:

"Not a glimpse of me does she get! There, she's gone in; but sure's you live she didn't want to!" They walked on. In front of their hotel he clutched his companion again. A young man of commanding figure stood near, deeply immersed in a telegram. The drummer whispered an oath of surprise.

"That's him now! the young millionaire she reject-ed on the trip we all made together! What's he here for?—George! he looks as worried as her!"

"How do you know she rejected him?"

"How do— Now, look here! If I didn't know it do you s'pose I'd say so? Well, then! Come, I'll introduce you to him— O he's all right! he's just as white and modest as either of us; come on!" March proved himself both modest and white, and as he walked away,

"This's a stra-a-ange world!" moralized the commer-cial man. "'Tain't him I'm thinking of, it's her! She's in trouble, Tom; in trouble. And who knows but what, for some mysterious reason, *I* may be the

only one on earth who can—O Lord!—Look here; I'm
not goin' to do any business to-day; I'm not goin' to be
fit; you needn't be surprised if you hear to-night that
I've gone off on a drunk."

Meantime Barbara had lifted the latch and gone in.
No hat was on the rack, but when she turned into the
parlor a sickness came to her heart as she smiled and
said good-morning to Henry Fair. He, too, smiled, but
she fancied he was pale.

They mentioned the weather, which was quite pleasant enough. Fair said the factories that used water-
power would be glad of rain, and Barbara seemed interested, but when he paused she asked, in the measured
tone he liked so well:

"Who do you think took us all by surprise and spent
last evening with us?"

Fair's reply came tardily and was disguised as a
playful guess. "Mister—"

"Yes—"

He sobered. "March!" he softly exclaimed, and let
his gaze rest long on the floor. "I thought—really I
thought Mr. March was in New York."

"So did we all," was the response, and both laughed,
without knowing just why.

"He ought to have had a delightful time," said Fair.

Barbara meditated pleasedly. "Mr. March always
lets one know what kind of time he's having, and I
never saw him more per-fect-ly sat-is-fied," she said, and
allowed her silence to continue so long and with such
manifest significance that at length the suitor's low
voice asked:

"Am I to understand that that visit alters my case?"

"No," responded Barbara, but without even a look of surprise. "I'm afraid, Mr. Fair, that you'll think me a rather daring girl, but I want you to be assured that I know of no one whose visit can alter—that." She lifted her eyes bravely to his, but they filled. "As for Mr. March," she continued, and the same amusement gleamed in them which so often attended her mention of him, "there's always been a perfect understanding between us. We're the very best of friends, but no one knows better than he does that we can never be more, though I don't see why we need ever be less."

"I should call that hard terms, for myself," said Fair; "I hope—" And there he stopped.

"Mr. Fair," the girl began, was still, and then—"O Mr. Fair, I know what to say, but I don't know how to say it! I admit everything. All the good reasons are on your side. And yet if I am to answer you now—" She ceased. Her voice had not faltered, but her head drooped and he saw one tear follow quickly after another and fall upon her hands.

"Why, you need not answer now," he tenderly said. "I told you I would wait."

"O Mr. Fair, no, no! You have every right to be answered now, and I have no right to delay beyond your wish. Only, I believe also that, matters standing as they do, you have a perfect right to wait for a later answer from me if you choose. I can only beg you will not. O you who are so rational and brave and strong with yourself, you who know so well that a man's whole fate cannot be wrapped up in one girl unless he weakly chooses it so, take your answer now! I don't believe I can ever look upon you—your offer—differently. Mr. Fair, there's one thing it lacks which I think even you overlook."

"What is that?"

"It—I—I don't know any one word to describe it, unless it is turn-out-well-a-bil-i-ty."

Fair started with astonishment, and the tears leaped again to her eyes as she laughed, and with new distress said: "It isn't—it—O Mr. Fair, don't you know what I mean? It doesn't make good poetry! As you would say, it's not good art. You may think me 'fresh,' as the girls say, and fantastical, but I can't help believing that in a matter like this there's something wrong—some essential wanting—in whatever's not good—good——"

"Romance?" asked Fair; "do you think the fact that a thing is good romance——"

"No! O no, no, no! I don't say being good romance is enough to commend it; but I do think not being good romance is enough to condemn it! Is that so very foolish?"

The lover answered wistfully. "No. No." Then very softly: "Barbara"—he waited till she looked up—"if this thing should ever seem to you to have become good poetry, might not your answer be different?"

Barbara hesitated. "I—you—O—I only know how it seems now!"

"Never mind," said Fair, very gently. They rose and he took her hand, speaking again in the same tone.

" You really believe I have the right to wait for a later answer?"

Her head drooped. "The right?" she murmured, " yes—the right——"

"So also do I. I shall wait. Good-by."

She raised her glance, her voice failed to a whisper. " Good-by."

Gaze to gaze, one stood, and the other, with reluctant step, backed away; and at the last moment, with his foot leaving the threshold, lover and maiden said again, still gaze to gaze:

" Good-by."

" Good-by."

---

## LXXIV.

### COMPLETE COLLAPSE OF A PERFECT UNDERSTANDING

The door closed and Barbara noiselessly mounted the stairs. At its top an elm-shaded window allowed a view of some fifty yards or more down the street, and as she reached it now the pleasantness of the outer day furnished impulse enough, if there had been no other, for her to glance out. She stopped sharply, with her eyes fixed where they had fallen. For there stood John March and Henry Fair in the first bright elation of their encounter busily exchanging their manly acknowledgments and explanations. Lost to herself she stayed, an arm bent high and a knuckle at her parted teeth, comparing the two men and noting the matchless bearing of her Southerner. In it she read again for the hundredth time all the energy and intrepidity which in her knowledge it stood for; his boyish openness and simplicity, his tender belief in his mother, his high-hearted devotion to the fulfilment of his father's aspirations, and the impetuous force and native skill with which at mortal risks and in so short a time he had ranked himself among the masters of public fortune. She recalled, as she was prone to do, what Charlie Champion had once meditatively said to her on seeing him approach: "Here comes the only man in Dixie Jeff-Jack Ravenel's afraid of."

After an instant the manner of the two young men became more serious, and March showed a yellow paper —"a telegram," thought their on-looker. "He's coming here, no doubt; possibly to tell me its news; more likely just to say good-by again; but certainly with nothing—nothing—O nothing! to ask." For a moment her hand pressed hard against her lips, and then her maiden self-regard quietly but strenuously definitely rebelled.

The telegram seemed to bring its readers grave disappointment. March made indignant gestures in obvious allusion to distant absentees. Now they began to move apart; Fair stepped farther away, March drew nearer the house, still making gestures as if he might be saying —Barbara resentfully guessed—

"You might walk slow; I shan't stop more than a minute!"

She left the window with silent speed, saying, in her heart, " You needn't! You shan't!"

As March with clouded brow was lifting his hand toward a tortuous brass knocker the door opened and Barbara, carrying a book and pencil in one hand, while the other held down her hat-brim, tripped across the doorstep.

The cloud vanished. " Miss Barb—good-morning!"

" O!—Mr.—March." Her manner so lacked both surprise and pleasure that he colored. He had counted on a sweet Southern handshake, but she kept hold of the hat-brim, let her dry smile of inquiry fade into a formal deference, and took comfort in his disconcertion.

" I was just coming," he said, " I—thought you'd let me come back just to say good-by—but I see you're on your way to a recitation—I—"

Her smile was cruel. " Why, my recitations are not so serious as that," she drawled. " Just to say good-by ought not to con-sti-tute any se-ri-ous de-ten-tion."

John's heart sank like a stone. Scarcely could he believe his senses. Yet this was she ; that new queen of his ambitions whose heavenly friendship had lifted first love—boy love—from its grave and clad it in the shining white of humility and abnegation to worship her sweet dignity, purity, and tenderness, asking for nothing, not even for hope, in return. This was she who at every new encounter had opened to him a higher revelation of woman's worth and loveliness than the world had ever shown him ; she to whom he had been writing letters half last night and all this morning, tearing each to bits before he had finished it be-

cause he could see no life ahead which an unselfish love
could ask her to live, and as he rent the result of each
fresh effort hearing the voice of his father saying to him
as in childhood days, " I'd be proud faw you to have
the kitt'n, son, but, you know, she wouldn't suit yo'
dear motheh's high-strung natu'e. You couldn't ever
be happy with anything that was a constant tawment
to her, could you ? "

These thoughts filled but a moment, and before the
lovely presence confronting him could fully note the
depth of his quick distress a wave of self-condemnation
brought what seemed to him the answer of the riddle :
that this was *rightly* she, the same angelic incarnation
of wisdom and rectitude, as of gentleness and beauty, to
whom in yesterday's sunset hour of surprise and ecstatic
yearning he had implied things so contrary to their " perfect understanding," and who now, not for herself self-
ishly, but in the name and defence of all blameless
womanhood, was punishing him for his wild presump-
tion.    O but if she would only accuse him—here—this
instant, so that contrition might try its value !    But
under the shade of her hat her eyes merely waited with
a beautiful sort of patient urgency for his parting word.
The moment's silence seemed an hour, but no word did
he find.    One after another almost came, but failed,
and at last, just as he took in his breath to say he knew
not what—anything so it were something—he saw her
smile melt with sudden kindness, while her lips parted
for speech, and to his immeasurable confusion and terror
heard himself ask her with cheerful cordiality, " Won't
you walk in ? "

It would have been hard to tell which of the two turned the redder.

"Why, Mr. March, you in-ti-ma-ted that you had no ti-i-ime!"

They stood still. "Time and bad news are about the only things I have got, Miss Barb. Wrapped up in your father's interests as you are, I reckon I ought to show you this." He handed her the telegram doubled small. "Let me hold your book."

Barbara unfolded and read the despatch. It was from Springfield, repeated at New York, and notified Mr. John March that owing to a failure of Gamble to come to terms with certain much larger railroad owners for the reception of his road into their "system," intelligence of which had just reached them, it would be "useless for him," March, "to come up," as there was "nothing more to say or hear." She read it twice. Her notions of its consequences were dim, but she saw it was a door politely closed in his face ; and yet she lingered over it. There was a bliss in these business confidences, which each one thought was her or his own exclusive and unsuspected theft, and which was all the sweeter for the confidences' practical worthlessness. As she looked up she uttered a troubled "O ! " to find him smiling unconsciously into her book where she had written, "I stole this book from Barbara Garnet." It seemed as if fate were always showing her very worst sides to him at the very worst times ! She took the volume with hurried thanks and returned the telegram.

"It would have been better on every account if you hadn't come up at all, wouldn't it ? " she asked, bent on self-cruelty; but he accepted the cruelty as meant for him.

"Yes," he meekly replied. "I—I reckon it would." Then more bravely: "I've got to give up here and try the West. Your father's advised it strongly these last three weeks."

"Has he?" she, pensively asked. Here was a new vexation. Obviously March, in writing him, had mentioned the rapid and happy growth of their acquaintance!

"Yes,"˙ he replied, betraying fresh pain under an effort to speak lightly. "It may be a right smart while before I see you again, Miss Barb. I take the first express to Chicago, and next month I sail for Europe to——"

"Why, Mr. March!" said Barbara with a nervous laugh.

"Yes," responded John once more, thinking that if she was going to treat the thing as a joke he had better do the same, "immigrants for Widewood have got to be got, and they're not to be got on this side the big water."

"Why, Mr. March!"—her laugh grew—"How long shall you stay?"

"Stay! Gracious knows! I must just stay till I get them!—as your father says."

"Why, Mr. March! When did—" the questioner's eyes dropped sedately to the ground—"when did you decide to go? Since—since—yesterday?"

"Yes, it was!" The answer came as though it were a whole heart-load.

The maiden's color rose, but she lifted her quiet, characteristic gaze to his and said, " You're glad you're going, are you not ? "

" O—I—why, yes! If I'm not I know I ought to be! To see Europe and all that is great, of course. It's beyond my dreams. And yet I know it really isn't as much what I'm going to as what I'm going from that I ought to—to be g-glad of! I hope I'll come back with a little more sense. I'm going to try. I promise you, Miss Barb. It's only right I *should* promise—*you!* "

" Why, Mr. Mar—" Her voice was low, but her color increased.

" Miss Barb—O Miss Barb, I didn't come just to say good-by. I hope I know what I owe you better than that. I—Miss Barb, I came to acknowledge that I said too much yesterday!—and to—ask your pardon."

Barbara was crimson. " Mr. March ! " she said, half choking, " as long as I was simple enough to let it pass unrebuked you might at least have spared me your apologies ! No, I can't stay ! No, not one instant ! Those girls are coming to speak to me—that man "— it was the drummer—" wants to speak to you. Good-by."

Their intruders were upon them. John could only give a heart-broken look as she faltered an instant in the open door. For reply she called back, in poor mockery of a sprightly tone : " I hope you'll have ever so pleasant a voyage ! " and shut the door.

So it goes with all of us through all the ungraceful, inartistic realisms of our lives ; the high poetry is ever there, the kingdom of romance is at hand; the only trouble is to find the rhymes—O! if we could only find the rhymes!

---

## LXXV.

### A YEAR'S VICISSITUDES

It was during the year spent by John March in Europe that Suez first began to be so widely famous. It was then, too, that the Suez *Courier* emerged into universal notice. The average newspaper reader, from Maine to Oregon, spoke familiarly of Colonel Ravenel as the writer of its much-quoted leaders; a fact which gave no little disgust to Garnet, their author.

Ravenel never let his paper theorize on the causes of Suez's renown or the *Courier's* vogue.

"It's the luck of the times," he said, and pleasantly smiled to see the nation's eyes turned on Dixie and her near sisters, hardly in faith, yet with a certain highly commercial hope and charity. The lighting of every new coke furnace, the setting fire to any local rubbish-heap of dead traditions, seemed just then to Northern longings the blush of a new economic and political dawn over the whole South.

"You say you're going South? Well, now if you want to see a very small but most encouraging example of the changes going on down there, just stop over a day

**in** Suez!" Such remarks were common—in the clubs —in the cars.

" Now, for instance, Suez! I know something of Suez myself." So said a certain railway passenger one day when this fame had entered its second year and the more knowing journals had begun to neglect it. " I was an officer in the Union army and was left down there on duty after the surrender a short while; then I went out West and fought Indians. But Suez—I pledge you my word I wouldn't 'a' given a horseshoe-nail for the whole layout! Now!—well, you'd e'en a'most think you was in a Western town! The way they're a slappin' money, b' Jinks, into improvements and enterprises—quarries, roads, bridges, schools, mills—'twould make a Western town's head swim! "

"What kind of mills?" asked his listener, a young man, but careworn.

"O, eh, saw-mills—tanbark mills—to start with. Was you ever there?"

"Yes, I—before the changes you speak of I——"

"Before! Hoh! then you've never seen Lover's Leap coal mine, or Bridal Veil coal mine, or Sleeping Giant iron mine, or Devil's Garden coke furnaces! They're putting up smelting works right opposite the steamboat landing! You say you're going South—just stop over a day in Suez. It'll pay you! You could write it up!—call it 'What a man just back f'm Europe saw in Dixie'—only, you don't want to wave the Bloody Shirt, and don't forget we're dead tired hearing about the 'illiterate South.' *I* say, let us have peace; my son's in love with a Southern girl! Why, at

Suez you'll see school-houses only five miles apart, from Wildcat Ridge—where the niggers and mountaineers had that skirmish last fall—clean down to Leggetts-town! School-houses, why,"—the speaker chuckled at what was coming—"one of 'em stands on the very spot where in '65 I found a little freckled boy trying to poke a rabbit out of a log with an old bayon——"

"No!" exclaimed the careworn listener, in one smile from his hat to his handsome boots.

He would have said more, but the story-teller lifted a finger to intimate that the bayonet was not the main point—there was better laughing ahead. "Handsome little chap he was—brave eyes—sweet mouth. Thinks I right there, 'This's going to be somebody some day.' He reminded me of my own son at home. Well, he clum up behind my saddle and rode with me to the edge of Suez, where we met his father with a team of mules and a wagon of provisions. Talk about the Old South, I'll say this: I *never* see so fine a gentlemen look so *techingly* poor. Hold up, let me —now, let me—just wait till I tell you. That little rat —if it hadn't been for that little barefooted rat with his scalp-lock a-stickin' up through a tear in his hat, most likely you'd never so much as heard—of Suez! For that little chap was John March!"

The speaker clapped his hands upon his knees, opened his mouth, and waited for his hearer's laughter and wonder; but the hearer merely smiled, and with a queer look of frolic in the depths of his handsome eyes, asked,

"How lately were you in Suez?"

"Me? O—not since '65; but my son's a commercial tourist—rattling smart fellow—you've probably met him —I never see anybody that hadn't—last year he was in New England—this year he's tryin' Dixie. He sells this celebrated 'Hoptonica' for the great Cincinnati house of Pretzels & Bier. Funny thing—he's been mistaken for John March. A young lady—Southern girl —up in New England about a year ago—it was just for an instant—O of course—Must you go? Well, look here! Try to stop over a day in Suez—That's right; it'll pay you!"

The two travelers parted. The Union veteran went on westward, while the other—March by name—John March—was ticketed, of course, for Suez.

Some ten days before, in London, having just ended a four weeks' circuit through a region of the Continent where news of Suez was even scarcer than emigrants for Widewood, he had, to his astonishment, met Proudfit. The colonel had just arrived across. He was tipsy, as usual, and a sad wreck, but bound for Carlsbad, bright in the faith that when he had stayed there two months he would go home cured for life of his "only bad habit." March was troubled, and did not become less so when Proudfit explained that his presence was due to the "kind pressu' of Garnet and othe's." He knew that Garnet, months before, had swapped his Land Company stock to Proudfit for the Colonel's much better stock in the Construction Company and succeeded him as president of the latter concern.

"As a matteh of fawm—tempora'ily—du'ing my ill health," said the Carlsbad pilgrim, adding, in an unfragrant stage-whisper, that there was a secret off-setting sale of both stocks back again, the papers of which were in Mrs. Proudfit's custody. Mrs. Proudfit was not with her husband; she was at home, in Blackland.

John knew also how nearly down to nothing the price of his own company's first-mortgage bonds had declined; but the Colonel's tidings of a later fate fell upon him like a thunderbolt. He stood before his informant in the populous street, now too sick at heart for speech, and now throbbing with too resolute a resentment for outward show, but drawn up rigidly with a scowl of indignant attention under his locks that made him the observed of every quick eye. The matter—not to follow Proudfit too closely—was this:

The Construction Company, paid in advance, and in the Land Company's second-mortgage bonds, for its many expensive and recklessly immature works, had promptly sold those bonds to a multitude of ready takers near and far, but principally far. When the promised inpour of millers and miners, manufacturers and operatives, so nearly failed that the Land Company could not pay, nor half pay, the interest on its first-mortgage bonds and they "tumbled," these second-mortgage bonds were, of course, unsalable at any figure. The smallest child will understand this—and worse to follow—at a glance; but if he doesn't he needn't. At this point Ravenel, who had kept his paper very still, "persuaded" Gamble and Bulger to buy, at the prices their holders had paid for them, all that smaller portion of these second-mortgage bonds, as well as all small lots of the Land Company's stock, held in the three counties. "The *Courier*," he said, with his effectual smile, "couldn't afford to see home folks suffer," and he presently had them all well out of it, Parson Tombs among them.

"Thank God!" rumbled March. "And then what?"

Then Ravenel, as trustee for the three counties—Uncle Jimmie Rankin was the other, but shrewdly let Jeff-Jack speak and act for him—privately combined with the Construction Company, which, Proudfit pathetically reminded John, was a loser by the Land Company in the discounts at which it had sold that Company's second-mortgage bonds. They went on a still hunt after the first-mortgage bonds, "bought," said Proudfit, "the whole bilin' faw a song," foreclosed the mortgage, and at the sale of the Land Company's assets were the only bidders, except Senator Halliday and Captain Shotwell, whom they easily outbid.

"Right smart of us suspicioned those two gentlemen were bidding faw you, John."

March, who was staring aside in fierce abstraction, started. "I reckon not," he said, and stared in the other direction. "So, then, Widewood and all its costly improvements belong half to the three counties and half to Garnet's construc——"

"John"—the Colonel lifted his pallid hand with an air of amiable greatness—"*my* construc', seel view play! Not Garnet's. *I*—Proudfit—am still the invisible head of that comp'ny. Garnet acknowledges it privately to me. He and I have what you may call a per-perfect und-und-unde'standing!"

"Perfect und'—O me!" interrupted March, with a

broken laugh and a frown. Proudfit liked his air and tried to reproduce it, but got his features tangled, rubbed his mouth, and closed his eyes. March stared into vacancy again.

The tippler interposed with moist emotion. "John, we're landless! My plantation b'longs t' my wife. I can sympathize with you, John. As old song says, 'we're landless! landless!' *We* are landless, John. But you have price—priceless 'dvant'ge over me in one thing, vice-president; you've still got yo' motheh!"

"O!" groaned March, blazing up and starting away; but Proudfit clung.

"My dea' boy! let me tell you, that tendeh little motheh's been a perfect hero! When I told her—in— in t-tears—how sorry I—and Garnet—and all of us— was,—'O Curl Prou'fit,' says she—with that ca'm, sweet, dizda-ainful smile of hers, you know—'it's no sup-prise to me; it's what I've expected from the begin-ning.' "

## LXXVI.

### AGAINST OVERWHELMING NUMBERS

During the boom Tom Hersey's Swanee Hotel—re-paired, enlarged, repainted—had become Hotel Swanee. At the corner of the two streets on which it fronted he had added a square tower or "observatory." But neither guests nor "resi*dent*ers" had made use of it as he had

designed. Its low top was too high to be reached with
that Southern ease which Northern sojourners like, and
besides, you couldn't see more than half the earth anyhow
when you got up there.

Early, therefore, it had been turned into an airy bed-
chamber for Bulger. He, however was gone. He had
left Suez for good and all on the same day on which
John March arrived from abroad, being so advised to
do by Captains Champion and Shotwell, who loved a
good joke with a good fat coward to saddle it on, and
who had got enough of Bulger on the day of the skirmish mentioned a page or two back. The tower room he
left came to be looked upon as specially adapted for the
sick, and here, some eleven or twelve months after the
wreck of the Three Counties Land and Improvement
Company, Limited, John March lay on his bed by night
and sat on it by day, wasted, bright-eyed, and pale, with
a corded frown forever between his brows save in the
best moments of his unquiet sleep.

On the hither side of one of the two streets close
under him, his office—the old, first one, reopened on his
return—stood closed, the sign renovated and tacked up
once more, and the early addendum, *Gentleman*, still
asserting itself, firmly though modestly, beneath the new
surface of repair. In and from that office he had, for
these many months, waged a bloodless but aggressive
and indomitable war on the men who, he felt, had
robbed, not merely him, but his mother, and the grave
of his father, under the forms and cover of commerce
and law; yet from whom he had not been able to take
their outermost intrenchment—the slothful connivance

of a community which had let itself be made a passive
sharer of their spoils. Now, in that office his desk was
covered with ten days' dust. " If you don't shut this
thing up straight off and go, say, to Chalybeate Springs,"
the doctor had one day exclaimed, " you'll not last half
through the summer." March had answered with jesting
obduracy, and two nights later had fainted on the stairs
of Tom Hersey's hotel. For twenty-four hours afterward
he had been "not expected to live." During which
time Suez had entirely reconsidered him—conduct, character, capacity—and had given him, at the expense of
his adversaries, a higher value and regard than ever,
and a wholly new affection. It would have been worth
all the apothecary's arsenic and iron for someone just to
have told him so.

A Suez physician once said to me—I was struck with
the originality of the remark—that one man's cure is
another's poison. Not even to himself would March
confess that this room, so specially adapted for the average sick man, was for him the worst that could have
been picked out. It showed him constantly all Suez.
Poor little sweating and fanning Suez, grown fat, and
already getting lean again on the carcass of one man's
unsalable estate!

" Come here," said Fannie Ravenel behind the blinds
of her highest window, to one who loved her still, but
rarely had time to visit her now, " look. That's John
March's room. O sweet, how's he ever again to match
himself to our littleness and sterility without shriveling
down to it himself? And yet that, and not the catching of scamps or recovery of lands, is going to be his

big task. For I don't think he'll ever go 'way from here; he's just the kind that'll always feel too many obligations to stay; and I think his sickness will be a blessing straight from God, to him and to all of us who love him, if it will only give him time to see what his true work is—God bless him!" The two stood in loose embrace looking opposite ways, until the speaker asked, "Don't you believe it?"

"I don't know," said the other, gently drawing her away from the window.

Fannie yielded a step or two and then as gently resisted. "Sweetheart," she cried, with a melting gaze, "you don't suppose—just because I choose to remember what he is and what he is suffering—you can't imagine— O if *you* mistake me I shall simply perish!"

"I know you too well, dear," caressingly murmured the guest, and they talked of other things—"gusset and band and seam"—for it was Saturday and there was to be a small occasion on the morrow. But that same night, long after the house's last light was out, the guest said her prayers at that window.

The windows of March's chamber, albeit his bed's head was against the one to the east, opened four ways. The one on the west looked down over the court-house square and up the verdant avenue which became the pike. Here on the right stood the *Courier* building! There was Captain Champion going by it; honest ex-treasurer of the defunct Land Company. His modest yet sturdy self-regard would not even yet let him see that he had been only a cover for the underground doublings of shrewder men. Yonder was the tree from

which Enos had been shot by his own brother—who
was dead himself now, killed, with many others, in that
"skirmish" which John could never cease thinking
that he, had he but been here, might have averted.
Over there were the two churches, and one window of
Ravenel's house.  March had not been in that house a
fourth as many times as he had been prettily upbraided
for not coming.

"Fannie's grea-atly cha-anged!" Parson Tombs said,
with solemn triumph.

John had dreamily assented.  The change he had
noticed most was that the old zest of living was gone from
her still beautiful black eyes, and that her freckles had
augmented.  He had met her oftenest in church.  She
had the Suez Sunday-school's primary class, and more
than filled the wide vacancy caused by Miss Mary
Salter's marriage to the other pastor.  These two wives
had grown to be close friends.  On the Sunday to which
we have alluded they had their infants baptized
together.  Fannie's was a girl and did not cry.  Johanna, in the gallery, did, when Father Tombs, with
dripping hand, said,

"Rose, I baptize thee."

Tears had started also in the eyes of at least one
other: Fannie's guest, as we say, whose presence was
unusual and had not escaped remark.  "The wonder
is," Miss Martha had said, "that she has time, or any
strength left, to ever come in to town-church at all, with
that whole overgrown Rosemont on her hands the way
it is!  If I had a sister no older than she is—with that
look on her face every time she falls into a study"—

she stopped; then sharply—"I tell you, that man
Garnet "—and stopped again.

From the tower's south window there was a wide view
up and down the Swanee and across the bridge, into
Blackland. March never looked that way but he
found himself staring at those unfinished smelting works.
Smart saplings were growing inside the roofless walls,
and you could buy the whole plant for the cost of its
brick and stone.

The north window view hurt still worse. The middle
distance was dotted with half a dozen "follies" "for
sale," each with its small bunch of workmen's cottages,
some empty, some full, alas! and all treeless and grass-
less under the blazing sun. Far beyond to the right,
shading away from green to blue, rose the hills of Widewood—lost Widewood!—hiding other "tied-up capital"
and more stranded labor. For scattered through those
lovely forests were scores, hundreds, of peasants from
across seas, to every separate one of whom the
scowling patient in this room, with fierce tears perpetually in his throat, believed he owed explanation and
restitution.

Garnet!—owned half of Widewood! March's con-
finement here dated from the night when he had at
length unearthed the well-hid truth of how the stately
Major had acquired it. No sooner had Ravenel and
Garnet got the Land Company into its living grave,
than Gamble and Bulger, with Leggett looming mys-
teriously in their large shadows, forced the Construction Company into liquidation by a kind demand upon
Mattox, Crickwater, and Pettigrew for certain call

loans of two years' standing, accepted in settlement their
shares of the Widewood lands wrested from the Land
Company, and then somehow privately induced Garnet
to take those cumbersome assets off their hands at a
round cash price.  That was the day before March had
got home and Bulger had cleared out.  Gamble had
departed much more leisurely.  Whenever money was
at stake Gamble had the courage of a bear with
whelps.  Whenever he said, "I can't afford to stay
here," it meant that his milk-pail was full and the
cow empty.  This time it meant he had, as Shotwell
put it, "broken the record of the three counties—
pulled the wool over Jeff-Jack's eyes;" for he had
sold his railroad to a system hostile to the fortunes
of Suez.

The other half of Widewood was public domain.

"Thank Heaven for that!" said March, lying
dressed on his bed.

"Suez thanks Mr. Ravenel," melodiously responded
his mother.  Parson Tombs had brought her up here
and slipped out again on creaking tiptoe.

"Why, mother, it was I made it so in my original
plan!"

"O my beloved boy, it was in Mr. Ravenel's original plan when he lent your poor father the money to
send you to school.  I have it on good authority."

The son gave a vexed laugh.  "O, as to that, why
Cornelius Leggett suggested it when——"

"John! forbear!" Mrs. March was not prejudiced.
She could admit the name of a colored person in a
discussion ; but *that* miscreant had lured her trusted

Jane to the altar and written back that she was one of the best wives he had had for years.

John forbore. He was profoundly distressed, but tried to speak more lightly. "Law! mother, one reason urged by Major Garnet for our privately reserving that trifling scrap of sixty acres on the west side of the creek was so's to make each half of the company's tract an even fifty thousand acres, one for the three counties and the other—O! there's another thing. I never thought to tell you because it was hardly worth remembering. On Major Garnet's suggestion, and so's to never get it mixed up with the Company's lands—you know how carelessly our county records are kept—I made a relinquishment to you of my half of your and my joint interest in those sixty acres. I never supposed I was going to make it one day the only piece of Widewood left you."

"Ah!" sighed the hearer, "half as many dollars would be far better for a helpless widow."

John was scowling in another direction and did not see her pretty blush. His voice deepened with indignation. "I'll give you double—right here—now—cash!"

"Will you write the receipt for me to sign?" she sweetly asked.

He started up, wrote, paid, and smiled as he shut his empty purse. His mother sighed in amiable pensiveness, saying, "This is a mystery to me, my son."

"No more than it is to me," dryly responded John, angered by this new sting from his old knowledge of her ways. It was her policy always to mystify those who had the best right to understand her. "I shall try to solve it," he added.

"I should rather not have you speak of it at once," she replied, almost hurriedly. "You'll know why in a few days." Her blush came again. This time John saw it and marvelled anew. He tossed himself back on his bed, fevered with irritation.

"Mother"—he fiercely shifted his pillows and looked at the ceiling—"the chief mystery to me is that you seem to care so little for the loss of our lands!"

"I thought you told me that Major Garnet considered those sixty acres as almost worthless."

"I believe he does."

Her voice became faint. "I would gladly explain, son, if you were only well enough to hear me—patiently."

He lay rigidly still, with every nerve aching. His hands, locked under his head, grew tight as he heard her rise and draw near. He shut his eyes hard as she laid on his wrinkling forehead a cold kiss moistened with a tear, and melted from the room.

"Mother!" he called, appeasingly, as the door was closing; but it clicked to; she floated down the stairs. He turned his face into the pillow and clenched his hands. By and by he turned again and exclaimed, as from some long train of thought, "'Better off without Widewood than with it,' am I? On my soul! I begin to believe it. But if you can see that so clearly, O! my poor little unsuspicious mother, why can't you even now understand that they were thieves and robbed us? Who—who—*what*—can have so blinded you?"

He left the bed and moved to his most frequent seat, the north window. Thence, in the western half of the view, he could see the three counties' "mother of learning and useful arts," fair, large-grown Rosemont, glistening on her green hills in each day's setting sun, a lovely frontispiece to the ever-pleasant story of her master's redundant prosperity. Her June fledglings were but just gone and she was in the earliest days of her summer rest. "Enlarged and superbly equipped and embellished," the newspapers said of her in laudatory headlines, and it was true that "no expense had been spared." Not any other institution in Dixie spread such royal feasts of reason and information for her children, at lavish cost to herself, low price to them, and queenly remuneration to the numerous members of the State Legislature who came to discourse on Agriculture, Mining, Banking, Trade, Journalism, Jurisprudence, Taxation, and Government.

How envied was Garnet! Gamble and Bulger were thrifty and successful, but Gamble and Bulger had fled and envy follows not the fleeing. Halliday had attained his ambition; was in the United States Senate; but the boom had sent him there, "regardless of politics," to plead for a deeper channel in the Swanee, a move that was only part of one of Ravenel's amusing "deals," whereby he had procured at last the political extinction of Cornelius Leggett. Moreover, for all the old General's activities he had kept himself poor; almost as poor as he was incorruptible; who could envy him? And Ravenel; Ravenel was still the arbiter of political fortune, but it was part of his unostentatious wisdom never to let himself be envied. But Garnet, amid all this business depression upon which March looked down from his sick-room, wore envy on his broad breast like a decoration. There were spots of tarnish on his heavy gilding; not merely the elder Miss Kinsington, but Martha Salter as well, had refused to say good-by to Mademoiselle Eglantine on the eve of her final return to France; Fanny Ravenel had, with cutting playfulness, asked Mrs. Proudfit, as that sister was extolling the Major's vast public value, if she did not know perfectly well that Rosemont was a political "barrel." And yet it was Garnet who stood popularly as the incarnation of praiseworthy success.

John March begrudged him none of his triumphs—at their price. Yet it was before *this* window-picture his heart sunk under the heaviest and cruelest of his exasperations. Other bafflements tormented him; here alone stood the visible, beautiful emblem of absolute discomfiture. For here was the silent, lifted hand which forbade him pursue his defrauders. Follow their manœuvres as he might, always somewhere short of the end of their windings he found this man's fortune and reputation lying square across the way like a smooth, new fortification under a neutral flag. Seven times he had halted before them disarmed and dumb, and turned away with a chagrin that burnt his brain and gnawed his very bones.

There came a footstep, a rap at the door, and Parson Tombs entered, radiant with tidings. "John!" he began, but his countenance and voice fell to an anxious tenderness; "why, Brother March, I—I didn't suspicion

you was this po'ly, seh. Why, John, you hadn't ought
to try to sit up until yo' betteh!"

"It rests me to get out of bed a little while off and on.
How are you, these days, sir? How's Mrs. Tombs?"

"Oh, we keep a-goin', thank the Lawd. Brother
March, I've got pow'ful good news."

"Is it something about my mother? She was here
about an hour ago."

"Yass, it is! The minute she got back to ow house
—and O, John, it jest seems to me like her livin' with
us ever since Widewood was divided up has been a
plumb provi*dence!*—I says, s'I, 'Wha'd John say?'
and when she said she hadn't so much as told you,
'cause you wa'n't well enough, we both of us, Mother
Tombs and me, we says, s'I, 'Why, the sicker he is the
mo' it'll help him! Besides, he's sho' to hear it; the
ve'y wind'll carry it; which he oughtn't never to find it
out in that hilta-skilta wa-ay! Sister March, s'I, 'let
*me* go tell him!' And s'she, jestingly, 'Go—if you think
it's safe.' So here I am!" The old man laughed timorously.

"Well?" John kept his hands in his lap, where
each was trying to wrench the fingers off the other.
"What is it?"

"Why, John, the Lawd has provided! For one
thing and evm that the smallest, Sister March's Widewood lands air as good as hers again!"

"What has happened?" cried the pale youth.

"O, John, the best that ever could! What Mother
Tombs and I and the Sextons and the Coffins and the
Graveses and sco'es o' lovin' friends and relations have

been a hopin' faw all this year an' last! Sister March
has engaged her hand to Brother Garnet!"

"I think I'll lie down," said John, beginning to rise.
The frightened Parson clutched him awkwardly, he
reeled a step or two, said, "Don't—trouble"—and fell
across the bed with a slam that jarred the floor. The
old man moaned a helpless compassion.

"It's nothing," said March, waving him back. "Only
my foot slipped." He dragged himself to his pillow.
"Good-by, sir. I prefer—good-by!" He waved his
visitor to the door. As it closed one of his hands crept
under the pillow. There it seemed to find and rest on
some small thing, and then a single throe wrenched his
frame as of an anguish beyond all tears.

At Rosemont, as night was falling, Doctor Coffin,
March's physician, the same who had attended him in
boyhood when he was shot, stood up before the new Rose
of Rosemont, in the greatly changed reception-room
where in former years Bonaparte had tried so persistently to cross the Alps. She had left the room and
returned and was speaking of Johanna, as she said,
"She'll go with you. Have your seat, Doctor; she's
getting ready and will be here in a few minutes."

The Doctor made a glad gesture. "I know how hard
it must be for you to do without her," he said, "but if
you can get along somehow for three or four days, why
—you know she's away yonder the best nurse in the
three counties—it'll make a world of difference to my
patient."

"I hope he'll like her ways," replied the young mistress. "There's so much in that."

"Don't fear!" laughed the Doctor. "He hasn't looked so pleased since he first took sick as he did when I told him I was going to fetch her. By the bye, how do you sleep since I changed yo' medicine this last time; no better? Ain't yo' appetite improved any? I still think the secret of all yo' trouble is malaria; I haven't a doubt you brought it with you from the North! I wish I could find as good an explanation of yo' father's condition.—I just declare it's an outrage on the rights of a plain old family chills-and-fever doctor, for a lot of you folks to be havin' these here sneakin' nerve and brain things that calomel an' quinine can't—O! here's Johanna."

On his way through town again, with the black maid beside him in his battered top buggy, he paused at the Tombses' gate, hailed by the fond old Parson. "You haven't got her? Why, so you have!—'Howdy, Johanna, you're a bless'n' here to-night,' as the hymn says. Doctor, I hope an' trust an' pray Sister Proudfit's attack won't turn out serious——?"

The Doctor was surprised. "*I* ain't been called to her; didn't know she was sick."

"Well, I say!" exclaimed the Parson. "Why, it's all over town that you *wuz*, and that you found her so prostrated with relaxation of the nerves that her husband couldn't hold her still! You've heard, of co'se, that he's got back at last? Isn't it pathetic? I've been talkin' about it to Brother Garnet—you passed him just now, didn't you?—and as he says, her husband goes off, a walkin' ruin, to be gone three months, stays twelve, and arrives back totally unexpected on

this mawnin's six-o'clock train, a-callin' himself *cu'ud !*
Brother Coffin, *you* don't believe that, *do* you? Why,
as Brother Garnet says, the drinkin' habit is as much a
moral as a physical sickness, and the man that can
make common talk of it in his own case to ev'y Tom,
Dick, and Harry, evm down to the niggehs, ain't so
much as tetched the deepest root uv his trouble, much
less cu'ud! Why, Doctor, Brother Garnet see him,
himself!—a-tellin' that C'nelius Leggett!—and pulled
him away! Po' Brother Garnet! Johanna, I wish,
betwixt the Doctor an' you, you could make him look
betteh. His load of usefulness is too great. I declare,
Brother Coffin, he was that tiud this evenin' that evm
here, where you'd expect him to seem fresh and happy
in his new joy, he looked as if, if it wa'n't faw the
wrong of the thing, he'd almost be willin' to call upon
the rocks and the mountains to fall on him and hide
him.—But I mustn't detain you!"

The physician drove on, and by and by was leaving
directions with Johanna and her protectors, Tom Hersey
and his wife. "And, Tom, mind you, *no visitors.* It's
his own wish. Good-night.—O !—that young Mr. Fair.
March tells me he's expecting him any time within the
next few days, to help lay the corner-stone of this new
building up at the colored college; Fair Hall, yes.
Whenever he comes take him right up to see March.
I promised John you would!"

## LXXVII.

### " LINES OF LIGHT ON A SULLEN SEA "

FROM the first hour of Johanna's attendance March began to mend. Whence she came, whither she went, as she moved in and out so pleasantly, he never thought to ask, and never found out that her bed was a pallet laid on the stair-landing just at his door.

The young bloods down in the street were keenly amused. " Doctor, if he was anybody but John March aw she anybody but Johanna "—the rest was too funny for words. " How is he to-day, anyhow ? Improving rap'—well ! good fo' that ! Come, gentlemen, let's— Come, Shot. Doctor, won't you—" And as they went they all agreed that the dark maiden's invincible modesty was like some "subtle emana-ation," as Shotwell expressed it, which charmed all evil out of the grossest eye.

True it was in the convalescent's case, that while Johanna's mere doings had their curative value, her simple presence had more. Yet her greatest healing was in her words ; in what she told him. She only answered questions ; but these he lightly plied on any and every trivial matter that promised to lead up—or around—to one subject which seemed to allure him without cessation. Yet always at her first pause after entering upon any phase of this topic, he would say, " But that's not what—hem !—I was speaking of," and starting once more, at any distance away, would begin to steal yet another approach toward the same enticing theme.

So the brief time of her appointed service came to its end, neither the Doctor, nor the convalescent, nor even her young mistress, for one moment imagining what dear delight, yet withal what saintly martyrdom to Johanna, this three days' task had been.

In its last hour, when she, to end all well, prepared and brought up the captive's evening meal, she found him sitting up in bed talking to Henry Fair.

"Doctor thinks I can go down to my office Monday. Yes, I knew what ailed me better than he did. I began to recover the moment I quit trying to convince the Lord that He ought to run this world in my private interest. Ah! Johanna, so this is the last, is it? I'm pow'ful sorry! Mr. Fair, you remember Johanna, don't you?"

Mr. Fair remembered, the maid courtesied, and March, a trifle unduly animated, ran on—"Johanna's the salt of the earth, Mr. Fair. Don't often see best salt that color, do you?" Then dropping hist one—"O! you know, if my chief concern were still, as it was at first, to recover my fortunes, or even to vindicate my abilities, I reckon I could make out to accept defeat— almost. For, really, I'm just about the only sufferer— outwardly, at least. Of course, there's an awful shrinkage here, but all our home people have made net gains —unless it is Proudfit; I—eh—Johanna, you needn't stay in here; only don't go beyond call."

The maid closed the door after her, took her accustomed rocking-chair and needle on the stair-landing,

"Fair," she heard him say, "—why—why, Fair, that's a mighty handsome offer to come from such a prudent business man as you. My George! sir, men don't often put such valuable freight into a boat that's aground. Why—why, you spoil my talk; I positively don't know what—what to say!" There was a choke in his voice. Fair made some answer which March gratefully cut short.

"O! I wish I could! It hurts me all over and through to decline it. But I must; I've got to! 'Think it over'—O! I've thought it over probably before you ever thought of it at all! I know my capabilities. I'm not in such a fierce hurry for things as I used to be, but I've got what brains I ever had—and spine, too—and I know that even without your offer there's a better chance for me North than here. But— O! it's no use, Fair, I just can't go! I mustn't! Yes. Yes. O! yes, I know all that, but, my dear sir, I can't afford— You know, this Suez soil isn't something I can shake off my shoes as you might. George! I'm part of it! I'm not Quixotic—not a bit! I'm only choosing between two sorts of selfishness, one not quite so narrow as the other; but—I've got to stay here."

Fair, after a short silence, asked if this was his only reason.

"Only reason? Why—why, yes, that's my only reason! To be sure, there's a sense in which—why, conscience! isn't it enough? O! of course, I could *think up* other considerations, but they're not reasons— I don't allow them to bias me at all! Fact is, I was never before quite so foot-free. Why did you Did you fancy I might be contemplating marri O, go 'long! why, my good gracious, Fair, I—it honest fact—I haven't even *been to see* one marriag girl since I came back from Europe! No, the rea give is *the* reason. It covers everything else.

"O! if you are thinking of debts, I could them at least as fast if I went as if I stayed. T not large, the money debts. O! no; it's—F spent a year in Europe coaxing men to leave mother-country for better wages in this. Of cours was all right. But it brought one thing to my that when our value is not mere wages, it isn' man who's got the unqualified right to pick up a out just whenever he gets ready. Look out th dow. There's the college where for five years I education—at half price!—and with money b here in Suez! Look out this one. Mr. Fai down there in those streets truth and justice a wounded and half-dead, and the public conscien ing drugged! We Southerners, Fair, don't bel man's as good as another; we think one man in place is worth a thousand who can't fill it. My here!—No! let me finish; I'm not fatigued How I'm to meet this issue God only knows, b even try to do it if I don't? Halliday's too Ravenel looks on as silent as a gallows! P poor old Proudfit hasn't been sober since th got home. Father Tombs has grown timid sighted, and the whole people, Fair, the whol have let themselves be seduced in the purse an

and being quite as human as if she had been white, listened. Fair's words were very indistinct, but March's came through the thin door-panels as clean as rifle-balls. "O! yes," was one of his replies, "I know that with even nothing left but the experiences, I'm a whole world richer, in things that make a real manhood and life, than when I was land-poor with my hundred thousand acres. As far as *I* am concerned, I can afford to deny myself all the reprisals, and revenges too, that litigations could ever give me. I've got sixty acres of Widewood to begin over with— By Jo'! Garnet, himself, began with less!" He let go a feverish laugh.

"If I come to that," he added, "I've got, besides, a love of study and a talent for teaching, two things he never had." Fair asked a question and he laughed again. "O! no, it was only a passing thought. If anybody 'busts Rosemont wide open' it'll have to be Leggett. O! no, I——" He played with his spoon.

Fair's response must have been complimentary. "Thank you," said March; "why, thank you!" Then the visitor spoke again and the convalescent replied:

"Ah! a 'diligent and vigilant patience'—yes, I don't doubt it would serve me best—provided, my dear sir, it didn't turn out simply a virtue of impotency; or, worse yet, what I once heard called 'the thrifty discretion of a short-winded courage!'"

When Fair responded this time March let him speak long. Johanna bent her ear anxiously. Her patient seemed to be neglecting his food; but as he began to reply she resumed her needle.

"Fair," she heard him say, "—why—why, Fair, that's a mighty handsome offer to come from such a prudent business man as you. My George! sir, men don't often put such valuable freight into a boat that's aground. Why—why, you spoil my talk; I positively don't know what—what to say!" There was a choke in his voice. Fair made some answer which March gratefully cut short.

"O! I wish I could! It hurts me all over and through to decline it. But I must; I've got to! 'Think it over'—O! I've thought it over probably before you ever thought of it at all! I know my capabilities. I'm not in such a fierce hurry for things as I used to be, but I've got what brains I ever had—and spine, too—and I know that even without your offer there's a better chance for me North than here. But— O! it's no use, Fair, I just can't go! I mustn't! Yes. Yes. O! yes, I know all that, but, my dear sir, I can't afford— You know, this Suez soil isn't something I can shake off my shoes as you might. George! I'm part of it! I'm not Quixotic—not a bit! I'm only choosing between two sorts of selfishness, one not quite so narrow as the other; but—I've got to stay here."

Fair, after a short silence, asked if this was his only reason.

"Only reason? Why—why, yes, that's my only reason! To be sure, there's a sense in which—why, conscience! isn't it enough? O! of course, I could *think up* other considerations, but they're not reasons— I don't allow them to bias me at all! Fact is, I was

never before quite so foot-free. Why did you ask?
Did you fancy I might be contemplating marriage?
O, go 'long! why, my good gracious, Fair, I—it's an
honest fact—I haven't even *been to see* one marriageable
girl since I came back from Europe! No, the reason I
give is *the* reason. It covers everything else.

"O! if you are thinking of debts, I could cancel
them at least as fast if I went as if I stayed. They're
not large, the money debts. O! no; it's—Fair—I
spent a year in Europe coaxing men to leave their
mother-country for better wages in this. Of course, that
was all right. But it brought one thing to my notice:
that when our value is not mere wages, it isn't every
man who's got the unqualified right to pick up and put
out just whenever he gets ready. Look out that window. There's the college where for five years I got my
education—at half price!—and with money borrowed
here in Suez! Look out this one. Mr. Fair, right
down there in those streets truth and justice are lying
wounded and half-dead, and the public conscience is being drugged! We Southerners, Fair, don't believe one
man's as good as another; we think one man in his right
place is worth a thousand who can't fill it. My place is
here!—No! let me finish; I'm not fatigued at all!
How I'm to meet this issue God only knows, but who'll
even try to do it if I don't? Halliday's too far off.
Ravenel looks on as silent as a gallows! Proudfit—
poor old Proudfit hasn't been sober since the day he
got home. Father Tombs has grown timid and slow-
sighted, and the whole people, Fair, the whole people!
have let themselves be seduced in the purse and are this

day betrayed as foully in their fortunes as in their souls!" The speaker ended in a high key. He was trembling with nervous exhaustion. In an effort to jerk higher in the pillow his knee struck the tray, the crockery slid and crashed, and Johanna found him in the middle of the room, fiercely shaking the skirt of his dressing-gown.

"O! never mind me; get the milk out of the bed!"

She saw how overwrought he was, yet turned to obey. Fair, to aid her, snatched away the pillows. A small thing from under them fluttered out upon the carpet and lay before the three. With a despairing murmur the invalid picked it up, and the two men stood facing each other. Fair colored slightly, March slowly crimsoned. Then Fair smiled. March smiled too, but foolishly. Johanna made herself very busy with the bed, but she saw all. Fair pushed forward a rocking-chair, into which March sank. Then with gentle insistence he drew from March's hand the worn photograph—for such it was—leaned against a window and gazed on it, while March turned his brow into the cushioned back of his chair and wept as comfortably as any girl.

Johanna took out the tray and its wreck, and in a moment was back with fresh sheets. March had lain down on the bare mattress and, with his cheek on a pillow, was smiling in mild amusement at Fair's account of a brief talk he had had with Leggett while the train waited at Pulaski City.

"Yes," said March, moving enough to let the bed be made, "he pretends to keep a restaurant there now; but where he gets all the money he spends is more than I

can make out, unless it's from men who can't afford to
let him tell what he knows."

A servant of the house tapped at the door and
said Major Garnet was in the office, waiting for
Johanna. March rose to his elbow and gave her a
hand.

"Why, I shan't ever know how to be sick without
you any mo'!" he said, as her dark fingers slipped tim-
idly from his friendly hold. "Johanna!—now—now,
don't you go tellin' things you'd oughtn't to; will you?"

"No, seh," came from the maid slowly, yet with a
suspicious readiness quite out of keeping with the limp
diffidence of her attitude.

"Hold on a moment, Johanna," he called, as she
turned to go. "Just wait an instant—sounds like——"
He rose higher. Fair stepped to the west window. Loud
words were coming from the sidewalk under it. March
started eagerly. "That's Proudfit's——" Before he
could finish the bang of a pistol rang, evidently in the
office door, another, farther within, roared up through the
house, and a third and fourth re-echoed it amid the wailings of Johanna as she flew down the stairs crying:

"Mahs John Wesley! O Lawdy, Lawdy! Mahs
John Wesley! Mahs John Wesley!"

At the same instant came Tom Hersey's voice,
remote, but clear:

"Stop! Great God! Stop! Don't you see he's
dying?"

Fair was already on the staircase and March was
whipping on his boots, when Shotwell, coming up by
leaps, waved them back into the room. "It's all ova,

Mr. Fair. Po' Proudy's gone, John. He fi-ud an' missed, and got Garnet's first bullet in his heart an' the othe's close to it. Garnet's locked himself into Tom Hersey's private room an' sent for Fatheh Tombs, to——"

"Fair!" interrupted March, "go! Go tell her he's safe and will not be—interfered with! I'll make your word good; go, Fair, go!"

But Fair answered with hardly less emotion, "I cannot, March! It isn't a man's errand! It isn't a man's errand!"

"Take Mrs. Ravenel!" cried March, and read quick assent in his friend's face. "But make her go dressed as she is; you've got to outrun rumor! Captain, go tell Tom to give him Firefly, won't you? She's mine, Fair," he continued, following to the stairs; "she's the mare I cured for Bulger; perfectly gentle, only—Fair!—don't touch her with the whip!"

"If you do," drawled Shotwell to Fair, as they hurried down into the lamplight, "you'll think the devil's inside of her with the jimjams. Still, she's lovely as long as you don't. Ah me! this is no time to jest! Po' Proudfit! He leaves a spotless characteh!"

Through the unnatural bustle, amid which Crickwater at the door of the closed office stood answering or ignoring questions and showing his intimates where Proudfit's wild shot had chopped out a large lock of his hair, they went to Hersey's door and so on to the stable. "Garnet's the man to pity, Mr. Fair. I couldn't say it befo' March, who's got family reasons—through his motheh—faw savin' Garnet whateveh he can of his splendid reputaation, but I'm mighty 'fraid they won't be a rag of it left, seh, big enough for a gun-wad! Mr. Fair, you've got a hahd drive befo' you, seh, an' if you'll allow me to suggest it, seh, I think it would be only wise, befo' you staht, faw us to take a drink, seh."

"Thank you," said the Northerner, "I hardly think— Do you suppose Major Garnet's firing those last two shots after——"

"Will ruin him? O Lawd, not that! We all know, and always have, that he's perfectly cra-azy when he's enra-aged. No, my deah seh, Miz Proudfit has confessed! She says——"

"Are you not surprised that Major Garnet was armed?" Fair interrupted.

"O! no, seh, Colonel Proudfit was too much of a gentleman to be lookin' faw a man, with a gun, an' not send him word! And, besides, Miz Proudfit's revela-a-tions——"

But the horse and buggy were ready, and at last March—to whom, as he stood at his window fully dressed, the few moments had seemed an hour—saw Fair drive swiftly by and fade into the gloom. Charlie Champion came toward the hotel, bringing Parson Tombs. March put on his hat, but for many minutes only paced the darkening room. Finally he started for the stairs, and half way down them met the Doctor.

"Why, bless my soul, John," he good-naturedly cried, "this is quite *too* fast."

"I reckon not, Doctor; I believe I'm well. I don't understand it, but it's so." He endured the Doctor's hand for a moment on his wrist and temples.

"Why, I declare!" laughed the physician with noisy pleasure, "I believe yo' right!" As they descended he explained how such recoveries are possible and why they are so rare, citing from medical annals a case or two whose mention John thought very unflattering.

"I should like to know what's become of Johanna," said March at the foot of the stairs.

"Johanna? O they say she ran all the way to Fannie Ravenel's, and they harnessed up the fast colt and put off for Rosemont, Johanna driving!"

"Why, of course! I might have known it! But"—John stopped—"Why, then, where's Fair?"

"O I saw him. He drove on to overtake 'em. He'll have a job of it!"

"Firefly can do it," said March, picturing the chase to himself. "But I—I wonder what—This is no time— Why—why, what did he want to do it for?"

"O he may have had the best of reasons," said the amiable Doctor, and departed.

Outside a certain door—"Why, John March!" murmured Tom Hersey. The voices of Garnet and Parson Tombs could be heard within. They ceased as the landlord modestly rattled the knob, and when he gave the visitor's name Garnet's voice said:

"Ask him in."

As March entered, only Parson Tombs rose to meet him. He had a large handkerchief in his fingers, his eyes were very red, and he gave his hand in silence. Garnet, too, had been weeping. He shaded his downcast eyes from the lamp. March had determined to give himself no time for feelings, but his voice was sud-

denly not his own as he began, "Major Garnet," and
stopped, while Garnet slowly lifted his face until the
light shone on it. March stood still and felt his heart
heave between loathing and compassion; for on that
lamp-lit face one hour of public shame had written
more guilt than years of secret perfidy and sin, and the
question rushed upon the young man's mind, Can this
be the author of all my misfortunes and the father of?
—he quenched the thought and driving back a host of
memories said:

"Major, Doctor Coffin has just pronounced me well.
I am at your disposal, sir, for anything that ought to
be done."

Garnet shaded his eyes again. "Thank you, John,"
was his subdued reply. "It's such a clear case of self-
defence—I hear there will be no arrest. Still, I shall
remain here to-night. Johanna's gone home, I believe.
There's only one thing, the deepest yearning of my
heart, John; but before I ask that boon, I want you to
know, John, that I acknowledge my sin! my awful,
awful sin of years! O my God! my God! why did I
do it?"

Parson Tombs wept again. "He's confessed everything, John," he said with eager tenderness.

"God knows," responded Garnet, "God knows I
never concealed it but to save others from misery! and
while I concealed it I could not master it! Now I
have purged my sin-blackened soul of all its hideous
secret and evil purpose! The thorn in my flesh is
plucked out and I cast myself on the mercy of God and
the charity of his people!"

"Pra-aise Gawd!" murmured Parson Tombs, "no sinneh eveh done that in va-ain!"

"O John," moaned Garnet, "God only knows what I've suffered and must suffer! But it's all right! all right! I pray He may lop off every unfruitful branch of my life—honors, possessions—till nothing is left but Rosemont, the lowly work He called me to, Himself! Let Him make me as one of his hired servants! But, John," he continued while March stood dumb with wonder at his swift loss of subtlety, "I want you to know also that I feel no resentment—I cannot—O I cannot—against her who shares my guilt and shame!"

"Great Heaven!" murmured March, with a start as if to turn away.

"No, thank God! her vanity and jealousy can drive me to no more misdeeds! She made me send Mademoiselle Eglantine to Europe, when she knew I had to sell her husband's stock in both companies to bribe the woman to go! John, the cause of her betraying me to him at last was my faithful refusal to break off my engagement with your mother!"

"Major Garnet, I prefer——"

"Will you tell your mother that, John? It's the one thing you can do for me! Tell her I beseech her in the name of a love——"

"Stop!" murmured March in a voice that quivered with repulsion.

"—A love that has dared all, and lost all, for hers——"

"Stop!" said John again, and Garnet turned a beseeching eye upon the pastor.

"John," tearfully said the old man, "let us not yield to ow feelings when the cry of a soul in shipwreck"— he stopped to swallow his emotions. "Ow penitent brother on'y asks you to bear his message. It's natu'al he should cling to the one pyo tie that holds him to us. O John, 'in wrath remembeh mercy!' An' yet you may be the nearest right, God knows! O brethren, let's kneel and ask Him faw equal love an' wisdom!"

Garnet rose to kneel, but March put out a protesting hand. "I wouldn't do that, sir." The tone was gentle, almost compassionate. "I don't suppose God would strike you dead, but—I wouldn't do it, sir." He turned to go, and, glancing back unexpectedly, saw on Garnet's face a look so evil that it haunted him for years.

---

## LXXVIII.

### BARBARA FINDS THE RHYME

BARBARA walked along the slender road in front of Rosemont's grove. The sun was gone. Her father had not arrived yet with Johanna, but she questioned every stir of the air for the sound of their coming. A yearning which commonly lay very still in her bosom and ought in these two long years to have got reconciled to its lovely prison, was up once more in silent mutiny.

With slow self-compulsion she turned toward the house. The dim, vacated dormitories grew large against the fading after-glow. The thrush's song ceased. Remotely from the falling slope beyond the unlighted house the voices of a negro boy and girl, belated in the milking-pen, came to her ear more lightly than the gurgle of the shallow creek so near her feet. Suddenly the cry of the whip-Will's-widow filled the grove— " whip-Will's-widow ! whip-Will's-widow ! whip-Will's-widow ! "—in headlong importunity until the whole air sobbed and quivered with the overcharge of its melancholy passion. Then as abruptly it was hushed, the echoes died, and Barbara, at the grove gate, recalled the other twilight hour, a counterpart of this in all but its sadness, when, on this spot, she had bidden John March come the next day to show Widewood to Henry Fair.

And now Henry Fair "some day soon," his unexpected letter said, was to come again. And she was letting him come. One of his sweet mother's letters— always so welcome—had ever so delicately hinted a hope that she would do so, the fond mother affectionately imputing to the father's wisdom the feeling that Henry's present life contained more uncertainties than were good for his, or anyone's, future. He was coming at last for her final word, and in her meditations, his patient constancy, like a great ambassador, pleaded mightily in advance.

Henry Fair, gentle, strong, and true, will come ; *the other* never comes. The explanation is very simple ; she has made it to Johanna twice within the year : a strained relation—it happens among the best of men— between him and Rosemont's master. Besides, Mr.

March, she says, visits nowhere. He is, as Fannie herself testifies, more completely out of all Suez's little social eddies than even the overtasked young mistress of Rosemont, and does nothing day or night but buffet the flood of his adversities. As she reminds herself of these things now, she recalls Fannie's praise of his "indomitable pluck," and feels a new, warm courage around her own heart. For as long as men can show valor, she gravely reflects, surely women can have fortitude. How small a right, at best—how little honest room—there is in this huge world of strifes and sorrows for a young girl's heart to go breaking itself with its own grief and longing.

The right thing is, of course, to forget. She should! She must! But—she has said so every evening and morning for two years. Old man! old woman! do you remember what two years meant when you were in the early twenties? Even yet, with the two years gone, by hard crowding of the hours with cares, as a ship crowds sail or steam, it seems at times as if her forgetting were about to make headway; but just then the unexpected happens—merely the unexpected. O why not the romantic? She hears him praised or blamed; or, as now, he is ill; or she meets him in a dream; or between midnight and dawn she cannot sleep; or, worst of all, by some sad mischance she sees him, close by, in a throng or in a public way—for an instant—and, when it is too late, knows by his remembered look that he wanted to speak; and the flood lifts and sweeps her back, and she must begin again. The daylight hours are the easiest; there is so much to do and see done, and just the dear, lost, silent-hearted mother's ways to follow. One can manage everything but the twilights with their death of day, their hush of birds, the mind gazing back into the past and the heart asking unanswerable questions of the future. For the evenings there are books, though not all ; especially not Herrick, any more ; nor Tennyson, for it opens of itself at " Mariana," who wept, " I am aweary, aweary. Oh, God, that I were dead ! "

Barbara walked again. Moving at a slow pace, so, one can more soberly—She heard wheels. A quarter of a mile away they rumbled on a small bridge and were unheard again, and while she still listened to hear them on the ground others sounded on the bridge. She hurried back to the steps of the house and had hardly reached them when Johanna drove into the grove and Fannie's voice called,

"Is that you, Barb ? "

"Yes. Where's pop-a ? Has anything happened ? "

" He's got to stay in town to-night. Barb," said the visitor, springing to the ground, " Mr. Fair's just behind. He's only come so's to take me back to my baby."

" Fannie, something's happened ! "

" Yes, Barb, dear, come into the house."

About midnight—" Doctor, her head hasn't stopped that motion since it touched the pillow," murmured Fannie. Fair had gone back and brought the physician. But the patient was soon drugged to slumber, and Fannie and Fair started for town to return early in the morning. The doctor and Johanna watched out the night. At dawn Fair rose from a sleepless couch.

At sunrise he could hear no sound through March's door; but as he left the hotel he saw Leggett come up from the train, tap at Garnet's door and go in.

Barbara awoke in a still bliss of brain, yet wholly aware of what had befallen.

"Johanna"—the maid showed herself—"has Miss Fannie gone home?"

"Yass'm. But she comin' back. She be here ve'y soon now, I reckon."

Barbara accepted a small cup of very black coffee. When it was drunk, "Johanna," she said, with slow voice and gentle gaze, "were you in the hotel?"

"Yass'm," murmured the maid. "I uz in Mr. March's room. He uz talkin' wid Mr. Fair, an' knock' his suppeh by acci*dent* onto de flo', an'"—she withdrew into herself, consulted her conscience and returned. "Miss Barb——"

"What, Johanna?"

Johanna told.

Long after she was done her mistress lay perfectly still gazing into vacancy. But the moment Fannie was alone with her she dragged the kind visitor's neck down to her lips and with unaccountable blushes mingled her tears with bitter moanings.

By and by—"And Fannie, dear, *make* them stay to breakfast. And thank Mr. Fair for me, as sweetly as you can. I don't know how I can ever repay him!"

"Don't you?" dryly ventured **Fannie**; but her friend's smile was so sad that she went no farther. Tears sprang to her eyes, as Barbara, slowly taking her hand, said,

" Of course pop-a can't keep Rosemont now. If he tries to begin a new life, Fannie, wherever it is, I shall stay with him."

Fair gave the day mainly to the annual meeting of the trustees at Suez University. The corner-stone was not to be laid until the morrow. March reopened his office, but did almost no work, owing to the steady stream of callers from all round the square coming to wish him well with handshake and laugh, and with jests which more or less subtly implied their conviction that he was somehow master of the hour. When Ravenel came others slipped out, although he pleasantly remarked that they need not, and those who looked in later and saw the two men sitting face to face drew back. " That thing last night," said Weed to Usher, going to the door of their store to throw his quid into the street, " givm the *Courier* about the hahdest kick in the ribs she evva got." But no one divined Ravenel's errand, unless Garnet darkly suspected it as he waited beside Jeff-Jack's desk for its owner's return, to ask him for ten thousand dollars on a mortgage of his half of Widewood, with which to quiet, he serenely explained, any momentary alarm among holders of his obligations. And even Garnet did not guess that Ravenel would not have telegraphed, as he did, to a  ık in Pulaski City in which he was director, to grant the loan, had not John March just declined his offer of a third interest in the *Courier*.

At evening March and Fair dined together in Hotel Swanee. They took a table at a window and talked

but little, and then softly, with a placid gravity, on
trivial topics, keeping serious ones for a better privacy,
though all other guests had eaten and gone. Only Shotwell, unaware of their presence, lingered over his pie
and discussed Garnet's affair with the head waitress, an
American lady. He read to her on the all-absorbing
theme, from the Pulaski City *Clarion;* whose editor,
while mingling solemn reprobations with amazed regrets,
admitted that a sin less dark than David's had been
confessed from the depths of David's repentance. In
return she would have read him the Suez *Courier's* much
fuller history of the whole matter; but he had read it,
and with a kindly smile condemned it as "suspended in
a circumaambient air of edito'ial silence."

"I know not what co'se othe's may take, my dea'
madam, but as faw me, give me neither poverty naw
riches; give me political indispensability; the pa-apers
have drawn the mantle of charity ove' 'im, till it covers
him like a circus-tent."

"Ah! but what'll his church do?" The lady bent
from her chair and tied her slipper.

"My dea' madam, what *can* she do? She th'ows
up—excuse the figgeh—she th'ows up, I say, her foot to
kick him out; he tearfully ketches it in his ha-and an'
retains it with the remahk, 'I repent!' What *can* his
church do? She can do jest one thing!"

"What's that?" asked the lady, gathering his dishes
without rising.

"Why she can make him marry Miz Proudfit!"

The lady got very red. "Captain Shotwell, I'll
thaynk you not to allude to that person to me again,

seh !" She jerked one knee over the other and folded her arms.

"My dea' madam ! I was thoughtless ! Fawgive me ! " The Captain stood up. "I'm not myself to-day. Not but what I'm sobeh; but I—oh, I'm in trouble ! But what's that to you?" He pulled his soft hat picturesquely over his eyes, and starting out, discovered March and Fair. He looked sadly mortified as he saluted them, but quickly lighted up again and called March aside.

"John, do you know what Charlie Champion's been doin'? He's been tryin' to get up a sort o' syndicate to buy Rosemont and make you its pres—O now, now, ca'm yo'self, he's give it up; we all wish it, but you know, John, how ow young men always ah; dead broke, you know. An' besides, anyhow, Garnet may ruin Rosemont, but, as Jeff-Jack says, he'll neveh sell it. It's his tail-holt. Eh—eh—one moment, John, I want to tell you anotheh thing. You've always been sich a good friend—John, I've p'posed to Miss Mahtha-r again, an' she's rejected me, as usual. I knew you'd be glad to hear it." He smiled through his starting tears. "But she cried, John, she did !—said she'd neveh ma' anybody else ! "

"Ah, Shot, you're making a pretty bad flummux of it ! "

"Yes, John, I know I am—p'posin' by da-aylight ! It don't work ! But, you know, when I wait until evenin' I ain't in any condition. Still, I'll neveh p'pose to her by da-aylight again ! I don't believe Eve would 'a' ma'd Adam if he'd p'posed by da-aylight."

The kind Captain passed out.  He spent the night in his room with our friend, the commercial traveler, who, at one in the morning, was saying to him for the tenth time,

"I came isstantly! For whareverss Garness's troubl'ss my trouble!  I can't tell you why; thass my secret; I say thass my secret!  Fill up again; this shocksh too much for me!  Capm—want to ask you one thing: *Muss* I be carried to the skies on flow'ry bedge of ease while Garnet *fighss* to win the prise 'n' sails through bloody seas?  Sing that, Capm!  I'll line it!  You sing it!"  Shotwell sang; his companion wept.  So they closed their sad festivities; not going to bed, but sleeping on their arms, like the stern heroes they were.

"Why, look at the droves of ow own people!" laughed Captain Champion at the laying of the corner-stone.  And after it, "Yes, Mr. Fair's address was fi-ine!  But faw me, Miz Ravenel, do you know I liked just those few words of John March evm betteh?"

"They wa'n't so few," drawled Lazarus Graves, "but what they put John on the shelf."

The hot Captain flashed.  "Politically, yes, seh! On the *top* shelf, where we saave up ow best men faw ow worst needs, seh!"

Fair asked March to take a walk.  They went without a word until they sat down on the edge of a wood. Then Fair said,

"March, I have a question to ask you.  Why don't you try?"

"Fair, she won't ever let me!  She's as good as told me, up and down, I mustn't.  And *now* I can't!  I'm penniless, and part of her inheritance will be my lost lands. I can't ignore that; I haven't got the moral courage! Besides, Fair, I know that if she takes you, there's an end of all her troubles and a future worthy of her—as far as any future can be. What sort of a fellow would I be—Oh, mind you! if I had the faintest reason to think she'd rather have me than you, I George! sir——" He sprang up and began to spurn the bark off a stump with a strength of leg that made it fly. "Fair, tell me! Are you going to offer yourself, notwithstanding all?"

"Yes. Yes; if the letter I expect from home tomorrow, and which I telegraphed them to write, is what I make no doubt it will be; yes."

March gazed at his companion and slowly and soberly smiled. "Fair," he softly exclaimed, "I wish I had your head! Lord! Fair, I wish I had your chance!"

"Ah! no," was the gentle reply, "I wish one or the other were far better."

A third sun had set before Barbara walked again at the edge of the grove. Two or three hours earlier her father had at last come home, and as she saw the awful change in his face and the vindictive gleam with which he met her recognition of it, she knew they were no longer father and daughter. The knowledge pierced like a slow knife, and yet brought a sense of relief—of release—that shamed her until she finally fled into the open air as if from suffocation. There she watched the west grow dark and the stars fill the sky while thoughts shone, vanished, and shone again in soft confusion like the fireflies in the grove. Only one continued—that now she might choose her future. Her father had said so with an icy venom which flashed fire as he added, "But if you quit Rosemont now, so help me God, you shall never own it, if I have to put it to the torch on my dying bed!"

She heard something and stepped into hiding. What rider could be coming at this hour? John March? Henry Fair? It was neither. As he passed in at the gate she shrank, gasped, and presently followed. Warily she rose up the front steps, stole to the parlor blinds, and, peering in, saw her father pay five crisp thousand dollar bills to Cornelius Leggett.

In her bed Barbara thought out the truth: that Cornelius still held some secret of her father's; that in smaller degree he had been drawing hush money for years; and that he had concluded that any more he could hope to plunder from the blazing ruin of his living treasury must be got quickly, and in one levy, ere it fell. But what that secret might be she strove in vain to divine. One lurking memory, that would neither show its shape nor withdraw its shadow, haunted her ringing brain. The clock struck twelve; then one; then two; and then she slept.

And then, naturally and easily, without a jar between true cause and effect, the romantic happened! The memory took form in a dream and the dream became a key to revelation. When Johanna brought her mistress's coffee she found her sitting up in bed. On her white lap lay the old reticule of fawnskin. She had broken the clasp of its inner pocket and held in her hand a rudely scrawled paper whose blue ink and strutting signature the unlettered maid knew at a glance was from her old-time persecutor, Cornelius. It was the letter her father had dropped under the chair when she was a child. Across its face were still the bold figures of his own pencil, and from its blue lines stared out the *secret*.

Garnet breakfasted alone and rode off to town. The moment he was fairly gone Johanna was in the saddle, charged by her mistress with the delivery of a letter which she was "on no account to show or mention to anyone but——"

"Yass'm," meekly said Johanna, and rode straight to the office of John March.

A kind greeting met her as she entered, but it was from Henry Fair, and he was alone. He, too, had been reading a letter, a long one in a lady's writing, and seemed full of a busy satisfaction. Mr. March, he said, had ridden out across the river, but would be back very shortly. "Johanna, I may have to go North to-night. I wonder if it's too early in the day for me to call on Miss Garnet?"

"No-o, seh," drawled the conscientious maid, longing to say it was. "H-it's early, but I don't reckon it's *too* early," and was presently waiting for Mr. March, alone.

Hours passed. He did not come. She got starving hungry, yet waited on. Men would open the door, look in, see or not see her sitting in the nearest corner, and close it again. About two o'clock she slipped out to the Hotel Swanee, thinking she might find him at dinner. They said he had just dined and gone to his office.

She hurried back, found it empty, and sat down again to wait. Another hour passed, and suddenly the door swung in and to again, and John March halted before his desk. He did not see her. His attitude was as if he might wheel and retrace his steps.

Mrs. March had broken off her engagement promptly. But when Garnet, by mail, still flattered and begged, the poetess, with no notion of relenting, but in her love of dramatic values and the gentle joy of perpetuating a harrowing suspense, had parleyed; and only just now had her tyrannical son forced a conclusion unfavorable to the unfortunate suitor. So here in his office March smote his brow and exclaimed,

"O my dear mother! that what is best for you should be so bad for me! Ahem! Why—why, howdy, Johanna? Hmm!"

With silent prayers and tremors the girl watched him read the letter. At the first line he sank into his chair, amazed and pale. "My Lord!" he murmured, and read on. "O my Lord! it can't be! Why, how?— why—O it shan't be!—O—hem! Johanna, you can go'long home, there's no answer; I'll be there before you."

At the post-office March reined in his horse while Deacon Usher brought out a drop letter from Henry Fair. But he galloped as he read it, and did not again slacken speed till he turned into the campus—except once. At the far edge of the battle-field, on that ridge where in childhood he had first met Garnet, he overtook and passed him now. As he went by he slowed to a trot, but would not have spoken had Garnet not glared on him like a captured hawk. The young man's blood boiled. He stood up in his stirrups.

"Don't look at me that way, sir; I've just learned your whole miserable little secret and expect to keep it for you." He galloped on. When, presently, he looked behind, Garnet had turned back—to find Leggett. That search was vain. Cornelius and his "Delijah," kissing their hands to their creditors, were already well on their way into that most exhilarating of all conundrums, the wide, wide world.

From Pulaski City Garnet returned on the early morning train to Suez, intending to ride out to Rosemont without a moment's delay. But on the station platform he came face to face with John March. They went to the young man's office and sat there, locked in, for an hour. Another they used up in the court-house and in Ravenel's private office with him between them in the capacity of an attorney. Yet when the three men parted Ravenel had neither asked nor been told what the matter was which had occasioned the surprising legal transaction that they had just completed.

"Now," said Garnet, briskly, "I must hurry home, for I want to leave on the evening train."

He rode out alone upon the old turnpike and over the knoll where Suez still hopes some day to build the reservoir, and reached the spot where he and his young adjutant picked blackberries that first day we ever saw them. There he stopped, and looking across the land to the roofs of distant Rosemont, straightened up in the saddle with a great pride, and then, all at once, let go a long groan of anguish and, covering his face, heaved with sobs that seemed as though each tore a separate way up from his heart. Then, as suddenly, he turned his horse's head and rode slowly back. Twice, as he went, he handled something in the pocket of his coat's skirt, and the third time drew it out—a small repeater. He did not raise the weapon; he only looked down at it in his trembling hand, the old thimbles still in the three discharged chambers, the lead peeping from the other two, and, thinking of the woman who shared his ruin, said in his mind, "One for each of us."

But it never happened so. He often wishes, yet, that it had, although he is, and has been for years, a "platform star;" "the eloquent Southern orator, moralist and humorist"—yes, that's the self-same man. He's booked for the Y. M. C. A. lecture course in your own town this season. His lecture, entitled "Temptation and How to Conquer It," is said to be "a wonderful alternation of humorous and pathetic anecdotes, illustrative, instructive and pat." I have his circular. His wife travels with him. They generally put up at hotels; tried private hospitality the first season, but it didn't work, somehow.

They have never revisited Dixie; and only once in all these years have they seen a group of Suez faces. But a season or two ago—I think it was ninety-three—in Fourteenth Street, New York, wife and I came square upon Captain Charlie Champion, whom I had not seen for years, indeed, not since his marriage, and whom my wife, never having been in Suez, did not know. Still he would have us up to dinner at his hotel with Mrs. Champion. He promised me I should find her "just as

good and sweet and saane as of old, and evm prettieh!"
Plainly the hearty Captain was more a man than ever,
and she had made him so! He told us we should meet
Colonel Ravenel and also—by pure good luck!—Mr.
and Mrs. Henry Fair. You may be sure we were glad
to go.

Ravenel had to send us word from the rotunda beg-
ging us to go in to dinner without him and let him join
us at table. Champion neglected his soup, telling us of
two or three Suez people. " Pettigrew?—O he left Suez
the year Rosemont chaanged haynds. Po' Shot!—he's
ow jail-keepeh, now, you know—he says one day, s'e,
'Old Pettie may be in heavm by now, but I don't
believe he's happy; he'll neveh get oveh the loss of his
sla-aves!'"

Fair spoke of John March, saying his influence in
that region was not only very strong but very fine.
Whereto Champion responded,

"—Result is we've got a betteh town and a long
sight betteh risin' generation than we eveh had befo'.
I don't reckon Mr. Fair thinks we do the dahkeys justice. John says we don't and I don't believe we do.
When it comes to that, seh, where on earth *does* the
under man get all his rights? But we come neareh toe
it in the three counties than anywheres else in Dixie,
and that I *know.*"

I dropped an interrogative hint as to how March
stood with Ravenel.

The Captain smiled. " They neveh cla-ash. Ravenel's the same mystery he always was, but not the same
poweh; his losin' Garnet the way he did, and then

John bein' so totally diffe'nt, you know—John don't ofm ask Jeff-Jack to do anything, but he neveh aasks in vaain.—John's motheh? Yes, she still lives with him.—No, she ve'y seldom eveh writes much poetry any mo', since heh book turned out to be such a' unaccountable faailu'e. She jest lives with him, and really "—he dropped his voice—" you'd be amaazed to see how much she's sort o' sweetened and mellered under the influence of—Ah! there's Colonel Ravenel——"

He broke off with a whisper of surprise. At a table near the door Garnet's wife sat smiling eagerly after her husband as if it was at her instigation he had risen and effusively accosted Ravenel; and both she and Garnet knew that we all saw, when Ravenel said with an unmoved face and colorless voice,

"No. No, I'm perfectly sure I never saw you before, sir." It may have been wholly by chance, but in drawing a handkerchief as he spoke he showed the hand whose thumb he had lost in saving Garnet's life.

The "star" hurried back to his seat and resumed conversation with the partner of his fate—for a moment. But all at once she rose and went out, he following, leaving their meal untouched.

Wife, as it was right she should, fell in love with Mrs. Fair on the spot, and agreed with me by stolen glances I knew how to interpret, that she was as lovely and refined a woman as she had ever met. Boston had not removed that odd, winning drawl so common in the South, and which a Southerner learns to miss so in the East. But when wife tried to have her talk about Suez

and its environs she looked puzzled for an instant and
then, with a light of mild amusement in her smile,
said,

" O !—I never saw Suez ; I was born and brought up
in Chicago."

" No," said Ravenel, " it's Mrs. Champion who can
tell you all about Suez."

" That's so ! " cried Champion, and turning to his
wife, added, " What the Saltehs don't know about Suez
ain't wuth knowin', is it, Mahtha ? "

That night I told wife this whole story. As I
reached this point in it she interposed a strong insinua-
tion that I am a very poor story-teller.

" I thought," she continued, " I thought I had heard
you speak of John March as a married man, father of
vast numbers of children."

To the last clause I objected and she modified it.
" But, anyhow, you leave too much to be inferred. I
want to know what Garnet's fatal secret was ; and—
well, I don't care especially what became of the commercial traveler, but I *do* want to hear a little about
Barbara ! Did she marry the drummer ? "

I said no, apologized for my vagueness and finished,
in effect, thus :

Before Barbara came down-stairs, at Rosemont, that
day, to see Mr. March, she sent him Leggett's letter.
Cornelius had caught scent of the facts in it from
Uncle Leviticus's traditions and had found them in the
county archives, which he had early learned the trick
of exploring. The two Ezra Jaspers, cousins, one the
grantee of Widewood, the other of Suez, had had, each,

a generous ambition to found a college. He of Suez
—the town that was to be—selected for his prospective
seat of learning a parcel of sixty acres close against the
western line of Widewood. Whereupon the grantee of
Widewood good-naturedly, as well as more wisely,
"took up" near the *Suez tract* the sixty acres which
eventually became Rosemont. Both pieces lay on the
same side of the same creek and were both in Clearwater County, as was much, though not the most, of
Widewood. Moreover, both were in the same "section" and "range," and in their whole description
differed scarcely more than by an N and an S, one being in the northwest and the other in the southwest
corner of the same township. On the ill-kept county
records these twin college sites early got mixed. When
Garnet founded Rosemont his friends in office promised
to tax that public benefaction as gently as they dared,
and he was only grateful and silent, not surprised, when
his tax-bill showed no increase at all. But while Rosemont was still small and poor and he seriously embarrassed by the cost of an unsuccessful election, came this
letter of Leggett's to open his eyes and complete his
despair. There across it were his own pencilings of
volume and page to show that he had seen the record.
In one of his mad moments, and in the hopeful conviction that the mulatto would soon get himself shot or
hung, he paid him to keep still. From that time on,
making Leggett's silence just a little more golden than
his speech, he had, "in bad faith," as the lawyers say,
been pouring all his gains, not worse spent, into property
built on land belonging to the Widewood estate; that

is, into Rosemont. When Judge March found his
Clearwater taxes high, he was only glad to see any of
his lands growing in value. When John came into
possession, Garnet, his party being once more in power,
had cunningly arranged for Rosemont not to be taxed
on its improvements, but only on its land, and March
discovered nothing. In the land boom Garnet kept the
odd sixty acres, generally supposed to be a part of
Widewood, out of sight, and induced John to deed it
to his mother. But when John came back from
Europe landless, there arose the new risk that he might
persuade her to sell the odd sixty acres, and, on looking
into the records to get its description, find himself and
his mother the legal owners of Rosemont.

"That's why the villain was so anxious to marry
her!" said John to himself audibly as he paced up and
down in the Rosemont parlor.

"Mr. March," said Barbara's slow voice. She had
entered as she spoke.

"Miss—Miss Garnet!"

"Please be seated." There was a tempest in her
heart, but her words were measured and low. "You
were very kind to come." She dragged her short sentences and at the same time crowded them upon each
other as if afraid to let him speak. He sat, a goodly
picture of deferential attention, starving to see again her
old-time gaze; but she kept her eyes on the floor. "Mr.
March, of course—of course, this is terrible to—me. I
only say it because I don't want to seem heartless to—
others—when I tell you I thank God—O please don't
speak yet, sir"—her hands trembled—"I thank God

this thing has come to light. For my dear father's own sake I am glad, gladder than I can tell, that he has lost Rosemont. The loss may save him. But I'm glad, too, Mr. March, that it's come to you—please hear me—and to your mother. Of course I know your lost Widewood isn't all here; but so much of it is. I wish——"

March stopped her with a gesture. "I will not—O I cannot—hear any more! I'm ashamed to have let you say so much! Rosemont is yours and shall stay yours! That's what I came to say. Two properties were exchanged by accident when each was about as near worthless as the other, and your mother's family and my father's have lived up to the mistake and have stood by it for three generations. I will not take it! My mother will not! She renounced it this morning! Do you understand?"

Barbara gave a start of pain and murmured, "I do." Her heart burned with the knowledge that he was waiting for her uplifted glance. He began again.

"The true value of Rosemont never came out of Widewood. It's the coined wealth of your mother's character and yours!" He ceased in a sudden rage of love as he saw the colors of the rose deepen slowly on the beautiful, half-averted face, and then, for very trepidation, hurried on. "O understand me, I will not be robbed! Major Garnet cannot have Rosemont. But no one shall ever know I have not bought it of him. And it shall first be yours; yours in law and trade as it is now in right. Then, if you will, you, who have been its spirit and soul, shall keep it and be so still.

But if you will not, then we, my mother and I, will buy it of you at a fair price. For, Miss—Miss——"

"Barb—" she murmured.

"O thank you!" cried he. "A thousand times! And a thousand times I promise you I'll never misunderstand you again! But hem!—to return to the subject; Miss Barb—I—O well, I was going to add merely that—that, eh—I—hem!—that, eh—O—However!" She raised her eyes and he turned crimson as he stammered, "I—I—I've forgotten what I was going to say!"

"I can neither keep Rosemont nor sell it, Mr. March. It's yours. It's yours every way. It's yours in the public wish; my father told me so last night. And there's a poetic justice——"

"Poetic—O!"

"Mr. March, didn't we once agree that God gives us our lives in the rough for us to shape them into poetry— that it's poetry, whether sad or gay, that makes alive— and that it's only the prose that kills?"

"Oh! do you remember that?"

"Yes." Her eyes fell again. "It was the time you asked me to use your first name."

"O! Miss Barb, are you still going to hold that against me?"

"Rosemont should be yours, Mr. March. It rhymes!" She stood up.

"No! No, no! I give it to you!" he said, springing to his feet.

"Will you, really, Mr. March?" She moved a step toward the door.

"O Miss Barb, I do! I do!"

"But your mother's consent——"

A pang of incertitude troubled his brave face for an instant, but then he said, "Oh, there can be no doubt! Let me go and get it!" He started.

"No," she falteringly said, "don't do it."

"Yes! Yes! Say yes! Tell me to go!" He caught her hand beseechingly. As their eyes gazed into each other's, hers suddenly filled and fell.

"Go," was her one soft word. But as he reached the door another stopped him:

"John——"

He turned and stood trembling from head to foot, his brow fretted with an agony of doubt. "Oh, Barbara Garnet!" he cried, "why did you say that?"

"Johanna told me," she murmured, smiling through her tears.

He started with half-lifted arms, but stopped, turned, and with a hand on his brow, sighed, "My mother!"

But a touch rested on his arm and a voice that was never in life to be strange to him again said, "If you don't say 'our mother,' I won't call you John any——"

Oh! Oh! Oh! men are so rough sometimes!

THE END.